The Miseducation of Caroline Bingley

LINDZ McLEOD

Recycling programs for this product may not exist in your area.

ISBN-13: 978-1-335-00171-9

The Miseducation of Caroline Bingley

Carina Press
22 Adelaide St. West, 41st Floor
Toronto, Ontario M5H 4E3, Canada
Harlequin.com

HarperCollins Publishers
Macken House, 39/40 Mayor Street Upper,
Dublin 1, D01 C9W8, Ireland
www.HarperCollins.com

Printed in U.S.A.

26 27 28 29 30 LBC 5 4 3 2 1

Praise for Lindz McLeod and *The Unlikely Pursuit of Mary Bennet*, book one of the Austentatious series

"A triumph of a book, and an utter delight from start to finish."

—Thomas D. Lee, *Sunday Times* bestselling author of *Perilous Times*

"From the brilliantly witty opening line, this sparkling tale of love between two of Jane Austen's beloved characters had me captured. It makes perfect sense that Mary Bennet, the studious, piano-playing younger sister of Elizabeth Bennet, would one day fall in love with Charlotte Collins, a woman who married for practical reasons, but has never known real love. This was the sweetest of delights!"

—Emily H. Wilson, author of The Sumerians Trilogy

"A love story so charming it will sweep you off your feet. *The Unlikely Pursuit of Mary Bennet* is a splendid queer spin on Austen that will delight her many, many fans."

—*BookPage*

"With Charlotte as the sole narrator, the mystery of whether she's reading Mary's signals correctly keeps the pages turning right up until the moment their passion erupts. The result is an unabashedly escapist, feel-good romance."

—*Publishers Weekly*

To Z, who understands why I could never—would never—look back

Author's Note

During the canonical events of *Pride and Prejudice*, Miss Georgiana Darcy is sixteen; she has turned seventeen by the end of the book. To avoid writing a minor entering into a relationship with someone older—especially given the problematic nature of Miss Darcy's previous experience with Wickham—I decided to age Georgiana up by three years, making her twenty at the start of *The Miseducation of Caroline Bingley.* Caroline is three years her senior, making her twenty-three, and thus the power dynamic has been somewhat rebalanced.

Chapter One

A book was an abominable thing, Miss Caroline Bingley decided, for no matter which book you picked up, their stories were already set in stone, and one's own tastes or opinions—no matter how excellent—could never prevail upon them to change.

Satisfied by the philosophical insight of such a thought, she strolled across the Darcys' library again. Her journey took her past the sofa where Miss Georgiana Darcy—younger sister of the man who had, only a week prior, married Miss Elizabeth Bennet—was curled up like a contented cat. It was the third time in half an hour that Caroline had taken a turn around the room, and the third time that Georgiana had, once again, ignored Caroline's delicate sighs in favour of concentrating on the book in her hands. Though the library at Pemberley was large and the seating arrangements—two long couches upholstered in an elegant shade of burgundy, accompanied by several matching chairs set into alcoves along the wall—were comfortable enough to please any numbers of readers, Caroline found herself in dire need of fresh entertainment. After all, one could only stare at the paintings of the ancestral Darcys on the wall for so long before one began to feel them staring back. She hesitated in front of a moustached man, who glared down at her from under a set of eyebrows so grey and hairy they looked like two mating caterpillars, and felt a shiver roll down her spine.

Swallowing her discomfort, Caroline selected yet another handsomely-bound book from the shelves. Flipping idly through it, she discovered only dry descriptions about land management. With a frown, she returned the book to its rightful home. "Pray tell me," she complained, turning to face her companion, "what is the use of having a library in one's home if one does not actually stock anything worth reading?"

"I recall that, not so long ago, you could find no fault whatsoever with my brother's tastes," Georgiana said, without looking up.

"I'm afraid I do not know what you mean. Surely even your brother does not spend his evenings deeply absorbed in"—she craned her head to the side, the better to see the title on the spine of the book which she had just put back—"*A Dissertation on the Chief Obstacles to the Improvement of Land, and Introducing Better Methods of Agriculture Throughout Scotland*?" Her lip curled in a sneer. "A thrilling read, to be sure."

"You are standing in the wrong area if you wish to be amused." Georgiana still hadn't looked up, though she pointed a finger at the opposite side of the room. Tendrils of perfectly curled fair hair framed her handsome face, which currently wore an expression of placid contemplation. "We keep what few novels we have over there."

Caroline crossed to the desired section, but the titles there did not inspire much hope: *Gulliver's Travels. The History of Tom Jones. The Life and Opinions of Tristram Shandy, Gentleman.* She rolled her eyes. Other countries, world history, their own mundane lives—these were topics upon which men loved to lecture at length, but she had rarely found those conversations stimulating. "I am sure that these will be equally as dry as the first one I picked up. Really, it is a wonder that the whole room does not burst into flames whenever the candles are lit."

Miss Darcy heaved a sigh of her own, which was much louder and more irritated than the ladylike sighs Caroline had been so lately emitting, and dropped the book she had been reading onto her lap, though her finger remained on the page to mark her place. "Perhaps it is not the fault of the books, then, but of the reader herself. What say you to that?"

Caroline advanced to the hearth, where a small but merry fire burned in the grate, and took a moment to warm her hands. Though it was early summer, there was still a slight chill in the air, no doubt caused by the housekeeper's insistence on keeping the windows open all night to freshen the room. Caroline's blue dress, which had served her perfectly well whilst upstairs in the guest room with a blazing fire, felt rather thin and insubstantial down here.

"Nothing at all," she retorted, "seeing as the argument makes no sense whatsoever. How can the fault of a book lie with a reader?"

"What I mean to say is that I do not think you possess the attention span to truly enjoy a book," Georgiana said, leaning back on the sofa. The dress she was wearing was a simple one—moss green, with lace trim at the hem and bosom—but it brought out the hues in her brown eyes to great advantage. She was as fair-haired as her brother was dark, but those beautiful eyes were a familial trait. "For it would require you to live another's life for a few minutes, perhaps even an hour or two, which I do not think you could abide, particularly if the character's views did not align perfectly with your own."

"I do not think that there is anything wrong in preferring to be one's own self," Caroline huffed. "You make it sound like some great defect of character."

The flames in the handsome fireplace crackled, filling the silence. Georgiana opened her mouth as if to add something, then closed it again, perhaps thinking better of it. "Not necessarily," she said, after a moment's thought. "But do not you think it may be a matter of being reluctant to give up control in some way? One cannot influence a book to comply with one's whims and wishes, after all."

This came remarkably close to what Caroline had been thinking only a minute prior, though she wasn't about to admit that now. "Certainly not."

Georgiana's lips twitched. "Hmm."

Caroline glared at her. "I believe you are laughing at me, Miss Darcy."

The smile which she had been repressing now made itself plain. "I believe you are being ridiculous, Miss Bingley."

"What are you reading?" Caroline asked, pointing at the edition in Georgiana's lap. Dutifully, Miss Darcy turned the book so that Caroline could see the cover. "*The Mysteries of Udolpho*, eh? Well, that explains it!" she exclaimed. She had no real idea what *The Mysteries of Udolpho* was about, but the title suggested an air of grandness and mystique. "There must be two hundred books in this room, and yet, you are hoarding the only interesting one."

"Four hundred, actually. At least, at last count. And you're welcome to this one." Georgiana closed the book and offered it. "I would love to hear your thoughts upon it."

With a delighted grin, Caroline accepted the novel, plopped down on the couch next to Georgiana, and began to read. To her surprise, the story began with a young lady called Emily bemoaning the manner in which she had been obliged to part from her love, Valancourt. This interested Caroline for a minute or two, as it seemed that some delicious gossip must be forthcoming, but in truth, very little reason for the separation was provided. She read on, hopeful of gleaning a juicy morsel or two, but could only discover that Valancourt had pleaded with Emily to remember him at sunset. Why sunset specifically, Caroline could not tell. Perhaps it had some significance to the lovers, or even to the author, though she could not determine what that significance might be.

Within another page or two, even the romance faded away, and with it vanished any hope of gossip. Before long, Caroline grew restless with the description of Emily's journey through a landscape she did not recognise. She quickly tired of the references to Alpine shrubs amidst the crags, fluffy clouds, and delightful villages. Those things could be found in almost any place in England; why would one bother to write about something everyone could see whenever they liked?

Lowering the book to her lap, she stared out of the long windows which so beautifully framed the view of the Pemberley estate. It was such a lovely day outside; the sky was a beautiful, deep blue, with only a few puffy clouds chasing each other across it like playful children. There was hardly a breeze, and the trees which she could see through the window were barely trembling at all. The hedges, which lined the paths and walkways of Pemberley, had lately been trimmed back, though not nearly enough for her liking—her brother, Charles, kept the hedges at Netherfield as straight and neat as soldiers awaiting their marching orders. In the distance, she could see only a slender sliver of the stream, though it sparkled as brightly as any jewel. From a window on any of the upper floors, one could see more clearly how it opened out into wider banks, becoming a stately river of some importance, though here in the library, the view was far too impeded by thick woodland to see such a thing.

A bird flapped past the window at speed, catching her eye. The room in which she and Georgiana now sat was north-facing, which rendered it much dimmer than the drawing room on the south side of the house. Despite the attractiveness of the drawing room, painted in a pretty shade of light blue and—perhaps more importantly—with far fewer Darcy ancestors scowling down disapprovingly, Georgiana much preferred the library and spent most of her days here. It was not an inelegant room by any means, wallpapered in a pale yellow flock which had remained the same as far back as Caroline could remember. Miss Darcy's late mother had apparently preferred this room above all others, and her daughter seemed to have inherited the same inclination.

"Perhaps we ought to take a turn around the garden," Caroline suggested, closing the book with a snap, already thinking about which bonnet would match her blue dress best. "I have heard that it is not good for the complexion to spend too much time indoors, especially when summer shall be over soon."

"We have only just entered June, and we took a turn around the garden only an hour ago," Georgiana reminded her, flicking through yet another book, as if it were the most interesting thing in the world. Perhaps *The Mysteries of Udolpho* had only been a kind of decoy, designed to distract Caroline from poaching the book Georgiana truly desired to read—the one now in Miss Darcy's hands.

A cunning trick, Caroline thought, delighted to have caught on to the scheme, *but you shall not outfox me.* She pointed to the book in question. "What is that one?"

"It is called *The Parsonage-House*, by a Miss Elizabeth Blower."

"What is it about?"

Georgiana sighed. "Perhaps if you stopped interrupting me every two minutes, I might read long enough to find out."

Despite the chiding words, her tone was mild. Undeterred, Caroline plunged onwards, lest Georgiana become so absorbed again that she forgot her guest existed. "Do you know if your brother intends to pack any books to take with him?"

"On his first trip alone with his new wife?" Georgiana's eyebrows rose until they almost disappeared into her hair. "Why, I have no idea. They will be busy touring England and . . . er . . . Well." She cleared her throat, a pink tinge blooming on her cheeks. "I hardly think they will be doing much reading."

Caroline turned back to face the fire, repressing a sudden urge to hurl *The Mysteries of Udolpho* into the flames; Emily and Valancourt and their ridiculous obsession with sunsets could burn in hell for all she cared. "I have no doubt they will be reading plenty, for Miss Elizabeth Bennet loves a good book, does she not?" Despite her best efforts, the words came out rather bitter. "I seem to recall a certain conversation in which she made plain that she felt her fondness for reading made her very superior to—"

"If you are so concerned about my brother's literary habits, then why don't you ask him about them tonight?"

Startled, Caroline spun so fast, the book almost slipped from her fingers. "They are coming here? Tonight?" she exclaimed. "Why did you not tell me?"

"*They* are not," she corrected. "Only Fitzwilliam is returning home to Pemberley. I received his letter this morning, but he was clear that—"

"I have not heard any news from Charles on the matter," Caroline interrupted.

Her brother was married to Jane, the eldest Bennet—Elizabeth's older sister and the only Bennet whose company Caroline could tolerate for more than a single minute. Charles was not the world's most constant letter-writer, but he ought to have updated her on his plans.

"As I said, only my brother is coming home," Georgiana repeated patiently. "I believe Charles plans to stay with the ladies at Netherfield, so that they may spend a last week or two with their parents before the party rejoins Fitzwilliam at Birmingham, whereupon both couples will travel together to Bath for several weeks. At least, that is the plan at present, as far as I know."

Whenever Caroline thought about Mrs Bennet—which was thankfully not often—she couldn't help a shudder of revulsion. It was bad enough that poor, sweet Jane was saddled with dreadful sisters, but to have an ill-tempered old goat of a mother was really too bad. *What are the other sisters called? Catty? Libia?* She frowned, trying to remember. *Something like that.* And then there was the short, serious one who played the pianoforte well enough but had all the social graces of a half-cooked goose. Really, in comparison, Miss Elizabeth Bennet seemed almost desirable company.

Almost.

"Charles puts up with such ridiculous things, does he not?" she said, unable to help the note of sourness which infused her voice. "Sometimes I wonder about him."

"Some people," Miss Darcy said, the book rising from her

lap as slowly and steadily as a sunrise, to take up residence once again directly in front of her face, "occasionally put themselves in situations of varying degrees of discomfort for the sake of others whom they love." The book lowered only slightly, just enough for Caroline to see beautiful dark eyes narrowed in exasperation. "As you will see tonight, when I will no doubt be called on to entertain an entire party when I have not the least desire to do any such thing."

Caroline was no longer listening. She tossed the book onto the nearest table—no point returning this one to a shelf when she had no idea which section it had come from in the first place—and stood up. "How large a party? And what on earth for?"

"Merely a few select friends, who wanted to wish my brother congratulations on his marriage."

Wonderful. Just wonderful. Now she was going to have to spend an entire evening hearing every single detail about the Bennet sisters and their recent felicities. "Could they not have written letters?"

"One would think you disliked parties almost as much as I."

"I merely . . ." Caroline hesitated, but there was no real explanation she could give which did not invite either further questioning or reveal some vulnerability which she was not prepared to do at any time of day but certainly not before lunchtime. "Well, I suppose I ought to go and get myself ready."

"For tonight?" Georgiana glanced at the clock. "The party is not for another six hours."

"One can never be too prepared, my dear," Caroline declared, before sweeping out of the room.

Chapter Two

Caroline had to admit that the housekeeper, Mrs Reynolds, had outdone herself yet again. The drawing room was amply lit with two dozen candles in silver holders, each so polished that the flames looked like twice the number. Caroline had often seen Mrs Reynolds adjusting and readjusting said candlesticks—sometimes even with a measuring tape in hand to ensure that each adhered to precise intervals—and so, she knew only too well how careful the placement of each had been, yet the housekeeper's positioning managed to look artful rather than uniform.

Two long tables had been brought into the drawing room and placed under the large windows which overlooked the south side of the estate. One table groaned under the weight of cold meats, cheeses, and four different types of cake, while yet another held platters of sweetmeats and pastries, including a large plate of Mr Darcy's favourite apple puffs. Servants moved to and fro amongst the crowd, ensuring that each guest had a suitable drink and that everything was very much to everyone's satisfaction. The party was larger than Caroline had expected—around thirty people, most of whom she recognised on sight as being friends of the Darcy family. Amongst them were several gentlemen of her brother's acquaintance, and she was obliged to conduct three separate—though equally tedious—conversations before she could reach the opposite end of the room, where Georgiana stood resplendent in a dove-grey gown.

Miss Darcy looked the very picture of elegance and beauty, though she had once complained to Caroline that this was her least favourite dress, for although the material shimmered and shone to wondrous advantage in the candlelight, it was almost unbearably itchy.

"Thank goodness," she said, upon seeing Caroline emerge from the crowd. "Do distract me from this infernal dress or else I fear I shall tear it off right here and now." From Georgiana's lips, the threat seemed even more scandalous than it would have from anyone else's.

"If it is really that bad, then why on earth are you wearing it?" Caroline inquired.

"It was a present from my brother," said she. "A couple of hours of pain on my part seems a small price to pay for making him happy." She rolled her shoulders, evidently repressing the desire to scratch. "Perhaps it will have an accident tomorrow after he is gone. Dresses sometimes fall into fires of their own accord, do they not?"

"Alas, the pattern of such unfortunate incidents is well known," Caroline murmured. "A shame to waste something so gorgeous, though. Do they not say that beauty comes at a cost?"

"A price I am unwilling to pay, if it means enduring this." Miss Darcy rolled her shoulders a second time, though the action seemed to offer little relief. "Good grief, it's as if a thousand tiny insects have been ordered to nibble on my flesh. Only a man would purchase something so damned itchy. It's not as if they have to put up with anything remotely similar."

Caroline scanned the crowd again but was unable to locate a familiar figure with dark, curly hair. "Speaking of our guest of honour, where is he?"

"Oh, you just missed him. He's gone off to show his new horse to Lord Braithwaite. Though I rather think he was looking for an excuse to leave the party for a while." Georgiana shifted again, grimacing. "You know, he is never quite comfortable amongst a large crowd, even comprised of his friends."

Surprised, Caroline raised an eyebrow. "Did not he invite these people in the first place?"

"Such a thing was expected of him, so he did it. One may say many things about we Darcys, but at least we always adhere to the standards society has set. However ridiculous they might be," she added under her breath.

The unexpected bitter edge of Georgiana's tone made Caroline glance at her, startled. Perhaps the itchiness of the dress was causing her ill-temper to escalate—but the next moment Miss Darcy was all smiles. "Mr Warwick, how lovely to see you!" she exclaimed, as a man stepped out of the crowd and came towards her. "I'm so glad you could make it. And where is your lovely daughter?"

The man bowed, smiling back. "Emmeline sends her apologies, Miss Darcy. I'm afraid she has rather a bad cold at the moment and regretfully did not feel she was fit to attend."

"Oh dear. In that case, I shall have the cook send you home tonight with her special remedy. It is quite awful, I admit, but it will ensure that Emmeline's cold will be cleared up in no time." She turned, dropping her voice so that only Caroline could hear. "Unfortunately, I must leave you now to do my duty as hostess, whether I like it or not. There are still several acquaintances I have not yet welcomed."

Caroline watched as Georgiana moved through the crowd, blushing and bestowing a sweet, shy smile on everyone who greeted her. A young man standing near the window gazed at Miss Darcy with clear admiration and only stopped when his companion jostled his elbow and leaned over to whisper something in his ear. The young man paled and stared into his wine glass. *What on earth was that about?* Caroline wondered. She had no time to investigate, though, for after a round of enthusiastic pleading begun by Mr Warwick, Georgiana finally acquiesced to play a song on the pianoforte.

Her voice was truly a delight—a pleasing, resonant timbre, not too high or shrill—and her range was most impressive. Caroline watched Georgiana's fingers dance up and down the keys with incredible dexterity. She herself could play, of course, as all well-heeled young ladies ought, but very few could compare to Miss Darcy's natural talents. Yet Georgiana bent her head as if checking the sheet music—strange, for Caroline had seen her play this piece a hundred times without ever needing to do so—and for a moment, the smile slipped from her face. When Miss Darcy lifted her head, however, the smile was back in place and as bright as ever.

Caroline shook herself. *Silly.* She must have imagined it. *What young lady with such obvious talent would not want to be the centre of attention? Particularly in front of an illustrious crowd who applauds her every move.* After shouts of encouragement, Georgiana was obliged to play yet another song on the pianoforte, followed by a third on the harpsichord. As the last few notes of this third song faded away, Mr Darcy entered the room with Lord Braithwaite on his heels. Dressed in a black jacket and crisp white shirt, a black cravat tied perfectly at his throat, Darcy looked as handsome as ever. *He would have been a perfect husband,* Caroline thought. *As perfect as a man could ever be, anyway.*

"Brava!" Mr Darcy cried, gesturing to Georgiana, who shot him a grateful look before getting up. "What a talent my sister has, do you not agree?" He turned to the crowd. "Those closest to us will remember that she was playing before she could walk, though I confess I am glad she mastered the latter skill as well."

The crowd laughed, turning their attention to Mr Darcy, each one congratulating him personally on his recent felicity in marriage. Despite Caroline's feelings about his new wife, she crammed an apple puff into her mouth and circulated the room again, intent on reaching him to do the very same. Unfortunately, she managed to get no more than a few steps each time before being accosted by yet another gentleman who either knew her brother or father or both. The Bingleys were not such an old and revered family as the Darcys, of course, but they were wealthy and good-looking, which more than made up for the rest. It helped that Caroline's brother and father were charming men who were extremely well-liked in all circles—a little too well-liked, in Caroline's opinion. *One should not seek to recommend one's self to everybody, but only to those whose acquaintance could benefit one in some way. Anything else is really a waste of one's time and energy.*

Charles had never understood that idea, and had frequently protested that everyone, regardless of status, deserved equal kindness. Mr Darcy, on the other hand, had shared Caroline's sensible opinion up until the point where he'd met Miss Elizabeth Bennet. Soon afterwards, he had changed for the worse, altering his former strict judgements into more kind, liberal ones. Really, it was enough to make one feel quite sick.

As a captain from the local militia regaled her with tales of his exploits, Caroline nodded, though her mind was entirely elsewhere. *What could Darcy possibly see in Miss Elizabeth Bennet?* The girl was pretty, certainly, though nowhere near being a true beauty like her sister Jane. Her tongue was sharp, though Caroline had never heard her actually insult anyone. She was obstinate and bold, which had been evident from the first—imagine walking miles in the rain and mud on your own two legs just to confirm that your sister had a mild cold!—and these untoward traits had been verified by Lady Catherine's tale of their brief meeting. Caroline had only a passing acquaintance with the de Bourghs through the Darcys, but that had been quite enough. Anyone standing up to the might and manner of the old battleaxe was certainly no coward. Caroline herself would rather have faced an actual dragon if given the choice; at least a dragon could only take your life, whereas Lady Catherine could murder your good name.

"And then later, I was faced with even worse peril," the captain declared. "My ship was a little damaged, for you remember, the cannons which we fired at the raiders had been returned in kind and—"

"Goodness gracious, how lovely," Caroline said absently, forcing a pleasant smile. She hadn't heard a word of the previous story and didn't intend to listen to this one either. "Do tell me more."

Perhaps it had been the bravery Miss Elizabeth Bennet had shown in the face of Lady Catherine's wrath which impressed Darcy so much. Perhaps there had been other moments to which Caroline had not been privy, where Miss Bennet had bewitched the gentleman with unsuitable and unladylike attributes. Confidence where there ought to have been coyness. Wit where there ought to have been demurity. Truculence where there ought to have been obedience.

Seduction where there ought to have been modesty.

Caroline scowled, then remembered she was supposed to be listening with rapt attention and corrected her expression to one of polite wonder. To think that all these traits might have combined to form a woman which Darcy thought not only pleasing but actually desirable was baffling in the extreme. Really, it was deeply frustrating not to know precisely how or why the pair had made their match.

And why did it not happen with me?

Caroline downed her second glass of wine, then picked up a third. By the time she was halfway through yet another piece of spiced honey cake, the green irritation festering in her stomach had blossomed into full-grown maggots, wriggling around in pale discomfort. When the guests had begun to disperse in twos and threes, shaking hands and calling farewells to their neighbours, Caroline approached Mr Darcy with a sunny countenance plastered onto her face that she certainly did not feel.

He turned, a half-drunk glass in his hand. "Ah, good evening to you." He made a short bow, his eyes flitting around the room. "Have you had a pleasant time at the party?"

"Good evening. Indeed, I did." She waited until the last few stragglers had crossed over the threshold, leaving them alone. Georgiana was nowhere to be seen, for which she was exceedingly grateful. A solitary fox was more easily cornered than a pair. "Did you enjoy yourself tonight?"

"It has been a delightful evening," he confirmed. "Though I confess I am now rather tired and have a long ride ahead of me tomorrow."

He bowed again, but before he could bid her goodnight she found herself blurting a question she had never dared voice before. "Why not me?"

Darcy blinked, his lips parting in surprise, and it took him a moment to find his own voice again. "Excuse me?" His hand went to his hair, fingers running through the thick curls, a habit she had seen only on occasions when he was truly unsettled by something or someone.

"I would like to know"—and perhaps she'd had a little too much wine and cake, for now the words were spilling out of her in a tumble—"why you never saw me as a real match?"

"Come now, Ca—Miss Bingley," he said, shifting uncomfortably on the balls of his feet, as if he'd like nothing more than to flee from the room at top speed. "It is best not to ask questions when one does not really wish to hear the answers."

Miss Bingley, she seethed. Never mind that it was appropriate for a now-married man to keep other women at arm's length—she was not just any woman. She had known him for years. She had eaten countless meals with him, had hundreds of conversations. She had stayed in his beautiful home several times and walked his grounds often enough that she could do it in her sleep. "I am all astonishment, sir! What on earth makes you think I do not wish to hear the answer if I asked the question in the first place?"

At this, he made no reply.

"I am not some wilting flower who cannot abide the slightest gust of wind," she pressed. "Pray, tell me honestly."

Darcy quirked an eyebrow. "Trust me, you do not wish to—"

"I bloody well do," she retorted, startled by the heat of her own temper.

A flush had risen in his cheeks, his dark eyes reflecting the sparkle of the candlelight. Lord, but sometimes he was almost as pretty as his sister, though he had far less patience.

"In that case," he said, his voice tight, "let me list the reasons."

He lifted a hand into the air between them, raising a finger for each item on his imaginary list. "You are vain. You are arrogant. You are stubborn. You consider yourself superior to most, and while I admit you have good reason to do so, you do not possess the ability to humble yourself. You are haughty and frequently uncharitable, and—" He'd run out of fingers, though he didn't seem inclined to start again. Instead, his hand curled into a fist and dropped to his side. "You do not know when to hold your tongue." Darcy took a deep breath, then bit his lip. "In short, you reminded me far too much of myself."

Caroline's jaw dropped. She certainly had not been expecting that answer.

"It took Lizzy to show me the darkest, most bitter parts of my soul. Then, once I was . . . well"—he cleared his throat—"made aware of my faults, it was up to me to decide whether to work on them or not. And I chose to do so, because I wanted to be a better man for her." He stepped towards Caroline, his voice lowering. "Look, neither you nor I would have made each other better people. In fact, in all likelihood, we would have made each other much worse. We never would have made a good match, for all that you have convinced yourself of the fact. Search your heart and tell me if you find my words false."

Caroline ground her teeth together. She had meant only to needle him, not to feel the pierce of his words like a thousand arrows. "I am glad, sir," said she, her voice cracking only slightly, "that you feel yourself so much improved compared to me. How low I must look to you from your lofty position."

"You misunderstand me," Darcy complained, his fingers flitting once again to his hair, smoothing it back. "I simply—"

"Thank you, but I need hear no more," she said, putting up a hand to stem the flow of his words. "You have said quite enough, sir."

"But as a friend, I must insist on making my meaning plain. For we are friends, are we not?"

She did not feel particularly friendly, and so, chose not to respond. He mistakenly took her silence as encouragement.

"It is my strong belief that if you do not mend the error of your ways," he continued, "then you will never find such happiness as I have done. A love match, no less, supported by respect and perfect understanding on both sides." His eyes were sincere and glittering in the candlelight. "It is a lonely life without love, Miss Bingley. Trust me. I lived it. Fortune and a good name can only take one so far forward."

"And you think that if I were more like your wife, then I should land myself a happy marriage?"

"I did not say that, precisely, although you would do well to mark her behaviour and character. There would be worse ladies to emulate." At this, his lips twitched. "Forgive me, but I cannot think of two women less alike than you and Lizzy."

"Nonsense! I could be just like her if I wanted to," Caroline insisted. "Better, in fact. I am exceedingly capable of falling in love. I could do so at any moment I choose." She ought to stop there, but anger had taken the reins and was driving her tongue inexorably onwards. "And you need not act as if your wife were perfect. She is far from it."

Any trace of amusement vanished. "I did not claim she is anything of the sort. But you shall have to forgive me if I doubt the veracity of your declaration. I have never seen you in love with anything apart from your own good opinion."

She bit back a gasp as the arrows in her soul twisted, digging their barbs in more deeply. Caroline pulled her shoulders back and fixed him with her iciest glare. “Goodnight, Mr Darcy. I wish you the utmost happiness. Both of you.”

Darcy bit his lip, regret already pooling in his dark eyes, but Caroline spun on her heel and fled the room before he could catch sight of the tears spilling down her cheeks.

Chapter Three

In the privacy of the guest room, Caroline curled up on the armchair in front of the fire and sobbed with wild abandon. *Blasted Elizabeth Bennet!* Everyone was so enamored with her, but she was simply an ordinary girl with too much confidence for her station and a witty remark for every situation. How could such a woman possibly have changed Mr Darcy for the better? And if she had indeed done so—though Caroline could not imagine how such a transformation had taken place, or precisely what the girl had done to garner such unwarranted accolades—then was Caroline really doomed to remain as she was without a suitor to likewise show her the error of her ways?

The inventory of Caroline's flaws, which Darcy had seemed only too ready to list off, had been comprehensive. Despite her protests, Caroline had to admit—however grudgingly—that several of his arrows had found their target. She could be a touch arrogant at times, she knew, though it was not without cause. She was perhaps a little vain from time to time, though what pretty woman was not? And as for stubbornness, had that not been a particularly notable trait found in Miss Elizabeth Bennet's own character? Why, then, was it a vice for Caroline when it had been a virtue of Miss Bennet's? This seemed like a terribly unfair double standard.

Love really does blind one to the object of one's affection's flaws, she thought, her lip curling. Unable to sit still a moment longer, she got up and began to pace from door to window and back again.

The guest room had been furnished to Caroline's exacting standards, since she stayed in it so often of late. A small writing desk had been placed to the left of the large window to best catch the morning sunshine. An elegant set of high-backed chairs were situated in front of the ornate fireplace, opposite a bed whose frame was slightly higher than her own at home. Fresh flowers in pretty vases adorned the windowsill, as well as the small tables which sat on the left-hand side of each chair, filling the room with a soft fragrance which was pleasant without being overpowering. She personally preferred pink camellias, which brightened up any space, and Mrs Reynolds had always made certain that the room was stocked with them during her visits.

Unfortunately, not even pink camellias could improve Caroline's mood right now. The more she paced, the more she considered Darcy's words and the more suspicious she became that he had—in some small way—been right. She stopped in front of the fireplace, pressing the heels of her hands into her eyes, her head throbbing. Good God, she couldn't actually be considering taking his advice. How would she even go about improving an already excellent character?

Wait a moment. Her hands fell to her sides, her jaw dropping as an idea formed. *Who better to show me how to act than the best and most perfect young lady of my acquaintance, who is right now in this very same house?*

Yes, it was a superb idea. She and Georgiana knew each other well enough by now for her to ask such a favour. They had been acquainted for three years, and this past twelvemonth had seen Caroline at Pemberley on no less than four separate occasions. Georgiana, although she could be rather quiet and distant at times, was easy company, even if she did prefer books to gossip and merriment. Caroline did not have many friends, but her relationship with Georgiana was the closest she had come to anything like real companionship. And through this wonderful scheme, they would no doubt become closer still.

Sisters, even!

The idea was so flawless, it had to be acted upon immediately. Caroline burst out of her room, marched along the hallway to Georgiana's chamber, and flung open the door without consideration for the occupant. Miss Darcy was already in bed, her fair curls lying loose around her shoulders, with *The Parsonage-House* propped on her knees. She looked up, her expression startled, the single candle on the bedside table guttering in the sudden draught. "Good Lord! Is something on fire?"

Rather too late, Caroline remembered that one ought not to burst in upon one's acquaintances without knocking, but what was done was done. "This is an emergency of a personal nature. I have a favour to ask."

"A favour suggests the opportunity to decline, which I do not think you intend to give me." Georgiana squinted in the darkness, her suspicious expression fading into concern. "Have you been crying? Is something the matter?"

"I need your help. Please." Caroline dropped to her knees beside the bed and clasped her hands together in supplication.

"Get up, for goodness' sake. What is it?"

"I need you to help me to become as kind and good as Miss

Elizabeth Bennet. Ideally in the next fortnight." She nodded, thinking it over. Yes, that was a more than sufficient period of time. How long could the endeavour possibly take, after all? "A shorter time, if you can manage it. I am sure you can. You are a very capable young woman, after all."

"Pardon?" Georgiana gaped at her. "You need me to . . . what?"

"To teach me to embody those characteristics in that young lady which you deem to be most attractive to a potential match."

The silence lengthened. Georgiana's eyes were as wide and round as saucers, her mouth opening and closing without words coming out.

"Really, it is not a difficult concept to grasp," Caroline sniffed. She'd expected some resistance, but this seemed overdramatic. "I am not asking you to help me fly to the moon."

"No, indeed," Georgiana exclaimed, finally finding her voice. "All you want is a total alteration of character. Frankly, flying to the moon would be an easier achievement."

"I beg to differ," Caroline corrected, pushing down another sharp pang of hurt. To hear it stated clearly that her character had been examined and been found deficient by a man whom she'd considered a potential match had hurt; to hear it indirectly from his sister, whom she considered a friend, somehow hurt even more. Besides, she did not wish a true alteration of her character, only to learn how to put the costume of kindness on and glitter enough to draw every gaze.

Georgiana's fingers pressed into her eye sockets in a move that seemed designed to alleviate some pressure, then sighed into her palms. "I simply meant to point out that you and Lizzy do not share many traits. I am not sure how you could possibly become—" Her hands dropped to her lap. "Why on earth would you . . . No, don't tell me. I do not even want to know how or why you've come up with this scheme."

"It was your brother," Caroline interrupted, ignoring the plea. "He made me realise that I have been somewhat . . . unkind of late. Uncharitable, even."

The word lodged in her throat, and for a moment, anger burned brightly inside her again. She dearly wanted to shove Darcy's charity somewhere society would have frowned upon.

"Oh?" Georgiana raised an eyebrow. "Did he, indeed? What precisely did he say? And what did you say to provoke him so? For I know you must have done something to incur such a rebuke. My brother is not often in the habit of uttering such things as would wound any friend of ours."

Caroline held out against Miss Darcy's steely gaze for a full ten seconds before she caved. "I may have asked him why he never considered me as a suitable match," she muttered.

"Oh, Caroline." Sympathy flashed across her face. "I hadn't realised that his marrying Lizzy would hurt you so much."

"Then he listed all my faults," Caroline continued, ignoring this. She did not need sympathy. She needed a plan of action. "And then he told me that I reminded him too much of himself, that love had changed him, and that without a similar change, I am doomed to spinsterhood. Well, he did not say it quite like that, but it was what he meant, I am sure," Caroline sniffed. "Look, I am three-and-twenty, and my fortune and family are secure enough to land me a decent match. Before Mother attempts to wed me to someone of her own choosing, I think it wise to seek out a man who fits my preferences."

"So then . . . do it." Georgiana waved a hand around the

room, as if alluding to a veritable crowd of unseen suitors. "Marry anyone you like. You have had offers before, have you not? I am sure I've heard you mention them."

"No one up to my standards," she corrected. *Or Mother's.* "And no one who truly adored me."

"Wait a moment. Are you telling me that you have decided to seek a love match?"

She thought about this for a moment. Darcy had certainly intimated that she wasn't capable of one, so it seemed like an obvious goal. Anything he had declared she couldn't do, she damn well would do. Rubbing his stupid, handsome face in her success would be the crowning glory on top of her own happiness. "Precisely. I am determined to fall in love."

Georgiana stared at her, then blinked. "Caroline, if that's what you want, then I have no idea why you require my assistance. You move in many lauded circles in society. You are constantly surrounded by men. Surely, one of them can be easily induced to fall in love with you, and you with him."

"But I have too many flaws," Caroline cried. "Your brother said as much. He said I must try to correct them first before anyone will even want me. You must teach me your ways—your modesty, your grace, your sweet disposition." She paused. "How long do you think it will take? Four days? Five?"

"Oh, good grief. I'm going to get up early just to shake Fitzwilliam so hard his teeth will rattle." Georgiana pinched the bridge of her nose. "You're not going to give up this idea, are you?"

"Your brother also called me stubborn," Caroline supplied helpfully.

Miss Darcy sighed.

"A character once formed can be changed, can it not?" Caroline pressed on, sensing weakness. "Isn't that what is always happening in those novels you like so much? I simply want to be seen as—I mean," she corrected, as Georgiana's eyebrow arched, "I simply want to try to be as good and kind as yourself and Miss Bennet. I think it is high time that I acknowledge that perhaps . . ." Even saying the words out loud made her want to grind her teeth again until they were nothing but powder. "Perhaps I have not always embodied those tender characteristics for which young ladies are most prized. I am eager to learn how to be a better version of myself. No, not better—the best version of myself! I must not settle for anything other than the loftiest of ideals. I shall become the best woman you have ever met, in every single respect, and I shall land a gentleman of equal geniality. Do you not want that for me, Georgie? Do you not want to see me happy?"

In fact, Georgiana looked as if she did not know whether to laugh or to cry or to fling herself out the window, but Caroline plunged on regardless. "And you are considered such a perfect young lady. Many would call you the most perfect young lady of their acquaintance, in fact. Therefore, you are the ideal teacher to—"

"I am far from perfect. I—"

"Nonsense, nonsense," Caroline said, cheerfully barrelling over Georgiana's protests. "You are the embodiment of everything that society deems wonderful, and thus, are the ideal person to teach me. But . . ." she trailed off, her smile becoming cunning, "if you do not agree with the list of faults your brother provided, then do say so, and I will consider myself remedied with no need for further application to amend my character."

Miss Darcy bit her lip in a manner that was very reminiscent of her brother. Clearly she did agree but to do so out loud would mean confirming that Caroline was in need of tutoring. *Caught between a rock and a hard place*, Caroline thought triumphantly. *Or perhaps the other expression suits better: between the devil and the deep blue sea?*

"Well . . ." Georgiana began. "If I agreed to help you in some way—"

Caroline grabbed her by the shoulders and squeezed hard. "Thank you, my dear Georgie! Thank you!"

"Hold on, I said 'if'! If I agreed to teach you," she repeated, extricating herself with some difficulty, "then you would have to agree to my terms."

"Terms?" Caroline repeated, a faint echo of suspicion sounding low in her gut. "What terms?"

Georgiana held up three fingers. "One, that you must not waste my time." She put down a finger. "Two, that you must do everything I say." She put down another finger, rendering the hand a clenched fist. "Three, that you must be open to all new experiences."

"Why, those seem no trouble at all. I am perfectly open to new experiences."

Miss Darcy levelled a long-suffering look over the top of her now closed fist. "We shall see."

"You shall not regret this," Caroline promised, squeezing Georgiana again.

"On the contrary, Miss Bingley," came the reply, muffled as it was against Caroline's bosom, "I rather think I shall."

Chapter Four

To my currently-not-dear brother,

Miss Bingley was in my room last night, face still wet from weeping, begging me to help her become a nicer person. Someone had told her that unless she altered her entire character, she would never find a match. That someone then fled by the dawn's light, leaving me the only person in this house capable of agreeing to the ridiculous scheme she has cooked up. That same someone ought to think very, very carefully about what sort of a present he should bring back from Bath for his darling sister.

It had better be horse-sized, Fitz. I do not jest.

Yours with an affection which depends
entirely upon my future gift,
Georgiana

P.S. There was no need to be quite so callous. I admit that she's rather ~~aggravating~~ ~~trying~~ strident at times, but I also think that, perhaps under all those layers of bluster, there might be something truly worth excavating.

Caroline woke early the next morning with a mild headache as a result of all the crying she'd done the night before. Tears were an infrequent occurrence for her, but when she thought of the way that Darcy had looked at her—that flash of anger, fading into pity—the tears threatened to break free again. She shook herself. His words had wounded her, had cut deeply into her soul in a way that she'd never expected, but there was no need for weeping now that she had a plan. It would work, especially now that she had Georgiana on her side. Miss Darcy had never failed at anything, as far as Caroline knew, and so, there was no reason to suppose that she was about to start any time soon.

Buoyed by this reassurance, she washed her face before slipping into a cream dress the colour of a new moon and then went down to break her fast. The Pemberley dining-parlour was one of the most elegant rooms in any house Caroline had ever visited. Tall windows rendered it light and airy, while butter-yellow walls enhanced the effect, making it look as if sunshine were always present, regardless of the weather outside. The curtains were a darker shade of yellow, leaning towards flaxen, and were hemmed perfectly so that the bottoms brushed the floor with only the slightest of caresses. The floor was a pale hardwood, worn smooth by the passage of many feet, and was polished highly enough to reflect the blue sky filtering through the windows. The only paintings on the walls were landscapes of Scotland, which the late Mrs Darcy had loved very much. Caroline gazed up at her particular favourite, which featured a sun-dappled glen through which a bold buck walked, his head held high, majestic antlers rising several feet above his graceful head. The painter had somehow managed to make the animal's flank look almost as if it were heaving, and one quite expected it to turn its head any moment to snort a plume of steamy breath into the soft summer air.

To her left, someone quietly cleared their throat. Caroline startled on the threshold, realising only now that she had been too lost in her own thoughts to see that there was another person in the room. Her momentary spike of panic that it might be Darcy himself receded as she swung round to find Mrs Reynolds lingering at the table, clad in a black dress which looked just as neatly-pressed as the lady herself. The housekeeper's smile was a little strained; she'd evidently been expecting Georgiana, who was usually up long before anyone else in the house. Caroline's gaze swept the table, noting the lack of used cutlery; unfortunately, it appeared that she was the first one to arrive this morning. Glancing over her shoulder into the great hall, Caroline saw that the pair of large riding boots which had lain on the mat the night before had disappeared. It was possible Darcy had left already, though it would be unlike him to do so, since he took every available opportunity to spend time with his sister. Then again, last night's confrontation might have prompted him to escape early, so as to avoid any more unpleasant scenes with Caroline.

Rude, she thought. He ought to have left her a letter of apology for all that he'd said. Or at the very least, he might have waited long enough to have a buttered roll thrown at his head.

"Good morning, ma'am," Mrs Reynolds said, drawing Caroline once again out of her reverie.

Normally, Caroline would have simply nodded, but a voice in her head prompted her to start as she meant to go on. *What would Miss Elizabeth Bennet do?* she wondered. *She probably charms every servant she meets as if each were a queen.* "Good morning, Mrs Reynolds," said she, addressing the housekeeper with the same warm tone that she'd heard Georgiana muster. She glanced at the table, where the settings were arranged with their usual uniformity. "What a lovely, er . . ." She paused. *Blast. How does one compliment a servant?* "Crockerial arrangement," she finished, feeling rather pleased with herself.

The housekeeper's expression did not change, though Caroline got the distinct impression that Mrs Reynolds could not have been more surprised if Caroline had strolled through the door nude and flung a dead rabbit onto the table. "Thank you, ma'am," she said, after the briefest hesitation, pulling out a chair for Caroline. "And how would you like your toast this morning?"

"Light," Caroline said, her attention distracted as Georgiana entered the room, wearing a pretty pink dress that complemented her fair curls perfectly. "The sort that is barely a moment beyond hot bread."

"Very good, ma'am."

"Good morning to you both," Georgiana said, eyeing Mrs Reynolds, who glanced at Georgiana before disappearing through the door in a manner that wasn't quite her usual bustle, but wasn't quite a scuttle either. "Heavens, it is not even nine on the clock and already you seem to have frightened my housekeeper out of her wits. What on earth did you say to her?"

Her plan was off to an inauspicious start. "I merely said good morning," she protested.

Georgiana stared at her. "Yes, that would have done it. You've never said good morning to any of the staff before."

Annoyed, Caroline poured herself tea, then added a heaped spoon of sugar. In an ordinary household, the servants were expected to actually serve; in such a grand place as Pemberley, one might assume one would receive exceptional treatment as a matter of course, yet Miss Darcy preferred to break her fast with no one waiting on her but Mrs Reynolds, and even then, she preferred that the housekeeper do as little as possible. When Mr Darcy was present, things proceeded in the usual way, but when he was gone, Georgiana lapsed into what Caroline often thought of as her *common woman* act—serving herself, dressing herself, maintaining her own fires, and so on. Caroline had learned to accept this quirk, though it did not make any sense to her; the effort of reaching a few inches to obtain her own condiments did not particularly signify one way or another.

"You speak as if I have no manners at all," she complained, "when you know very well that nothing could be further from the truth."

"You have very pretty manners indeed," Georgiana allowed, seating herself one place away from Caroline and reaching for a platter of cold ham. She stabbed a thick slice with her fork and moved it onto her plate before lifting a cloche to peer at the eggs underneath. "Though, if my memory serves me, you generally do not apply them to servants."

"It is all part of my Great Endeavour," Caroline declared, enunciating the words to make it plain that the plan was capitalised in an appropriately formal way. "Do not tell me you have forgotten what we discussed last night."

"I had rather hoped that was all a bad dream," Georgiana muttered, sliding two eggs onto her plate. "And I am not sure 'discussed' is the right word either. What I recall is you barging in and making a series of demands. Or rather, one large demand."

"That is a terrible misrepresentation of the matter. I simply begged for your help, and you"—Caroline flashed her most charming smile at Georgiana, who looked completely unimpressed by it—"agreed to help me in my hour of need. As any true companion might. We are friends, are we not?"

"*Friends* is a strong—" Georgiana muttered, then raised her voice. "You seem much recovered this morning. Is there really any need to—"

"I am completely set upon my course," Caroline interrupted. "And you already gave your word."

"I hardly think that it is fair to hold me to something which you threw at me without a moment's notice." Georgiana caught Caroline's pout and sighed. "Yes, all right. I shall assist you in your . . . what did you call it?"

"My Great Endeavour."

"It sounds like a ship about to set sail on some dangerous voyage."

"Nonsense. I hardly think that you teaching me to be kinder can be dangerous in any way."

Georgiana emitted a small *hmm*, but declined to comment. A moment later, Mrs Reynolds brought in a rack of warm toast, lightly done, and set it on the table in front of Caroline, who refrained from offering more than a tight smile in case she scared the woman further. If she could not even bid a servant good morning without causing alarm, then perhaps she needed more help than she had realised. Some unfamiliar emotion twinged in her chest, as red as embarrassment, though nowhere near as warm. "Will your brother be joining us this morning?" Caroline asked, selecting the most appetizing-looking slice.

"Why? Looking for another list of your flaws?"

Indignation stung as hard as a wasp. "I believe I already have a thorough inventory of them, thank you," Caroline retorted, buttering the toast so hard, her knife gouged through the bread and scraped the plate. "I do not think there is a single rock left in my soul that your brother has not pried up and shone a light underneath."

She cut a corner off and crammed the toast into her mouth, then buttered a second slice with even more venom than the first, risking removing the very pattern on the admittedly beautiful china plate. Georgiana chewed slowly, her eyes tracking every erratic movement of Caroline's knife. "May I ask a question?"

Caroline swallowed, hardly tasting her mouthful. "Certainly."

"Did you ever love Fitzwilliam?"

"Of course," she replied immediately. "We all love your brother. Such a dear man."

"I mean, were you ever in love with him?"

Caroline's knife halted above the butter dish. *What a ridiculous question.* "Goodness, no."

"I did not think so." Miss Darcy cocked her head. "When you talked about him, it was clear you thought him handsome and interesting, but I never really got the sense you truly . . . adored him."

An astute observation, and closer to the truth than Caroline had been prepared for at such an early hour. "Do you think that is why he was never interested in me in return?"

"Partly, yes."

"Oh." She put the knife down.

"Have you ever been in love?" Georgiana persisted.

"Never. Love renders one foolish and nonsensical."

"So why do you wish to be in it now?"

"Well, I . . ." She floundered. That was a very good question, and one she didn't really have an answer for, other than it was something Darcy had seemed to think she couldn't possibly achieve. What higher motivation could there be to want to accomplish something than someone declaring that you could not possibly manage it?

"And why on earth do you think I am capable of assisting you with such a thing?" Georgiana continued.

"You always master everything you try," Caroline said, though to her mind, the answer was obvious. "Bach. Haydn. All the most difficult *contredanses*."

"You are a person, not a piece of music. Nor are you a series of steps."

"Even so." She picked up her steaming cup, savouring the heavenly scent. "I have every faith in your ability to master and manage the most complicated of affairs. Perhaps this is an excellent test for you, too. A chance for you to succeed in something far more impressive than needlework and concertos."

"Oh yes," Georgiana said, sarcasm lacing her tone. "I can easily see all the ways in which teaching you will benefit me. I am definitely not thinking about all the ways in which trying to reform you into a mirror-image of Lizzy will drive me into an early grave."

The idea of Elizabeth Bennet's face in a looking glass distracted Caroline for a moment. That was another thing; the girl was appealing to anyone with eyes to see her feminine charms. She had not her sister's looks to be sure, for Jane was by far considered to be the real beauty of the family by anyone with taste and sense, but the animation in Lizzy's fine, dark eyes certainly did lend a certain warmth to her countenance. Even her mouth was appealing, with pink lips that curved in an impertinent smirk at every available opportunity, yet softened into genuine loveliness whenever she . . . whenever she . . .

Caroline couldn't quite remember what line of thought had brought her to this conclusion. A faint, incomprehensible blush heated her cheeks as she stared down into her tea. Shaking her head to free herself from the attractive mental image of Miss Elizabeth Bennet—witty and amiable paragon of all Hertfordshire, may God burn it to the ground whenever He so desired—she returned to the destruction of her toast with renewed vigour.

Georgiana sighed. She'd been doing a lot of that over the past day, Caroline had noticed. "I have two further questions."

Caroline arched an eyebrow. "Only two? My, my, this interrogation is light. Are you feeling quite well?"

Georgiana ignored this jab; she was far too well-versed in the art of sparring to be waylaid by such a simple riposte. "My first is this: one is generally advised on such things by one's relations rather than one's friends. Why, therefore, do you insist on receiving my help in particular?"

"I told you precisely why last night. You are the societal ideal of what a young lady ought to be. Everybody thinks so. I have quite lost count of the number of times I have overheard that declaration from other young ladies and their mamas, as well as from eligible gentlemen."

"Mmm." She poured herself another cup of tea. Caroline wasn't quite sure why she had the feeling that these questions were a test, or why she suddenly felt like she was failing. "And secondly," Georgiana continued, picking up her fork and spearing another piece of ham, "how exactly do you propose to begin?"

"Well, I . . ." She faltered. "I assumed that you would know what to do next."

"You thought that you could demand I assist you in this endeavour and that once I agreed, I would take on the entire responsibility for producing all ideas and activities related to it?"

"Exactly." She smiled, relieved. "I'm so glad we're on the same page, Georgie."

This time, Miss Darcy sighed so hard that the curtains actually fluttered.

"Don't sigh so, my dear friend," Caroline chided. "You'll give yourself sad lung."

Georgiana blinked, a forkful of ham faltering on the way to her mouth. "What on earth is sad lung?"

"It's something Mother used to remind Louisa and I about when we were small. One should only ever emit delicate, ladylike sighs or else one depresses one's lungs to such an extent that one will not be able to breathe properly in one's old age."

Georgiana stared at Caroline over the rack of toast, which was rapidly dwindling. "I do not think that is a real condition."

"Why, it certainly is. Mrs Rotheringham died of sad lung in Bath only four years ago."

"Mrs Rotheringham drowned," Georgiana corrected.

"A terrible accident which she might well have survived," Caroline pointed out, "had she not possessed sad lungs to begin with. Weakened, you see, by all the vigorous sighing."

Georgiana mouthed the words *sad lung* at her plate, then evidently gave up pursuing that particular line of inquiry. "If we are committed to this scheme, I suggest we begin here."

"At the breakfast table?"

"In the house," Georgiana clarified. "Once you have eaten your fill, we shall go around the place, room by room."

"And do what?"

"You shall see. Do you intend to eat the rest of your toast

this morning, or would you prefer to continue mutilating it beyond all recognition?"

"It will be far more mutilated where it is going," Caroline muttered, but she put down her knife anyway and acquiesced to choke down another piece of toast, calmed a little by the idea that the Great Endeavour was about to begin.

Chapter Five

After they had finished eating—or rather, after Caroline had shifted in her seat enough times that Georgiana had sighed again and got up from the table, gesturing for her friend to follow—they ended up in the library. Caroline supposed she shouldn't be surprised by this; it was, after all, Georgiana's favourite room in the house, which she loved even more than her personal sitting room, but Caroline had thought that the Great Endeavour might begin in a more exciting place than the very same room they sat in day after day.

She slowed to a stop as Georgiana spun to face her, eyes alight with amusement. "Your first lesson begins here," Miss Darcy said. "We will go on a tour of the house, and I wish you to find at least two or three things to praise in every room."

"That does not seem so hard." Caroline glanced around. Her mother had always imposed on her the care and attention with which one ought to pay to the smallest of details, and Pemberley offered ample opportunity to wax poetic. "Why, in this room alone I could find a dozen such objects deserving of the highest compliments. The fireplace, for example—did not your brother once tell me that the mantelpiece was made of marble?" She cast an approving eye towards the object in question, noting that even though the stone was dark, it had been polished enough to glint in the flickering light of the fire below. "It is one of the most elegant I have ever seen."

"Very good."

Caroline wasn't finished, though. She had been set a challenge and was determined that she would pass it with flying colours. "I have long admired the candlesticks, too, for this room needs a little more light than others. And the portraits, particularly this one"—she gestured at the only painting in the room which did not frighten the life out of her—"of your . . . paternal great-grandmother?"

"You are correct." Georgiana smiled at the depiction, which featured a woman seated, hands folded in her lap, long, fair hair cascading down her back.

Something which had been nagging at Caroline for the last few days tripped off her tongue without thought. "Though I do think that, perhaps, the room could benefit from a little . . . refreshment." She had, after all, completed Georgiana's task, so surely, she ought to be allowed her opinion now, particularly if it could help refine the room into a perfect, stylish haven.

"Refreshment?" Georgiana blinked. "You mean a tea trolley?"

"No, my dear friend. I mean that these couches, while beautiful, are rather old-fashioned now. At the very least, this one requires a complete reupholstering. Look," she said, bending to poke at the nearest one. "There's very nearly a hole worn through here. Whatever would a visitor think?"

Before she could straighten, a hand closed around her other wrist, tugging her firmly away. "Please do not touch that," Georgiana said. Her voice was calm, but a muscle jumped in her jaw.

Surprised, Caroline dropped her hand to her side. Miss Darcy was not prone to fits of temper or indignation. "Suit yourself. I am sure that your brother could easily arrange for it to be altered. Why, you would not need to be inconvenienced at all. In fact, my father spoke of a fellow who could, for an additional fee, complete a task overnight, which really—"

"Let us proceed," Georgiana said, and then marched from the room.

Caroline followed, equally baffled by this response and by the stiffening of Georgiana's shoulders, but by the time they'd reached the picture gallery, Miss Darcy seemed to have reverted to her usual, placid self. "And what of this room?" she asked, this time not turning to face Caroline, but stopping to stare up at the two magnificent portraits of her parents which hung in the centre of the room.

The picture gallery was, by anyone's standards, a lovely place to linger. The portraits here were more modern and looked far less foreboding than the ones which hung in the library. Caroline's gaze was drawn, as it always was, towards the image of the late Mr and Mrs Darcy, who had been painted individually. Mr Darcy, with his mop of curly fair hair, looked so much like Georgiana that it was uncanny; the same straight, perfectly-shaped nose, the same gentle curve to the lips, which signified a happy soul at rest. Fitzwilliam had evidently inherited his mother's black hair and angular jaw, though Mrs Darcy's beautiful dark eyes lived on in both of her children. Georgiana cast only a cursory glance over her parents, moving quickly to stand in front of several framed drawings.

Caroline followed, peering over her shoulder. These were Georgiana's own creations—really, was there anything the girl could not do with grace and elegance?—and each rendered some person or scene in exquisite detail. Any visitor to the house with even a passing acquaintance with the family would easily recognise Darcy himself, lounging in a meadow while his horse grazed in the background, or the exterior of Pemberley, drawn with the most minute attention paid to every brick.

"I suppose that is the source of all your talents, really," Caroline said, not quite meaning to say it out loud.

Georgiana glanced at her, a slight frown creasing her forehead. "Pardon?"

Caroline gestured at the drawings. "You pay such attention to detail. Much more so than other people."

"Do you think so?"

"Oh, certainly. People are not so observant as one would always hope, you know," Caroline said loftily. Though there was only three and a half years between them, she had always felt the urge to instruct Georgiana on all her views. When one had such excellent opinions, it was one's duty to spread them as far and wide as possible; she would be doing a disservice to the world to keep them to herself. "They do not pay attention to what is most important."

"Indeed," Georgiana said, her lips twitching. "And you do?"

"Of course I do. For example, I note that here"—she pointed at the rendering of Darcy—"you have drawn most carefully that lock of hair which insists upon falling over his left eye, no matter how he has it cut. And this is the horse which, if I am not mistaken, lived to a great old age and sired many of the creatures in your stable today."

In fairness, the beast was an unmistakable one, for it had a distinctive blaze running from forelock to nose. "Newton," Georgiana supplied. "The best horse who ever lived. Apart from my Swift, of course."

Caroline pulled a face, making sure Georgiana could not see it. She'd never really understood Georgiana's bond with animals of all sizes. To her, a horse was simply a carriage that required more upkeep. A carriage, at least, did not have to stop at regular intervals on the road to excrete. Swift was a rather handsome beast by horse standards, but he was still just a horse in Caroline's opinion, and as such, was interchangeable with any of a dozen others.

"Wait a moment," Caroline said, only now noticing a new picture which had been added on the left. "That was not here last time I visited." She leaned closer, a tendril of Georgiana's hair tickling her cheek. Jane and Charles, looking into each other's eyes as they danced, his hand on her slender waist, her hand on his shoulder. Their smiles were joyful and pure, full of love, as if they had forgotten that the rest of the world existed.

"I drew the original picture as a present for them to hang in Netherfield, if it pleases them to do so, but the image of their happiness was so beautiful that I couldn't help replicating it here. Besides, it's nice to have pictures of friends as well as family."

Georgiana's tone was surprisingly wistful. With a stab of annoyance, Caroline realised that a similar picture of Miss Elizabeth Bennet and Mr Darcy would likely follow in due course. What would they be doing? Dancing, or walking together, or reading their beloved books, side by side? Her lip curled in distaste.

"I am working on one now, in fact, though I cannot quite seem to get it right." Georgiana shook herself, as if remembering what they'd come here for. "In any case, observing my drawings is not a compliment."

"Whyever not? I did say they were exquisite, did I not?"

"I am loath to contradict you, but you merely commented that my attention to detail was . . . How did you phrase it? The source of all my talents?" She looked amused.

"Sometimes I forget that you cannot hear my very thoughts." Caroline stepped back, giving Georgiana room to turn around. "Very well. I shall repeat out loud that your drawings are exquisite, though you already know this to be true."

"I know no such thing."

Caroline rolled her eyes, turning to face the rest of the room. "This room has a very pleasant air to it. I might even call it contemplative. It speaks to the reverence with which you and your brother hold your family. And of course, you know that your mama and papa were both very handsome. I cannot imagine that there is a single person in your family who could not be described as exceedingly handsome." She turned to look at the portrait of Lady Catherine de Bourgh, who was Georgiana and Fitzwilliam's aunt. "See? Stern, yes, but an undeniably pretty woman." *Stern* hardly covered it, for the lady seemed to glare out of her painting as if the very act of being captured on canvas personally affronted her. Yet in the dark slash of her eyebrows, the high cheekbones, the perfect rosebud mouth, one could see at a glance that here was good breeding indeed. "You know, these chairs really do not suit this room. They are far too high-backed. And where are the cushions? How can you expect someone to sit and regard these magnificent portraits in comfort?"

Georgiana's look of annoyance did not go unnoticed. "Come. Let us go upstairs."

"You needn't be so huffy. I am doing what you asked of me," Caroline protested as they left the picture gallery and climbed the stairs in the main hall.

"You are, but then you undo all your good work by providing additional comments about what ought to be improved."

Caroline cocked her head. "I do not see the problem."

"One may have an opinion," Georgiana said, casting a long-suffering look at her, which Caroline did not feel she had at all merited, "and yet keep it to one's self from time to time."

"Not give my opinion?" Caroline repeated, horrified, as she trailed Georgiana along the hall. "Whyever not? Did you not ask me to give my opinion as my first task?"

"I asked you to give compliments," Georgiana corrected. "And that was merely a foundational test, for it is easy enough to give a compliment about something which you already like. Now we will move on to something more advanced . . . if you think yourself capable of doing so."

"Of course I am," Caroline said indignantly. "Besides, it is almost too easy to achieve the task you set before me when everything in your house has been chosen with such taste and elegance. Few other houses could boast of having so much splendor and beauty to admire on a daily basis."

Georgiana paused outside the door to her chamber. Despite Caroline's prior visits to the Pemberley estate, she had never before been invited into Georgiana's private chambers. The previous night, the room had been in relative darkness, and she had been too consumed with her own plight to really take in her surroundings. "You may begin," Georgiana said, swinging the door open.

Caroline stepped inside, then groaned inwardly. Even a single glance told her that this room provided a much harder test than the rest of the house put together.

"Well, there are so many . . . things in this room," she said, desperately scanning for something to praise. Everywhere she turned, she was met with a clutter of mismatched old furniture. Evidently Mrs Reynolds hadn't been permitted to bring her measuring tape into this room, for the candles which stood upon the mantelpiece were of differing heights and had apparently been put there entirely at random, so that some stood far too close to others. The desk, which was probably the only beautiful piece of furniture in the room, was so covered in parchment and books that not a single square inch of its surface was visible. The table by the window held the ugliest vase in the world, which was evidently meant to resemble some sort of headless, scaly reptile and was a colour Caroline could only describe as fish-vomit green. The grotesque vase was only slightly ameliorated by the beautiful roses it held, each as dark red as a pricked finger, filling the room with a sultry scent.

"So many lovely things, indeed," she continued, sweeping the room with another glance. "The curtains are such a delicate shade of red, though they are a little thicker than you need. One really ought to let the sun wake you, especially in the summer mornings. It is best for—"

Georgiana cleared her throat.

"And have I mentioned the rug?" Caroline added hastily, lest she fail this test mere seconds into beginning it. "It ties the room together wonderfully."

Threadbare rug, she pronounced mentally. *Heavy curtains. God forbid one should have a modicum of taste and share it for the betterment of others. Is that not, after all, a selfless act of utter charity?*

"Anything else?" Georgiana asked. "What about this blanket? My old nanny stitched it for me."

Caroline had been purposefully avoiding looking at the patchwork blanket on the bed. It was possible that the thing had once been a vibrant rainbow of colours as would please any infant eyes, though it was hard to imagine now. Really, how could one possibly be expected to compliment a ratty old blanket? And why on earth would Georgiana bother to keep such a thing when she could so easily purchase a beautiful new one?

"You forget that I have not complimented you yet," Caroline said, deciding that changing the subject was the only way to escape this conversational trap.

Georgiana blinked. "Me?"

"You did say that I was required to compliment something in every room and every person in the room, did you not? And are you not the only other person in the room, and are thus deserving of my compliment?"

"Well, I . . ." A blush tinged Georgiana's cheeks, making her look even lovelier. "Go on, then."

Praise for Georgiana's beauty and figure came almost too easily, for Caroline had long admired Miss Darcy's proportions. "You are tall and stately, like a young queen."

"I said a compliment, not flattery."

"Firstly, they are one and the same thing. One cannot compliment something without flattering it, and vice versa. Secondly, I mean it," Caroline insisted. "You have a very regal bearing. I have always admired it. Though you really mustn't stoop, Georgie. Embrace your height. Do not be ashamed of it."

"I do not like being so tall," Georgiana muttered. "When I am in a crowd of young ladies, it makes me feel like a goose among ducklings."

"Do not say a goose, say instead a swan." Caroline crooked her hand, imitating a swan's neck with the curve of her wrist. "On the contrary, my dear, it makes you stand out. And what young lady does not desire to stand out among her peers?"

Again, a flash of something on Georgiana's face that was not pleasure at the compliment, but it was gone in the blink of an eye. "I am loath to extract another compliment from you, but is there something in my character that you might flatter, rather than my looks?"

A baffling request, but Caroline was keen to keep Georgiana sweet in case she changed her mind about assisting with the Great Endeavour. "Why, of course! You are most proficient in the musical arts. And your embroidery is exquisite." She cast about for a specific example. "That rosebush you created last year? Perfection itself." It really had been a wonder, with every tiny rose stitched so neatly and gracefully that the flowers seemed to bloom right off the fabric. "In fact, I'd rather been hoping that you would make me one, but then you moved on to cameos."

This did not seem to entirely satisfy, though Georgiana only nodded. "I do get bored rather easily, I'm afraid, and tend to jump from one fancy to another."

This struck Caroline as an odd thing to say, when so many of Georgiana's talents involved hours and hours of practice. Why, she had surely sat at the harp and the pianoforte every day for no less than three hours between the ages of ten and fifteen, and still kept up her practice with regularity. Perhaps once one reached a certain level of proficiency, it did not feel like a chore anymore and was more like unfettered joy. Her playing had certainly brought her family many hours of pleasure, as well as the guests at all the Darcys' many parties. And yet—

She thought of the way Georgiana had looked before she'd begun playing the night before. That had certainly not been an expression of unfettered happiness. *Curious*, she thought.

"—and in any case," Georgiana was saying, and Caroline blinked, aware that she'd missed a large portion of the conversation, "I think it wise that we give you a little more practice before our first outing."

Ooh, an outing! She had almost forgotten what it was they were supposed to be doing. "What need have I of more practice?" she demanded. "Have I not proven to you this morning that I am capable of being a star pupil?"

"Your performance has been good," Georgiana allowed, though Caroline did not miss the flicker of doubt in Miss Darcy's eyes. "But this lesson is not about splendor. It is about appreciation."

"Are those not one and the same thing?"

Georgiana raised an eyebrow. "You said that about compliments and flattery."

"So I did." Caroline turned, glancing around the room again. "Enlighten me."

"Anyone may appreciate beauty and splendor, as you put it," Georgiana said slowly, as if she'd never had to voice the thought before. "But those are merely superficial glamours. Beauty can be found in most things, if one cares to look a little deeper. What we appreciate, truly appreciate, ought to be more than what we see at first glance."

"If a thing is not beautiful, shouldn't it be made to be so? That is the easiest solution."

"The easy solution is not always the best solution. Or the right one."

Caroline spread her hands, gesturing at Miss Darcy's bedchamber. "Then what am I to do? You put me in magnificent rooms"—*not counting this one*, she thought, and was careful not to say out loud—"surrounded by wonderful art, furniture which has been carved with every possible care and a considerable degree of talent, and yet, you ask me to look deeper. To what end? How much depth can there be here?"

"That is a fair point, well-made," Georgiana said. "When one is surrounded by beauty, it is easy to be beautiful."

"Where are we going on our outing?"

"Somewhere that your new status as star pupil, as you so confidently put it, will be tested a little harder."

"I'm ready," Caroline declared.

"We shall see," was all Georgiana would say upon the subject. "Though we are going nowhere today. Now, are you ready for a spot of tea?"

Chapter Six

Dear daughter,

I am writing from the coast, where I intend to stay for a couple of months with Louisa, in hopes that a trip will rejuvenate us both. I do not know when you plan to return home to Hadley Hall, but remember that you ought not to linger at Pemberley like a bad smell. A friendship, once it has left the safety of harbour, can be sunk in any number of ways.

Yours,
Arianna Bingley

Caroline stared down at the letter, a cold coil of disappointment winding through her stomach. It wasn't as if she particularly wanted to go to the coast—by which her mother might equally have meant Bath or Lyme Regis—but it would have been nice to be asked.

It would have been nice to be wanted.

Worse, the letter had been dated more than two weeks prior, suggesting a clear lack of urgency on the part of the sender. She folded the page up again, unable to look at her mother's handwriting a moment more. Louisa had always been their mother's favourite, and Charles had been their father's, which had left Caroline feeling rather left out all her life. They had aunts and uncles, of course, but most lived in another county and visited infrequently.

Hadley Hall, the family house in south Lancashire, was beautiful and elegant, furnished with her mother's discerning eye, but it had never felt much like a home to Caroline. Pemberley, in spite of all its stately grandeur, exuded a feeling of cosiness that Hadley Hall could never hope to achieve. One could never be quite comfortable there, all too aware that a person, along with every decoration in every room, was also on display at all times and was therefore expected to exude the same glittering, polished perfection as any vase. Mrs Bingley had at least approved of her children spending time with the Darcys, who were an old family and very well-connected, though she seemed to think that friendships ought to be cultivated like rosebushes—watered often and pruned frequently. Caroline's mother did not actually know Fitzwilliam or Georgiana herself, though she ate up every scrap of gossip and chatter as if she were a hungry little sparrow with a nest of babies to feed. Not that Caroline actually wished her mother to visit Pemberley; she was sure Mrs Bingley would have preferred Darcy the way he'd been last year, all cool haughtiness and superiority, and although there was nothing one could possibly criticise about Georgiana, Caroline did not want to risk it. Miss Darcy was too nice of a person to endure even a moment of Mrs Bingley's chilly temperament.

She realised that the parchment was trembling in her hands, and stood abruptly, not quite knowing what to do with herself. Restless anxiety drove her out of her seat and along the corridor. Though an early riser by nature, surely even Georgiana was unlikely to be up at such an hour, when the sun had barely begun to ascend from its own bed. Caroline herself had only awakened when the maid had crept in to leave the letter on her dresser—something which ordinarily wouldn't have awoken her, for she slept like the dead, had the girl not stumbled over the rug on her way out and uttered a soft yelp of alarm.

In the great hall, Caroline unhooked her coat from the peg in the cloakroom and wound a light scarf around her neck lest she should catch an unattractive cold. A walk would do her wonders and would certainly sweep away the sticky cobwebs of this awful feeling of abandonment which had crawled into her chest. In the middle of that tangle, the plump spider of loneliness spun new threads. Her mother was wrong; she was neither intruding on Georgiana's time nor her space.

Am I?

She slipped out of the main door, which was oiled so often it never creaked, and headed down the stone steps which led to the courtyard. The fountain bubbled quietly as she passed it, but the friendly sound was nowhere near enough to quell her agitation. Caroline settled into a brisk pace, marching down the path which led to the shrubberies without a particular destination in mind. Before long, she emerged out the other side. The landscape lay before her, green and inviting, the treetops ahead only just kissed by a pale sunrise which promised later warmth. The air was cool, though not cold, and dew brushed the hem of her skirt. Somewhere on the left, a blackbird trilled, and Caroline swung towards the friendly sound, desperate for any shred of comfort.

Perhaps Mother thinks she is doing me a kindness by not inviting me along, she tried to convince herself. *Perhaps she thinks that Louisa is in need of some special attention at the moment, since she is not yet with child.* This was a lie, of course. Mrs Bingley and Louisa had often taken little trips together, sharing confidences in a way that Caroline could never hope to. Tears prickled, spilling over before she could blink them back, forcing her to dab at her face with her scarf. Really, it was too ridiculous to cry twice in one week. She was almost certainly going to get sad eyes if she did not get a hold of herself.

Caroline trudged through the trees, her steps slowing as she realised her path was taking her towards the lake. A pleasant, calming view might aid her in this moment. The fountain had been too active, too cheerful, but the morose stillness of a lake would be a perfect match for her mood. However, by the time she was thirty feet away from the shore, she could see that the water was not still at all. Instead, ripples wrinkled the surface and, in the very middle, a small, dark thing bobbed around. *What on earth is that?* she wondered, drawing closer. *Some sort of animal? An otter, perhaps, or a stoat. Or—oh!*

"Good heavens, Georgie," she called. "At first I mistook you for a stoat."

Miss Darcy's head turned sharply at the sound of Caroline's voice. For a moment, she did not respond, her dark eyes narrowing.

"A terrifyingly large stoat, I should think," Georgiana called back, before cutting through the water with easy strokes that brought her within reach of the shore in mere seconds. "Your ability to identify woodland creatures is extraordinarily deficient. Did your governess never take you outside?"

"No, she imprisoned Louisa and me in a stuffy room all day," Caroline groused, halting by a towel which lay neatly folded on the shore. "Hence why I enjoy being out of doors now." She cocked her head. "Though not, it seems, as much as you."

Georgiana hauled herself to her feet and strode forward, dripping water with every step. Until this moment, Caroline had not actually imagined what Georgiana might have been wearing for a swim in the lake. If she had, she might have concluded that something shapeless and dark would be an appropriate garment for such a ridiculous activity. She certainly wouldn't have pictured only a single white petticoat, rendered almost entirely transparent by the soaking, clinging to Georgiana's every curve like a barnacle.

Caroline gaped, unable to form coherent thought. She'd been aware that Georgiana, like other people, had a body upon which her head sat. She'd always been appreciative—and openly complimentary—of Miss Darcy's figure. But there was a world of difference between seeing a body artfully swathed in layers of silks in the dim light of a ballroom, or cloaked in cotton across the breakfast table, versus seeing it now, in the light of day, flushed and rosy under a single layer. And good Lord, that layer seemed thin. Insubstantial, as if questing fingers might press right through—

"What?" Georgiana twisted, staring down at herself. "Do I have something on me? Some strand of grass, perhaps?"

"No, not at all." Caroline swallowed hard. Words suddenly seemed rather difficult to string together in an adequate manner. She stooped and picked up the towel, offering it to Georgiana. "Here, dry yourself off before you catch your death of cold."

"I promise you," said she, though she accepted the towel gratefully and wiped her face, "that I shall be fine. I have been doing this at least thrice a week for the last decade."

Caroline hadn't even known that Georgiana could swim, far less that she was doing so in a disgusting, muddy lake with routine regularity. "Is not the water unpleasant?" Without waiting for an answer, she dipped a finger in the lake and drew back with a shriek. "Why, it is freezing! Beyond freezing!"

"If it were beyond freezing, it would be ice," Georgiana pointed out. "Which would make swimming rather impossible."

Caroline wiped her finger on her dress. The tip was already numb. "My dear Georgie, this is madness. You surely cannot actually enjoy such a thing."

"And yet I do."

"It is torturous to do this to one's self," she insisted. "You are behaving like those monks who live in a bare cell and eat only one meal a day."

Georgiana swivelled to stare at Pemberley, the enormous house now equally kissed by sunrise. "Our living conditions seem rather a long way away from what you describe."

She peeled a section of soaked petticoat away from her stomach, then let it slap back into place. Caroline's stomach did a strange somersault, as if she'd unexpectedly missed a step on a staircase. Georgiana leaned sideways, wringing her dripping hair onto the grass before toweling it vigorously, an activity which caused a noticeable—if Caroline had to call it anything—jiggling of other bodily parts.

"Fitzwilliam does the same thing, you know," Miss Darcy added, while Caroline wondered what to say next, casting her eyes up to the heavens as if checking to see if it might rain. The few clouds which had gathered were grey, though none yet looked expectant with rain-children. "Likes to dive in off that little pier after he's had a long, hot journey on horseback. He says there's nothing quite like it to cool off." She pointed to a tiny jetty about thirty feet away. "As children, we swam here together very often." She wrapped the towel around her waist and chest, covering up those parts of her which had been most on display, filling Caroline with a surge of relief. "I could never dive as well as he, but then he could never swim as fast as I."

"Indeed?" Her voice sounded rather croaky. Caroline cleared her throat, then cleared it again. Really, it was very strange that the sight of Georgiana's petticoats should have such an effect. Why, Caroline had seen her mother and sister thus undressed—and more besides—and even an aunt or two. Was it simply that Georgiana was not family? Yet she did think of Georgie as family, in a way. Certainly Miss Darcy had been a better sister to her than Louisa, though there was something decidedly unsororal in the way Caroline's stomach swooped. Her gaze was still averted, but out of the corner of her eye, she could still see the . . . the . . .

The *jiggling.*

Good grief. Was it really necessary to shake one's bosom so much? She'd never noticed them bobbing around so much before, though perhaps they'd been held in like penned sheep by the fit of Georgiana's dresses and only now were allowed to roam freely upon the hills of her—

"—and so I said to Mrs Reynolds," Georgiana was saying, apparently oblivious to Caroline's sudden distraction, "if it were true that one caught a cold every time one had wet hair outside, then I ought to have had a thousand colds in my lifetime. And yet I can count the number of colds I have actually had on the fingers of one hand."

"I expect she simply worries."

A sodden strand of Georgiana's hair was still plastered to her face. Without thinking, Caroline reached out, plucked it away, tucking it behind Georgiana's ear. Miss Darcy looked at her, a strange expression on her face. "Your cheeks are flushed. Are you feeling well? And what are you holding?"

Caroline had entirely forgotten she was holding anything in her other hand. It was rather crumpled now, for her hand had clenched into a fist, although she wasn't sure whether that had happened before she'd left the house or in the last two minutes. "Oh, it is nothing. Just a letter from my mother."

"Ah." Georgiana's expression softened at once. "What says she?"

"She is going to the coast with Louisa for a couple of months."

"The coast? Which one?"

The cold coil of hurt, which had receded from the moment Georgiana stepped out of the water, came flooding back full force. Caroline shrugged. "Your guess is as good as mine."

"Are you not planning to—"

"I was not invited," she said, relieved that her tone was only edged in bitterness rather than dressed in it entirely. The Darcys would never have treated their children so, choosing favourites among them. Nor would they have suggested that friendships could sink if one actually dared to spend time with their companions. Did even her own mother think her company so unbearable? First Darcy, now this. Her very soul felt crushed. "I suppose I ought to go home," she said, though she couldn't imagine anything she wanted to do less than travel back to Lancashire simply to sit alone in an empty house for several weeks. Her mother's words rattled around her skull until she felt like she could scream. *You ought not to linger. You ought not to linger.* "I've imposed on you quite enough."

"Imposed?" Georgiana repeated, looking surprised. "But what about your marriage scheme?"

"Oh, do not pretend that you really want to be part of such a silly thing. I am aware that I forced it upon you from the start." It wasn't at all what she'd meant to say, but she couldn't simply announce her real feelings; they were too wrapped up in hot humiliation and shame as dark and rippling as the depths of the lake. How could she profess to be lonely when her family were still alive, and Georgiana's parents were not? How could she identify this nameless need, when even acknowledging its existence made her feel like her world was crumbling apart? A sudden yearning stole her breath, yet she could not even say what it was that she wanted, or why. *Is it too much to hope that I could belong somewhere?* Without meaning to, she squashed the parchment into an even tighter ball.

Miss Darcy stared at her, then at the letter in her hand. "What did your mother say?"

Embarrassment burned in her chest, and now the tips of her ears were hot. "What makes you think—"

"Even a stranger could see that you are entirely unsettled. Therefore, your mother must have said something to upset you." Georgiana's hand closed around Caroline's other wrist, fingers cool and still damp. "May I read it?"

Caroline thrust the letter at her. Miss Darcy took it but didn't let go of Caroline's wrist with her other hand, her fingers sliding down until they entwined with Caroline's own. This was not usual for them—they embraced as friends did, but they had never held hands before. Caroline flattened her palm, seeking every inch of contact she could find, and drew a long, slow breath while Georgiana read. Without warning, Miss Darcy crumpled the letter, then reared back and flung it as hard as she could into the lake. It bobbed on the surface for a moment before taking on water and sinking out of sight. "There," said she. "That is what I think of your mother's suggestion. What use is there in going to Hadley Hall when none of your family will be there to greet you?"

Mutely, Caroline shrugged. *Because Mother likes to order me around*, she did not say. *Because the world must act as she says, regardless of what anyone actually wants.*

"Well, too bad. I demand your company for a week or two yet, for if you leave, I shall be quite alone here," Georgiana added, squeezing Caroline's hand gently. "Besides, we have a scheme to work on. And we have already begun, have we not? I am sure that your mother will be delighted when you return home with the happiest of news."

She swallowed, an unexpected surge of gratitude overtaking her. Another person might have agreed to her return home, might have failed to see through her façade or even been relieved at being provided with an escape route from her madcap marriage scheme, but not Georgiana. "You really are a very good person," she murmured. "And an excellent friend."

This ship shall never sink, she thought, an unexpected fierceness coursing through her. *Whatever my mother says.*

Now it was Miss Darcy's turn to blush. "You will not say that when we are fighting over the last picce of cake."

Caroline felt her shoulders relax at Georgiana's gentle, teasing tone. "Friendship is one thing. Baked goods are quite another. I believe I would don armour and go to war to defend Mrs Addlecombe's pear cake."

"I would fight beside you," Georgiana admitted, her shoulder bumping Caroline's as they turned to head back to the house. "The things that woman can do to a piece of fruit are downright sinful. I feel certain that God cannot possibly approve."

Sinful. The word echoed around Caroline's brain, her throat suddenly dry. For some reason, her eyes flicked to Georgiana's bosom, which was only partially concealed by the tightly-wrapped towel. She was extremely glad when they arrived in the main hall and Georgiana made a hasty exit to change into dry clothes, promising to meet Caroline in a few minutes for breakfast, followed by a truly tremendous amount of cake.

Chapter Seven

My dearest Caroline,

I hope this finds you the picture of health and happiness. We are already having the most splendid time, and we have not even left Meryton yet! I do so love being around a large family—Jane and I are both of the opinion that a sizable brood of our own would be a wonderful thing. Mrs Bennet is extremely ~~fervent vehement~~ conscientious about the happiness of all her children, which must be admired as one of the great traits of motherhood. I have been shooting with Mr Bennet twice, though neither of us had much success.

I look forward to meeting Darcy and continuing our journey, as I think ~~Miss Elizabeth~~ Mrs Darcy must be missing him so very much. I know if I were to be parted from my sweet Jane for even a moment, it would be hard, yet the idea of our meeting again after a period of longing would be so sweet that I confess myself torn between the two. Oh, how wondrous strange love is!

Please send my best wishes to Georgiana. Such a sweet girl. I am so glad that you have become friends.

Your devoted brother,
Charles

A red-haired maid held out a silver tray as the ladies finished breaking their fast. "A letter for Miss Bingley, ma'am," the girl said, performing a neat, if rather shallow, curtsey.

For a moment, Caroline froze, half-expecting a follow-up from her mother, but the address on the front had been written in an effusive, rounded hand which she recognised in an instant. "Charles," she said, in answer to Georgiana's questioning look. "Look, even his alphabet is unbearably cheerful."

Georgiana snorted before requesting more tea. The maid curtseyed again, much deeper this time, and trotted off to fulfill the order while the ladies made their way into the library. Despite Caroline's complaints about the worn upholstery the day before, she found herself rather glad of it now. Nothing at Hadley Hall would ever be permitted to remain long enough to endure the rigours of daily life, which meant that nothing from Caroline's younger years had survived to wax nostalgic about. Not even her precious dolls, which had been given away without her consent and replaced with more stylish ones as soon as her mother saw fit to do so. Appearances, after all, were everything, while attachments were only temporary.

"What says your brother?" Georgiana asked.

Caroline unfolded the letter, cleared her throat, and began to perform a perfect impression of Charles, which had Georgiana in actual tears by the end. "The fool," she said fondly, folding the letter back up. "Mrs Bennet could stand over him in the marital bedchamber, issuing the sternest and most detailed instructions, and he'd only smile and thank her for all her maternal attentiveness."

"Caroline, really!" Georgiana dissolved into another helpless fit of giggles. "He is not that bad." She had said nothing further about the letter from Mrs Bingley during breakfast, for which Caroline was grateful, and apologised now before disappearing afterwards for a couple of hours, reappearing in the parlour mid-morning with ink-stained hands that had evidently already been scrubbed repeatedly. Georgiana did not explain the state of her hands, but neither did she complain when Caroline asked to take a turn around the garden. Caroline had spent the morning alone, accompanied only by two slices of Mrs Addlecombe's delicious fruitcake; the taste of candied lemon peel, both bitter and sweet at once, lingered in her mouth as they strolled down the path towards a cluster of rosebushes.

"We ought to discuss the next stage of the Great Endeavour," Caroline said.

"You read my mind. I was engaged with the scheme all morning." Georgiana waggled both hands at Caroline, though the ink stains were now hidden by beautiful white gloves.

"Really? In what manner?"

"Writing letters to my acquaintances to discover what balls and parties are forthcoming over the next month." She flashed a satisfied look at Caroline. "I am certain that you will find suitors enough at such events. Therefore, we ought to work now on your . . . on those traits which you feel you may be lacking. Particularly your sweetness and your humility. You shall have a chance to practice them this afternoon."

"I do not recall that I mentioned anything about my humility," Caroline said, sensing a trap. "Which, in any case, I— Wait, what do you mean? Where are we going?"

"You must have forgotten," Georgiana said, as they rounded a corner, "that I promised you an outing. Or else you would have already harangued me about where and when we were going."

It took Caroline a moment to remember what she was talking about. "Oh, the outing!" she exclaimed. "Why, yes, I did forget."

"You astonish me," Georgiana teased. "What happened to all your enthusiasm for the Grand Endeavour?"

"The Great Endeavour," Caroline corrected. "Although I'm sure it will also be grand. I was merely a little distracted this morning, but my commitment to the Great Endeavour never wavered, I assure you."

Miss Darcy's gaze softened. Not wishing to be pitied, Caroline rushed on, "Are you going to tell me now? Withholding details of an outing is not merely cruel, it is impractical. I must know our destination in order to decide how best to dress. Will what I am wearing now suffice, or ought I change?"

"If I tell you, then you may decide for yourself. We shall take the carriage and call upon a friend of mine, Miss Beatrice Merryhill," Georgiana said. "In my opinion, the visit will require nothing more than an ordinary dress, so you need not go to any—"

"Merryhill?" Caroline screwed up her face. "I never heard you mention the name before." She caught sight of Georgiana's expression and quickly corrected her own, smoothing it out into a passably civil one. *A completely ridiculous name, and no doubt a completely ridiculous person*, she thought. *Surely none of the gentry have ever been called Merryhill.* "And where precisely does she live?"

Georgiana hesitated. "Why do you ask?"

"I am merely ascertaining the location, geographically speaking. A question confirming facts, nothing more." Nothing could be further from the truth. If she knew the name of the estate, she would be able to glean several important details which would furnish her with enough interesting topics to keep the conversation going. There were several large estates nearby, though as far as Caroline had been aware, none of them had been let out to anyone with such a silly name.

Georgiana's expression had gone carefully blank, exactly the sort of look she wore at balls and parties while moving through a crowd of people. "She lives on the outskirts of the village, in the house across from the church. Is that a problem for you?"

Caroline bit her lip. She could not bring such a house to mind immediately, but she knew exactly the sort of place it was: small, ugly, inhabited by those with neither fortune nor status. Mrs Bingley had always impressed upon her children the need to appear only in exalted company, and never to mix with any of the lower classes, far less visit any of their houses. One did not simply call upon the peasants. "Poverty is not catching, is it?"

It was only half a jest.

"Not as far as I know." Georgiana raised an eyebrow. "Did you think this plan to reform you into an amiable and darling creature would only take place in the most elite of social circles, and would never induce you to step out of your comfortable life for even a moment?"

"Well, I . . . Hold on. Am I not darling already?"

"God forbid that you breathe the same air as people who

have less than one thousand a year," Miss Darcy said, neatly sidestepping the question. "If you do not feel yourself ready, then we can delay, of course. I merely thought that your boast about being a star pupil—"

"Yes, yes," Caroline interrupted. "You've made your point. I did make the claim, and as such, I shall stand by it."

A Merryhill, though! she thought, with no little scorn. *Who lives in the village, of all places!* Ordinarily, Caroline would never have been caught dead there. Unbidden, Mr Darcy's words rose to her mind: *It is my strong belief that if you do not mend the error of your ways, then you will never find such happiness as I have done.*

A lonely life, he'd said.

She pictured herself an old lady, sitting alone in a vast and empty room filled with glittering objects inherited from her mother. Going nowhere. Speaking to no one. Visiting Charles only twice a year and seeing his happy family, only to come home to an empty house of her own. Or rather, empty with the exception of her mother, which was somehow a much worse thought. Seeing Louisa in London, surrounded by children. The thought made her want to cry again, but thrice in the span of a single week was certain to bring on sad eyes, an affliction from which one might never fully recover. "Besides, I have often longed to visit the . . . the outskirts of the village," she said, forcing herself to sound cheerful.

"Have you?" Georgiana's dark eyes narrowed in suspicion. "It's only three miles away."

"One rarely purposefully visits one's own back garden," Caroline declared, hoping it would sound like profound words of wisdom. "Or in this case, the back garden of one's dear friend. And has this Miss Merryhill sent us an invitation?"

"She has."

"Wonderful. Wonderful." She considered risking a third *wonderful*, caught sight of Georgiana's expression, and subsided.

Clearly this Miss Merryhill was not wealthy or well-connected, therefore Caroline couldn't see any reason for the friendship to exist in the first place. She had been prepared to do quite a lot to achieve the Great Endeavour, but bestowing her time and attention on a charity case seemed like asking rather a lot. Unfortunately, she had agreed and now couldn't back out of the deal without losing face, or worse, losing Georgiana's mentorship. Besides, Miss Elizabeth Bennet would probably have been delighted to spend hours upon hours with the local poor, talking of . . .

Caroline frowned. *What on earth do poor people talk about?*

She supposed she was about to find out.

In the privacy of the guest room, Caroline changed into a pretty cornflower-blue dress, which brought out the bright shade of her own eyes, and paired it with fashionable blue kid-leather shoes which her mother had assured her were all the rage in London. *Not that anyone from the village is likely to recognise high fashion, far less appreciate it*, she thought gloomily. She would have to be on her guard today, though surely Georgiana was not such an unforgiving teacher that a slip-up or two would convince her to call off the entire Great Endeavour. Or would it? *No*, she thought, shaking her head. *She claimed she would only take me on as a pupil as long as I did what she said. None of her conditions were dependent upon my success in every area.* The thought relieved her slightly, though perhaps it would be best to come up with a few words of praise now, and practice them while she could, so as to give the impression that she had devised them on the spot.

"What a lovely home," she said into the looking glass, and produced her sweetest smile. "I particularly like your, um . . . the . . ."

What did people compliment? It was hard to say without actually seeing the house in question, though all houses had certain things in common. "Your front door," she finished, feeling rather pleased with herself.

Surely that would impress her friend long enough for Caroline to pass this ridiculous test. She was almost certain that no one had ever taken Miss Elizabeth Bennet to a village and demanded that she mix with people below her station. Really, the whole thing was rather unfair, though she was equally certain that making such an argument to Georgiana would result in Caroline failing the test before she had even begun, which felt even more unfair.

Well, it is only one afternoon, she consoled herself. *How bad can it possibly be?*

Chapter Eight

My dearest sister,

While I quite understand and sympathise with your consternation over Miss Bingley's wounded feelings, I might take the opportunity of reminding you that the lady in question is a woman grown, who cornered me and extricated those comments under no little duress. That, of course, does not excuse my candour, though I will apologise for the harsh tone in which I delivered my response.

~~*In my defense*~~

~~*The thing is*~~

I am of the firm belief that one ought not ask questions to which one does not really wish to hear the answers. I told Miss Bingley as much at the time, and yet she insisted on hearing that which she must have known could only hurt her. I fear that I forgot one of the most important points on that list; her inability to leave well enough alone. This, above all other faults, may be her undoing someday. If you have agreed to such a scheme, and I assume you have, for you have never been able to ignore any creature in need, then you would do well to bear that in mind.

Your affectionate—whether you return my love or not—brother,
Fitzwilliam Darcy

P.S. Stallion or mare?

The sky was overcast now, the clouds amassing into one large grey blanket which blotted out the sun. Caroline was glad of her navy wrap, for a newly-sprung breeze caused goosebumps to rise along her arms in the short time it had taken she and Georgiana to leave the house and climb into the carriage. The footmen and driver looked as resplendent as ever in starched uniforms and neatly combed hair, but none of them wore the same terrified expressions as Mrs Bingley's servants often did. Before they'd even reached the front gates of Pemberley, Georgiana's nerves became apparent, her fingers twitching in her lap. "I just wanted to say—" she began, then stopped. "Perhaps this was a mistake. It is rather soon after your first lesson, is it not?"

"You act as though I am some wild animal recently purchased from a faraway land, who must be muzzled lest she start running amok and biting the ankles of the general populace." Caroline frowned. "Do not forget that I was out in society a full three years before you."

"That is not what I . . ." Georgiana sighed, her expression turning apologetic. "Pray excuse my incivility. I did not mean to suggest that you do not know how to conduct yourself. Nor that you bite ankles."

"Not without being asked first, anyway."

Georgiana's lips twitched. "And yet," she added, fixing Caroline with a semi-serious glare, "you did ask me for help to become a kinder person. Which means that you acknowledge deficiencies in your own character and seek to rectify them. And given that—"

"Is there any need to refer to them as *deficiencies*?" The word recalled Darcy's comments a little too closely for comfort, and while she'd decided to take his advice—albeit in her own peculiar way—she did not particularly wish to relive those humiliating moments when he'd listed her worst qualities. Or at least, what he'd decided were her worst qualities.

"Oh? What might you have called them?"

"Something far softer. Quirks, perhaps. Tiny flaws. Even a precious jewel may have one or two slight . . . er . . . scratches upon its surface that, in being ground away or otherwise polished, renders the gem of a much higher value and beauty. This is merely my polishing, Georgie."

Miss Darcy raised an eyebrow. "And here I thought you were asking to be dug out of the ground."

"Do you plan to stop needling me before we arrive at Miss Merrybank's house or is this to be an all-day treat?"

"Merryhill," Georgiana corrected.

"Yes, yes," Caroline said, waving an impatient hand. "You were saying? About my so-called imperfections?"

"Well, I merely wish to remind you of what I said the other day. About keeping your opinions to yourself. Not every word which flits through that beautiful head of yours need be spoken out loud. Remember that we discussed the need for your words to always be amiable and graceful, whatever the situation or whomever the company might be. If your opinion is not a complimentary one, please do not share it."

Caroline preened. "You think my head beautiful?"

Miss Darcy closed her eyes for a moment, her lips moving

as if in prayer. "Please pay attention. Today, your test is to be charitable and complimentary, regardless of how you might actually feel. Just because Miss Merryhill does not live on a large estate or move in the highest of society circles does not mean that she is not deserving of respect and kindness."

Caroline opened her mouth to say that, *Actually, in my opinion it means exactly that*, but then decided against it. After all, they'd only just made it onto the main road, and if Georgiana was pushed too far, she might decide to forgo the outing entirely. "Tell me," she said, as the carriage rumbled down the road, "how did you come to be acquainted with this young lady in the first place?"

"What makes you think her a young lady?"

Caroline blinked. "Oh. I had assumed, since she was Miss Merryhill and not Mrs, that—"

"In fact, she is a spinster. I do not know her precise age, but I expect she is in her late thirties."

That certainly put a different spin on the afternoon ahead. "I see."

"We met at church," Georgiana continued. "She plays the organ there sometimes, and very well, too. We exchange sheets of music and talk of what we have heard played. She has excellent taste, and a splendid ear. Only needs to hear something once before she can play it." She smiled, evidently recalling a fond memory. "A singular talent. I wish I possessed such a thing."

Caroline nodded, digesting this news. Georgiana was very keen on music, fervent about it in a way that few other young ladies of their acquaintance were; it made sense, therefore, that she had formed an attachment to an unsuitable friend on the basis of a common interest. Caroline could hear her mother's voice in her head, warning her that while a Darcy might have reputation and status enough to show compassion to those of lower classes, a Bingley was not yet so removed from tradesmen and therefore must be extremely careful about whose company they kept. She felt a pang of guilt but pushed it down. What harm could one visit really do, as long as no one from the proper circles found out about it?

As long as Mother never finds out about it.

"Oh look, we're almost there," Georgiana said airily, sitting up straight and smoothing her dress down.

Caroline turned to stare out of the carriage window as it rolled to a stop, and only just resisted the urge to sigh loudly. Miss Beatrice Merryhill's house was precisely as Caroline had suspected. It was exceedingly small, barely even a house at all by her standards, since it stood only two storeys tall and perhaps only forty feet wide. The gardens—if one could really call them that, for Caroline had seen bigger picnic blankets—were hardly more than a few tragic squares of lawn, edged with wilting flowerbeds. The woman who waited at the door was in her late thirties, of rather plain countenance, and so broad in the shoulders and hips that the overall impression reminded Caroline of a water pitcher.

Caroline frowned as she descended from the carriage and followed Georgiana down the narrow path. Meeting one's guests by one's self was a little odd. Was it possible that Miss Merryhill was too poor to afford any servants at all? And if so, what on earth were they doing here, spending time with such a person? If this was to be a lesson in holding her tongue when the situation so clearly called for judgement, then she was about to have a very difficult afternoon indeed.

"Miss Darcy," Miss Merryhill said, her voice unexpectedly soft and mellifluous. "How perfectly lovely to see you. You shall have to excuse the state of the house today, for Mrs Wimple has been called away to deliver another baby."

Georgiana waved away the excuse with a smile and turned to Caroline, who was wondering who on earth Mrs Wimple was. "Allow me to introduce my friend, Miss Bingley."

"Why, Miss Bingley, it is so lovely to meet you! Miss Darcy has talked of you often."

"In glowing terms, I hope," Caroline said, smiling.

In response, Miss Merryhill only smiled back, though it did not quite reach her eyes, which were as pale blue as a December sky. "Come in, come in. The others are already here."

"Others?" Caroline muttered, as she and Georgiana followed their hostess into the dark hallway. "You never said there would be others."

"I wasn't aware there would be, Miss Bingley," Georgiana muttered back, a warning tone in her voice. "Is that a problem?"

Caroline subsided sulkily, choosing instead to glare first at the back of Georgiana's head—beautiful as ever—then at the walls, which were painted a shade of muddy brown that no person with even a single fragment of taste in their body would have allowed within a hundred feet of their home. The wooden floor was a moderately dark oak, whorled and grainy, and looked as if it had been swept recently but not polished. There was not a scrap of carpet to be seen anywhere, nor an inch of wallpaper. Since she was at the end of the small procession, Caroline allowed herself a single satisfying eyeroll. Miss Darcy's shoulders looked stiffer than usual, though that was hardly Caroline's fault; she hadn't given her opinion on anything yet, though she'd certainly formed some rather large ones in the few seconds they'd been inside.

Somewhere in the distance, the cool green scent of mint

mixed with something sharper and richer. Caroline sniffed the air. Cheddar, perhaps? It was almost too much to hope for.

Good God, let there be decent cheese at least, Caroline prayed, as Georgiana ducked her head slightly in order to step into the next room. *I can withstand almost anything, as long as there is cheese.*

The parlour was as small and dreary as Caroline had feared. Two rose-coloured couches faced each other over a low wooden table like two frustrated chess players. A high-backed armchair, in a shade of lighter pink that neither matched the couches nor complemented them, sat at the opposite end of the room, as if overseeing the whole tasteless affair. The walls were painted a cold, passionless white, quite unbecoming of a supposedly cosy room, and the presence of three people already seated there did nothing to alleviate the stark effect. The party stood when their hostess led Caroline and Georgiana inside, smiling towards the newcomers. An impossibly tall young man in a black jacket bowed jerkily, his movements hampered by the equally tall young woman who clung to his arm as if she were drowning and he was the only slender log for miles around.

"May I introduce Mr and Mrs Grimley?" Miss Merryhill said, stepping aside to allow for a fuller inspection.

Good grief, Caroline thought. *Their children will be able to build chimney stacks without need of a ladder.*

She swept the two with a glance that took everything in at once: A loose thread hanging from the sleeve of his jacket, which would have looked old-fashioned on her father. A grass stain on the side of the lady's left shoe. His hair, mussed so much it looked as if it had never so much as heard of a comb, far less seen one. Her rouge, which looked as if it had been drawn on by a shaky-fingered, weak-sighted child. "Good morning," the Grimleys chorused in unison, sending a shiver of horror down Caroline's spine.

Aware that Georgiana was watching her closely, Caroline offered a nod that was far more gracious than either of the Grimleys deserved. "Good morning."

"And this," Miss Merryhill said, turning to the other gentleman, "is Mr Acton. This is Miss Bingley, a friend of Miss Darcy's."

"Good afternoon, Miss Darcy, Miss Bingley," Mr Acton said, nodding to each of them in turn. His manners were handsome enough, as was his face, though his waistcoat was frayed, and his hands, though evidently scrubbed, still bore traces of paint.

"Come, sit down," Miss Merryhill said, ushering them in. Caroline waited until Georgiana had seated herself on one of the couches before hurriedly sitting beside her. Their hostess disappeared into the hallway as the other guests seated themselves, too.

"Who is Mrs Wimple?" Caroline murmured.

Georgiana blinked in confusion, evidently taking a moment to recall the brief mention of the name from their arrival. "She is Miss Merryhill's recently widowed sister."

Ah. Caroline nodded. That explained a lot, though it left one glaring question: Why was this lady's sister out delivering babies? Did not babies generally deliver themselves? There was, after all, only one route outwards into the world. Where else would they go? She had a sudden image of a woman holding a candle, coaxing a baby out into the light like an animal from its burrow, and had to stifle the giggle with a cough.

Miss Merryhill returned a moment later bearing a tray, upon which sat an assortment of sandwiches. She set them down on the low table in front of Caroline, who eyed them cautiously, before she disappeared again. When Miss Merryhill returned a second time, she was laden with two trays—one holding several plates piled high with cake, and a larger dish which contained a variety of fresh fruit. It wasn't a terrible spread, Caroline had to admit. Nothing close to Pemberley's standards, of course, but it didn't look entirely like something a ploughman might be presented with after a hard morning's work doing . . . whatever ploughmen did.

Ploughing, presumably.

"Thank you very much," Mr Acton said, casting an appreciative glance at their hostess as Caroline reached for a cheese sandwich. "Is this your famous apple cake?"

Miss Merryhill blushed. "It is indeed."

Caroline nibbled the sandwich cautiously and then, finding it tolerable, continued. The cheddar was creamy and tart, and the bread was soft with a delicious, seeded crust—a far cry from the stale loaf and tasteless cheese she had envisioned. Perhaps the poor ate better than she'd previously thought. Mrs Grimley reached for a slice of apple cake, though she made no attempt to eat it. Instead, she brought it to her husband's lips. "You simply must try this cake, Mr Grimley."

"Why thank you, Mrs Grimley." He accepted the cake with far more gusto than Caroline thought appropriate outside of the bedchamber, his lips coming dangerously close to his wife's fingers and lingering suggestively.

"What do you think of the flavour, Mr Grimley?" his wife inquired anxiously, as if awaiting the most important news of her life.

"Why, Mrs Grimley," said he, staring into her eyes with the kind of rapturous adoration Caroline had only ever seen on the faces of cherubim on church frescoes, "I think it the most marvellous cake I ever tasted. You simply must try it." As if executing the moves of some hitherto agreed-upon dance, he picked up a piece of cake in turn and fed it to his wife.

"Why, Mr Grimley, I am quite in agreement," she said breathlessly, as soon as the morsel touched her lips. "It is marvellous cake indeed."

Caroline felt hysteria bubbling inside her. She wanted very much to look elsewhere—in fact, would have paid quite a lot to remove this entire scene from her mind forever—but seemed unable to actually turn her head away. The exchange held all the grim interest of a carriage accident; one did not necessarily wish to see any actual carnage, but simply could not help gawking at it just the same. She would have given half her entire fortune to have Lady Catherine de Bourgh present in this moment; the ensuing verbal slaughter would have surely satiated Caroline for the rest of her life.

"My excellent wife, you have the most perfect taste of anybody I have ever met," declared he.

"My excellent husband," said Mrs Grimley, blushing, "I think the very same of you."

"So, Mr Acton," Georgiana said, more loudly than she ordinarily spoke, and Caroline at last managed to tear her eyes from the awful scene unfolding in front of her. "How goes your painting? The last time I saw you, I believe you were painting something for the tenant of the estate near the valley, were you not?"

"It goes well enough, Miss Darcy." Mr Acton smiled at Georgiana, and Caroline thought she could sense a touch of relief in it. "You are kind to ask, and your memory is as excellent as ever." He cradled a cup of tea in his hands, his expression tender. "It took a little longer than I had expected, but I finished my latest commission a fortnight ago."

"You surely cannot yet know, Miss Bingley, that Mr Acton paints wonderful landscapes," Miss Merryhill said, her voice warm and affectionate. "I never saw such beautiful paintings in all my life."

"And yet you will not let me give you one," said he, smiling, and the tips of Miss Merryhill's ears pinked.

"You mean I will not let you give me another one," she corrected, "for I keep *Chrome Hill During a Rainstorm* upstairs." Her ears turned a darker shade of pink. "The morning light suits it best," she added, as if justifying her decision.

Upstairs? Caroline wondered, suddenly far more interested in the conversation. *In her bedchamber, perhaps?*

"I seem to recall," Mr Grimley said, still gazing at his wife with tender affection, "that you once admired a painting of Mr Acton's, did you not, Mrs Grimley?"

"Oh, Mr Grimley, how sweet you are to remember such a trifling detail!" she cried. "Indeed I did."

Caroline reached for another sandwich and stuffed it into her mouth. *If my mouth is constantly full*, she told herself, *then I am at no risk of saying something which will displease Georgiana and cause me to fail my test.* She chewed, doing her best to focus on the sharp taste of the chutney, but the temptation was so strong, and these people were so unbelievably ridiculous. *This is how victims of torture must feel*, she decided miserably. *Minus the cheese, of course.*

Mr Grimley turned to Mr Acton. "Do you still possess that painting, sir?"

"Do you recall which one it was?" the artist inquired.

Mrs Grimley frowned. Evidently, thinking of something other than Mr Grimley required significant effort. "It was a lovely rendering of the village," she eventually managed, "and I believe that the stream ran in a bright slash down the right-hand side."

"Ah, yes, *A Sunday Morning Before Church Bells Toll.* I still have it." Mr Acton's smile was rueful. "I still have most of my paintings, unfortunately."

"Would you consider selling that painting to us?" Mr Grimley asked.

"I would be delighted to," said he, smiling. "Though the lord who commissioned my latest piece has been kind to me, as have several people in the surrounding area, I am afraid it is not what you might call a steady income. I am very grateful indeed to make any sale."

"There, Mrs Grimley," her husband said with some satisfaction. "You shall have your heart's desire, and Mr Acton shall have his, too."

"Oh, but you are my heart's desire, Mr Grimley," she said, fluttering her eyelashes at him in a manner no doubt designed to be coy, but which merely made her look as if she were about to faint.

That was the last straw. "If I have to hear one more address from either Grimley to the other," Caroline murmured, as the conversation continued around them, "then I am going to throw myself out of the window."

"We are on the ground floor, Miss Bingley," Georgiana pointed out, barely moving her lips.

"Thank you for the reminder, Miss Darcy. In that case, I shall run upstairs first."

Georgiana shot her a sidelong glance which spoke as loudly

as any shout. Sullenly, Caroline subsided and helped herself to a third sandwich. Did Georgiana really expect her to spend an entire afternoon with these people? She wasn't even sure if she could get through the next hour. She'd expected a test, certainly, but this was less of a gentle examination and more of a trial by fire.

There weren't enough cheese sandwiches in the world to ameliorate this descent into hell.

Chapter Nine

"I finished a new painting only yesterday," Mr Acton declared. "And I was rather hoping that you will all give your opinion." He turned to Caroline and Georgiana. "Miss Bingley, Miss Darcy, if you would be so kind as to bestow yours upon me too, I would be most grateful. And do not hold back for fear you will wound my tender feelings. I seek to improve myself constantly."

"Is that what you left in my kitchen earlier?" Miss Merryhill said, her eyes alight with curiosity. "Do bring it in and show us."

The artist rose and disappeared through the doorway, returning with a large cloth-covered rectangle. This he settled on the floor, with considerable care paid to the precise angle and tilt, before pulling the cloth away in one smooth motion. Caroline wasn't sure what she had expected to see—perhaps something amateur, or garish. This was neither; instead, it showed sloping hills in muted, though not tedious, shades of green and yellow. In the middle of the painting, a small herd of sheep grazed close to a shepherd, who was asleep with his hat shading his eyes. A lamb had wandered a little way from the flock and was staring down at the valley below. The landscape was clearly beloved by the beholder, and that adoration could be seen in every stroke of the brush.

As Miss Merryhill exclaimed over each and every detail, Caroline noted how Mr Acton's eyes followed her every move. *A man in love*, she thought. It would have been rather romantic, had not the Grimleys been in the room as a reminder of how disgusting such feelings of *amor* could be.

"I quite agree," said Georgiana, shaking Caroline out of her reverie. "It is a magnificent specimen. I have seen several of your works now, Mr Acton, and I think this might be my particular favourite."

"Thank you very much," he said, and though he looked pleased, there was something searching in his gaze. "And you, Miss Bingley?"

Caroline heard Georgiana's intake of breath and felt a sharp elbow nudge her in the ribs. Really, there was no need. The man had asked for her honest opinion, after all.

"I like it very much," she said, "but it is lacking something, is it not?"

Four pairs of scandalised eyes turned to Caroline, but she ignored them. Mr Acton was frowning at the painting. "You have hit on my problem precisely, Miss Bingley. I agree that it lacks something, though I am at a loss to discover where or what that missing something might be. Can you tell me—"

"The sky," she said promptly. "There ought to be something else there, though I know not what."

"Yes, I see what you mean," said he, staring at it. "Yes, indeed!"

"Could you perhaps add an extra cloud?" Mrs Grimley suggested.

"It has quite a lot of clouds already," her husband pointed out.

"Why, you are perfectly right, Mr Grimley!" she exclaimed. "How clever you are to have noticed all the clouds."

Caroline gritted her teeth. God help her, she couldn't endure another round of that. "A bird, perhaps?"

Mr Acton shook his head. "I tried a ring-necked dove, then a skylark. Neither seemed to fit."

"What about a bird of prey?" She pointed at the lamb. "Something looking for the opportunity to swoop upon a young animal while it is otherwise unguarded and vulnerable."

"A buzzard or golden eagle, perhaps?" Georgiana offered.

"Precisely!" Caroline exclaimed. "It might lend a slightly darker air to the painting, but perhaps that is what your buyers are looking for. Something which displays the full gamut of nature, from the peaceful and pastoral to the brutal and savage."

The party broke out into excited chatter about precisely how big a buzzard was and whether anybody had ever seen a golden eagle in the skies of Derbyshire, so it was a few tumultuous minutes before Caroline could get a word in edgewise. While the artist himself was nobody special, the same could not be said of his work; it was a shame that such talent had been overlooked, when everybody ought to be able to gaze upon such beauty. A sudden idea sprang to mind—a way to turn the Grimleys' simpering into something that might aid this poor man.

"I have heard it said," Caroline declared, when there was a moment's quiet, "that all the great marriages of the past insisted on having their portraits painted together, so that their love could be admired long after they themselves had passed." She turned to the Grimleys, bestowing one of her most dazzling smiles upon them. "Perhaps you, with your equally great love, might consider employing Mr Acton to do the same. After all, his evident talent makes him an ideal candidate for the job. And of course, knowing you both as he does, surely he would be best suited to . . . to . . ." She hesitated, seeking a careful path through the thorny maze of honesty. "Imbue the painting with all the fervour of that passion and tenderness which you both possess."

It was a truthful statement, yet conveyed none of her real feelings. Caroline mentally patted herself on the back. *I am, in fact, a genius of the highest order. Perhaps even some sort of kindness savant.* She risked a single glance at Georgiana, whose eyebrows had lifted so high, they were in danger of losing themselves in her hairline.

"A capital idea!" Mr Grimley exclaimed. "Capital indeed! I cannot believe we did not think of it before. Miss Bingley, we are truly in your debt. Mr Acton, I beg of you to consider bestowing this great honour upon us."

"Oh, please say you will, Mr Acton," Mrs Grimley cried. "You simply must immortalise us with your brush!"

Mr Acton shot a grateful glance at Caroline, though she suspected it was also tinged with some dread at the idea of spending a few hours alone in the Grimleys' presence. "I would be delighted to do so."

"And I am sure," Caroline continued, directing her words again towards the Grimleys, "that once your friends have seen the result of all Mr Acton's hard work and talent, that more will wish to have their portraits painted, too. One happy customer begets another. Is that not correct, Mr Acton?"

"I have certainly heard it claimed," he said, smiling in a

way that made his eyes crinkle, "though I cannot comment on the veracity of such a statement. Perhaps in a few months I shall be able to."

Georgiana was looking at her with a new expression that Caroline had never seen before and couldn't decipher. Something about it brought to mind the lake memory, which Caroline had managed to forget for almost a whole hour. "Perhaps you and I ought to have our portraits painted together too, Miss Darcy," Caroline said, her mouth suddenly dry. "Would that show how deep and true our friendship runs?"

The words had been spoken in jest, but Georgiana's dark eyes caught hers, and there it was again—that strange lurching feeling in her stomach, as if someone had dropped a small frog into it.

"I rather think we—" Miss Darcy murmured, but whatever she had been about to say next was drowned out by the Grimleys exclaiming over the late hour and declaring that, despite their wishes to the contrary, they had to leave that very instant.

Chapter Ten

My dear Charles,

I'm so glad you're having a wonderful time. Netherfield is so close to Longbourne—why, it's almost like living in one's mother-in-law's lap, a thing that every young man dreams of, I am sure. How perfectly delightful for you.

I wanted to ask, if you do not think it a strange or impertinent question: What is it like to be in love?

Your devoted sister,
Caroline

By the time they had said their goodbyes and got into the carriage home, Caroline was bursting with impatience to give her opinion on everything and everyone she'd seen. The moment the door clicked shut, she gave voice to all her thoughts. "Are you not impressed with how well I held my tongue, Georgie? I said nothing of the terrible brown paint in the hallway, nor did I comment on how mismatched the furniture was in the parlour. And did you see the colour of those couches? Lord, they were absolutely dreadful."

Instead of lavishing her with praise, Georgiana sat back, the contented look on her face vanishing in an instant. She regarded Caroline, her expression cool. "Are you really asking me to commend you for not openly insulting the home of a person who invited you to tea?"

"Well, I . . ." When put like that, it did sound rather impolite. Caroline stared out of the window as the small house receded from view. "You told me that I should not speak my every opinion aloud, an order which I dutifully accepted." When she glanced back at Georgiana, she was surprised to see a muscle jumping in Miss Darcy's jaw. "You needn't look so upset. I did not actually say anything untoward, did I?"

"But you thought it."

A sharp wave of disappointment swept Caroline's jubilation away. "Are thoughts crimes?" she inquired. "I wasn't aware that the law had changed."

"Obviously not. But they did not remain thoughts, for you just spoke them aloud to me. Do not forget, Caroline, that you are speaking of a dear friend of mine. Did you imagine that your poor opinion of Miss Merryhill's house would be well-received?"

In truth, Caroline had thought so; Georgiana did have functioning eyes, after all. "Are you saying that you think her house beautiful?"

Georgiana stared out of the window, her hands flexing in her lap. "I am saying that it would have behooved you to try to find something nice to say, regardless of your first impression."

"Is that the standard of a perfect woman, then? To choose a pretty lie over an ugly truth? I thought you valued honesty more than that."

To this, Georgiana made no reply.

"You are being impossible," Caroline declared, already fed up with the conversation. "And you might consider the possibility that criticising me for what I did not do, rather than praising me for what I did do, is rather an inefficient way to teach good behaviour. When we left, I felt rather pleased with myself, but now I . . ." She swallowed. "You are not even applying your own lesson, if you cannot acknowledge even one good thing I did or said."

The silence stretched on. Caroline's skin prickled horribly, her stomach hot and tight with embarrassment and injustice.

"Mrs Darcy," Georgiana said, her voice quiet but firm, "would never have spoken so."

"Then she is a perfect fool!" Caroline cried, humiliation giving way to exasperation. "I am sure even your perfect Lizzy could not see the need to spend time with people like Miss Merryhill and her acquaintances. They are not of our particular circles and cannot advance us in any way."

"That does not signify," Georgiana snapped. "Kindness should not be dependent on what the other person can offer you but should be extended to all people regardless of class or social standing."

"According to whom?" she retorted and was surprised to see hurt flash across Miss Darcy's face.

"It is a truth generally held amongst those people who are considered to be upstanding members of society."

The implication was that Caroline, who did not share this opinion, could therefore not be counted as an upstanding member of society. Stung, Caroline folded her arms across her chest and flopped against the hard backrest of the carriage.

"You act as if only the most superior in society are worth noticing," Georgiana continued, "though they are simply a small group. The rest of the world may not be handsome or wealthy or well-connected but that does not make them any less deserving of respect. Or love. Does not the Bible say we ought to love all creatures great and small?"

Caroline changed tack, sensing that picking a fight with God as well would not be the most sensible decision in the present moment—one should avoid warring on two fronts at the same time. "Those Grimleys are absolutely unbearable. We shall agree on that at least. You cannot tell me that spending an hour or two in their company has improved me any as a person. If anything, it may have made me worse."

"They may be a trifle tiresome at times," Georgiana admitted, "but not nearly so much as you are making out. And they are good people at heart, who evidently adore each other very much. They do not deserve outright contempt."

"Oh, Georgie, really! I am all astonishment! Did I not expand their happiness by suggesting a portrait? Did I utter a single unkind word in their presence?"

"You said you wanted to throw yourself out of the window," Georgiana reminded her. "Or have you forgotten?"

"That was for your ears only," she complained. "Am I not allowed even a single pithy aside? If so, life will hardly be worth living."

"Do you not think it possible that you were simply jealous at the sight of two newlyweds so in love?"

"Jealous?" Caroline had experienced two emotions happening at the same time before, though it was an infrequent occurrence in her life, but they had never been this particular combination of outrage and confusion. "Of the Grimleys? Are you feeling quite well? Why on earth would I be—"

"Only of their wedded bliss."

"I am no such thing, I assure you. The very sight of them made me feel quite sick. Why on earth would you think that?"

"Because you asked me to help you become a kinder person," Georgiana pointed out. "And you did specifically say that you intend to become so in pursuit of a suitable match. A love match, no less. And this all happened mere weeks after Fitzwilliam's marriage to—"

"For goodness' sake!" Caroline snapped, annoyed to discover that Georgiana's words held a kernel of truth. Seeing the Grimleys act in such a lovesick manner had made her feel on the verge of regurgitating her luncheon all over her beautiful blue shoes, and yet, something about the way they'd looked at each other had made her feel slightly bitter. They had found each other—and frankly, two such fools deserved each other—but when would Caroline find her own match? And what if she never did? "You know that I wasn't in love with your brother. I thought I had already made that very clear to you, but if I must do so again, then I am delighted to clarify further."

"I am not suggesting that—" Georgiana bit her lip. "I only meant that you might be envious of their felicity."

Caroline opened her mouth to retort, found she had nothing loaded on the gun of her tongue, and closed it again with an audible snap of her teeth. "You misunderstand me," she said, though in fact, Georgiana had understood her very well. "I simply meant that I could not imagine ever being so awful with my own betrothed. So . . . simpering. It entirely put me off my luncheon."

"You had five sandwiches," Georgiana pointed out.

"In a *spiritual* sense, Georgie. One must eat to keep one's strength up. You would not wish me to be swooning all over the place from lack of sustenance, would you?"

"I cannot believe you would ever swoon." Georgiana still wasn't smiling, but her shoulders had loosened. "One rather feels that your body would have to petition your mind for approval for such an act, and that your mind would deny the suit."

Caroline began to relax. They'd been on the brink of an argument, and now it looked as if they had managed to safely steer themselves back to firmer footing. She'd never actually argued with Georgiana before, not properly. Miss Darcy was too patient for that, and far too ready to consider the other party's side and give it all the same quarter as her own, though in Caroline's opinion, Georgiana went too far. Surely one could be kind to all beings without actually being forced to like all of them.

"Mr Acton possesses considerable talent," she said. "Do you not think me clever for suggesting the idea of a portrait to the Grimleys?"

"It was an excellent idea," Georgiana allowed. "Though I would feel more impressed had I not also suspected that you were entertained by the idea of mocking the Grimleys in a way they could never understand. Or by the notion that Mr Acton now has to spend hours in their company."

"Does that matter?"

"Everything matters," Georgiana muttered, steadying herself with a hand on the seat beside her as the carriage went over a slight bump in the road.

"It's not as if you have to be there, too." Caroline cocked her head. "Do not tell me you have feelings for the man? He is so below your station, it would be entirely out of the question."

Miss Darcy rolled her eyes. "I do not harbour romantic feelings for Mr Acton, I assure you. Nor is he interested in me. He is simply a talented artist of low means who has struggled to gain appreciation for his work." She bit her lip. "I often think that if he had been born a young lord, that his life so far would have been very different. He has had to work hard, Caroline. Scraping pennies here and there in order to live. Such a life might have turned another into a bitter man, yet Mr Acton is patient and good-natured, with an eye for beauty and an appreciation of all life's little pleasures. I think his disposition, with those circumstances in mind, is very commendable indeed."

"And he is quite in love with Miss Merryhill. Have you noticed?"

"Of course I have. And I feel rather sorry for him," Georgiana admitted. "I gather that he cannot afford to marry, though he loves her dearly. She has never told me directly how she feels upon the subject, for she is a shy creature, but I am certain that she feels the same way."

"Oh, she reciprocates, I have no doubt. Did not you notice her comment about the painting he gave her? She keeps it upstairs, probably in her chamber where she can look upon it every day. That is not the action of a woman who does not care." The carriage rolled on, the only sound that of the footman murmuring something to the driver, which produced a quick barking laugh. Caroline tapped her thumb against her bottom lip, thinking the situation over. Through the window, she could see the gates of Pemberley approaching; vast, iron, foreboding enough to a stranger but an immensely welcoming sight for a family friend. "Though I cannot see why he is so interested in Miss Merryhill. She is sweet enough, I grant you, but a painter surely wishes to look at beauty every day. What could such a wife offer him?"

She'd meant it as an offhand comment, but Georgiana stiffened again. "I knew you could be judgemental, but I did not think you could be cruel. Beauty is so much more than a pretty face or shapely figure."

Caroline stared at her, entirely lost. "But it is not as if she is here to hear me. Cruelty would have been saying the words to her face, and trust me, I have known some who would do just that."

"That does not make it right to say it at all."

"From what I've heard, your own aunt does not mince words. In fact, Lady Catherine de Bourgh is rather known for her forthright nature, is she not?" Caroline arched an eyebrow. "Did she not visit Miss Elizabeth Bennet only a few months ago? I had heard a rumour that—"

"Lady Catherine, while possessing many virtues," Georgiana said tightly, "is not necessarily the person on whom I would recommend one base one's commitment to kindness. Look, I am merely asking you to take a moment to consider how your words sound. Imagine, for a moment, that someone unknown to you met us both at a party, and upon their returning home to their family, they declared similar opinions of you. How would that make you feel?"

"But I am neither poor nor ugly. I cannot see how—"

"Good heavens, I am only asking you to think before you speak, not impale yourself permanently on the sword of humility!" Miss Darcy exclaimed, as the carriage slowed to a halt outside of the house. "Miss Merryhill may not be a great beauty, but she is a gracious and generous woman with whom I have been friends for a great many years. After my parents passed, she walked to Pemberley once a week to bring a cake she had baked herself, and to check in on me when Fitzwilliam was away. She did so without expecting anything in return. Her friendship, and the friendship of others which you consider so beneath us, became indispensable to me. I will not hear her abused even a little." Her hands clenched into fists, her knuckles pale. "Heavens, I was prepared for you to be irritating today, but I had no idea you were going to be downright insufferable."

Georgiana flounced out of the carriage without a backwards glance, leaving Caroline staring after her with her mouth hanging open. *Insufferable?* She followed Georgiana into the hallway, whereupon the latter tugged off her gloves and threw them with gusto onto the side table.

"I think it a little dishonest to pretend that everyone is worthy of the same amount of respect, no matter how they look or act," Caroline said. "I disagree that it is unkind to express a preference for one person over another, or to express one's taste. Nor do I think it unkind to acknowledge that the Grimleys, however you slice it, rather embarrassed themselves today. They may be young and in love, but they lacked decorum."

Georgiana whirled on Caroline. "You spend far too much time looking outward at everyone else and no time at all looking inward."

Surprised, Caroline cocked her head. "That's simply not true. I think about myself every single day."

"I am talking," she said through gritted teeth, tearing off her wrap with quick, jerky movements, "of self-reflection. It's a wonderful thing. You ought to try it sometime."

The action revealed the full glory of Miss Darcy's considerable bosom; it was truly terrible timing, but Caroline could not help a quick glance at the soft skin, the way it heaved and—

"Are you even listening to me?"

"Of course I am!" Caroline said, more heatedly than she felt, feeling the need to cover up her sudden lapse in attention. "And how does one reflect on one's self? Ought I find a looking glass?"

"If you're not going to take me seriously, then I shall stop talking. And what's more"—Miss Darcy glared at her—"I shall stop helping with your Great Endeavour."

If even Georgiana's patience was running out, then there was surely no one on earth who'd put up with Caroline long enough for her to achieve her goal. "No, wait," she said hastily. "I'm listening. What do you mean by 'self-reflection'?"

"Well, you might consider sitting in a quiet room and writing about your feelings."

"Whatever for?"

Georgiana's long-suffering sigh was almost certainly going to induce sad lung, though now did not seem like a good time to remind her of the dangers of such a condition. "In order to discover what lies inside you, if indeed anything does." Georgiana disappeared into the library for a moment and returned with a pretty leather-bound journal, which she shoved unceremoniously into Caroline's hands.

Caroline turned the journal over, admiring the cover, which had been embossed with an intricate floral pattern. "What am I supposed to write?" she asked, but Miss Darcy was already halfway up the stairs.

"You're so clever, I'm sure you'll figure it out," Georgiana called over her shoulder. "Until you do, I shall be otherwise engaged."

Caroline stared down at the journal. The journal stared back blankly.

Fine, she thought. *If Georgiana wishes me to examine the very deepest recesses of my soul, then examine I shall. What could possibly go wrong?*

Chapter Eleven

Caroline took off her wrap and folded it neatly before laying it on the side table. Next, she tugged off her own gloves, which were as soft and blue as the shoes she currently wore, and placed them neatly on top of the wrap. She couldn't help doing the same for Georgiana's wrap and gloves—really, one couldn't simply walk away from articles of clothing lying around all askew, for it made the place look untidy—and if performing a small task gave her a moment's reprieve from carrying out what she'd been ordered to do, well, that was merely a happy coincidence.

Finally, lacking anything further to fold bar the furniture, Caroline carried the journal into the library, settled herself at the writing desk in the corner, and placed the open book in front of her. Selecting a quill from an array of Georgiana's favourites, she opened an ink bottle and dipped the nib. Before she could touch quill to parchment, she hesitated. What on earth was she supposed to say? A soul must surely be like the sea, deep and dark, and one could not simply dive in without dipping one's toe in the water first to test the temperature.

Dear Self, she wrote. That seemed a sensible way to begin.

I spoke the truth earlier about Miss Merryhill's house and the gathering we attended today, and yet Georgiana was angry with me when I voiced my opinions.

She hesitated again.

I suppose I understand that one may feel defensive if one's friends are criticised in some way, even if the opinions expressed are correct. I would never stand for anyone criticising Georgiana so, even if they were right about—

"Oh," she breathed, realisation slamming into place.

Georgiana had told Caroline explicitly that she and Miss Merryhill were friends, but Caroline had not entirely believed it, due to the difference in status. She had assumed that the relationship had to have been, in part, a sort of charity; that Georgiana, out of the goodness of her heart, had simply deigned to offer Miss Merryhill a little of her time and energy. It had never actually occurred to Caroline that perhaps it was a real friendship, or that the kindness might run in both directions. It took several attempts to picture Miss Merryhill walking miles simply to bring a cake to an orphaned, lonely Georgiana, but once she had the image fixed in her mind, she suddenly felt rather guilty.

And of course, someone as good and kind as Georgie would feel any slight against her friend as if it were magnified. She may look as gentle as a lamb, but she protects those she cares for as well as any lion.

As she scribbled furiously, another thought took hold. Georgiana had given Caroline a very specific task for her first lesson at Pemberley—to praise something about each room—and yet Caroline had forgotten to apply this instruction entirely to Miss Merryhill's house. Everything she'd said had been a criticism, unameliorated by any praise, which must have made it seem as if that lesson had never taken place; as if Georgiana had taught her nothing.

The idea became clearer with every word she wrote.

While I am sure there is something to be said for honesty and a clear eye, I forgot to look for something to praise, too. That was the point, after all, which I entirely missed. I shall correct my failing here, beginning with Miss Merryhill's house, for though I thought the brown paint in the hallway ugly—

She paused, then scribbled over the last few words. *Praise only*, she reminded herself. Surely that could not be so hard. Biting the feathery end of the quill, she closed her eyes and recalled the scene.

The couches in the parlour were of a pleasant firmness, and the legs elegantly carved in dark wood. The furniture appeared well-cared-for and well-used, indicating that it had been passed down through the family for some generations. Miss Merryhill's dress was ~~a worn~~

~~a shapeless~~
~~an inexpertly~~

"Oh good grief," Caroline said, exasperated, scratching out yet another description.

Of the thousands of dresses in the world, Miss Merryhill's gown had the advantage of belonging to that number.

She surveyed her words with no small pride. That would do nicely. Now she ought to move into praise for the party themselves.

Mr Acton is a talented painter, and I feel sorry that few will ever know of his skill. Miss Merryhill was kind enough to invite me along to tea when she did not even know me, and served us by her own hands without shame. The Grimleys—

Here, she paused, momentarily bereft of appropriate language. A mortal woman could only do so much in the face of explicit revulsion.

The Grimleys are nauseating together, but it is clear that they love each other dearly. There is something to be said for treasuring the happiness of another over your own, and of seeking to further that happiness in every way possible.

With surprise, she found she meant what she'd written. Caroline regarded the page with satisfaction. *There.* She had experienced a Revelation, with a capital *R*. Georgiana's hurt, her wounded look, had cut Caroline deeply. If being kinder meant that her friend—her dearest friend—never looked like that again, then kinder she would bloody well be. This went far deeper than her urge to best Miss Elizabeth Bennet. Making her way upstairs, Caroline swallowed before knocking on the door of Miss Darcy's bedchamber. Georgiana did not immediately answer, and it took a second, firmer knock to elicit a response.

"Come in," Miss Darcy said, her tone neutral, gaze firmly fixed on the half-written letter in front of her. The quill clutched in her right hand trembled very slightly as it moved across the page. "How may I help you?"

"I wrote in the journal." Caroline waved it. "As you so desired."

"This isn't about what I want," Georgiana corrected. "It's about what you want, is it not? What you asked me to help you to achieve?"

Caroline drew in a deep breath. "You're right. And I am sorry," she said, her voice sounding far too loud in the quiet room. "Really, I am."

Georgiana's quill paused its scratching, though its wielder still did not look up. "How do I know that you are not simply apologising so that I will agree to continue with your Great Endeavour?"

"You may think what you will, but I'm saying it because I really am sorry. I know that I hurt your feelings by speaking so of your friend, and, well, I suppose I thought that no one could ever really be angry with me for speaking the truth, however hurtful. That habit may not easily be broken, I'm afraid. It may take some time for me to get used to a new one. A better one."

Georgiana looked up, finally meeting Caroline's gaze. The expression in Miss Darcy's eyes was cautious but curious. "I've always wondered why you were so quick to judgement."

"I suppose I . . . because I expect people to judge me quickly, too." The low flame of discomfort flickered in Caroline's chest. "My mother instilled the idea in me early on that we always had to be on our guard because we were always on display, and I suppose the notion took hold a little too well." She swallowed. This was different from dipping a toe in the waters of her soul. Instead, this felt like slicing it open. "The Bingleys are not an old family like yours, Georgie. We do not have status borne from long histories, nor the same level of wealth. We cannot afford to make any mistakes regarding our connections. My cautiousness led me to callousness."

"Putting others down does not necessarily lift yourself up," Georgiana pointed out.

"I know." Guilt lanced through her again, the blade twisting at the remembrance of Georgiana's expression in the carriage. "Though I confess I wasn't thinking so much of height and depth but more of . . . distance. The space between *them* and *us*, as Mother would say. Here, you may read what I have written." She offered the journal, but Georgiana waved it away.

"No, that is for your own personal use. Write in it whenever you need to work something out. That's what I do."

Caroline knelt beside Georgiana and clasped her hands earnestly. "I henceforth vow to be better, if only you'll show me how."

"Did we not already have this conversation?"

"True, but when first I asked you to help me, I did not quite know what I was asking. I think I comprehend a little more now. I shall stumble often on the road to becoming a better person, but what I do know is this: You are the only one who can help me walk that path." Caroline widened her eyes and pouted her lips, creating the best puppyish expression she possibly could.

Georgiana looked alarmed. "Do not twist your face so. It makes you look ill."

"Why, I am ill," Caroline exclaimed, pressing a hand to her forehead in the most dramatic fashion she could manage. "I sicken with your dubiety. I swoon with your suspicion. I am feverish with—"

"Yes, alright, you've made your point." Miss Darcy shook her head. "I really do not know why I agreed to go along with your ridiculous scheme in the first place, but I feel compelled to see it through now, for better or worse."

"Your good opinion means the world to me," Caroline admitted, watching Georgiana's eyes widen. "And I hate to think that I might have lowered myself in your estimation. I know I do not always say the right thing. In fact, I rarely . . . And I am aware that I am a long way from . . ." She trailed off, shifting uncomfortably. "Do you forgive me? Say you do, for my knees are beginning to hurt dreadfully."

"Of course I do, you goose. Please get up."

Caroline clambered to her feet, relief spreading through her entire body in a cool wave. "And who knows, perhaps teaching me will furnish you with something, too."

"An early grave, no doubt," Georgiana muttered, though she was smiling. "I need a little more time to finish my correspondence. Can you amuse yourself for an hour or so? I shall come and fetch you, for it looks as if it is clearing up outside and I expect you would like a nice, long walk before dinner."

"You know me well." Caroline leaned down and pressed a kiss against Georgiana's cheek. "Thank you for being such a good friend."

Georgiana turned away, though not quickly enough; Caroline caught a flash of the pretty blush that crept across her face. "Out, you devil, before I change my mind."

Beaming, Caroline obeyed.

Chapter Twelve

My dear Caroline,

Lyme Regis is quite lovely this time of year, if still a little cold. I feel that Mother's spirit is much improved by our long walks on the promenade, though she complains about the wind every day. There are few shops worth our time here, but never fear, I shall bring you back a shiny bauble as I always do. My husband is overseeing a few repairs to our house in Grosvenor Square. Once it's complete, you shall have to come to London and spend a month or two with us there. You have been at Pemberley a good while already, have you not?

Charles has written to me from Bath and seems exceedingly pleased with his new bride. With our brother now wed, ~~Mother thinks~~ I think it might be time to turn your thoughts towards marriage as well. I would hate for you to feel left out, and ~~Mother has~~ we have made some very interesting new acquaintances here . . .

Your affectionate sister,
Louisa

Groaning, Caroline balled up her third attempt at a letter to Louisa. Each had been worse than the last, sounding increasingly stilted and angry. Why on earth did her family keep insinuating that Georgiana would be glad to be rid of her? It wasn't as if they themselves were waiting back at Hadley Hall to receive her with open arms. Caroline picked up Charles' letter and read it again, feeling a twinge of relief. At least her brother had not suggested her presence at Pemberley was as unwelcome as hungry rats in a fully stocked larder.

She glanced around the room, seeking distraction, and her gaze landed on *The Mysteries of Udolpho*, which lay untouched on the small table beside the bed. In truth, she hadn't read a single page since the first day she'd obtained the book, and while Georgiana hadn't pursued the matter much since, Caroline knew she was going to ask about it eventually. Caroline crossed to the bed and flopped onto it, forcing herself to pick up the book. She flipped through another few pages, but nothing interesting seemed to be happening, and she lacked the patience to continue in the hope that something did. The problem was that no tale could please her. Perhaps she ought to write one, for her own story could surely be controlled and made to fit all her smallest whims to her greatest satisfaction. The idea pleased her immensely until she thought of the time and effort it would likely take to produce a whole book.

Days. She shuddered. *Perhaps even a whole week.*

Really, it was a wonder that anyone ever wrote anything at all.

Caroline let *The Mysteries of Udolpho* fall onto her chest with a soft thump. Speaking of things that could please her, she ought to be picturing her perfect match so that, when she finally met him, she would know whether he satisfied her ideals exactly. A grand house must play a part, of course, perhaps not as grand as Pemberley but at least as pretty as Netherfield Park, Charles' home. It ought to have large gardens in which she could walk, with plenty of flowerbeds. That sort of thing was easy enough to decide upon, although the man who went with the dream house was more difficult to imagine. He ought to be a little on the short side, for she did not like tall men the way some women did. *Perhaps about Georgiana's height*, she mused. Miss Darcy really was the perfect height; tall enough to loom over Caroline by two or three inches, but short enough to kiss without Caroline having to crane her neck. Yes, a shorter man would do nicely. What else?

He should dress well, of course, she thought. *His hair ought to be . . .*

Her imagination stuttered to a halt. She'd always admired Darcy's dark head of curls, but now that she was actually picturing her ideal suitor, he had much lighter hair. Not yellow like Charles', but something paler, more flaxen, like Georgiana's. Once that was decided on, her imagination faltered again. Clothes and hair were one thing; it was easy to dress a man in one's mind like a doll, but impossible to picture facial features with any degree of clarity. None of the men she knew suited much. Oh, Darcy had been handsome enough, but the thought of him smiling down at her did not make her pulse quicken. Perhaps someone with whiskers? She pictured a bearded mouth pressing against her own, then shuddered.

Absolutely not.

Very well. Someone clean-shaven, then. Ideally, he'd have pretty eyes; not blue, like the rest of her family, but the darkest of browns. Some men had eyelashes so long that it made women jealous, and she had always enjoyed the sight of long, dark lashes resting upon pale cheeks. While eyelash length was not exactly the kind of thing one ought to base a prospective marriage on—she bit back a laugh at the idea of taking a ruler to parties and balls to see who passed this test—it was certainly a start to the winnowing process. Besides, if the man had favourable looks, then he would naturally pass them down to their children too, should they have any.

Caroline frowned. She wasn't sure how she felt about the idea of children. They were pleasant enough to be around when they were well-behaved, but terrors when they were not. She couldn't picture herself holding a baby in her arms any more than she could picture a suitable man in front of her fantasy house. Oh well, perhaps it did not matter much. Perhaps fate had someone else in store for her already. Perhaps she would walk into a ball one day and simply see the man of her dreams, turning to face her, thunderstruck by her beauty. He would be so overcome by her grace and nobility that he would propose on the spot. Yes, that would be sufficiently dramatic and would make for a wonderful tale; she would be the envy of all the ton. It almost did not even matter who the man was or what he looked like, in that case—the story was the thing, something by which she could distinguish herself as being special. He'd pick her rightfully out of a crowd as the prettiest, most charming, most eligible young lady in all of England. He'd want her. He'd need her.

He'd see me.

The yearning sent a pang of longing through her. Plenty of people watched her in ballrooms or at parties, men and women both, but that was something quite different. *Watching* was not the same as *seeing*. One could watch a brick wall if one so desired, could watch a thousand handsome figures dancing, but it wasn't the same as someone approaching, excited, hopeful, their eyes studying your every curve and angle.

The image of Georgiana emerging from the lake came to mind again, entirely unbidden, but extremely insistent. The yearning moved lower, building into a slow heat, and Caroline groaned. *Not again*, she ordered her body, which paid her no heed whatsoever, the familiar ache building between her thighs. And yet—

She paused, licking her lips.

Perhaps her body was trying to tell her something. Swallowing, she allowed herself for the first time to recall every detail of that moment; the droplets of water beading on Georgiana's forehead, her sturdy thighs flexing as she heaved herself out of the lake. Caroline's hand began to drift downwards. *Yes*, she thought, *if there was a man in the world who looked exactly like Georgiana Darcy, that would suit me very well indeed. Perfect height, long eyelashes, firm and supple arms. Soft, fair hair that practically begs one to run one's fingers through it.*

But the image that formed in her mind wasn't a man. It was Georgiana herself, dark eyes fixed on her, mouth set in a wicked smile, fingertips ghosting over the sodden fabric of her petticoat and—

Caroline gasped, arousal spiking low and sudden. Her hand stilled on her stomach as she fought for control, but it was no use. Clearly, the idea was plaguing her for some reason. Perhaps she simply had to exorcise this devilish thought from her mind. It was like that silly childhood game she and Charles had played called Pink Cow; the more one tried not to picture a pink cow, one could only picture pink cows. This must be the very same thing, just a little more . . .

Sensuous?

Not that it was hard to imagine anything more sensual than a pink cow. Even so . . .

With a shameful twinge, Caroline let her head tip back, her pulse quickening. Guilt wrestled with lust as her hand drifted lower. Was she really going to do this? Was she really going to think of Georgiana while she—

A knock sounded on the door. "What? Yes? What?" she yelped, flinging her legs to the side of the bed and standing with such haste that she almost tipped over.

"Shall we go down to dinner?" Georgiana popped her head inside. "I hear that Mrs Addlecombe has cooked us a delightful—" She squinted at Caroline. "You look flushed again. Are you well?"

"What?" Caroline repeated, her heart still pounding. She'd almost touched herself thinking of Georgiana. That had been foolish. A moment of silly weakness, nothing more. "No, I'm—I mean, yes, I'm perfectly fine."

Georgiana approached, placed cool fingers against Caroline's forehead, and oh dear, the touch did nothing to quell the low blaze burning inside her. Caroline couldn't repress the shiver that ran through her, making Georgiana eye her with genuine concern. "Are you developing a cold, perhaps? Ought I send for a doctor?"

"No, no," Caroline said, catching Georgiana's hand with her own. Why on earth did she suddenly want to kiss that hand? Impulsively, she did so, her lips touching Georgiana's knuckles for a mere moment. "You are very sweet to me, but I am quite well, I assure you."

Now Georgiana was the one who looked flushed. She hadn't pulled away, though her fingers hadn't curled around Caroline's own. Instead, her hand lay limp and unprotesting, her dark eyes studying Caroline's face. "If . . ." she said, then cleared her throat and finally pulled her hand back. "If you're sure. But I shall be keeping a close eye on you, Miss Bingley. Shall we head to dinner?"

"Lead the way," Caroline said weakly, really hoping that wouldn't be the case.

Chapter Thirteen

My dearest brother,

There is truth in what you say, for I fear that Caroline's stubbornness stretches far and wide across the plains and valleys of her character, taking on entirely new colours and angles. On certain subjects she does indeed resemble a dog with a bone, though I think that tenacity something to admire; too many people are weathercocks, their every opinion blown about by a prevailing wind. To encounter someone who insists on pursuing her own path and thoughts regardless of others, who knows her own mind firmly, is refreshing indeed. Our lessons so far have been ~~exhausting~~ ~~deeply alarming~~ somewhat productive, and I feel confident that I can help her become a better version of herself, even if that is not precisely the version she currently imagines.

Oh, and you know very well that I do not care for the sex of my horse—whichever is the brightest and boldest will suit me fine. If you bring me some prancing pony who loses its head over every little fence and stile, I shall adorn it in ribbons and confess to all our visitors that it belongs to you.

Yours affectionately,
Georgiana

Dinner was indeed delicious—flaky fish cooked in a white sauce, preceded by a light salad—but Caroline was too distracted to really enjoy it properly. How had she never before noticed the way candlelight played upon Georgiana's features, picking out the beautiful curve of her lips? How had she failed to see that, while her friend had always been beautiful, she was also entrancing? A door had been opened inside Caroline, though it was a problem entirely of her own making. If she simply hadn't allowed herself to recall Georgiana's soaked body, then she wouldn't be sitting here now, squirming awkwardly with only half an appetite.

Or rather, an appetite for something that was not salad-based.

No, it is not my fault at all, actually, she decided, forcing her discomfort down until it was little more than a whisper. *I was not the one who decided to start emerging out of lakes and encroaching upon innocent passersby who were minding their own business. It is, in fact, not remotely my fault. If anything, I am a victim here.* She gave a little nod. *Yes. A victim of . . . watery allure.*

She looked up to find Georgiana watching her over the rim of her wine glass. "You look like you are arguing with yourself. And I am certain that you haven't listened to anything I've said for the last five minutes."

"I apologise. Pray, repeat whatever it was you said."

"I am delighted to inform you that my correspondence this morning has proven extremely fruitful. We have received several invitations already, and may go through them if you wish, although I have ascertained which are most likely to be attended by eligible bachelors. There is to be a picnic at a lake nearby in two days' time, which I believe would suit your Great Endeavour perfectly."

Caroline stared down at her plate, a muscle under her eye twitching. Good God, was she to be tormented by lakes for the rest of her life?

"I am sure there will be at least a dozen prospective suitors there," Georgiana added, "if not more, for I believe they intend to hold a boat race. That ought to draw a good range of gentlemen. Lady Lennox takes dinner with illustrious company, since her husband is a baron and her sister-in-law married an earl, so I would be surprised if she did not have at least a few lords in their company."

"Indeed?" Caroline perked up. Being surrounded by available men would surely chase away whatever strange notions had entered her mind of late. "Even better. I shall double my efforts to improve myself, so that I can present an excellent first impression."

Perhaps she could obtain an orphan child or a wounded puppy to bring along, so that the men could see her feeding the little creature and praise her for being saintly and good. Had not both Miss Bennets once cooed over a darling lamb that had become briefly separated from its flock? And had not the men exchanged amused yet reverent glances about the maternal instincts shown by their beloveds? *Georgiana would probably never let me do such a thing, though*, Caroline sulked, as Mrs Reynolds took away their plates. *And hiding a lamb, however small, under my skirts would be difficult indeed. I don't believe they fold well.* Mentally, she pictured all the ways in which a lamb might be neatly compacted to, say, the size of a reticule, and then repressed a sigh. *No. Too much leg.*

Really, sometimes it was as if the entire world conspired against her.

"Shall we retire to the drawing room now?" Georgiana

suggested, rising to her feet. The candles were perfectly positioned to throw pools of light onto her ample bosom, making it beam brightly.

Caroline swallowed hard, averting her gaze. "You go on ahead. I shall meet you there in a moment."

She retreated to her room upstairs, filled the basin to the brim with cool water from the pitcher, then stuck her face in it and screamed. This produced suitably dramatic bubbles but did not actually make her feel much better. "Calm down," she told her dripping reflection. "You did not actually do anything earlier."

Her reflection stared back accusatorially. *No*, it seemed to say, *but you were about to, had Miss Darcy not knocked when she did. And what then? Might you have imagined her peeling that petticoat off? Touching her bare flesh underneath? How dreadfully sinful. You would have finished thinking of her, and that surely cannot be the behaviour of a perfect woman.*

The truth was difficult to argue with. Still, Caroline had only been trying to get rid of the urge, not to savour it. She couldn't possibly be held responsible for the strange, unknowable things one's body did. Reassured by the solidity of such reasoning, Caroline patted her face dry, smoothed down her hair, then headed for the stairs, determined to have a perfectly normal evening.

The music already drifting from the drawing room was soft and tender, entirely unlike the performances Georgiana usually gave at parties. The melody itself was delicate, overlaid on a bed of earthen notes, deep and dark. Georgiana halted, her fingers stuttering to a halt on the keys, when Caroline edged over the threshold.

"Pray do not stop on my account," said she. "It sounds rather lovely. What is it?"

"Gluck," Georgiana said, smiling, though she looked a little hesitant. "It's from his opera *Orfeo ed Euridice*."

Caroline knew very little about opera, though she had enjoyed the few performances she'd seen in London. She crossed to the nearest couch and sat, pleased to note that Mrs Reynolds had provided a bowl of grapes and neatly-cut cubes of cheese. "Oh? What is it about?"

"In short, a woman dies, and her lover journeys to the underworld to fetch her back."

"Fashionably morose," Caroline declared, leaning back and crossing her legs at the ankle. The couches in the drawing room were not nearly as comfortable as the ones in the library, though they were far more stylish, with ornately carved legs. The price of beauty was one Caroline would gladly pay, though after an hour or three, her posterior would disagree vehemently with that sentiment. "Is there anything more delicious to hear about than someone else's tragedy? One may experience all the thorny pleasure of the anguish while experiencing none of the real consequences." She selected a grape from the bowl and popped it into her mouth, where it burst with sweetness. "And does he succeed?"

"Well, he—Orfeo—is told that he can bring her back to life with the power of music, but he only has one opportunity to lead her from the underworld of the dead out into the land of the living, and he must not look back at her at any point. If he does, she will be lost to him."

Caroline scoffed. "Rather easy. One would think they would make it more difficult to test his love."

"Indeed. Yet Orfeo fails the test."

"What?" She blinked. "Do they deceive him?"

"Well, it's . . ." Georgiana hesitated, her fingers picking up the melody again. "Euridice faints, you see. And so Orfeo feels compelled to look back."

"Even after being told not to? Seems like rather an obvious trick." Caroline picked up another grape. "I myself would never be so fooled."

"Indeed." Georgiana smiled, watching her own fingers glide over the keys. "I suspect you would end up staying and ruling the underworld by sheer force of will."

"It sounds as if it needs a little more ruling, if demons are running amok setting ridiculous traps for people. Do not they have proper work to do? Tending to hellfire and, er . . ." She wasn't quite sure what tasks demons might be reasonably entrusted with, now that she thought about it, but hazarded a guess anyway. "Boiling cauldrons and poking people with hot irons and so on?"

"The thing is," Georgiana said, as her right hand played a series of notes that sounded like twinkling stars, "it's not about the look. It is what is behind the look. The emotion, you see. Does Orfeo trust her to follow him even if he is not leading her? Is that not what love is?"

Caroline opened her mouth to reply, then closed it again. She honestly had no idea if that was love, though what Georgiana said did make rather a lot of sense. Curiosity pricked her. "Is that what you think love is?"

Georgiana didn't seem to hear the question, her eyes lost and focusing on some distant point in the room as her hands roved over the keys, the melody fading away. After the final notes, her hands dropped into her lap, and she sat quite still. "He receives a reward anyway."

"Orfeo? But you said he failed the test," Caroline protested, annoyance flaring. Composers simply could not be trusted to write a straightforward tale; really, they were almost as bad as novelists. "This is rather a confusing story."

"I promise it all makes sense once you see it. Cupid—the god of Love—sees Orfeo's fidelity and restores Euridice to life, so they can be together once more. It's a rather happy ending, really."

"But that is not fair." Caroline sat up straighter, irritation blooming bright as a summer flower. "He failed! He ought not to have received any reward. How very like a man. I do not suppose that if it had been the other way around—this Euridice going into the underworld to rescue her lover—that she would have been quite so fortunate if she had failed her task."

"I believe that Gluck's interpretation is a more romantic one than the original, where Euridice is forever condemned to the underworld after Orfeo fails, though I—"

"Any sensible woman would not have looked back in the first place," Caroline interjected, not content to let the point lie.

"In the Bible, Lot's wife is told not to look back when Sodom and Gomorrah fall," Georgiana reminded her, "and when she does, she is turned into a pillar of salt."

"Yes, well." She sniffed. "Rather odd how in both cases, the woman is the one punished, regardless of which member of the party actually looked back."

Georgiana laughed. "If you had only been born a man, you would have made a wonderful lawyer."

"If I had been born a man," Caroline retorted, "I would have aspired to be the kind who could employ wonderful lawyers to make arguments on my behalf. Will you perform something else?"

"What would you have me play?"

"Anything you like."

Georgiana began to play something she often trotted out at parties—a pretty little melody designed to be pleasantly unobtrusive—but Caroline stopped her, holding up a hand. "No, no, none of that. Something you want to perform, not something you think I want to hear. I'm tired of watching you suffer through these tunes."

For a moment, Georgiana's gaze held hers, burning with a sudden, fierce look that stole Caroline's breath away. But when she blinked, the look was gone, replaced with an expression of warm gratitude. "I wasn't aware that anyone had observed my . . . suffering. I hope it was not too obvious."

"Not at all. I notice more than you give me credit for, Miss Darcy."

"And I credit you more than you notice, Miss Bingley." She began to play, something ominous and slow, which sounded like a scythe swinging in tall grass. It was entirely unlike anything Caroline had heard her render before, and yet it suited Georgiana somehow. Caroline recalled the scent of Miss Darcy's bedchamber, the roses as dark and sultry as spilled blood. There was another side to Georgiana that few saw, if any.

Perhaps the lake runs deeper than you think, a voice in her mind supplied. Caroline swallowed and did her best to focus on the music. Now was not the time to think about lakes again.

"And now, something for the lady," Miss Darcy said, smiling over at Caroline. "Allow me to please you in turn."

Surprised, she blinked. "Well, I remember seeing a performance of *Dido and Aeneas* two or three years ago, which I thought very beautiful. Might you know something from—"

Before she could even finish her sentence, Georgiana played the first few drawn-out notes from Dido's famous lament, then beamed at the look of surprise on Caroline's face.

She sat, entranced, as Georgiana's playing conjured the memory of the opera as if it were happening all over again right in front of her: Dido, queen of Carthage, clasping the hand of her maid Belinda, begging the girl to remember her mistress but to forget Dido's fate, which had always seemed to Caroline like a rather impossible request; one could hardly remember a person but forget what had happened to them. Nevertheless, it was a beautiful and poignant piece which had touched Caroline deeply. Georgiana played the rest, allowing the tune to die down into a whisper before roaring back to life with a thunderous peal that brought Dido's vocal ascent perfectly to mind. Caroline applauded loudly, causing a blush to pink her friend's cheeks.

"I do not know how you can keep all those melodies in your head at once and pluck from them as easily as one takes a book from a shelf," she declared. "It is a mystery to me."

"It is a skill I have always possessed." Georgiana shrugged. "Perhaps my head is not full of much else."

"That is certainly not true." Caroline admired Georgiana's figure in the candlelight, reassuring herself that it was perfectly normal to do so. Why, it was natural that she should be envious of Miss Darcy's curves; a clever young lady should seek to acquaint herself with the competition wherever possible. Not that Georgiana was competition, of course. Who could ever compete with such a gorgeous, talented woman?

"Whatever made you think of this particular opera?" Georgiana asked.

"I am not entirely sure." Caroline hesitated, forcing her gaze towards the nearest candle flame, which flickered with every breath. "I recall that it begins with the queen of Carthage complaining about her attraction to the Trojan prince and then her handmaidens arguing that a marriage between the two would bring peace to their queen as well as their respective cities. Something like that, anyway."

Miss Darcy nodded. "She is a widow, is she not? I seem to recall that much of her reluctance to wed stems from her promise never to remarry."

"That is part of it, indeed, but I believe she is concerned that love in any shape or form will make her a weak monarch."

"And do you agree?"

"With what?"

Georgiana's gaze was curious. "Do you think love makes one weak?"

"I am no queen," Caroline said, though the jest fell rather flat. "So it hardly matters how weak or strong I am."

"You did not answer the question, Miss Bingley."

"I do not have a suitable response for you, Miss Darcy. I have never been in love, so how could I possibly comment on how it might make me feel?"

Georgiana opened her mouth to reply, but Caroline interrupted, uncomfortable with the direction the conversation had taken. "I wish I had your talent," she added, finding herself surprisingly wistful. "I can play the pianoforte well enough, but I always wanted to learn the harp. Mother insisted it was better for me to stay with the pianoforte. Harps were only for angels, she said." She picked another grape, then shot a glance at Georgiana, unable to help but smile. "I suppose she was not wrong on that account."

"Why, you ought to have said so sooner! I could teach you," Georgiana said, hands stilling on the keys. "I could have you playing something recognisable in mere days."

"Oh, you needn't go to any trouble." An unfamiliar shyness twinged in her chest.

"Your mother isn't here, Caroline," Georgiana said, softly. "And even if she were, you are a woman grown who can pursue her own ends. You may do as you wish when there are no eyes to judge. If you want to learn the harp, pray allow me to teach you."

Caroline hesitated, but Georgiana was right—why shouldn't she learn something if she wanted to? Playing the harp was unlikely to get her into trouble of any kind. She was no timid girl of twelve, afraid of her mother's scoldings. "If you insist."

"I do." Georgiana rose, leaning over Caroline to select a few grapes from the bowl. "Come on."

"What, this instant?"

"Oh, I'm sorry. Do you have a full dance card this evening?" Georgiana inquired, her smile mischievous.

Caroline rolled her eyes, then rose and re-seated herself on the stool at the opposite side of the room, the harp firmly wedged between her thighs. "Very well. What ought I do?"

"Try plucking a string," Georgiana suggested, and Caroline complied, though the string twanged strangely under her fingers. Miss Darcy smiled. "Ah, I am afraid that you must learn to let it go straight away. Do not hold on, for you will mute the sound. Here, let me show you."

Caroline had expected her to bend forward, but instead, Georgiana moved until she was standing behind Caroline, then leaned down and placed her arms around Caroline's own. Miss Darcy's breath was hot against Caroline's ear, eliciting a strange shiver. "Watch how I do it," Georgiana whispered, and Caroline watched those elegant fingers pluck, release, pluck, release. Each note reverberated in the air, as pure and cold as a single snowflake.

"Now you try it." Georgiana still had not moved, her bosom pressing into Caroline's shoulder blades, her warmth sending distracting tingles down Caroline's spine. Caroline focused on her own hands, which were trembling slightly, and strummed the required string.

"Again," Georgiana murmured, and Caroline obeyed, making sure she released quickly. "Very good! We shall make an excellent musician of you yet. Now, I shall show you a few notes. Watch my hands and do as I do."

The next quarter hour passed in a hazy blur, and by the time Georgiana had stepped back and straightened up, Caroline could feel beads of sweat rolling down her sides. It had been one thing to see Georgiana wet and almost naked and quite another to have their bodies pressed together. They had embraced from time to time, of course, as all friends did, but never for so long nor so close. There had been a lady at an inn last summer, with eyes as green as fresh moss, who had passed Caroline alone on the stairs and made sure their bodies brushed, her gaze lingering in a knowing way that Caroline hadn't understood at the time and wasn't sure she wanted to understand now. That experience had left her trembling for days, and it had only been a single encounter, barely lasting two or three seconds; Georgiana had been flush against her for long minutes.

"And remember, you can practice the harp any time you like," Miss Darcy said. "You are my esteemed guest, after all. I give full permission."

Apart from a slight blush, Georgiana looked perfectly normal. She couldn't possibly have any idea of what was roiling through Caroline, nor did the close proximity seem to affect her in the same way. "Thank you," Caroline said, her voice unexpectedly hoarse. She cleared her throat. "I suppose I might have spent my life cowering from the harp if not for your insistence."

"One must always go after what one wants," Georgiana declared. "I would have thought you, of all people, would espouse that opinion."

Caroline forced a chuckle. "As long as one knows what one wants, then certainly."

Georgiana returned to the pianoforte and began to play a livelier song that often accompanied dances at balls. The rest of the evening passed in this merry way, with occasional performances in between discussions of opera and music. Caroline watched Georgiana and could not remember having ever seen Miss Darcy so animated before. It was as if Caroline's earlier comment about having perceived her friend's suffering had opened up some door that had previously been bolted shut.

"Would you like a sherry before we retire?" Georgiana asked, getting up and strolling to the cabinet where the bottles were kept.

"Perhaps a small one," Caroline acquiesced. "But only a small one, please. I do not wish to be at risk of sad liver."

Georgiana did not turn, though her shoulders stiffened slightly. Caroline had the sneaking suspicion her friend was trying not to laugh, though Miss Darcy's tone was perfectly serious when she repeated, "Sad liver? Is that"—there was the slightest hitch in her voice, though her tone remained somber—"related to sad lung at all?"

"All organs are prone to depression of one sort or another, Georgie." Caroline sniffed. Really, Miss Darcy's governess must have been very deficient in important matters. "It's a simple fact of medical science."

Georgiana poured sherry into two glasses, taking far more care than one really needed to over such a simple action. "And is this purely a female complaint?"

"Er . . ." Caroline cast her eyes up to the ceiling, following the pattern of the crown moulding as she considered her answer more fully. "No. At least, I do not think so. Perhaps women are simply more susceptible."

Georgiana still hadn't turned around. "What other organs are sad? May I hear the full list? I feel I ought to know, lest I be beset upon by a sudden affliction of—"

"You're making fun of me," Caroline accused.

"I would never dare do any such a thing," Georgiana said, casting a glance over her shoulder. Her mouth was pressed into a tight, straight line, though her eyes were dancing with merriment. "Pray continue."

Caroline's own lips twitched, though really, it was no laughing matter. "I shan't tell you if you continue to mock me."

"But I simply must know which of my organs are at risk of being melancholy." She passed Caroline a glass of sherry and sat down on the couch beside her, tucking her feet under her thighs in a manner most unladylike. "Would you dare risk your dear friend catching such an affliction when it could be easily avoided?"

"Well, you may get sad knees sitting in such a manner," Caroline pointed out. "Mother always said a lady ought to sit thusly." She demonstrated with both feet on the ground, her knees firmly together and slanted to the right.

Georgiana swallowed hard, though she held on to her composure. "I see. Pray, do go on."

"Well, the entire body is at risk, depending on what one eats and drinks and how one behaves. And . . . well . . ." Caroline blushed as she thought of a particularly embarrassing conversation with her mother, after being caught alone in her room doing something that felt very nice but which she was swiftly informed could cause *sad womb.* It was bad enough, Mrs Bingley had said, that the womb could go wandering about the body, causing women to become hysterical and moody, without sadness being willfully inflicted upon it as well. Since then, Caroline had been naturally afraid to touch herself there and only permitted the urge when it became a hunger so overwhelming it could not otherwise be satiated.

"And what?" Georgiana's eyes were suddenly sharp, as if scenting an opportunity for more teasing. If she had been a dog, her ears would have been pricked up to their fullest extent for the slightest sound of stag or hare.

"Never you mind." She sipped her sherry, which was, of course, delicious. Perhaps a slightly depressed liver could be tolerated from time to time.

"Tell me," Georgiana wheedled, leaning closer. "I promise I can keep a secret."

Her lips glistened in the candlelight, and Caroline found herself momentarily at a loss for words. The memory of Georgiana arising from the lake returned with all the insistence of a bee buzzing against a window, certain that there must be a way inside. Miss Darcy had looked like a nymph from an ancient story, come to tempt stray travellers into the deep, dark water. Those lips had pressed against each other, wet and pink and—

Caroline cleared her throat. Good Lord, what was wrong with her? "Perhaps another day. If you're good."

"How cruel!" Georgiana pouted. "I thought you said I was always good."

"In certain areas and at certain times, you are the very best person I know. And at others, you are a mischievous little weasel."

"I thought you said I looked like a stoat earlier."

"Weasels. Stoats." Caroline waved a careless hand. "Who even knows the difference?" She sipped her sherry again, then glanced at it. "I did say a small one, did I not?"

"That is small. Look, compare it to mine." Georgiana raised her glass, which was almost a third bigger; in comparison, Caroline's sherry did look small. Thankful for the subject change away from sad organs and woodland creatures, Caroline cast about for another topic to keep her friend from pursuing the original. Before she could do so, Georgiana spoke.

"And how are you getting on with that book? *The Mysteries of Udolpho*?" Georgiana ran slender fingers through her hair absently, exposing her neck, and Caroline couldn't help watching them dip into the mass of now-dry curls, tugging gently. "For if you are not reading it, then I would quite like to return to—"

"Ah, yes." She had quite forgotten about the book. "I am very keen to keep reading it. In fact, perhaps it is best that I retire now, in order to spend more time with it, and see you in the morning."

Georgiana smiled up at her, her eyes crinkled in a most mischievous manner. "Goodnight, Caroline. I hope that your organs remain happy and healthy all night."

Back in the guest room, Caroline put the memory of Georgiana's bodily warmth firmly from her mind. Her strange notions were doubtless caused by the fact that she and Georgiana had been sequestered away by themselves for days without any other company, which doubtless explained some of her more unusual fixations of late. However, in a couple of days, they would attend a lakeside party where she would no doubt meet the man—or men—of her dreams. Caroline slid in between the sheets and stretched luxuriously. Her body still thrummed with need, but she couldn't possibly address the urge now in case the memory of a wet Georgiana came flooding back. Instead, she turned over in bed, tucking her hands under her chin, and blew out the candle.

The lake party would be the start of something wonderful. She could feel the certainty in her very bones.

Chapter Fourteen

Dear Self,

I am never certain precisely where the line between kindness and honesty lies. Is there one? For instance, if I were talking to a young lady at a dance, and I noticed she had a seed stuck in her teeth, Georgiana says I ought to tell her before her beau approaches. But what if I do not like the young lady—does that turn my lack of action into unkindness? And if I think her beau a fool she would be better without, does that turn my lack of action into kindness of a sort?

Georgiana says my ~~philosophies~~ ~~arguments~~ expostulations give her quite a headache.

Yours, and mine,
Caroline Bingley

To Caroline's delight, the day of the lake party dawned with the kind of radiance one did not often see until late summer. Birds fluttered past her window, chasing each other with the kind of ostentatious courtship displays she intended to attract for herself. It was a most excellent herald of what was surely to come, which further brightened her already good mood. Georgiana had agreed to assist her in locating the perfect dress for the occasion and Caroline felt relieved in an entirely different way—though her strangely lustful urges had remained, simmering quietly under her skin, today she would be able to channel that energy into the real task at hand: enticing a suitable gentleman.

"Oh, not that one." Miss Darcy shook her head as Caroline held up a dark green gown for inspection. "If you are to attract attention, you must stand out, not blend into the foliage."

"But it is such a lovely colour and suits my hair so well."

"I agree, and you look absolutely ravishing in it. However . . . Let me see." Georgiana nudged Caroline aside and began to rake through the closet. "Hmm. Have you nothing in pastels? Oh, this one would do nicely." She pulled out a pale pink dress. "I do not believe I have ever seen you wear this. Is it new?"

"I am yet to wear it because I remain unsure that it suits my complexion," Caroline admitted. *Ravishing? Really?* she wondered. "There is something rather too soft about it for my liking."

"And soft you must be today." Georgiana passed her the dress. "Try it on. Allow me to be the judge."

Caroline wriggled into the dress, aware of Georgiana's eyes following her every movement. "There," she said, smoothing it down. "Will you do my buttons?"

Georgiana obliged, buttoning up the back of the dress, her warm fingers brushing the sensitive skin of Caroline's nape. *Don't think about water, for God's sake,* she told herself firmly.

"You look the very picture of loveliness!" Miss Darcy cried, when Caroline finally turned. "Why on earth did you resist?"

Caroline shrugged. "Mother used to force me into pale colours when I was a child, and even then, I was aware that they did not suit. By the time I chose my own dresses, I preferred to resemble jewels. Dark, shimmering, polished. Elegant, rather than gentle." She patted her hair, though not a single strand had dared to move out of position in the last few minutes. The recollection of those childhood dresses made her stomach turn. It was all too easy to remember that she had never matched up to what her mother had expected. Louisa, with her soft brown curls and hazel eyes, had looked simply darling in mint green and buttercup yellow, and Charles' pale blue eyes had ensured that he looked dashing in any shade of blue known to man. "You do not think it makes me look as if I am wasting away?"

"Not in the slightest," Georgiana promised, clasping her hands together. "You look like a young goddess, freshly created from a flower in some glorious myth."

Preening, Caroline turned to the looking glass. Of course, she looked like nothing of the sort, but the slight blush in her cheeks accentuated her delicate face, while the muted pink of the dress made her dark hair seem even darker, and her blue eyes almost violet by comparison. Even so, there was something a little unnatural about pale colours. So soft, so wan, so . . .

Romantic.

Caroline wasn't sure she had a romantic bone in her body, but perhaps she'd have time to grow one during the two-hour carriage ride which lay ahead.

By the time they arrived at their destination, the hills rising so high around them that Caroline could not see the sky even after pressing her cheek to the cool glass of the carriage window, she was extremely glad to get out and stretch her legs. The afternoon sunshine was pleasant rather than blinding, though there was no breeze to speak of, and her stomach was already grumbling.

The trees were tall and stately, providing homes for many an unseen songbird as they made their way towards the party, which had taken up position only a few feet from where water lapped the shore of a sparkling lake. It was evidently a favoured spot, Caroline noted with interest, as the grass here was noticeably trampled underfoot and someone had built several campfires over which chickens were roasting on skewers, the smell drifting on the air and causing her mouth to water. A neatly-dressed servant manned each spit, turning the handle constantly, to ensure that the birds were cooked evenly on all sides.

A woman of around forty, even taller than Georgiana, came forward to meet them. "Miss Darcy," she cried in a surprisingly high-pitched voice considering her size. "I am so glad you came."

"Lady Lennox, I am delighted to introduce my dear friend Miss Bingley," Georgiana said, smiling back. Before Lady Lennox had even turned to Caroline, an equally tall man appeared on her right, followed by three gigantic young women—evidently her husband and daughters. In a moment, they were joined by three average-sized young men, who each took positions at the sides of their ladies, and thus the pleasantries began in earnest.

Caroline bobbed and smiled and tried to commit all their names to memory as best she could, though she had rarely been introduced to so many people in the span of a few seconds.

"Do not worry," Georgiana murmured, after cordialities

about the weather and the state of Derbyshire had been exchanged. "I shall keep you right. Though I do not know everyone assembled here, I know a fair few."

She steered Caroline past a group of men and towards a long table, prettily adorned with a snow-white tablecloth and fresh flowers, among which sat large jugs of lemonade and trays of delicacies. Lady Lennox followed them, still expounding on the wonders of the weather in this part of the world, but Caroline was no longer listening; a man with broad shoulders had glanced curiously in their direction as they passed, his gaze lingering longer than was polite. He was of average height, perhaps even a little short when compared to the men who stood by him, but his face was handsome and his body much more muscular than his fellows. His hair was dark and ruffled, hanging over one eye with a rakish air, and his eyelashes—though she could hardly tell for certain from such a distance—appeared to be long indeed. *Point one in his favour.* Caroline squinted at the small pier which held several small boats, all lashed safely to wooden posts. The man's build suggested he might be one of the keen rowers Georgiana had mentioned, which in turn meant that he had probably been educated at one of the larger universities. *Point two in his favour.* Fitzwilliam and Charles had both studied at Cambridge, though at different times due to their age difference, and they'd talked fondly about attending many competitive events to cheer on their friends against rival schools.

The man caught Caroline's eye and smiled. *And he has excellent taste in women—point three in his favour.* She returned the gesture demurely before focusing her attention back on Georgiana. She would have to confer with her friend on how to receive an introduction, though a lady could not make such gestures immediately for fear of looking over-eager. Upon her next glance, she was surprised to see the man already approaching with a glass of something dark in one hand.

Lady Lennox smiled at him, though Caroline did not detect the same fondness in it that she'd displayed for Georgiana. "Miss Darcy and Miss Bingley, this is Mr Radcliffe, a dear friend of our family."

Mr Radcliffe bowed. "I am very pleased to make your acquaintances." He turned to Georgiana. "I know your brother only a little, but what I know is enough for me to declare him one of the finest gentlemen I ever met."

"I quite agree, sir," Georgiana said, beaming at the compliment. "I would feel the same way even if he were not my brother, though I am glad he is."

"I believe he is recently married, is he not?" he continued. "I have not yet had the pleasure of meeting his wife, though I am sure any lady he chose must surely be the very best of women."

Caroline forced herself to keep smiling. Must the notion of Elizabeth Bennet's greatness be foisted on her at every available opportunity? Would she never be allowed to forget that the young lady had already achieved what she herself was still a long way from accomplishing? *Is there any place left in England where I might be safe from the mention of that name, or have all the local crofters heard of her, too?*

"Indeed," Georgiana said, casting a sidelong glance at Caroline. "My new sister is a darling woman."

In short order, Mr Radcliffe introduced a few of his friends. They were pleasant enough, albeit a little keen to show off by talking of the large bets they'd placed on who might win the upcoming boat race.

"Perhaps I shall place a bet, too," Caroline declared, and Mr Radcliffe turned to her, interest lighting up his blue eyes.

"Do you like to gamble, Miss Bingley?"

"Not at all, sir," she replied. "But I do like to win."

"Difficult to achieve one without the other," he said, amused. "And whom shall you place your bet upon?"

"Why, whichever team you are on." This was perhaps over-doing it a little, she knew, but subtleties hadn't yet been part of the Great Endeavour's curriculum. She ignored Georgiana's raised eyebrow and kept her attention on her target.

Mr Radcliffe chuckled, giving Caroline an appraising look. "You believe me to be a victor, Miss Bingley?"

"It is not what I believe, sir," said she. "For I know very little of the sport, that much is true. But I heard your friend Mr Howard say that when you declared your intent to row, several gentlemen immediately changed their bets. To have such support speaks of prior experience with your talent."

"Is that so?" he said, his eyebrows rising. "A sharp mind behind such a beautiful face, Miss Bingley. Twin dangers indeed."

Georgiana was watching them intently, her mouth hidden by the rim of her glass of lemonade. The other men, apparently too interested in their own conversations, had already wandered off to stand by the pier.

"What say we make the bet a little more interesting?" Mr Radcliffe suggested.

Now Caroline was the one intrigued. "What did you have in mind?"

"Money is beside the point. I expect you and I have enough of it already," he said, with a careless wave of his hand. "If I win, I would like to have the honour of your company for lunch."

Caroline allowed him the full force of her most charming smile, allowing the moment to drag on for a heartbeat longer than was proper. "Do you think that motivation enough to win, sir?"

He smirked back. "I am certain the opportunity will lend my arms hitherto unknown strength, Miss Bingley."

Caroline nodded her acquiescence, and Mr Radcliffe gave a short bow before strolling away. "Well," said she, the moment he was out of earshot, "that was something, was it not?"

"Indeed." Georgiana opened her mouth, seemed to think better of whatever she was going to say, and closed it again. "I am delighted that you have found a potential match."

"Hardly," Caroline scoffed. "One conversation is no basis for a marriage."

"People have fallen in love over less," Georgiana pointed out, studying Caroline. "A single look across a crowded ballroom, even."

"You need not fear the same from me, Georgie. If I am to fall in love, it will take time and many conversations. And many such looks, both in public and in private." Caroline cast a quick glance at Mr Radcliffe, who was entertaining his fellows with some jocular story that had them all in stitches. Flirting had always been fun for its own sake—and what young lady did not like attention being lavished on her by eligible men?—but when she looked at Mr Radcliffe, she did not feel any particular desire. Still, as she'd just pointed out to Georgiana, love could not be so easy as a single glance. "One ought to know the true nature of one's intended partner before one utters a weighty word such as *love*."

"Do not tell me you are getting cold feet about your Grand Endeavour now," Georgiana teased, nudging Caroline with her elbow.

"Firstly, I would have thought you'd encourage me to get to know a man before trying to wed him," Caroline countered, elbowing Georgiana back and eliciting a grin from her companion. "And secondly, you know very well that it is the Great Endeavour, not the Grand Endeavour."

"I know it indeed, but nothing pleases me so much as pulling your tail a little, just to see your claws emerge. I have always thought you at your prettiest when slightly peeved, Miss Bingley." Miss Darcy's dark eyes met her own, and the look in them was so intimate, so knowing, that for a moment Caroline entirely forgot that they were surrounded by people, forgot that there was a sky above and grass underfoot; forgot everything but Georgiana's tender smile, meant for her alone. Something in her chest twinged; not the soft pluck of a harp string, but something hard and sharp and—

Someone bumped into her, jostling her hard enough to nudge her off-balance for a moment, and Georgiana caught her by the elbow before Caroline fell flat on her face. "Why, Miss Chester," Georgiana said, turning to the offending party. "Are you injured?"

Caroline turned too, finding two ladies behind her. The younger of the pair—evidently sisters, with matching brown hair and grey eyes—was staring at the ground and had bent to massage her ankle. The girl, who now looked up in consternation, could not have been more than seven-and-ten. "Oh, Miss Darcy! My deepest apologies to your friend," she said, looking as guilty as if she'd just run Caroline through with a sabre. "I must have tripped on this tussock. I hope I did not injure either of you?"

Miss Darcy's hand was still on her elbow. Caroline swallowed as the warm fingers slipped away, wishing they could remain. "I am unharmed," she assured the group. "And you?"

"Perfectly fine," the girl said stoutly. "I am forever falling over things which are there, as well as things which are not."

"Miss Bingley, allow me to introduce Miss Emily Chester," Georgiana said, smiling, "and Miss Laurel Chester. We have met but twice before, have we not?"

"Indeed," Miss Laurel agreed. "Though it is our wish to get to know you far better, Miss Darcy. Not"—she threw a reproachful glance at her sister, who looked sheepish—"by tumbling into your acquaintances, let it be said."

Georgiana smiled. "But that is how one meets half of the most interesting people in all of England, is it not?" She turned back to Caroline. "It is said that Miss Emily Chester knows everything about every family of note in the entire country."

"Is that so?" Caroline said, looking at the younger Miss Chester with renewed interest. "What can you tell me about my brother, Charles Bingley?"

"Worth five thousand a year, recently married to a Miss Jane Bennet," the girl rattled off. "Resides at Netherfield Park just outside of Meryton. Very well-liked and always spoken of in glowing terms."

"Handsome, too," Miss Laurel added. "For I saw him at a ball in London, and he was very pleasing to the eye. I see that beauty runs in the family, Miss Bingley. You do not have any unmarried brothers that are in need of wives, perchance?"

"You are too kind," Caroline said, smiling, for the praise seemed genuine enough. "I fear my beauty hardly compares next to Miss Darcy. And I'm afraid I have only the one brother to spare, and as you know, he is already married."

"You know she only has one brother," Miss Emily whispered to Miss Laurel, loud enough for Caroline to hear.

"Remember your niceties, Em," her sister muttered, shooting her another sharp look.

"This party is well-attended indeed," Georgiana said smoothly, drawing their attention. "There are three earls and a baron. Oh, and a viscount too—Lord Ashbrook. I saw him talking with Lady Lennox earlier."

"Ashbrook?" Caroline repeated. The name sounded familiar, though she couldn't think why.

"Over there, under the large oak tree," Miss Laurel said. "He's the one in the blue coat."

The fair-haired viscount in question was standing with an equally fair-haired young man, though he did not seem to really be paying much attention to his companion's conversation and instead was staring into the crowd with an expression of deepest yearning. If pressed, Caroline would have guessed the lord was no more than eight-and-twenty, though he had the solemn, sad countenance of a man ten years his senior. The freckled boy was perhaps nine-and-ten, therefore surely could not be the viscount's son. Scenting intrigue, Caroline tried to follow Ashbrook's gaze, but it was impossible to tell who might have caught his attention. For a moment, as if feeling the weight of her gaze, his face turned towards her. She met his eye with interest, noting the full lips, the handsome set of his jaw, before he turned away again. From this distance, he could have been mistaken for being Georgiana's brother; the resemblance was striking.

"I say, he is rather fine, is he not?" Caroline said. "He might be the most handsome man I have ever seen in my life."

"I must agree." Miss Laurel giggled. "He is considered the

best catch for miles around, though no feminine angler has been able to ensnare him yet."

"Miss Chester, what can you tell us about Mr Radcliffe?" Georgiana asked abruptly, indicating the man in question with a slight jerk of her chin in his direction.

Caroline had almost forgotten about Mr Radcliffe's existence. *Focus on the Great Endeavour,* she reminded herself, *not on extremely handsome lords whose attentions have evidently been caught elsewhere. I need a fish without a hook already embedded in its cheek.*

Miss Emily looked delighted to be able to prove her skills yet again. "He is the owner of a large estate down in Wales. He is worth about three thousand a year. He won races for Oxford every year that he attended, though any man here could have told you that fact."

Caroline could already hear her mother's pronouncement on the subject: *A suitable catch indeed.* Mr Radcliffe was looking more and more promising by the minute.

"He was previously married," Miss Emily continued, "but his wife died after only two years."

Miss Laurel shot her a warning glance. "That'll do, Em."

"In childbirth—"

"That will do!" Miss Laurel snapped.

"And the baby died, too," Miss Emily mumbled, shooting an apologetic glance at her sister. "My apologies, but you know I cannot stop mid-stream."

"So he is a widower with no children?" Caroline asked, forestalling further bickering. *How perfect.* Not for him, of course, but his circumstances suited her very well indeed.

They passed the next half hour testing Miss Emily's capacity, with results that amused Caroline and elicited a few more glares from Miss Laurel. Caroline did not really see what the problem was; the girl had a tendency to be a little overly honest in her statements, but since they were all gossiping together, it hardly seemed to matter. Too many people in society placed importance on not uttering their true beliefs or waiting until they had ascertained what the majority thought in order to fall in line, and Caroline found herself appreciating Miss Emily's candour.

By the time the sun was highest in the sky, the men began to gather near the pier, some removing their jackets and loosening their cravats in preparation for the race. Mr Radcliffe's tight shirt did very little to hide his bulging muscles, and several ladies—both married and unmarried—seemed to find their eyes inexplicably drawn to his figure as he neatly stepped into his boat and took his seat. Caroline appraised his figure studiously, though her lustful urges seemed to have dissipated for the moment, and wondered what her mother would make of him. Three thousand a year was not to be sniffed at, though it would probably fall short of Mrs Bingley's expectation for her last unmarried child.

Caroline was surprised when the rowers began leisurely making their way across the lake with long, slow strokes of their paddles. Presumably they had decided to make the event more dramatic for everyone else by rowing to the other side first as a warm-up exercise before racing back towards the crowd on the southern shore. The boats reached the northern shore and milled around before arranging themselves into a neat line, evenly spaced so that no rower would be in danger of crashing into another. Good-natured shouts drifted back over the water, though they were too far away for her to clearly make out what was said.

A cry went up, though she knew not from whom, and the rowers were off, skimming across the water with powerful strokes. Caroline peered into the distance, shading her eyes from the glare of the sunshine. A welcome relief fell over her face as Georgiana provided a parasol.

"They are certainly going at speed," Miss Darcy commented. A slight breeze had picked up, teasing the curly tendrils which framed her face and wafting her familiar rosewater scent towards Caroline, who could not help drawing a deep breath. "Why, it hardly looks like they are touching the water at all," she added.

"Indeed." Caroline leaned close, indulging in Georgiana's perfume as the crowd around them buzzed with nervous anticipation. Miss Darcy smelled good enough to eat, a thought which distracted Caroline from the ongoing action. It was bad enough that she could remember precisely what had happened the last time she'd stood next to a lake. A ripple of warmth threatened to unseat her entirely, but she gritted her teeth, determined to pay attention.

A young man, barely older than six-and-ten, waited in another rowboat just a few feet away from the pier and as the rowers reached this unseen line, he was evidently the one who must indicate who had won the race. "The victory is Mr Radcliffe's!" the boy called, though it was hardly necessary to do so. Mr Radcliffe's boat had been a full length and a half ahead of the others at the moment of triumph.

The crowd burst into applause and cheers, and Caroline clapped along politely as Mr Radcliffe climbed out of his boat. He was a lot less graceful on land, and walked, she noticed now, with a slightly bow-legged strut, as if he were a rooster parading the barnyard, master of all he surveyed. The other rowers did not seem to care much that they had lost, and crowded around Mr Radcliffe to clap him on the back and offer congratulations.

Miss Laurel sighed. "He's so wonderfully talented."

He might be an excellent rower, Caroline thought, *but that is a skill rarely called for, and which surely cannot translate well on land.* She shook herself. *Remember to seek the good in people. Mr Radcliffe is evidently well-liked and respected here. He must have plenty of good qualities, therefore I shall make it my mission to discover every one.*

"So, Miss Bingley," said he, appearing at her elbow. "May I call upon you two days hence to take you and Miss Darcy to lunch? Say, around noon? You are staying with her at Pemberley, are you not?"

Caroline blinked. She hadn't expected the invitation to happen quite so swiftly, though she supposed if he were soon headed back to Wales, Pemberley would not require much of a deviation from any intended route south. "Indeed, sir. I am very much looking forward to it."

"Excellent." He bowed. The action brought with it a blast of male musk, earthy and dry, and it was all Caroline could do not to wrinkle her nose.

After a hearty lunch, which had consisted of nearly half a chicken and two large platefuls of salad, Caroline found herself nodding off in the carriage on the way home. Her eyelids drooped as the warmth of the air, to say nothing of the comfortable silence which lay between her and Miss Darcy, had lulled her into a daze. Georgiana's own eyelids had fluttered shut some minutes ago and her chest now rose and fell with gentle, steady breaths. Before Caroline could drift off entirely, Georgiana's head slumped onto Caroline's shoulder, sending a frisson of excitement through her.

She bit back a groan. *Not this again.* She'd managed to get through most of the day without thinking of Georgiana in this strange way. Steeling herself, Caroline pictured Mr Radcliffe again: strong arms, broad shoulders, handsome face. They would no doubt have beautiful, if rather short, children. But could she picture herself actually married to the man? Did the idea excite her as it should?

Not even remotely.

She frowned, adjusting the mental picture this way and that. She could see him shaking hands with Charles, charming Louisa, and yet . . .

She could not picture herself sitting across the table from Mr Radcliffe at dinner, nor walking arm-in-arm along the promenade in Bath. Nor could she picture herself in bed with him, a thought which ought to have drawn the most scandalous of blushes to her cheeks, but which only left her feeling helpless and perplexed. What was one supposed to feel? And what if, despite one's best efforts, one did not feel anything at all?

Did that make her strange? Odd? Broken?

And what did that mean for the Great Endeavour?

Chapter Fifteen

My dearest sister,

I hope this letter finds you extremely well. You asked me what it is like to be in love—it is impossible to describe something so all-encompassing in mere words, but nevertheless, I shall attempt it here.

~~*I now understand what the poets*~~

~~*She makes me*~~

Nothing seems to do this feeling justice, but I shall try again. My good mood seems to spill like sunshine into every moment of every day. It is a passionate joy beyond all my wildest dreams, and yet a domestic harmony so blissful I cannot imagine how I ever managed without it. Marriage is wonderful, and I thank God every day that He sent me the most perfect angel.

There, how is that?

Speaking of, Jane sends her most fervent best wishes to you too and hopes that she may see you once we return from our sojourn to Bath. I hope that one day you shall experience such delight in matrimony! Perhaps you were asking about love because you have lately felt its firm grip around your heart? I hope that is the case and look forward to meeting the fellow.

Your devoted brother,
Charles

Caroline descended the stairs the next morning to find Georgiana waiting in the great hall, armed with a bulging wicker basket and a rolled-up blanket.

"I thought you might enjoy a proper picnic today. Shall we head down to the lake?" Miss Darcy suggested.

"Oh." Caroline's stomach sank. She didn't think she could bear any more lake-based activities. "Why don't we go to the meadow instead? It would be so lovely to eat there amongst the flowers."

To her relief, Miss Darcy acquiesced without complaint. After Caroline had secured her bonnet, they strolled out of the house and down towards the shrubbery. Though the breeze was slightly cooler than she'd expected, the sun kissed the back of her neck with pleasant heat, making her shiver as they made their way towards the fields at the right of the estate. The meadow, a large one lined on three sides by trees which offered some privacy from the view of the house, was dotted with purple wildflowers, the vivid colour as loud as trumpets among the muted yellows and greens of the tall grasses. Georgiana spread a blanket upon the ground in a likely spot, partially under the shade of a large oak tree, and they settled themselves comfortably.

"I expect you're looking forward to lunch with Mr Radcliffe tomorrow," Georgiana said, casting a sly look at Caroline.

Caroline untied the strings of her bonnet and pulled it off, then patted her hair down. She rarely took her bonnet off outside but there was no need for formality with only Georgiana present, especially since Miss Darcy hadn't even worn one out of the house. The action bought Caroline a moment's thought, and a chance to school her features into something more amiable. She was aware that she ought to be excited for the forthcoming event, but whenever she thought about it, nothing sparked in her chest. Love was always being described in poetry and books as being like a kind of fire, but she couldn't summon up even a single candle's worth. Again, she couldn't help worrying whether something was wrong with her. Any sensible unmarried woman would be delighted to have lunch with a handsome gentleman who had singled her out for attention. Why, then, did she not feel excited by the prospect?

I did tell Georgiana that one ought to know the true nature of one's intended partner before one considers one's self in love, she reminded herself. *My feelings may change once I know him better, or I may discover that he is not the right man for me. Either way, I shall be a step closer to understanding what I do want.*

Lacking an answer, she decided to turn the tables on Georgiana. "Lord Ashbrook was very handsome, was he not? Would you like a viscount for yourself?"

"Oh, no," said she, looking surprised. "Not that I—I mean, his rank would not matter to me. I much prefer a person to a title. But I seek nothing at all, at least for the moment. Here, try the salted ham. It is quite delicious."

Not all young ladies had the privilege of such a position. "You never told me—would you prefer a love match for yourself?" Caroline asked, realising she had no idea what Georgiana might want in a husband. Her lip curled; it was difficult to imagine her closest friend on anyone's arm.

"You really do not like the idea of love, do you?" Miss Darcy asked, misinterpreting Caroline's expression.

"I am not against it, as a general rule. I simply do not understand it."

"What I do not understand," Georgiana said, buttering a piece of bread, "is why on earth you are seeking something you do not believe in."

"I never said I do not believe in it," Caroline corrected. "I said I do not understand it. The two are quite different. Love exists, of course, and I cannot argue otherwise. It is obvious between Charles and Jane, and between your brother and . . . Miss Elizabeth Bennet."

The breeze changed, coming now from the south, bringing with it the scent of lavender. Georgiana's lips twitched with amusement at the mention of the cursed name, and although she did her best to hide a smile, Caroline saw it and couldn't help feeling irritated.

"And yet . . ." Caroline hesitated again, wondering how to phrase the thought that had been plaguing her since Darcy's harsh words the night of the party. "Perhaps my greatest worry is that I am not actually capable of such a thing. That I lack whatever quality is necessary to allow love to blossom in the first place. Otherwise, would it not have struck me already? I am three-and-twenty, after all."

"Of course you are capable of it!" Georgiana took Caroline's hands in her own and squeezed them. "I think all people are capable of falling in some kind of love, though that may look different from person to person. Some may be content to have friends and companions, while some may find that kind of contentment only amongst family. While others seek passion and a different sort of . . ." She cleared her throat. "Intimacy. You may find that what is right for you may not be right for others, and vice versa."

Caroline felt her cheeks heat. They were still holding hands, which was perfectly natural, though perhaps Georgiana was not aware of the way her thumb had begun to stroke over Caroline's knuckles. The sensation made Caroline feel a little like she was falling, though she was seated on the ground with nowhere to go.

"I believe that you were in love once, were you not?" she murmured.

For a moment, she thought that Georgiana's temper might rise. Instead, Miss Darcy's dark eyes fluttered to meet Caroline's, then away again, like two restless summer butterflies. They'd never talked about George Wickham at any length before; Caroline knew that there once had been an attachment of sorts, and that, under mysterious circumstances, the man had disappeared from the Darcys' life only to turn up again in Meryton as part of a regiment. Darcy had been more furious than she'd ever seen him on hearing the name, though his fury tended to be the silent type. He was not the kind of man who would storm into a room and demand a duel at dawn, though she did not think for a moment that, if honour demanded such a thing of him, he would not immediately rise to the occasion. Caroline had watched as Wickham, handsome and sly, with tousled brown hair and broad shoulders befitting a member of the militia, had flirted openly with Miss Elizabeth Bennet. A mere common soldier, and yet, Miss Bennet had entertained his suit, laughing at his jokes. Caroline, who owed her nothing, had even deigned to warn Lizzy that Wickham was not as he seemed, that he had used the Darcys most terribly, but the impertinent girl had brushed her away with barely concealed scorn.

How often her thoughts slid back to the infernal woman. Really, the road was a well-trodden one at this point. She must try harder to—

"I believe I was," Georgiana murmured, drawing Caroline's attention back with a jolt.

"What was it like?"

Miss Darcy's hands did slip away then. The breeze changed direction once more, ruffling the stray tendrils of Georgiana's hair, and Caroline's fingers twitched as she fought the sudden urge to tuck one back behind Georgiana's ear. If she startled her friend now, perhaps she would not find out the story which she had always wanted to know.

"To be in love?" Georgiana let out a rather humourless laugh. "It is difficult to describe."

That was what Charles had said, though Caroline did not think that Georgiana necessarily shared his feelings of *spilled sunshine* upon the subject.

"It is . . ." Georgiana trailed off. "I mean, it was complicated. I was but fifteen at the time, and I enjoyed his attentions and affections. The way he looked at me as if I were the most interesting creature alive. And he actually listened to me."

I listen to you, Caroline thought. Unexpected jealousy, as bitter-green as raw asparagus, simmered in her stomach. At once, the idea of not knowing Georgiana's secret self was absolutely unbearable. Had her friend discussed opera with Wickham? Had she showed him how to play the harp, leaned close enough for him to feel her breath upon his cheek?

"He understood what it was like to be . . . to be expected to be something which you knew you were not," Miss Darcy continued. "At first, it was merely a flirtation, but after a few months, it developed into something more. And then he wanted to, er . . . take what married men have a right to." Georgiana's cheeks pinked. "I told him that I couldn't possibly do such a thing unless we were wed. He relented, after a time, but he wanted to tell my brother directly about our intentions. I suspect he thought it would make him seem more of an equal, for George always did have a bee in his bonnet about his station in life. But I knew that my brother would never allow the match. The only way—at least, the only way I thought he'd have to accept it—would be if we ran away to Gretna Green. If we were already married, then my brother would simply have to accept the matter."

"An elopement? With Wickham?" Caroline goggled, her jaw dropping. "Darcy would have been furious."

Good Lord, that was an understatement. Heads would have rolled.

"Well, yes, but I . . ." Georgiana shrugged, looking more uncomfortable than Caroline had ever seen her. "What was the alternative? Telling the truth? Having Fitz throw George out and forbid him from ever seeing me again? I knew how he'd react, and merely sought to . . ." She shrugged again. "Bypass it."

"That is certainly . . ." Caroline hesitated. She could see Georgiana's point, she supposed, but lying about something as large as this seemed like it was by far the worse option of the two. Darcy was far too good a shot; better to be honest to the gentleman's face and accept whatever consequences came as a result.

"It is the greatest regret of my life that I let my brother think the elopement was George's idea," Georgiana sighed.

"Hold on," Caroline said, sitting up straighter. "Why did you not simply tell him the truth?"

"You do not understand the pressure put on us," Georgiana continued, her lips pursing into a thin, pale line. "We lost our parents at such a young age, and Fitz always impressed upon me the strictest need to maintain pristine reputations. One slip, he said, and we might lose all that our parents had sought to endow us with." She shrugged, a muscle jumping in her jaw. "George took the blame for the elopement before I could even open my mouth, and I did not correct him. Fitz sent me out of the room in order to speak to George privately, and then I never saw George again. No final farewell, no letter of explanation. From that point until I debuted, my brother kept such a close eye on me that I could barely breathe. Afterwards, he made it clear that no young man anywhere was to so much as look at me twice. I cannot really blame him, and in truth, I did not really care. I was not eager to get into another relationship. It was only after Fitz met Miss Elizabeth Bennet that he . . . that he and I had a conversation." Georgiana hesitated, biting her lip.

Caroline could very well imagine Darcy's new approach: sympathetic, reconciliatory, kind. "Why did you not reveal the truth then?"

"I had planned to, but he revealed his own truth first, and that rather threw me. It turned out that he had offered George a significant amount of money to never see or speak to me again. The man who claimed to love me did not reject the idea out of hand, but instead bargained for more, which my brother gave gladly in order to be rid of him." Miss Darcy smiled as if she cared not a whit for this news, though the tense line of her jaw told Caroline otherwise. "I think people claim that they would do anything for love, until the right opportunity presents itself. Everyone has a price. That is my opinion, anyway. Now you may see why it is hard for me to trust, and why I have not sought a match of my own before now. I did not tell you because I did not want you to think less of me." Georgiana bit her lip again. "You do not, do you?"

Caroline opened her mouth to speak, then closed it again. Certainly, the idea of Georgiana marrying a man who would never amount to anything more than a mere soldier was an affront to dignity and added to the sour feeling churning in her stomach, but that was not a fair assessment of the affair, nor of Georgiana's part in it. Miss Darcy had been young and impressionable at the time, and evidently, Wickham had been charming enough to keep her convinced of his affections.

"No," she said slowly. "I do not think less of you for the affair." Georgiana looked relieved, and really, Caroline ought to have left the matter there, but she could not help adding, "Though I might have, if you'd married him. There did not seem, at least to me, to be anything extraordinary about the man. Certainly I would have thought you a fool for giving up so much for so little."

Georgiana sighed. "Then I cannot say you would be different from any of the other ladies of our acquaintance in that respect. I doubt any one of them would have kept up our friendship if I'd actually married him."

"Could he really have made you happy, though?" Caroline pressed. The idea of Georgiana in some tiny house, the wife of a common soldier, sharing his bed every night and his table for every meal, was increasingly abhorrent to her the more she thought about it.

"That is a difficult question to answer." Georgiana hesitated. "I know I loved him, though he was far from perfect. But one can never predict the future with any degree of real accuracy. Perhaps love would not have been enough."

Caroline coughed to cover the unladylike sound that bubbled out of her throat. What was so special about George Wickham that might make a woman such as Georgiana consider giving up her entire fortune, her status, her entire life? "I am afraid I do not follow," she said. "There is not a single man in the world who could elicit such feelings in me that would compel me to give up everything I have in order to love him. I can tell you that for certain."

"Then I pray that you are never presented with such a choice." Georgiana smiled, though it did not quite reach her eyes. "It is of no consequence, though, since all the men in our circles are likely to be worth a few thousand a year. You are surrounded by suitable options."

"Hmm. Do you ever think it odd that your former lover married your sister-in-law's sister?" Caroline mused. "Wickham might have married anyone, but he chose the youngest Bennet of all people." She remembered very little of the girl, but she'd seemed wild, a half-feral blaze of exuberance that drew the attention of every foolish man in the room. Another fifteen-year-old, if Caroline recalled correctly. Wickham clearly had a particular taste for girls too young to know better.

"I . . ." Georgiana blinked at her. "I hadn't actually thought of it like that. I suppose it is a bit odd, though when one moves in certain circles, one is bound to come across people with whom one has formerly been . . . acquainted."

Caroline did not particularly want to think about how well Georgiana and Wickham had been acquainted. She could see it now: that smug, satisfied smile of his, those strong arms snaking around Georgiana's waist. His lips upon hers, pressing his body close. To make matters worse, Wickham had tried to court Miss Elizabeth Bennet, too. *If only he'd managed it*, she thought wistfully. *Then I wouldn't have had to listen about how bloody wonderful she is.*

She scowled, then realised Georgiana was staring at her with some impatience. Evidently she'd been asked a question. "My apologies," Caroline floundered. "Pray repeat yourself. I was too busy wondering why, when England is clearly full of people, that there appear to be but seven or eight families in all the country who intermarry."

That earned a snort of laughter from Georgiana. "I asked if you would like some lemonade."

Caroline agreed that lemonade sounded lovely, and they busied themselves with the contents of the wicker basket for the next few minutes. Mrs Addlecombe had provided fruit scones liberally smeared with clotted cream, a bowl of glistening and luscious strawberries to accompany them, and two enormous slices of spiced cinnamon cake. Caroline plucked the raisins out of her scones and handed each to Georgiana, who ate them with relish.

"I really do not understand why you are so opposed to raisins," said she. "They are so delicious."

"I do not like their texture." Caroline glared down at the latest piece of offending fruit. "So wrinkled. So very . . . elderly and dry. Whatever the process entails, it seems a terrible thing to do to a perfectly good grape."

"What about wine?"

"That is quite different. In fact, one might argue that wine is a grape's natural ambition."

"So there is a spectrum, in your opinion."

"My dear Georgie, it is objective fact," Caroline argued. "If I were a grape, I would be delighted to become wine and extremely offended to be relegated to the fate of a raisin."

In this way, they passed the next half hour with pleasant bickering. After they had enjoyed their fill from the basket, they lay back on the blanket, side by side, and stared up at the sky. It was unusual for Georgiana not to disappear into a book at this stage of any picnic, but a quick glance into the basket proved that Miss Darcy had not even brought one with her. Caroline's earlier jealousy vanished, replaced by a fluffy, warm contentment. *Of course I am more interesting than any book*, she thought, *but it is nice to have confirmation of such a thing from time to time.*

It almost certainly didn't have anything to do with the fact that Georgiana had been a little more tactile than usual since the harp incident. Or perhaps Caroline was just aware of her friend in a way she had never been before; the heat emanating through Miss Darcy's thin dress made Caroline feel as if they were actually touching. Neither conclusion made her feel entirely comfortable, but she couldn't summon enough energy to move away.

"You asked why I never told you about Wickham before." Georgiana hesitated, staring upwards into the leafy branches of the oak tree. A single insubstantial cloud crawled overhead, as if hoping the blazing sunshine would not notice its progress across the sky. "We have been acquainted for three years, but we were not truly friends before."

This was news to Caroline. "Weren't we?"

"I mean, we are, now," Georgiana said, turning her head to study Caroline. "I suppose I am simply slower to open up than most. Besides, I could not be certain how you might react to something like this, so I was loath to mention it. You see, I had a former friend who had deduced a little of the affair. After it was over, she cut me in the street when next we saw each other. And she did not know the half of it."

"How perfectly awful," Caroline declared, outraged. "What kind of cut?"

"Excuse me?"

"What kind of cut?" she repeated.

Georgiana frowned at her. "Does it matter?"

"It may be of no consequence, I was just curious." Caroline shrugged. "There are four main cuts, you know, and each one is intended to impart a specific meaning. Clearly you have not been cut much, or have seen them done, or you would know each of them very well indeed."

Georgiana made no reply to this.

"Shall I tell you what they are?" she persisted.

Miss Darcy sighed. "I see that the explanation has been forced upon me from the start. Is there any escape?"

"No," Caroline said bluntly. "Not unless you run."

"In this dress," Georgiana said, gesturing down at the pale yellow silk which only just kept her ample bosom in check, and which was hemmed more tightly than her usual gowns, "you would catch me in mere seconds."

Caroline did her best not to look in the direction of Georgiana's gesture. She'd been doing so well today, with only a few stolen glances at her friend's curves, and even those had really been in admiration for the dress, hadn't they? "Precisely."

"Go on, then. Explain it to me."

"Well," said Caroline, wriggling until she felt herself in the most comfortable position possible, which required her right foot to be resting against Georgiana's in a purely platonic fashion, "there are four cuts."

"Upon my soul," Georgiana exclaimed, "are so many ways required to convey a person's displeasure?"

"Those are limitless, I am sure, but a cut is a very specific glance. One may simply look in another direction and pretend not to see an acquaintance—that is the cut indirect, which, to me, seems like the most cowardly. Then there is the cut direct, in which you look at a person's face but remain blank, as if they were nothing but a mere stranger to you. The cut infernal involves gazing down at the ground, perhaps adjusting your boot or admiring a cobblestone, until your acquaintance has gone past. And then there is the cut sublime, in which one raises one's eyes heavenwards."

"I see. It seems an awful lot of weight to place upon a simple movement of the eyes."

"Many a simple act conveys a complex behaviour, does it not?"

"I suppose you are right." Georgiana sat up, picked a daisy which was only inches from her nose, then another, and began to fashion a chain. Caroline had not done such a thing since she was a girl, and she watched with fascination at the careful preparation: the application of thumbnail to stalk, creating a slit through which the next stalk might pass, and the selection of only those daisies with petals tinged pink at the edges. Georgiana carried out the process with as much care and concentration as any jeweller. "She gave me the cut sublime. A shame, when it is the nicest sounding of the four."

"True," Caroline agreed. "One usually only hears the term

sublime in a positive context otherwise. How could something heavenly be otherwise?"

"Is there an opposite of a cut?" Georgiana paused, the daisy chain hanging limply from her hands. "For instance, four ways to look at someone to indicate pleasure. Is there no opposite for each cut?"

"Not that I have heard." Caroline pushed herself up on one elbow. "How would one perform the opposite of a cut sublime, for instance?"

"I am not sure. Perhaps one would have to look deeply into another's eyes and expect to see heaven there?" Georgiana finished her chain, and leaned forward, looping it carefully around Caroline's neck. Instead of pulling back, she brought her fingers to Caroline's chin, tipping it up gently and gazing into her eyes. "Like so."

Caroline's reply died on her tongue. All she could feel were the pads of Georgiana's fingertips, warm on the underside of her jaw, and all she could see were two dark pools, reflecting her own image back in miniature. Georgiana made to withdraw her hand but Caroline, hardly knowing what she was doing, grasped it and kept it there. Georgiana's eyes widened, a light blush spreading across her cheeks. She had tiny freckles on the very tops of her cheekbones, and Caroline's fingers twitched with the impulse to acknowledge each and every one. Instead, she stared back, willing her voice to stay calm. "You deserve so much more."

"Than what?"

She hadn't really thought that far ahead. "I . . . I don't know. I only know that you deserve someone who sees you for who you really are in all your glory."

"Thank you." Georgiana's breath ghosted over her lips,

warm and sweet, and Caroline swallowed hard as her vision blurred. Was it just her imagination or was Georgiana leaning closer?

Before she could wonder what to do—her body screaming at her to do nothing, something, or a nonsensical combination of the two—a bird squawked loudly in the branches above, making them both jump. “Shall we return to the house?” Miss Darcy said, smiling in amusement. “Lest another bird should frighten us both out of our wits?”

Caroline agreed, though her heart was still pounding. While they packed up the picnic, Georgiana chattered away, seemingly unaffected by the incident, but Caroline could think of nothing else on the way back to the house. For a moment, she’d thought that Georgiana truly looked like she wanted to kiss her. And for a moment . . .

Caroline had wanted that, too.

Chapter Sixteen

When they reached the house, Caroline excused herself while Georgiana trotted off to return the now-empty wicker basket to Mrs Addlecombe.

In the guest room, Caroline paced from side to side in a manner that was starting to feel like a familiar rhythm. The very idea of kissing Georgiana was preposterous. Completely absurd. *Women do not kiss other women, do they?* Her footsteps faltered in front of the window, and she stared unseeing at the blue sky beyond. Actually, Caroline had no idea whether women did this or did not do this. Louisa, who was five years her elder, had been her sole source of knowledge for all things salacious, though this font of wisdom admittedly had been rather dry on most subjects. Growing up, Caroline had very few friends bar Louisa's group of select girls, who were equally of an age with her sister and had not been inclined to share secrets and gossip with someone so much younger.

She spun on her heel, marching across the floor again as if the very boards themselves could have answers wrung out of them. Of course, one could argue that in society, women ought to kiss men—or rather, the other way around—only once married. Out of wedlock, nothing untoward should occur between the sexes, that was well-known, but between the same sex, might it be possible that people indulged in . . .

Hmm.

Caroline had only a loose idea of what happened in the bedchamber after a wedding, based on her mother's scant explanation a few days after she'd had her first blood, but that had been enough to turn her stomach. Yet when she pictured—and oh dear, wasn't even imagining such a thing a sin?—a woman next to her instead, breathing heavily, delicate hands reaching for her own body and clasping it with tenderness and—

Heat rushed to her cheeks, followed by an additional wave of warmth much further south. Physical affection had been largely absent from Caroline's life, apart from the occasional embrace from a friend or family. Her mother had not been the tactile sort, and her father, who had been much more warm-hearted, had been led by his wife's firm belief that too much tenderness resulted in weakness of character. The very small amount of kissing Caroline had experienced so far had been completed in the utmost secrecy. Her childhood friend Victoria had beautiful red ringlets which quite entranced Caroline; at twelve, they'd exchanged brief kisses on the lips as part of some playacting, which had made Caroline's stomach feel as if it were turning somersaults. Victoria's parents had moved away a year later, and Caroline had boxed up the memory as simply girlish foolishness. The breathless anticipation which she'd felt every time Victoria's lips had touched hers had been merely a reaction to her first exploration of the world.

Hadn't it?

Caroline frowned, marching back towards the window again. When she was sixteen, she'd allowed the neighbour's roguish son to kiss her several times, and while that had proved interesting, particularly when he'd introduced his tongue into the equation, it hadn't resulted in her falling in love. The young man had once tried to take things further, his hand creeping towards her breast, but she'd baulked, cutting off the affair—if one could even call it that—shortly afterwards. He had accepted the rejection with dignity and moved on swiftly, which had relieved her, for the idea of someone knowing a secret by which they might seek to control her or embarrass or, worse, ruin her reputation, would have been the most terrible thing in the world.

Caroline shook herself. She had been a mere child then, not a woman grown. Kissing when twelve or sixteen was very different from kissing at three-and-twenty; the fresh ache between her legs was proof enough of that. She threw up her hands in frustration, then covered her face with them and let out a low groan. It was impossible to think when her body thrummed with such urgent need, but there was no way of addressing it now, not when her mind was so full of Georgiana.

Would that be so bad? the little voice in her head asked. *To finally finish what you began a few days ago?*

Caroline swivelled, the bed catching her eye. The soft, inviting bed, where relief would find her very, very swiftly. *Oh dear.* The act would surely take no more than seconds, considering how wound up she felt. Yet if she gave in, it would be tantamount to admitting that her attraction, however ridiculous, was real. At the very least, it would be difficult to look Miss Darcy in the eye afterwards. *She is an excellent friend*, Caroline reminded herself, fingers pressed to her lips as if trying to keep a confession inside. *An excellent friend who is helping me in my Great Endeavour and who does not deserve repayment in sinful thoughts. An excellent friend who has the most delicious-looking—*

No. This would never do. She had to get a grip immediately. She had to think of nothing but her forthcoming lunch with Mr Radcliffe and his broad shoulders. Bunching her skirts in her hands, Caroline fled the room before she could succumb to any mattress-related temptation.

During the interminably long day that followed, Caroline prattled on about anything and everything, engaging Georgiana in the dullest and most unflirtatious discussion she could possibly think of, even going so far as to locate and read long passages from *A Dissertation on the Chief Obstacles to the Improvement of Land, and Introducing Better Methods of Agriculture Throughout Scotland* in the hopes of quelling her libido. By the time they said their farewells in the upstairs hallway that night, her mind was full of rippling fields of wheat, thoroughly ploughed furrows, and swelling buds bursting from the ground with only the lightest encouragement. She was beginning to wonder whether she was genuinely in the process of losing her mind. Georgiana, for her part, had borne it all with polite—if rather baffled—grace. It was at least nice to know that if one truly was descending into madness, that one's friends would tolerate the journey with good cheer.

Alone in her bedroom at last, Caroline performed her usual ablutions and got into bed, lying ramrod straight and trying to recall each of the obstacles to land improvement mentioned in the large book. When finally she drifted off, she found herself walking through a meadow, hands outstretched, tall grasses on either side brushing her palms with the lightest tickles. She could not say how long she remained in the meadow, for it was well-known that dreamtime did not pass in the same way as ordinary time did, but the moment when she emerged from the grass and stepped out onto the shore of the lake was both an unwelcome shock and somehow entirely unsurprising. Georgiana's dark head bobbed on the surface of the water, her shoulders two pale peaks on either side as she made her way slowly to the shore. Caroline braced herself, promising she would not look upon that which tempted her most, but when the moment came, God himself could not have torn her gaze away from the sight of Georgiana in a soaked petticoat.

Caroline groaned as Georgiana emerged from the water, the fabric clinging to every curve as it had done on that first day, but Miss Darcy did not stride forward as she expected. Instead, Georgiana stood there, fair hair plastered to her high cheekbones, her dark eyes full of longing, her gaze raking Caroline from head to foot.

Puzzled, Caroline looked down. She too was wearing only a single petticoat, and was equally soaked through, though she did not feel at all cold. When next she looked up, she found that Georgiana's hand was outstretched, as if inviting her to swim. Caroline took a step forward, cool water sloshing over her bare toes. There was hardly any resistance, which was not at all usual; instead, the water felt and looked more like shadowed air, dank and dim, like the inside of some long-forgotten coastal cave. Her grasping fingers found Georgiana's, and the smile which Miss Darcy gave her—not the practiced, polite smile of the ballroom, but something shyer and more hopeful—was enough to make her knees weak. Before Caroline could reach Georgiana, Miss Darcy turned, leading her down as the lakebed tilted at a sharp angle. Caroline had expected them to begin swimming at some point but instead they continued walking as if still on land. When the water slopped over her chin, she drew back, startled, but Georgiana kept going, her fingers slipping from

Caroline's grasp, and she was forced to decide whether to hold on or lose her to the darkness.

Caroline refused to let go, taking a deep breath as the water closed over her head, but in the next moment she found that she could manage well enough without air, though the water tasted of salt and sweat in a way that made her want to lick at it. The deeper they walked, the less Caroline could make out anything in front of her. The only constant was the shape of Georgiana and the hot press of her fingers around Caroline's. She opened her mouth to ask where they were going, but the answer came before she could get a word out.

Thirty feet ahead, a cave mouth yawned open, impossibly black even in this inky darkness. Caroline did halt then, a prickle of fear raising the hairs on her arms—for one did not simply walk into an unknown cave without any sort of discussion about what might lie inside—but the shape of Georgiana paused, turned, came back to her and pressed close enough for Caroline to feel every inch against her own. She rested her head against Georgiana's shoulder, her free hand winding around Georgiana's neck. She was determined to soak in the feeling, to absorb every detail that she could not possibly achieve when awake, but before she could properly relish the experience, her chin was being tilted up and her mouth firmly kissed.

Sudden warmth bloomed in her chest, the sharpness of the feeling both unexpected and shocking. Caroline gasped, her free hand flying up to tangle in Georgiana's curls, pulling Miss Darcy's head down in a much harder kiss. A current of water brushed her breasts and neck before seeping between her thighs, curling in a way that gave Caroline exactly what she'd needed for agonising days. One stroke, then two, and a third, and then—

Caroline woke facedown with a gasp still on her lips. She

rolled her hips once, twice, delicious shudders of pleasure rippling through her, before lying quite still, panting into her pillow.

Good heavens, she thought. *If only every day started like that, I should be in bed every night by eight on the clock.*

She couldn't feel guilty about it, since it had only been a dream. One could never be held responsible for what one did in one's dreams. Caroline buried her face in the pillow and rolled her hips one last time, squeezing the last frisson of ecstasy out. She certainly wasn't picturing Georgiana's body underneath her, nor behind her, equally sweaty and panting. Surely now that this—whatever it was—was out of her system, she would be able to concentrate once more on the Great Endeavour.

No longer shall I waver, Caroline thought with determination, as she swung her legs out of bed. *A Bingley never falters in pursuit of a goal.*

Miss Darcy was in the dining-parlour already, reading a book and spooning porridge into her mouth with apparently very little care for where she was aiming, judging by the splashes of porridge on her chin.

"Good morning, Caroline," said she, wiping her mouth with a napkin and looking rather sheepish. "I did not expect you quite so early. I must have been rather engrossed in my book if I did not hear you coming down the stairs."

Before Caroline could think of a suitably arch reply, Mrs Reynolds entered, carrying a tray of smoked kippers, which she laid on the table with all the pride of someone bearing the crown jewels. Caroline had to wait by her chair until the housekeeper bustled over to pull it out for her—good grief, would it kill Georgiana to have a single footman in the room?

Was she going to start laundering her own clothes, too?—and finally seated herself. "Good morning, Mrs Reynolds," she said.

"Good morning, ma'am." At least the housekeeper did not look surprised by the greeting today; however, rather than asking what Caroline wanted, Mrs Reynolds studied her for a moment, tapping one finger against her top lip. She was not an unattractive woman, Caroline allowed, despite the grey at her temples. If the housekeeper had been born into a higher class, she might have been considered elegant or even handsome, though in Caroline's opinion she was rather too thin to be truly pretty. "Let me guess. Toast, though I expect you want it twice as well-done as yesterday."

Caroline blinked. "Why, yes. How did you know?"

"Oh, Caroline." Georgiana groaned. "You just lost me another shilling."

"Take heart, ma'am," Mrs Reynolds said, with a surprisingly impish smile. "Your losing streak is most impressive."

"I . . . What?" Caroline said, utterly at sea.

"We take occasional bets on which of us can guess our guest's preferences," Georgiana explained.

Caroline raised an eyebrow. "And you lose often?"

Mrs Reynolds snorted.

"Not that often!" Georgiana protested. "It's simply that . . ." She glared at the housekeeper. "She's very good at being correct."

"That is why your brother employs me, ma'am." The housekeeper sashayed out of the room, still grinning.

Caroline stared in astonishment. She had never heard Georgiana and Mrs Reynolds speak so freely with each other. Being friends with Miss Merryhill was one thing, but being friends with one's own staff was quite another. Mrs Bingley would have had choice words upon the subject, and none of them good. Reaching for the kippers, Caroline speared two and laid them on her plate. "What did you choose?"

"Pardon?"

"What did you choose?" she repeated. "Since Mrs Reynolds selected toast for her side of the bet, I am curious to know what you thought I might order."

"Porridge," Georgiana said, staring ruefully down at her own bowl. "It's not as sunny as it was yesterday and you often choose porridge when the sky is grey. And you had toast yesterday, so I thought . . . Alas, Mrs Reynolds knows you better than I."

Caroline stared at her. "I had no idea you paid so much attention to my breakfast habits."

Georgiana shrugged. "When one is bored, one must make one's own entertainment."

Caroline had always enjoyed being looked at and admired. An appreciative glance or comment about her face or figure ordinarily made her feel wonderful, even powerful. To be perceived, on the other hand, set a warm glow alight in her chest that was very, very different. She doubted whether any of her family could have guessed her breakfast preferences, even if five thousand pounds had been at stake. "Does your brother know that you gamble with the staff?"

"Of course he does," Georgiana said, as Mrs Reynolds returned bearing a rack of well-fired toast. "He does it too, though he's even worse at it than I am."

"Your losses paid for many a pretty present for my children,

Miss Darcy," Mrs Reynolds said, and her smile was now the soft, kindly one she reserved for the Darcys alone.

"That does not make me feel any better," Georgiana muttered, though she grinned back at Mrs Reynolds with a look of equal fondness.

Caroline watched the interplay with bafflement. She'd known the Darcys were fond of all their staff, and of Mrs Reynolds in particular, but she'd had no idea that the relationship ran quite so deep. They must have gone to some lengths to keep this camaraderie hidden from their guests. So why were they now displaying it openly in front of Caroline?

What has changed? she wondered, but a satisfactory conclusion eluded her.

Chapter Seventeen

My dear Caroline,

William reports that the repairs to our London home are coming along splendidly—perhaps no more than a month—so we shall expect you there soon. How delightful it will be to see you again, for I have much in the way of gossip to impart, and you must by now be starved for such delicious morsels! Derbyshire is a pleasant place, but I cannot understand your desire to sequester yourself from society during the best months of the season. You do yourself no favours.

Your affectionate sister,
Louisa

Mr Radcliffe's carriage had been due to arrive at noon, but when half past the hour came and went without any sign of him, Caroline began to wonder whether he'd had some sort of terrible accident on the road. However, at precisely quarter to one, the familiar clip-clop of shod horses could be heard just outside. Caroline smoothed down her dress—the pretty green one she hadn't worn to the lake party, which Georgiana had complimented so heartily—and they went out to greet him.

Without getting out of the carriage or apologising for the lateness of his arrival, Mr Radcliffe introduced them to his sister, a dark-haired lady perhaps a year or two his elder, with whom Georgiana seemed not to be acquainted at all. He politely refused all offers of tea and insisted that they climb aboard and be on their way at once, for he claimed to be famished.

"Where are we going?" Caroline asked once inside, aware that Mr Radcliffe had neither offered the information nor asked their preference.

"Only the very best place to eat luncheon in all of Derbyshire!" he cried, though he supplied no more clues to their destination than that. "Sister, do you remember when they used to serve the pea soup? With little pieces of ham floating in it?"

His sister agreed that she did indeed remember, and that while she had thought highly of it, she did not think the dish comparable to the lamb stew. Mr Radcliffe retorted that the lamb stew utterly paled into insignificance next to the roast venison, and the rest of the carriage ride continued in much the same way, with each dish being judged against the rest in a kind of culinary hierarchy, meaning that by the time they arrived, Caroline's appetite was sharp enough to cut glass. Unfortunately, the inn, which had looked pleasant enough from the outside, had its interior ambience rather tainted by the heads of nearly a hundred stuffed and mounted animals, each staring glassily down on the diners as they ate. Caroline had seen a great number of hunting trophies displayed in fine homes over the years, but never to such a crowded degree. At the table they were led to, she was forced to inch her chair closer to Georgiana's to avoid putting her elbow directly in a stuffed fox's open mouth. Worse, there was a sad little rabbit at eye-height, which seemed to be almost as unhappy about being there as she was.

"Do not you think the place marvellous, Miss Bingley?" Mr Radcliffe asked.

Caroline hesitated long enough for Georgiana to nudge her under the table. "Am I to understand that hunting is one of your many interests, sir?" she asked. *Kindness, not honesty*, she reminded herself. *You can do this.*

"Indeed it is," he said, his broad chest puffing up with manly pride. "There is nothing more pleasing to me than an excellent shot and a clean kill. Why, my home in Wales has thrice the number of trophies you see here. I have gunned down almost every animal you can think of."

She could offer nothing more than a weak, "Oh?"

"Birds and beasts both," he went on. "Everything from the finest stag to a plodding hedgehog. Hunting truly is the most glorious sport, Miss Bingley. Nothing can compare to it."

Caroline bit her tongue to refrain from making any comment on how hedgehog execution seemed to her to be rather a pathetic pastime given how slowly the little creatures crawled, but before she could come up with something suitably polite, a server arrived at their table, and Mr Radcliffe ordered for all of them without consultation. Caroline made accidental eye contact with the stuffed rabbit again. *Oh dear*, it seemed to say. *Murderous and presumptuous, two of your least favourite traits.*

Fighting rising panic, she swivelled further in her chair to get away from the brush of silky fur, which only brought her closer to Georgiana. Miss Darcy shot her an unreadable glance, which softened when she took in Caroline's expression. "When will you be returning to Wales, Mr Radcliffe?" Georgiana asked.

"Immediately," said he, turning to his sister, who was gazing adoringly at half a wolf on the opposite wall, posed as if it were in the process of leaping through stone. "Jemima is marrying a splendid fellow in a fortnight, and we have a few arrangements left to make."

The ladies warmly congratulated Miss Radcliffe on her forthcoming nuptials, and the next few minutes were taken up with a description of her groom and the wedding party in general. "I am sure that you must both know the Walthropes already," Miss Radcliffe added. "They are a fine old family, and very well spoken of."

"I may have heard my cousin, Colonel Fitzwilliam, mention them," Georgiana supplied. "He has spent a little time in Wales and along the border in that part of the world."

"A colonel, indeed?" Miss Radcliffe's lip curled. "Ah. Well, I hope he has had the pleasure of meeting my husband-to-be, for he is, as my brother says, a very splendid gentleman." Her words were pleasant enough, but the tone was noticeably cooler than it had been only a few moments prior.

Startled by this sudden rudeness, Caroline glanced at Georgiana. She had never met the cousin in question, though, of course, she had seen his portrait in the picture-gallery at Pemberley, along with his handsome sister; Colonel Fitzwilliam was the nephew of Lady Catherine de Burgh, the younger son of an earl and, while very respectable, the man did not have much in the way of fortune. Miss Darcy made no immediate reply and her face remained politely impassive, though Caroline could see her hands curling into fists under the table. Torn between defending the Darcys and her new habit of being polite whatever the cost, Caroline cast about desperately for something to say that could achieve both ends and came up empty-handed. The food arrived a moment later, providing a much-needed distraction, and when the dishes were arranged to the Radcliffes' liking and each one appropriately complimented on the look and smell, they were finally allowed to eat.

"The party at the lake was most enjoyable," Caroline said, cutting up her venison. It was rather more well-done than she liked, but the Great Endeavour compelled her to appear agreeable, even inside this inn of horrors. Over Miss Radcliffe's shoulder, a beady-eyed boar armed with two enormous tusks gaped at Caroline as if coveting her meat. "It is always so pleasant to meet new people."

"Lady Lennox is an excellent woman," Mr Radcliffe proclaimed. "And her husband is a capital horseman."

"And the Chester sisters were delightful," Caroline added, aware that Georgiana hadn't said a word since the slight to Colonel Fitzwilliam.

The Radcliffes exchanged amused looks. "Really, Miss Bingley," said Miss Radcliffe, "your cheerfulness in the face of what was undoubtedly banal conversation must be a testament to your disposition, which I think the sweetest I have ever had the pleasure of meeting."

Beside Caroline, Georgiana quietly choked on a spoonful of soup. "That is a compliment which I certainly do not deserve," Caroline said, kicking Georgiana under the table. At least Miss Darcy looked far less stiff now than she had a few minutes ago. "Though I thank you for your kind words. And, Mr Radcliffe, how did—"

"Those Chester girls are dreadful," he interrupted. "You need not pretend in our company. One cannot hold her tongue, and the other is too afraid to say anything of note. I steer clear of them myself, and you ought to as well."

Caroline had rather liked the Chesters, but even if she'd disliked them, they hardly deserved such outright criticism. She cast an eye at Georgiana, who spooned pea soup into her mouth with all the placidity of a cow chewing cud, though her knuckles were pale around the handle of her utensil. Perhaps the Great Endeavour had been going too well, for Caroline might have found such opinions amusing a few weeks ago. Now, all she felt was deep discomfort about the censure of young ladies who had only ever been friendly towards her. *Wait*, she thought, a horrible realisation dawning. *Is this how my former behaviour appeared to others—critical and superior, without proper consideration given for virtues or accomplishments?*

No wonder Georgiana had thought her a lost cause.

"They remind me a little of Mr Walthrope's cousin's daughter," Miss Radcliffe said. "Do you remember? The one with the . . ." She gestured at her face, which did nothing to explain what she was referring to, but Mr Radcliffe laughed anyway. "Did not her brother row with you once or twice? And was he not responsible for a loss in your second year at Oxford?"

Seizing the opportunity to change the subject, Caroline pressed Mr Radcliffe to tell her tales of his exploits at Oxford, which he was more than happy to do. The conversation, if one could call such a thing which continued only on one side, reminded her of her mother. Caroline was now certain Mrs Bingley would approve of Mr Radcliffe, but the very idea of her mother approving the match put her off even further. The home which she had barely been able to envisage with Mr Radcliffe in the first place now seemed to hold echoes of Hadley Hall; all polished surfaces and pearly smiles, with not a single iota of genuine feeling or warmth underneath it all. Caroline was surprised to find herself longing to be back on the worn couch in Pemberley's library, which had at least been used by people who treasured it and genuinely liked each other's company.

They made it through the rest of luncheon without further incident, and Caroline breathed a sigh of relief when they were back in the carriage, though she still felt as if she had the weight of a hundred glazed eyes upon her. She would surely have nightmares about that inn for the rest of her life.

"I will be travelling through Lancashire in a couple of weeks," Mr Radcliffe announced, as they neared the gates of Pemberley. "I would very much like to take you to luncheon a second time, Miss Bingley. Your family rents Hadley Hall, does it not?"

Clearly he had vetted her with his fellows before offering his first invitation, though there was no need to put quite so much emphasis on *rents*. Many respectable families leased estates these days. "Oh, Miss Bingley has no plans to return home any time soon," Georgiana said coolly, before Caroline could answer. "We have been having such fun together here."

"That is true," Caroline said, trying not to bristle at being spoken for, "but I cannot encroach on Miss Darcy's hospitality forever." She was torn—with the Radcliffes staring at her expectantly, it was difficult to reject the offer, but she had no intention of ever being alone with them again.

"Then perhaps I shall see you at the Percys' next ball," he said in a warm tone, bestowing his most dashing smile on her.

"I have heard that they throw very grand parties," Caroline said. "Although—"

"Neither Caroline nor I have been invited to that particular event," Georgiana interjected. "Though I think it likely that we shall be busy that day, in any case."

Miss Radcliffe's expression plummeted, as did the temperature inside the carriage. "Our lack of invite is no fault of the hosts, for I know them not at all," Caroline said hastily, wondering just how injured she would be if she opened the door of the moving carriage and flung herself out. "However—that is to say—"

"Do not fret. I shall ensure the Percys send you a direct invite for you and your"—he glanced at Georgiana—"friend."

The carriage finally ground to a stop, and Caroline sent a silent prayer of thanks heavenward. "I would be most obliged, sir," Caroline said, swinging the door open as fast as she dared without causing insult. "I look forward to seeing you there. Come, Miss Darcy, we must hasten inside," she added, not daring to look up at the bright blue sky, which held not a single cloud of any shade, "for I fear it will rain any moment."

The instant they were inside the house with the door shut behind them, Caroline turned on Georgiana. "What on earth is the matter with you? I did not ask you to speak for me. Or do you think I am incapable of managing—"

"I do not think anything of the sort," Georgiana said, an angry red flush spreading down her neck. She took off her gloves, but rather than flinging them onto the side table like she usually did, she clutched them like a lifeline. "You are not even interested in the man, so why do you encourage him? Are you toying with him? It is rather poor form to do so if you have no intentions."

"I am not toying with him," Caroline said, attempting to keep her temper in check. "But it is difficult to extricate one's self from such a situation without causing offense, and you made that much harder than it needed to be."

"I—" A muscle jumped in Georgiana's jaw. "Very well. I

apologise. His sister was rude, and I could not forgive the slight, for I care for my cousins very deeply, and that has perhaps coloured my judgement and my temper. But if you are in love with Mr Radcliffe, then I shall endeavour to look past that."

"Heavens, no! I do not like him at all," Caroline admitted. "Did you not hear what he said about the Chesters? I would have thought you happy that I was not interested in a man for whom unkindness seems to be rather a sport. To say nothing of his compulsion to murder any animal unlucky enough to stray across his path. No, he and I are ill-suited indeed."

"And so," Georgiana pressed, stepping closer, "why not break it off cleanly? Why lead him on? Do you think you can simply use him as a means to connect yourself with his rich friends in the hopes of landing one of them? Is that why you asked so many questions about his friends from Oxford?"

Stung, Caroline glared at her. "I," said she, drawing herself to her fullest height, which made very little difference in comparison to Miss Darcy's, "may not have your wealth or name, but I am not so low that I need throw myself at the first man with three thousand a year. I merely wanted to get through luncheon, and then I fancied an invite to this grand ball, which sounded rather lovely, but neither was it an offer of marriage or an acceptance of such. I did not wish to humiliate the gentleman by rejecting his offer outright. You needn't— Oh!" She halted, struck by a sudden inspiration. "You're jealous," she breathed. "Of course. Why did I not see it before?"

"I— What?" Georgiana froze, her eyes wide. "No, I am not."

"You are!" Caroline watched as Georgiana spun on her heel and headed into the library, evidently escaping to her place of safety. She followed so closely behind that she almost trod on the back of Miss Darcy's slipper. "Why, Georgie, you needn't worry. As soon as I have locked down a match for myself, we can immediately set about the business of locating one for you."

Georgiana stopped short, and Caroline only just avoided crashing into the back of her. "You have me entirely wrong," she said, her tone clipped, turning to glare at Caroline.

"Then perhaps you want Mr Radcliffe for yourself?" Caroline suggested.

"That is not— I have no interest whatsoever in Mr Radcliffe!" Georgiana looked deeply wounded. "I could never desire such a person, obsessed with fortunes and titles, who doesn't care one whit for the real character of those around him. I cannot believe you would say such a thing, Caroline, even in jest. I thought you knew me much better than that."

The conversation was becoming more infuriating by the second. "Then if we are in agreement that neither of us is remotely interested in Mr Radcliffe, then why on earth are we fighting about him?"

"We are fighting because you have learned nothing. You seek to use Mr Radcliffe for his connections, like a stepping-stone to greater men. That is not kindness. That is not—"

"That is a very bad-faith interpretation of my actions," Caroline interrupted, barely tempering her annoyance. "And even if that were so, what would it matter? Should a man who has shown himself to be loathsome be cast aside entirely, which would not benefit anybody, rather than put to good use to better my situation?" Caroline threw up her hands. "Why are you acting as if you do not understand exactly why I did not reject him outright in front of his sister, nor why I accepted his offer to get us invites to a ball? For all your talk of courtesy and humility, you—"

"Oh, now I am not perfect? Is that it?"

"I did not say that."

"Remember why you asked me to help you in the first place?" Georgiana hissed. She put a hand to her chest and affected a simpering air. "Oh, Georgie, you are the embodiment of everything that society deems wonderful in a lady. You are perfect, you are a young saint, et cetera, et cetera."

"I do not sound anything like that!" Caroline spluttered, outraged. "How dare—"

"Do you know what your problem is, Caroline Bingley?"

Caroline's fists were clenched so hard, she was beginning to worry she might be doing permanent damage to her finger joints. "Oh, do tell me," she snapped. "Listing my flaws appears to be the preferred pastime of the Darcys. Why stop what your brother started?"

Georgiana approached with one finger held out and didn't stop until it was pressed against Caroline's right collarbone. "This process, or whatever you call it, is all about you."

"Well, yes," she agreed, her attention caught by the feel of Georgiana's finger against her bare flesh, of the dark eyes pinning her in place with a savage glare. Even furious, Miss Darcy was uncommonly beautiful; in fact, the anger heightened her attractiveness rather than diminished it, rendered her a wild creature of wind and fire rather than the poised, glossy perfection of the ballroom. *Pay attention*, Caroline scolded herself. "That was rather the point, wasn't it?"

"All about you," Georgiana repeated, jabbing her finger for emphasis. "Like everything else is. You clearly have not thought about me at any point."

Caroline blinked, baffled by the accusation. "I came to you

in the very first instance. I asked you for help. Clearly I thought about—"

"I mean about me as a person!" Georgiana turned and strode a few paces away, her chest heaving. When she turned back, her eyes were bright with hurt. At the sight, Caroline felt as if someone had slapped her across the face. "I am so tired," Georgiana whispered, her voice low and dangerous, "of being perceived as faultless. I am unable to make mistakes like a normal person, for the consequences of a fall from grace would be twice as hard. Perhaps it has never occurred to you that I too would like to be selfish sometimes. That, when in the company of people who disparage my dearest relations, I might like to do something other than smile politely and accept the blow. If we are really the dear friends that you keep insisting we are, then I do not understand why you did not stand up for my family and say something in support of them instead of fawning at the feet of your new acquaintances, no matter how many connections they have."

Caroline opened her mouth but could not think what to say. "You're being rather selfish now," was what came out. "You have insisted this entire time that I strive to be kind and polite, which is exactly what I did, and now you are saying that I ought not to have been? This is dreadfully unfair! Did you want me to leap across the table, grab that stuffed boar, and wield its tusks in defense of your family's honour? The Radcliffes are of no consequence whatsoever, so I shall not act as if they are equal to you or your family." She took a deep breath. "Peace, Georgie. They mean nothing to me, while you mean everything."

Georgiana marched towards her, the offending finger held

out again, and once again it made contact with Caroline's bare collarbone, sending a shiver rippling down her arms. "And yet you continued to flirt with him after his sister slighted my cousin," Miss Darcy said, though her voice held only half the temper it had a minute prior. "You show your loyalty in very strange ways."

Ah, this is the true crux of the matter, Caroline thought. Georgiana had assumed that Caroline's lack of reply meant that she agreed with the Radcliffes, or at the very least, thought along the same lines with respect to Colonel Fitzwilliam. While Miss Darcy had known where Caroline's principles lay on the subject of circles and status, she had evidently not expected it to apply to her own family, a topic about which she was extremely sensitive. Caroline was aware that she ought to apologise, but Georgiana's earlier comments still rankled.

"I did not flirt," said she. "I merely helped the conversation along in order to get us through the lunch. There is a vast difference."

"I never liked him." Georgiana's lip curled. "You have terrible taste in men. I hope the next will not be so uncouth."

"I never said Mr Radcliffe was to my taste," Caroline snapped. "And you do me a disservice to be angry at me when you're really angry at him and his sister. You cannot hold me responsible for the behaviour of a man I only just met, nor for any of his relatives' behaviour. Please be sensible, Georgie. I could not possibly have guessed at his bad habits and discourtesy before I got to know him, or else I should never have agreed to go to lunch. I cannot be expected to find out what I like in a man if I do not try to get to know a few, and if we discover their vices or cruel natures quickly, that is all the better. Or would you rather I marry the next suitor on sight alone and simply hope for the best? Never mind that he may be yet another rabid huntsman whose idea of fun is—"

"You—" Georgiana prodded at Caroline again, her lips pursed, and Caroline grabbed her hand, forcing it down to their waists.

"Stop poking me like a prize pig, Miss Darcy," she hissed.

"Then stop acting like a hard-headed goat, Miss Bingley. And what on earth do you mean, what you like in a man? Don't you know?"

"Well, I . . . certainly have more of an idea now of what I do not want." Caroline hesitated. She ought to let Georgiana's wrist go, but Miss Darcy had made no move to pull away, her pulse fluttering under Caroline's fingertips. "It is impossible to know what I like in a man. Other women seem rather sure of their tastes, but I am finding it difficult to . . . to . . ."

"To what?"

"To discern mine," Caroline cried, dropping Georgiana's hand. "For all of my talk and my opinions, I simply do not know what I like in men. Or if I particularly like them at all. There, are you happy? I am doing my best with what little I have, and what little I have is decidedly queer."

That was more than she had meant to say. Quite a lot more, in fact.

"Difficult to discern," Georgiana repeated, and Caroline knew, without quite knowing how she knew, that her friend was looking at her in an entirely new light. Long seconds passed, those glittering eyes raking her face with such intensity that Caroline could have sworn she felt her skin burn at the contact. "And let me ask you this: Has there ever been any man who—"

The reply was immediate, without requiring any thought. "No."

"Not even my—"

"Not even him."

Georgiana didn't move. They were still standing only a few inches apart, and Caroline became aware of Georgiana's closeness in a way she had not fully appreciated before. Those full, plump lips. That bosom, heaving with passion. Those dark eyes, so fiercely locked on her own.

"And," Georgiana breathed, barely moving, as if afraid Caroline would skitter away like a feral cat at the slightest provocation, "what about women?"

Caroline opened her mouth, ready to retort with something incisive, but nothing came out. Instead, a series of pictures filled her mind. Her childhood friend Victoria with the red ringlets. The green-eyed woman from the inn who had pressed against her so knowingly. *Miss Elizabeth Bennet.*

Oh, God. Oh, no.

Oh, hell, she thought, a split second before Georgiana Darcy lunged forward and kissed her full on the mouth.

Chapter Eighteen

It might have been minutes or years later that Georgiana attempted to pull away. Instead of complying as she ought, Caroline chased Miss Darcy's lips eagerly, unwilling to permit the lovely new sensation to end so quickly. The feeling, hot and heady, thrilled down her spine, her hands clenching and unclenching with nowhere to go, her world narrowed to a single point of focus where two mouths met and unmet in a clumsy clash of teeth and lips and oh good Lord, she was probably going to get sad tongue from kissing someone who was not her wedded husband but she couldn't bring herself to care one single whit because this was delightful and burning and passionate, and Georgiana's fingers were curling around her waist, pulling her still closer, and—

When they finally broke apart, panting, Caroline wasn't sure exactly what had happened, what had occasioned it, or what she might do to elicit such a response again. The realisation that she wanted it to happen again shocked and delighted her in equal measures. This was new indeed, and yet not unwelcome.

Perhaps too welcome.

Georgiana's fingers rose to cover her own lips as she backed away. "I apologise most heartily for—for—"

"For what?" Caroline blurted.

For a heartbeat, Miss Darcy looked at her as if she'd gone completely mad. "For kissing you," she whispered, sounding scandalised. "You are aware that I just kissed you, are you not?"

"I am not so sheltered that I do not know what a kiss is."

"You . . ." She shook her head. "No matter. In either case, I apologise."

"You needn't." The world was too sharply-focused, too crisp. Caroline was acutely aware of each and every thundering heartbeat, the dampness of her palms, the heat writhing through her veins. "You were not as bad as all that."

"I— Excuse me?" Georgiana stared at her. Clearly, her friend had expected Caroline to faint or flee.

"Why did . . . How . . ." Caroline hardly knew what one ought to be asking in such a situation, nor how to phrase the question in a suitable way. Floundering, she changed tack. "I must say, I had no idea that you—"

Georgiana's expression turned frosty, and she backed away, putting careful distance between them. "That I what?"

The change made Caroline's stomach drop. "I—I don't know," she stammered, her voice coming out uncharacteristically reedy and uncertain. How could they have gone from kissing heartily one moment and feel like damned strangers in the next? "Georgie, I really—"

"It is better that we do not talk of this ever again," Miss Darcy said stiffly. "I have letters to write. Pray excuse me, Miss Bingley. I shall see you at dinner."

Without another word, she turned and fled the room.

Caroline's knees gave way and she slumped onto the worn couch, one finger brushing against her now-swollen lips. Every time she recalled Georgiana's fingers clutching at her waist, her heart rate sped up so much, she thought she might actually faint. How on earth was she going to get through dinner without bursting into flames? How on earth was she going to achieve the Great Endeavour with such a distraction so close to hand?

And how on earth can I entice her to kiss me a second time?

After she felt herself suitably under control again, which took the best part of an hour, Caroline made her way up the staircase to the first floor. She paused on the landing and listened intently, straining to hear any noise coming from Miss Darcy's bedchamber.

Nothing.

Perhaps Georgiana wasn't even in her room; perhaps she had escaped elsewhere to avoid being cornered. Creeping closer, Caroline sidled along the hallway, avoiding the creakiest floorboards, and shamelessly put her ear to Georgiana's door.

Still nothing. No murmuring to herself. Not even the scratch of a quill or a sigh could be heard.

Frowning, Caroline lifted her hand to knock, then decided against it. The reasons for the kiss might be as murky as lakewater, but Georgiana's panicked flight had made some things crystal clear. Forcing a confrontation might not be the best course of action at the present moment, even if it was Caroline's first impulse. Inside the guest room, Caroline went first to her bed, lowering herself onto it with still-shaky legs, then bounced up again with renewed vigour. She had too much energy inside her to sit still right now, yet she could not simply keep pacing the floor lest she wore grooves in the hardwood. Crossing to the window, she settled herself against the wall and stared out at the sky. Though the sun was still an hour or two from setting, the deep blue which she had so admired earlier that day had begun to fade, tinged with a rosy glow. What was that old saying her governess had so loved—*red sky at night, shepherd's delight*? Though what shepherds had to be delighted about, Caroline had no idea. Perhaps a flock behaved better if they saw a particularly lovely sunset the night before. It was impossible to know what might matter to a sheep.

She rubbed her eyes, suddenly feeling exhausted. The first thing to do, presumably, was to ascertain why Georgiana had kissed her in the first place. Caroline hesitated. Was it a *why*? If not, then she wasn't sure what else it would be. Certainly not *how* or *where*—she knew both of those, and the memory brought a hot flush to her cheeks and a thrill to her stomach. No, perhaps it was not a *why*, but a *what*. She had been talking of men and her inability to determine what she liked about them in the marriageable sense, and then Georgiana had asked her about women. Caroline felt certain that her feelings must have shone clearly on her face in that moment, whatever those feelings were—and good Lord, that was a thought she ought to address at another time—and instead of being repulsed or outraged at such deviancy, Georgiana had . . .

Responded to it.

As if she too found women attractive.

At least one woman, anyway.

Caroline drew in a deep, ragged breath. *Well. That is certainly something.* She turned to the looking glass and stared at her reflection. The lady who stared back was gorgeous, stylish, and looked utterly lost. *I hardly think that you teaching me to be kinder can be dangerous in any way*, she'd told Georgiana only a few days prior. Caroline sighed at the memory, allowing the breath to escape unchecked without any consideration for sad lung. How absolutely wrong she'd been.

Well, there's a first time for everything, I suppose.

She turned back to the window and threw it wide open. The gust of fresh air which entered made her feel more grounded. *If one breath achieves that much*, she reasoned, *then surely several hundred will be even more reviving.* Decision made, she swept out into the hallway and made her way downstairs. She was halfway across the great hall when footsteps sounded in the passage behind her. Not Georgiana's, which she knew by heart and could have picked out in any crowd, but heavier, more stately.

"Good afternoon, Miss Bingley," said the housekeeper. "Is Miss Darcy upstairs, ma'am?"

"Good afternoon," Caroline muttered. She couldn't bring herself to make eye contact, not when she was so flustered, and made a great show of putting on her bonnet and gloves to avoid doing so. "I expect so. She left me only a short while ago to, er, finish her correspondence."

Mrs Reynolds nodded, though did not press the matter, and Caroline fled through the front door, relieved to escape any further questioning. She stalked down the path which led between high hedges and along a left-hand turn, which, in truth, was her least preferred route, until she reached the flowerbeds. She'd had some thought of sitting here on the bench for a while, but the rosebushes merely reminded her of Georgiana. Instinctively, Caroline reached for the nearest rose; dark petals, velvet-soft, simply begging to be touched and fondled and smelled and—

Good grief, she chided herself, yanking her hand back. *Are not even the flowers safe from your amorous intent?*

The thought made her chuckle, despite the strange way her stomach twinged at the thought of any kind of *amor.* Instead of sitting, she headed down yet another path, admiring the bright blaze of purple and white columbines and the tall stems of pink hollyhock. Not even the faint scent of lilac drifting on the breeze could distract her from the memory of the kiss, from the way Georgiana's lips had descended on hers, creating a storm cloud of passion, which had sent a bolt of lightning all the way down to her very toes.

One unassailable point of the matter was that Georgiana had kissed her—had kissed her first, in fact—and Caroline had kissed back. Miss Darcy had been right, of course, that they ought to leave it at that. One kiss was simply one kiss. It could be swept under the rug like any other indiscretion, could it not? Caroline found she'd taken another left, quite without meaning to, and was now en route back to the house. Her pace quickened as she considered the matter, as if by marching she could bring her thoughts closer and thus sort through them more efficiently.

The second unassailable point of the matter was that, even before the kiss had taken place, she'd desired Georgiana in a manner she had not quite understood. From the moment she'd seen Georgiana emerge dripping from the lake, Caroline had wanted to embrace Miss Darcy in a way that went very much beyond mere friendship. She was prepared to admit that it had taken her a ridiculously long time to reach this elementary conclusion, though this had hardly been her fault given how little she knew of these things, but now that they had kissed, and at least some future potential had been made plain to her, she could not simply close the door on the business without stepping through it again at least once. It need not interfere with the Great Endeavour, either, since Miss Darcy was not a man and would therefore have no interest in marrying her.

My reasoning, as ever, is perfectly sound.

She sped up until she was flat out running, bursting through the front door of Pemberley with a vehemence that was not at all ladylike before bolting up the staircase two at a time, ripping her bonnet off as she went. Panting, Caroline kicked the door of Georgiana's room open without knocking, strode inside, and swung the door shut behind her. Miss Darcy was sitting at her desk, quill in hand, though she'd been staring out of the window rather than at the correspondence in front of her, and flinched when she saw Caroline.

Georgiana was up and out of her seat in a moment, putting as much distance between them as possible. "It's considered polite to knock and wait to be admitted to a private chamber, you know."

Caroline ignored this. She hadn't been in the habit of remembering to knock before, and she wasn't about to start now. "It is my conclusion," she announced breathlessly, "that we ought to do that again."

Georgiana stared at her. "I beg your pardon?"

"We ought to kiss again," she said, advancing. "That is my conclusion."

"Your . . . your conclusion to what?" Georgiana backed up again until she was in danger of becoming lost in the curtains.

"The argument that you will undoubtedly make."

Georgiana blinked, her eyes sliding down towards Caroline's lips. Her shoulders, which had been up around her ears, relaxed minutely. "How do you know what sort of argument I will make?"

Caroline scoffed. "You cannot really be asking me that."

"Whyever not?" Miss Darcy straightened her shoulders, inching forward so that she was no longer trapped against the wall. Her gaze flickered past Caroline, presumably to the closed door, but Caroline had no intention of letting her run a second time.

"Because I know you, Georgie. I do." Her heart was beating so fast she felt rather light-headed, but she kept her eyes on Georgiana, intent on making her case plain. "I know you will say that it is improper, but no one ever need know. Besides, can an improper action truly be called so if there is no one to witness it?"

"How very philosophical of you. Is that your entire line of reasoning?"

She refused to let herself be deterred by such a jab. "No. I have other conclusions. Sub-conclusions, if you will. And they all amount to the same . . . peroration." *There.* She was rather proud of that summary. She waited, but Georgiana made no reply.

"Caroline, I do not think it a good idea. It may lead down a path which . . ." Miss Darcy pressed her lips together, as if clamping down on her own sentence. "It is simply an unwise course of action. Therefore . . . no."

Caroline hadn't expected Georgiana to leap into her arms immediately, but the abrupt dismissal stung. "No?" she repeated, incredulous.

"No. I cannot possibly—" Georgiana caught herself, then swallowed hard. "We could not possibly—" She halted again, clearing her throat. "No. My answer is no."

"I see." Caroline straightened, unable to help a smile creeping across her lips. If Georgiana had intended to reject her properly, she would have done so in a manner far more sympathetic, which took Caroline's own feelings into account. She knew Miss Darcy well enough to suspect that this panicked response was likely borne of the instinct to protect herself from something she found frightening. And why not, when her last dalliance had ended so badly? Not that Caroline would ever deign to compare herself with the likes of George Wickham. "Very well," she said mildly.

"What are you smiling about?" Georgiana demanded, staring at her.

"Nothing, my dear friend." She smiled even more widely. It was excellent to have another goal. Obtaining a single kiss was far more immediately achievable than the end goal of marriage which underpinned the Great Endeavour. That stubbornness which Fitzwilliam had accused her of, and which he'd been perfectly correct about, would serve her well here. "Nothing at all."

"You did hear me, did you not?" Georgiana said, a look of deepest suspicion suffusing her pretty features. "I said no."

"Of course, Miss Darcy." She turned, throwing a coy look over her shoulder. "Whatever you say shall be."

Chapter Nineteen

My dearest Georgiana,

Your plan to humiliate me, though cunning, would be easily thwarted if I were to own outright that I am fond of such a ridiculous, festooned pony. In fact, my reputation would not suffer from it, but would actually increase, for only the manliest of men could endure such an agonising fate and live to tell the tale. You shall have to work much harder to embarrass me!

I have found a beautiful mare for you, who has won several races against stallions. Though she is but two-thirds of their size, her fierceness and spirit outstrip them all. The beast rather reminds me of someone I know.

Your affectionate brother,
Fitzwilliam Darcy

Caroline had heard it said that love was war, and though she did not think this affair was likely to run along such tumultuous lines, she intended to meet her challenge with the fortitude and cunning of any good general. Therefore she wore her lowest-cut dress to dinner that evening—a weapon unfortunately beyond the reach of most, if not all, military men—and made sure to lean across the table to help herself to every single dish, whether she actually wanted it or not. Georgiana seemed as twitchy as a rabbit throughout and twice almost knocked over her wine glass. Though they were seated at least fifteen feet apart, making Caroline curse the length of the Darcys' handsome dining table, she was certain that she saw Georgiana's hands trembling. The blush which adorned Miss Darcy's fair cheeks was far easier to recognise, and much more satisfying.

Professing a sudden and inexplicable headache, which Caroline could explick very well indeed, Miss Darcy fled the room before dessert was served. Mrs Reynolds, who entered bearing two bowls of lemon posset only moments after said flight, stared at the empty chair and then at Caroline.

"Miss Darcy has a terrible headache," Caroline announced, trying her best to keep a straight face. "I cannot imagine one so afflicted would be able to consume even a single bite. No, no, leave both with me and I shall take care of them. I would not for the life of me have our wonderful Mrs Addlecombe saddened by the return of a full bowl of her heavenly creation."

"Of course, ma'am," Mrs Reynolds complied, casting a worried glance towards the door. "I shall take up a cold compress for Miss Darcy. It is unlike her to suffer from such aches."

"I am sure she would benefit greatly from something cold," Caroline said, pulling the first bowl towards her and tucking into the tangy mousse, humming a jaunty tunc as shc did so.

Dinner had only been a minor skirmish, in the grand scheme of things; the war was nowhere near won, yet she felt that every small victory ought to be celebrated, as surely each one brought her closer to her ultimate goal. In addition, it granted her new knowledge which she might arm herself with going forward—that Georgiana could be, and indeed was, very affected by the sight of a perfectly-framed bosom being aimed towards her with all the subtlety of cannon fire.

Patting her now-rounded stomach, Caroline left the dining room and paused in the great hall, wondering what to do next. One could harry the enemy as it retreated, if one so chose, but she did not intend to run Georgiana into the ground. It would be a hollow victory indeed if Caroline obtained a second kiss by means of an overwhelming onslaught, for that would in no way guarantee a third. And she did want a third, she realised. *Possibly even a fourth.* The trick here would be to lay such an enticing trail, over a series of encounters and days, that Georgiana simply could not resist following to see where it led. And if Miss Darcy were able to withstand all of her allures—

Caroline snorted, remembering the way Georgiana had flushed at dinner. No, she would have what she wanted; it was simply a matter of time. The prey would come directly to the hunter, if the hunter made herself tempting enough.

She went into the library, seated herself upon the stool next to the harp, and began to practice the simple tune Georgiana had showed her. This gave her something to pay attention to for the time being and stopped her from marching upstairs again and dragging her friend out of her room. Miss Darcy was stubborn, though she was no match for Caroline's obstinacy; Georgiana could, and would, be broken. *Good things come to those who wait*, she thought. *Very good things indeed.*

Caroline smiled to herself and began the scales again.

★

She wore another dress—this one verging on scandalous—to breakfast the next morning, which caused Georgiana to drop her spoon into her porridge with such force that flecks of it ended up spattered on the cloth runner. Miss Darcy muttered a terse greeting and continued to avoid her gaze, spending the rest of breakfast staring determinedly into her cup of tea as if it could provide answers to all of life's questions. Caroline sashayed out afterwards, leaving a trail of delightful perfume in the air behind her, and went off for a nice, long walk. When she finally returned, windswept but happy, the dulcet sound of the pianoforte indicated where she might find Miss Darcy.

Georgiana paused when Caroline sidled over the library threshold, but made no attempt to get up, no doubt assuming that the size of the pianoforte would afford her suitable cover for whatever was coming next. She stiffened in surprise as Caroline wandered towards her, positioned herself behind Georgiana, then purposefully leaned over Georgiana's shoulder as if to examine the sheet music more closely. "What were you playing?" said she, though she could read very well that it was Chevalier de Saint-Georges.

"*Adagio in F minor*," Georgiana muttered, then sucked in a breath as Caroline pressed against her more closely. Miss Darcy could have moved; she could have slid left and put distance between them again, but instead, she sat, teeth gritted, until Caroline withdrew.

Caroline gestured at an envelope which sat on the lid of the pianoforte. "What's this?"

Two heartbeats passed before Georgiana responded. "Another response to my earlier inquiries. There is to be a ball tonight, at a house on the other side of the village. I think it best we attend, to further your Great Endeavour."

"Splendid!" she exclaimed, accidentally-on-purpose dropping the invitation and bending over far more than was necessary in order to retrieve it.

She glanced over her shoulder. Georgiana's eyes were fixed on the ceiling, but the tips of her ears were a dark, luscious pink. Caroline turned away, hiding her smile. A ball was a perfect place to garner attention, serving both goals: to entice Georgiana, and to attract any suitable bachelors. There could be no downside to such a plan, for surely it was only a matter of time before she came across a gentleman who interested her just as much, if not more, as Miss Darcy did.

The ball itself was a reasonably large one, though the house was nothing particularly extraordinary in Caroline's opinion, and the two rooms in which the event chiefly took place were decorated with a lack of style that could be charitably described as inoffensive. She recognised several of the gentlemen who had attended Mr Darcy's party only a few weeks prior and made use of what little she remembered about each to make herself ingratiated to everyone she spoke to. By the end of the first hour, she had been invited to dance by no less than three gentlemen, all of whom she accepted with a gracious smile.

The sets took twenty minutes each, which meant she was obliged to keep up a steady stream of conversation with her first two partners for quite some time, and therefore could only sneak an occasional glance at Georgiana. Miss Darcy accepted two invitations to dance, though Caroline was certain her friend had only undertaken them out of duty and not for any particular love of the dance itself nor for either of her partners, who were both stately middle-aged men. Excusing herself to fetch another glass of red wine, Caroline watched as Georgiana danced, flowing from one position to the next with an easy grace entirely unmatched by anyone else in the room. When they finally had a moment alone together, Caroline nudged Georgiana's elbow and was delighted when Miss Darcy did not flinch away; she did not lean into the touch either, but it was a start.

"You dance uncommonly well, Miss Darcy," said she.

"I am good at many things which bring me very little pleasure, Miss Bingley." The look Georgiana gave her might have been placid and inscrutable to others, but Caroline thought she detected real sadness lingering underneath.

"Then we ought to remedy that. What shall we do that gives you real pleasure?"

Georgiana glanced sharply at her, apparently to ascertain whether this was meant as a flirtation. Upon seeing that Caroline was sincere, her expression softened. "A difficult question."

"On the contrary, it should be the simplest one in the world to answer."

"Pleasure may take many forms." Miss Darcy shifted uneasily from foot to foot. "One might argue that it is a pleasure to behave as a young lady ought."

"You are not addressing the royal court, Georgie. You may be honest with me." Caroline glanced at her. "Perhaps you should learn to speak truth, as I have learned to utter kindness."

"Swimming, then," Miss Darcy murmured. "Fencing. Riding—not sidesaddle, as a lady should, but galloping with Swift as if the devil himself is after me. Though I admit that these pleasures are difficult to indulge in here in Derbyshire, where everyone knows me, for I have a family reputation to uphold. And uphold it I shall."

Caroline's reply was cut short by the approach of her third dance partner. "Shall we, Miss Bingley?" he asked, extending a hand.

She nodded and let him lead her out onto the dance floor, trying to recall every detail about him. He had been standing with the captain of the local militia during Fitzwilliam's party, though he had not been a military man himself. *Stanhope*, she thought. *No, Stanwick. Or is it Stanley? Something like that, anyway.*

"And how do you know Captain St. John?" she inquired, a question which kept her partner busy and herself tolerably entertained for the next few minutes while they waited to dance down the set.

Her eyes flitted back to Georgiana, who was talking with some animation to a girl of perhaps eight-and-ten in a grey dress that did absolutely nothing for her rosy complexion. Caroline recognised the man standing between them as Mr Warwick, who had been so keen for Georgiana to play at Darcy's party, therefore the girl must be his daughter, Emmeline. She was making a poor show of hiding her interest in Mr Acton, who was standing across the ballroom and chatting with Miss Merryhill. Perhaps this was a new way in which Caroline might flex the muscle of kindness, which she had so recently grown into a substantial bulge. Biting back a smile at the thought, she waited for a lull in the conversation before artfully dropping in the mention of Miss Warwick to her partner.

"I had not the pleasure of meeting her at the last party," she said, "for if I recall correctly, she was suffering from a head cold."

"Ah yes." His smile brightened. "A lovely girl indeed, and very accomplished."

"Miss Darcy talks of her in glowing terms. And you know, it is the hope of all young ladies to dance with a handsome man of an evening. Perhaps Mr Acton might do his gentlemanly duty, if you were to introduce them? I do not think it would be a hardship to indulge such a pretty girl."

Mr Stanley—or Stanhope?—raised an eyebrow at her. "I take you for a clever woman, Miss Bingley. To my eyes, Mr Acton has not noticed a girl twenty years his junior, nor is he likely to with Miss Merryhill by his side. Why, then, do you seek to introduce him to another?"

"He has not yet danced," Caroline said, ensuring that she kept pace. *Turn, turn, hop, turn again*. "Nor has he pursued the quarry which would most like to be caught. Therefore, I must surmise that he has no enthusiasm for the hunt. Or perhaps it is courage he lacks."

"He is not a rich man," her partner said, evidently keen to gossip. "Poor men marry in haste and repent at leisure. Although, I have heard that he has recently been commissioned by a man who could change Mr Acton's fortunes if he should continue to paint well. Viscount Ashbrook, if my intelligence is correct."

Ashbrook had been at the lake picnic, Caroline recalled. *I knew I recognised the name!* The bubble of her satisfaction was immediately popped by also recalling that she had thought the handsome viscount looked like Georgiana. *Perhaps I do have a type*, she thought grimly. "It is my experience, sir," said she, as they whirled around the floor, "that a suitor who is reluctant to make his attentions known to a lady, for one reason or another, often cannot help doing so when another suitor shows those same attentions openly."

"That is a sentiment well observed." Mr Stan-whatever gave

her a shrewd look. "Well, I am all for creating a ruckus from time to time. Keeps life interesting, does it not? If you have a scheme in mind, I shall act my part in it."

"Introduce Miss Warwick to Mr Acton, then ask Miss Merryhill to dance," she suggested.

"Bold indeed." He chuckled. "This plan may misfire. What if Mr Acton falls for the girl? What if Miss Merryhill falls in love with me?"

"Then I suppose we shall all have our answers, one way or another. Is it not said that he who dares, wins?"

"But is it not also said," her partner countered, bowing as the dance came to an end, "that one must look before they leap?"

"In my opinion, that rather depends," Caroline said archly, unable to help another glance at Georgiana, who had joined Mr Acton and Miss Merryhill, "on where one is currently standing and where one intends to land."

They parted with a smile, and Caroline joined the small group. She hardly heard what was said between them, for an unfamiliar feeling of trepidation had come over her. What if Mr Stan-whatever was right? One could never predict the precise effects of one's intervention. It was too late to alter the plan, however, for the next moment her dance partner came bustling over with a blushing Miss Warwick. The introductions were made, the invitation extended and accepted, albeit with some evident bafflement on Mr Acton's part. Miss Merryhill took to the floor, glancing back over her shoulder at the artist, who wore a look of consternation as he escorted a chattering Miss Warwick.

"Are you playing matchmaker now?" Georgiana murmured, brushing Caroline's elbow with a gloved hand. "Or playing with fire?"

"They are often one and the same, I think." She crossed her

arms, the movement hiding her right hand, which stroked down Georgiana's arm. Her glove prevented her from feeling bare skin, but the way Georgiana shivered was unmistakable. "I told you that I see more than most, did I not?"

"Perhaps you see what you want to see," Miss Darcy said, her voice barely more than a whisper. "Just like everyone else."

"Then show me what I am missing," Caroline said, surprising herself with the urgency in her own voice. Her fingers itched to reach out again, to turn Georgiana towards her and shake some good sense into her. "Show me what you hide from the world, Georgie. Let me be the one who—"

Miss Darcy was saved from having to respond by the approach of a young man whose cherubic face was not at all aged by the bushy whiskers adorning his chin and rosy cheeks. He expressed his desire to become Caroline's fourth partner, and she confirmed her readiness to dance the next cotillion with a forced smile, hoping he would go away until then, but the man lingered, evidently hoping to converse. To Caroline's great relief, Georgiana took over the conversation with discussion of mutual acquaintances whom Caroline neither knew nor cared for, and she was able to watch her scheme playing out on the dance floor. Miss Merryhill appeared to be having a pleasant time with Mr Stan-whatever—Caroline made a mental note to learn his name in thanks—while Mr Acton was paying only the barest attention to his own partner. To the girl's credit, Miss Warwick did not look sour about her partner's interest lying elsewhere, but was being a lot less subtle about craning her neck to see where the painter was looking.

There, she thought with satisfaction. *Now their feelings are out in the open. If they do not do something about them, it is hardly my fault. I gave a push, and now the little birds must fly.*

With a murmured instruction to Georgiana to commit to memory every moment of Mr Acton and Miss Merryhill's conversation post-dance, Caroline reluctantly submitted to dancing the cotillion. She would have much rather stayed and observed for herself, but nothing short of an injury could have freed her from this obligation. A lady could not deny any invitation without denying all of them, for fear of humiliating a gentleman, and besides, the young man was rather pretty, even if he was too whiskered to suit her taste. *Time to turn my talents to advancing my own suit*, Caroline thought, and bestowed such a dazzling smile on the young man that he promptly tripped over his feet. She took great satisfaction in catching Georgiana scowling from the shadows at Caroline's partner, who seemed to be taking a great deal of his own satisfaction in touching her just as much as the dance allowed.

The night ended with a hot supper and two lively boulangeries, leaving all participants pleasantly exhausted and declaring that they had not had such a wonderful time in a twelvemonth.

After Georgiana had recited every word and look between Mr Acton and Miss Merryhill—apparently the conversation had been stilted and awkward, with both parties blushing furiously and unsure where to look, before Mr Acton had left early—Miss Darcy fell silent on the carriage ride back to Pemberley. Caroline busied herself with looking out of the window, enjoying the sight of the moon flitting between dark treetops. Thought it was often obscured, it always returned to her view, shining brilliantly, reflecting her own feeling of contemplative victory. Though Mr Acton had left the ball early, which hadn't been precisely Caroline's intention, this could only be considered a good thing in the larger scheme; the poor man had clearly been too affected and jealous to remain a moment longer, which spoke highly of his feelings towards Miss Merryhill. Caroline made no attempt to touch or otherwise engage Georgiana, who seemed now to be lost in her own thoughts. Better to wait until they were home, lest Miss Darcy feel trapped in such an enclosed space with her.

When they returned to the house, all was quiet. Mrs Reynolds appeared as if she'd been lying in wait for them, and after checking to see that neither lady required anything before bed, she retired for the evening. Caroline followed Georgiana into the candlelit library, where the faint smell of struck matches suggested that the housekeeper had anticipated their arrival perfectly, and poured two small glasses of sherry. She turned, holding one out for Georgiana, and made sure their fingers brushed. "Did you have a pleasant evening, Georgie? Would you like to have an even more pleasant one here?"

"I beg of you to stop this," Miss Darcy said, her voice quiet, strain evident in her tone.

"I do not know what you mean," Caroline said airily, pretending to examine the bookshelves.

"You know exactly what I mean," Georgiana snarled, advancing on Caroline. "Wearing your lowest-cut dresses. Bending over every two minutes. Flirting outrageously with me in private, then smiling at every gentleman in the room. Leaning close to me, so that I can smell that perfume which you know I—" She cut herself off, her free hand clenching into a fist. "Just . . . stop it."

"I absolutely will not," Caroline said, as sweetly as she dared. She could see that Georgiana was on the edge, and it would only take a moment of weakness to send them both over the precipice into the abyss. Romantically speaking, of course.

The delicious, delectable abyss.

"You will not?" Georgiana repeated. She turned away, taking a large gulp of her sherry, and placed the glass on the nearby table. "Caroline"—her voice caught—"why are you doing this to me?"

"I am not doing anything to you. I am merely displaying what is on offer, should you choose to imbibe it. And besides, when I enlisted your help in the first place, you told me that I had to agree to be open to trying new things. If this is one of those things, then know that I am very open to it. I only mean to make you acutely aware of that fact."

Georgiana looked as if she did not know whether to laugh or cry. "You know very well that I did not mean anything like this."

"Firstly, I do not know that at all. I have no idea what you were referring to when you said it, and you have not exactly elaborated since. And secondly, now that you have introduced the idea, I find myself . . . unable to stop thinking about it." She sidled closer, a spark of triumph flaring in her chest when Georgiana did not back away. "The truth is that I would very much like another taste of you, Miss Darcy."

Georgiana swallowed hard, her throat bobbing, yet she stood her ground. "You are incorrigible, Miss Bingley."

"Yes, so I've heard."

"We really shouldn't—"

"Did not you tell me recently that you were tired of being perceived as faultless? That you would like to be selfish sometimes? So why not be selfish with me? Why shouldn't we indulge ourselves in a pleasurable pastime?"

Using Georgiana's own words against her wasn't exactly fighting fair, but Caroline was beyond caring. *The ends justify the means*, she thought, *especially when the ends are so warm and sweet.*

Georgiana sighed so long and hard that Caroline instinctively clamped her hand over Georgiana's mouth. "Sad lung," she said, by way of explanation when Georgiana's eyes widened. "You really ought to be more careful, especially if you insist on swimming in that freezing lake." She released her hand, letting it drift down to Miss Darcy's shoulder, where it hovered. "I admit that I do not possess much in the way of expertise upon the subject of kissing," she added. Georgiana's bosom still rose and fell with sharp breaths, drawing her attention; her blood was already hot with jealousy and frustration, and introducing a competitive element into the situation would surely be the means by which Caroline won this particular battle. "But my opinion was that you performed the previous action with moderate skill, and therefore, I politely request a second kiss in order to pass better judgement on your talent."

"Moderate?" Miss Darcy repeated, her tone outraged, the flush on her cheeks darkening.

"Moderate," Caroline confirmed, holding Georgiana's gaze.

"You are so unbelievably infuriating," Georgiana hissed, before lunging at Caroline again, pulling Caroline towards her so hard, they fell onto the couch together in a tangle of lips and teeth and grasping, clumsy hands.

In an instant, their mutual irritation turned to passion. For a glorious moment, Caroline felt the warm satisfaction of knowing that she had got precisely what she wanted; the victory was sweet, and the reward was even sweeter.

Really, this is the way the world ought to be.

Chapter Twenty

Georgiana's hands settled on Caroline's hips and squeezed, eliciting a gasp of pleasure that seemed only to spur Miss Darcy onwards. Caroline's hands slid up into Georgiana's hair, finding the curls just as soft as she'd imagined, tugging gently at the roots. "Don't—" Miss Darcy panted, but whatever it was that she didn't want Caroline to do was entirely lost in a flurry of passion; she kissed like a dying woman, all desperation and desire to hold on.

By the time they eventually parted, Caroline's lips were sore and her entire body on fire. Slightly dazed, she watched Georgiana smooth the front of her dress down as if nothing out of the ordinary had happened. The only evidence of their embrace was that her face and neck were flushed a most becoming shade of rose and she was purposefully avoiding Caroline's gaze.

Had Caroline been a different sort of woman—one who was sensitive and easily wounded—she might have interpreted the avoidance as a slight. Instead, she smiled and reached out to take Georgiana's hand.

Georgiana seemed to deflate at the touch. "I tried my utmost," said she, her voice hoarse. "Let it be known that I tried to resist you. Lord knows I may be weak, but I am not as weak as all that."

Caroline hesitated. That one was a little more difficult to ignore; Georgiana might be evincing regret, in which case the tiny prick of hurt she herself felt was entirely justified, or perhaps it was that Caroline was simply so unbelievably enticing that Georgiana had not been able to withstand the sheer temptation of Caroline's bewitching beauty. The latter was a much more flattering interpretation and was therefore the one she chose to believe.

"Now you know I am not perfect," Georgiana added, in a voice barely above a whisper. "Far from it. I did warn you."

Oh. A third option. Caroline stared at her, then took Georgiana's hand. "Whatever can you mean by such a thing?"

Miss Darcy bit her lip and made no reply. Her hand lay limp in Caroline's, who squeezed it firmly and shuffled closer. "This seems as good a time as any to pick up our conversation from the ball," Caroline continued, when no answer was forthcoming, "when I was prevented from replying to your statements in the expeditious manner that I would have liked. Allow me to do so now. I wish to make it utterly plain that I do not care a whit if you fence or gallop or wear breeches around Pemberley every day or whatever else your heart desires. If one cannot do the things one likes in one's own home, then one is not truly free." The memories of Hadley Hall, cold and unloving, echoed in her mind. "In fact," she declared, "I do not think I care very much for Miss Georgiana Darcy, paragon of perfection. I much prefer you, whomever you are. I thought I knew you before, but you were correct—I knew only the face you presented to the world. There is far more to you than meets the eye, and I would very much like to know the real version."

The longing look Georgiana gave her, helpless and hopeful all at once, stole Caroline's breath. "Do you mean that?"

"To whom do you think you are talking? Am I not known for my honesty?"

Georgiana managed a watery laugh, and Caroline was surprised to see her friend on the verge of tears. "Come here," she said, tugging Georgiana into an embrace. "I promise that all your secrets are safe with me."

Caroline insisted that they finish their sherries while discussing the events of the ball, going over every detail of the conversation between Mr Acton and Miss Merryhill a second time, lest something had been forgotten during the first recital. By the time Georgiana's glass was empty, colour had returned to her cheeks and she seemed more like herself again. Caroline escorted her up the stairs and to the door of her bedchamber, lingering while they said goodnight.

"You know," Georgiana said, leaning closer, as if she were about to kiss Caroline again. "I would never have guessed that you would attempt to matchmake. It appears that I am not the only one to whom there is far more than meets the eye."

With an impish smile, she slipped into her room and closed the door behind her. Caroline chuckled, half-outraged and half-amused, and returned to her own room. Once inside, she closed the door and leaned back against it. A general who had triumphed ought to allow herself a moment or two to relive the finer points of the battle, particularly those parts which had involved breathy little moans. She lost herself in the memory a little longer than intended and began her usual ablutions with some reluctance. The cool water with which she washed her face managed to somewhat calm the fire which Georgiana had ignited in her. Once she'd brushed her hair, Caroline slid into the bedsheets with some eagerness; the sooner she slept, the sooner another day would begin, and the sooner another kiss could be procured.

Unfortunately, another dream overtook her. In this one, Caroline looked down to find herself wet to her knees in the lake, her petticoat clinging to her. The water which slopped around her lower thighs was not cold, as she had feared, but as warm as bathwater. When she looked to the shore, Georgiana was standing there, trembling like a leaf in high winds, though she was perfectly dry. This was a reversal of positions from the first dream, and Caroline did not know what to make of it. Beyond Miss Darcy's figure, the treeline looked wrong—smudged together somehow, as if someone had rubbed over a charcoal drawing. The sky was a brilliant black, glossy as a horse's mane. No sun of any colour hung in the sky, yet Georgiana's face was clearly visible as if lit by an internal candle.

She looked afraid, Caroline realised. No, more than that. Utterly terrified.

Of what? Of me?

Without thinking, she held out her hand. Georgiana hesitated for a long moment, then stepped closer. No words passed between them as Georgiana's eyes searched her own. Caroline knew not what her friend was searching for and kept her hand outstretched. *I won't harm you*, she thought, and Georgiana's eyes widened as if she'd uttered the words out loud. Before she could blink, Miss Darcy walked into the water and grasped Caroline's hand, holding on tightly, as if fearing she would drown without it.

Caroline drew her backwards, down into the inky depths where they had gone before, only now she was the one leading, the one who yearned for the darkness of the cave. She was certain, without knowing quite how she knew, that inside lay some great treasure or another. Whatever it was was not without danger, but the danger was worth the reward. Her hair had flown free of its fastenings with the pressure of the water, and dark curls tumbled around her head, obscuring her vision, but she walked on steadily. Something hot and insistent in her chest was ushering her forward, and if she would only rely upon its guidance, she was sure that all would be well.

Georgiana's fingers tightened their grip as they approached the cave. The great mouth yawned much wider than Caroline remembered from the first dream, though perhaps it was simply that they were closer this time. Nothing lay inside but the utter darkness of infinite night. This was the only exit, she was sure. Oh, one could walk onto the shore and wander around as one pleased, but those smudges pretending to be trees were no more woodland than a painting was. There was no escape on land. The only way out was through the cave, regardless of what lay ahead.

Unexpectedly, Georgiana's fingers loosened. Caroline panicked, reaching back to grab blindly in the darkness, but her hand found nothing to hold on to. *Lead*, Georgiana's voice said in her ear. *Lead and I will follow.*

Caroline took one halting step forward and then another. Blackness engulfed her, swallowing her, and the water which served as air grew thick and warm in her mouth and lungs. She took another step, then halted. She could hear nothing but her own heartbeat. What if Georgiana was not there? What if something had happened to her, or she had become lost? What if Caroline emerged from this place to find herself quite alone?

She couldn't bear it a moment longer. Whirling, she gazed at the entrance of the cave, which now seemed a long way away, to where a familiar figure stood. *You said you wouldn't look back*, Georgiana's voice in her ear accused, and the figure vanished.

Caroline woke with a cry, an unfathomable ache yawning inside her. Somehow, she had made a mistake and done what she had declared she would never do. She had a horrible, nagging feeling that she was missing something terribly important.

Yet, it was only a dream, was it not?

At breakfast, Georgiana's hair was still damp at the ends, suggesting she had gone for another one of her morning swims in the lake. Caroline seated herself, wondering how she might get herself invited along to the next one; rising at dawn might be tolerable once or twice a week as long as there was a particularly lovely view on display. They exchanged their usual greetings with warmth, which was a vast improvement on the previous day, causing the housekeeper to eye them both curiously as she laid a rack of browned toast on the table in front of Caroline.

"That is the perfect shade, Mrs Reynolds!" Caroline exclaimed. "I do not know how you manage it when I myself do not have any idea how well-done I want the toast until I enter this room."

The housekeeper beamed. "It is no sorcery, Miss Bingley, merely my own intuition." She glanced at Georgiana, who sighed. "That is another shilling lost, Miss Darcy."

"I must break my losing streak eventually," Georgiana declared, though she did not sound particularly confident.

"Many a gambler has said so," the housekeeper murmured, moving the kippers closer to Caroline's end of the table. She bustled around the corner of the table, to where a trolley was laden with hot dishes.

"Georgie, I have an excellent suggestion for what we might

do today, and I believe you will be most pleased by it," Caroline announced. "A lovely, vigorous activity to get the blood flowing."

Georgiana's mouth formed a small, horrified O, her eyes darting to Mrs Reynolds and back to Caroline.

"You have barely ridden Swift since I have been here," Caroline continued, biting back a smile, as the housekeeper busied herself setting out the plates of eggs and ham. Clearly, the memory of last night's kissing was still fresh in her friend's mind. Perhaps she'd even been thinking of repeating it. Caroline dearly hoped that was the case. "It is such a lovely day after all, and I fear we have been rather indolent of late. I would not like you to grow restless."

"But you do not like to—" Georgiana began, then closed her mouth with a sharp snap. "Ah yes, I remember you telling me only last night how, um, how much you longed to . . . ride more."

"Are you quite well, ma'am?" Mrs Reynolds asked, and Caroline stuffed half a kipper into her mouth to quell the burst of laughter that threatened to erupt. "Has your headache returned?"

Georgiana shot a murderous look at Caroline, which only made her want to laugh more. "I am quite well, I assure you. I am only surprised that Miss Bingley wishes to ride when she has so little experience on . . . horses."

Caroline almost choked on her mouthful. Outraged, she glared back across the table, where Georgiana now wore a triumphant expression.

"Indeed," Mrs Reynolds said, her polite smile managing to convey clearly that she thought them both quite mad. "Shall I ask Mrs Addlecombe to pack you a lunch, ma'am?"

The walk to the stables, though a pretty one which wound past several flowerbeds and hedgerows of uncommon beauty, was not one Caroline had taken often while at Pemberley. Georgiana had been correct; Caroline really did not like to ride much, for she distrusted most horses. The one exception was a short and rather plump white stallion called Edward, which she had ridden several times. He was a reliable horse, never spooked and always steady on his feet. One could probably ride him through a burning building without eliciting any reaction; in a strange way, the beast reminded her of her brother. Edward nosed at Caroline's shoulder, evidently hoping for a treat. Caroline fed him a carrot from a nearby barrel to placate him, then a second when Miss Darcy wasn't looking.

Georgiana was over by Swift's stall, caressing his enormous head. Caroline had often thought that Swift must have a lineage which included giants, for he was a truly enormous stallion to her eyes, standing sixteen hands high. His mane was a dusky roan, his coat a tawny brown which blended perfectly with the way the ground looked at the moment summer turned into autumn, though neither Georgiana nor Swift would probably appreciate the comparison to mere soil.

"I cannot believe you mocked my lack of experience at breakfast," Caroline said, stepping closer. Now that they were alone, and out of sight of the house, surely, another kiss was imminent.

"Was I wrong, Miss Bingley?" Georgiana gave Swift a final pat and turned to face her.

"No, but I . . ." Caroline dropped her voice to a husky whisper, though there was no one around to hear them. "That is only because I had not found anyone worth gaining experience with."

Georgiana swallowed, then picked up a carrot and offered it to her stallion. "I'm sure you shall."

That was not at all the reaction Caroline had hoped for nor expected. She frowned. She'd assumed after their conversation the night before, that it would be far easier to resume where they had left off, and she was disappointed to find otherwise. "Perhaps I have not made myself clear," she said, stepping forward until she was within arm's reach. "You are not going to make me beg for another kiss, are you?"

"What a strange question. I do not recall you begging for either of the others. I only recall you being utterly impossible and frustrating me to the extent that I—"

"Would you like me to?" Caroline asked, inching closer, her hand brushing Georgiana's arm.

Miss Darcy swallowed. "Would I like you to do what?"

"Beg."

Georgiana looked down at her, her jaw tight. Up close, her dark eyes were a luminous brown, speckled with amber. "You are straining my self-control again, Caroline."

"I thought we agreed that you had already given in? You did say last night, did you not, that you tried to resist me and failed. What, then, is the point of reviving your self-control? Consider it dead and buried where I am concerned."

"A thing, though buried, may still haunt a person from time to time. And mine is so newly entombed."

Caroline's fingers itched to touch Georgiana. *Why not? Why should I always wait for her to make the first move?* "I do not understand why you fight it so," she whispered, placing a hand gently on Georgiana's waist and tugging her closer. "Could we not simply give in to each other and enjoy whatever happens?"

Georgiana leaned in, then jerked back reflexively. Swift

whickered in his stall, watching them with interest, his ears pricked up. "You," she said breathlessly, "do not know what you ask of me. Such an affair may be easy to begin but difficult to end."

"Why must there be talk of endings when we have barely begun?"

"Caroline—"

"You will not put me off," she announced, tiring of all this talk. "I am determined upon this course, if you will join me on it. So I will ask again, Miss Darcy: Would you like me to beg?"

Georgiana's expression was not one Caroline had seen before and was far too complicated for her to parse. She waited, heartbeat thudding, to hear what her fate would be. "You would do that, Miss Bingley?" Georgiana breathed, leaning down until Caroline could feel warm breath ghosting over her lips. "You would really beg for me? Do you want my kisses so much?"

The answer was obvious and true. "Yes." Caroline pressed closer, tilting her head up, her fingers tightening on Georgiana's waist. "Please, Georgie," she whispered. "I want you so much, I cannot think of anything else. I—"

Her words were cut off as Georgiana surged forward, kissing her with so much passion that Caroline hit the stall door behind her with a thump. She kissed back just as fervently, relief flooding her, the heat inside her building.

Georgiana stopped after a few moments, though she did not pull away. Instead, she rested her forehead on Caroline's, breathing heavily. "We really ought not to do this," she said.

"There can be no harm in it," Caroline assured her. "No one will discover us. It can be our little secret."

"Are you perfectly sure?" said she, dropping her head to nuzzle Caroline's neck and planting a series of soft kisses there.

"Quite sure," Caroline gasped, groaning again when Georgiana's lips touched a particularly sensitive spot. She grasped at Georgiana's shoulders, pulling her closer, eliciting a hum of appreciation.

"Will you grant me a favour, then?" Georgiana did pull back then and unhooked the bridle which was hanging from the wall. "Ride with me on Swift today."

"Oh." Caroline stared up at the enormous horse. "Well, I suppose you were most obliging, and therefore, I ought to oblige you in return." She hesitated. "You're not going to gallop like the devil himself is after you, are you?"

Georgiana grinned. "I swear I will not. And I also promise that I will keep you safe from devils and demons of all varieties and statuses, should they appear."

Reluctantly, Caroline acquiesced and allowed Georgiana to help her mount Swift. This was not exactly her idea of a good time, for sitting astride the stallion made the ground seem uncomfortably far away. Before she could change her mind, Georgiana slipped into position behind Caroline and reached forward for the reins. Clicking twice, Georgiana twitched the reins and Swift dutifully obeyed, breaking into a trot. Caroline clung to the saddle, her palms damp, her anxiety only alleviated by the warm body pressed against her back. However, once Swift had settled into a sedate pace through the woods and Georgiana's arms had wrapped tightly around Caroline's waist, holding her securely, she was prepared to admit that, perhaps, she had overlooked some of the great benefits of riding.

Chapter Twenty-One

Georgiana pulled Swift to a halt somewhere to the far west of the estate, though not so far that Caroline could see the wall which marked the boundary between the Darcy grounds and the farmer's fields beyond. "Here," she said, alighting with ease and holding her hand up for Caroline. "Let me help you down."

Caroline slithered down with far less grace and stumbled into Georgiana's arms, earning herself a chuckle from Georgiana and an indignant huff from Swift, who promptly wandered off and began to pull mouthfuls of tender green grass as if they had personally injured his pride.

"I have rarely seen you look so inelegant, Miss Bingley." Georgiana made no move to let her go. "Usually you move with all the poise of a young queen."

"Well, usually the ground is level underfoot, and the staircases which I avail myself of do not have steps which are quite so large." Caroline blinked up at her, her hands trailing down Georgiana's arms. The more they embraced, the bolder she grew, though she was still wary of crossing some hitherto unforeseen line and causing Miss Darcy to retreat. Her fingers traced a path along Georgiana's jaw, causing a shiver.

"Come, help me lay the picnic out," she said, stepping back and clearing her throat.

Caroline acquiesced, placing the rug in a patch of dappled sunlight while Georgiana unpacked the wicker basket. They sat together, their knees touching, while Caroline exclaimed over the inclusion of plain scones rather than fruit ones. "Not a single raisin in sight!" she exclaimed, delighted by the prospect. "Mrs Addlecombe has finally achieved the highest understanding of good taste." The mention of raisins jostled something in her memory. "Oh! I thought you were going to kiss me at our last picnic," she added. "Do you remember? You placed the daisy chain over my head and then you leaned in rather close."

The silence stretched on far longer than Caroline had expected.

"I recall making a necklace of daisies, yes." Georgiana buttered a scone with far more exacting precision than was required, giving every crumb her undivided attention. An interesting flush crept up her neck, and Caroline wondered just how far down it spread.

"Were you going to kiss me then?" Caroline prompted.

"No, I—I wasn't going to kiss you."

Caroline frowned. She knew what she'd seen and felt. Perhaps she wasn't asking the right questions. Georgiana wasn't a very good liar, but she could be slippery and evasive at times if not pressed in the correct way. "But you were thinking about it, were you not? Did you want to?"

Georgiana's blush deepened as she swallowed. "Perhaps."

"I wanted you to." She leaned forward, making sure her bosom was angled to catch the sunlight. "I have been dreaming about you a lot lately, and often in states of undress."

"Good grief," Georgiana complained, fumbling with her knife and almost dropping it. "How is a woman supposed to enjoy her scones in peace when you keep flirting so incessantly? It is very distracting."

Caroline pouted. "If I allow you time alone with your precious scones, do you promise to kiss me afterwards?"

Miss Darcy huffed, though the smouldering look she levelled at Caroline was far from being truly aggravated. Caroline grinned and lounged back, content in the knowledge that more kisses lay on her horizon. "I have heard the name of the composer you were playing yesterday, though I confess I am not so familiar with his music as I ought to be. What do you think of his talents?"

"Chevalier de Saint-Georges?" Georgiana cocked her head, chewing thoughtfully. "They say he is a genius of the first order, and I see why. Not every composer can be, you know. Some are workhorses, who merely churn out serviceable pieces to please this lord or that king, while some shine brighter than any star in the sky. Now, if you consider what Mozart—"

A few weeks ago, Caroline might have been bored by talk of music with which she was not familiar. Now, every conversation was another window into Georgiana's real passions. This was the real Georgiana, who loved saturnine music and fast horses and, apparently, kissing young men and ladies who were entirely unsuitable for her. Caroline watched Miss Darcy, her dark eyes bright with animation, her hands flying through the air as she gestured, and thought that she had never before seen anything so lovely in all her life.

When they had finished all the baked goods, Georgiana plucked a perfectly ripe red apple out of the picnic basket. "Shall I be Eve?"

Caroline propped herself up on her elbows. "That depends. Are you offering me fruit, or temptation, or knowledge?"

"That depends," Georgiana echoed, smirking. "Which one do you want?"

Without taking her eyes off Georgiana, Caroline leaned over and sank her teeth into the apple. The skin gave way to ripe flesh, and she allowed her lips to press against the surface before she tore a chunk out and leaned back.

Georgiana's own lips parted in a gasp, her eyes darker than Caroline had ever seen them before. Caroline hardly had time enough to swallow her bite before Miss Darcy was on top of her, the press of her body hot and needy against Caroline's own and her mouth equally as hungry to taste and nip and soothe.

"All three, ideally," she murmured, when the blazing kiss had died down to embers. "That is, if you are amenable to the idea, Miss Darcy."

"As you wish, Miss Bingley," Georgiana breathed, and bent down to steal another kiss.

Back at the house, a slightly awkward silence settled between them. In the woods, Georgiana had seemed freer with her tongue and her hands, but here in the house, a placid, pleasant mask schooled her features again.

Caroline wandered into the library while Georgiana passed the now-empty wicker basket back to Mrs Reynolds, praising Mrs Addlecombe's baking to the highest degree. Once the housekeeper's steps had died away, Caroline felt, rather than heard, Miss Darcy hesitating on the threshold of the library.

"You once asked me," said she, stepping inside and touching the back of the worn couch with some reverence, "why I did not want to reupholster when the couches in this room are so in need of it."

Caroline wished she hadn't announced her bad opinion of the furniture. Of course it was entirely true, but she recognised now that she needn't have stated it quite so baldly.

"I did not want to change a single thing in here," Georgiana continued, "because I have kept it the same way it was on the day our parents died."

"Oh." Guilt roiled in her stomach. "I apologise. I had no idea."

"Why would you? I am not in the habit of sharing something so personal with even my closest friends. I kept the portraits the same too, for I used to talk to them," Georgiana said, her eyes bright with unshed tears. "I had no one else to talk to and I . . . They were the only family I had left, you see. Apart from Fitzwilliam, but even he could not be here constantly. He had only just left Cambridge, and he often had business in London which required his presence."

Caroline turned to look at the portraits. Now she saw what she had not been able to before—the expressions, which she had interpreted as intimidating and rather suspicious, now looked merely inquisitive, even protective. "They must have been somewhat of a comfort to you. Hardly a replacement for a brother in the flesh, though."

"Unfortunately, that comfort came with a price. They remind me every day that the weight of expectation is a heavy burden." A muscle jumped in her jaw. "That is why I—I do not want you to think that I don't—"

If this conversation had taken place a few weeks ago, Caroline might have interrupted here. Now, she stayed quiet, allowing Georgiana time to sort her own thoughts out.

"I do want you," Miss Darcy murmured, coming closer. "I hope you understand that I am likewise attracted to you. I am telling you this so that you understand that if we pursue this affair to both of our pleasurable ends, it should not be any more than that."

Caroline frowned. "Whatever do you mean? What else could there be?"

Georgiana smiled, though it didn't quite reach her eyes. "Nothing, my dear friend. As long as we are on the same page, then we may continue. As long as you are eager to do so, and that we shall remain friends afterwards, for I have so few that each and every one is dear to me. You especially have become dearer to me these past weeks."

Caroline had the feeling she was missing something large here, though she failed to see exactly what. She probably ought to press a little more, but the idea of a full-blown physical affair being dangled before her made it difficult to concentrate on anything else. "I am eager indeed. And I cannot imagine that we would not be friends, Georgie, whatever should happen. The very notion is preposterous."

"Very well." Miss Darcy took off her gloves. "Would you like another harp lesson to pass the time before dinner?"

Caroline agreed and showed off the scales which she had been practicing the day before. "That is most impressive," Georgiana said, raising an eyebrow. "Another lesson or two and perhaps you will be able to accompany me on the pianoforte. Perhaps we will be able to create a few pretty harmonies together. What say you, Miss Bingley?"

The smirk left Caroline in no doubt that Georgiana intended two entirely different meanings by the phrase, which caused her fingers to be clumsy over the next few notes. Still smirking, Georgiana approached and bent over, her mouth close to Caroline's ear.

"In order to play an instrument well," she murmured, sending shivers down Caroline's spine, "one must listen to one's own desires, as well as the instrument's desires, and find a way to bring them together."

"Is that so?" Caroline managed, proud of how calm her voice sounded despite her heart racing. She risked a glance downwards at Georgiana's bosom and immediately wished she hadn't. All memory of what she was supposed to be playing flew out of her head. "You shall have to teach me all that you know."

"I would be delighted to have such an eager pupil." Instead of moving away, Georgiana lowered her head and nipped at the sensitive spot on Caroline's neck again, leaving her shaking and helpless. "There," she murmured, smiling wickedly as she retreated a few inches, just enough for Caroline to read the hunger written on the lines of her face. "That is revenge for those hours which you spent torturing me with that which you knew I ought not allow myself to indulge in."

"Consider me thoroughly revenged, in that case. If you felt then even half of what I feel right now, then it is a wonder you did not give in much sooner." Caroline sighed, leaning her head against Georgiana's shoulder. "You quite undo me, Miss Darcy."

"Well, I . . ." Georgiana swallowed, then dropped a kiss against Caroline's cheek. "That is good, for I quite like you undone, Miss Bingley."

"Perhaps we could"—Caroline turned her head, pressing a kiss to the soft skin within reach, hearing Georgiana's breath hitch in a most interesting way—"see what else may be . . . unbuttoned?"

Whatever Miss Darcy might have said in reply was lost to the sound of footsteps in the hallway. They sprang apart just as Mrs Reynolds entered with a tea tray, and Caroline did her best to look angelic, like someone who was succeeding at playing a harp, not one who was doing her utmost to seduce—and being seduced by—the mistress of the house. Given the strange glance the housekeeper gave her, she probably wasn't succeeding at doing either. They were not doing a very good job of pretending to be merely friends, but surely, Mrs Reynolds would not interpret anything she saw as untoward. After all, who would think that two proper young ladies, both well brought up, each having status and fortune, would do such a thing with each other?

No, Caroline decided, as Georgiana poured the tea and Mrs Reynolds left the room without a backwards glance, *our new affair is surely cloaked beyond all possible recognition.*

Chapter Twenty-Two

My dear Louisa,

Thank you for your kind offer—of course I shall join you in London later, though I expect after such a long trip with Mother, you shall be glad to spend a little time in your glorious, finished abode with your dear William. I am sure he has been missing you dreadfully.

How is Mother faring? Does she plan to return to Hadley Hall immediately or does she feel herself well enough to visit London for a time? The answer, of course, will influence my plans for the next few weeks.

Your devoted sister,
Caroline

Caroline scowled down at the letter; what she had written was true enough, though Louisa would not be able to detect her true meaning. Caroline had no intention of going back to Hadley Hall any time soon, and particularly not if her mother was there alone. She would rather spend the next three years in Louisa's London home, listening to William Hurst gamble and belch and rant at length about the depth and complexity of his cook's ragout, which wasn't even particularly good. Miss Darcy had been gone for most of the morning and afternoon, though this time, she had assured Caroline that it was merely her correspondence which kept her. If Caroline had doubts about the veracity of such a claim, the promise of later kisses had soon erased them.

They enjoyed a long walk around the garden in the late-afternoon sunshine, and after an excellent dinner of roast pheasant and boiled potatoes, followed by another posset—this time, a raspberry one which was as tart as it was smooth—Caroline spent a pleasant evening listening to Georgiana alternating between playing the pianoforte and wandering about the room, reciting the history of this or that ancestor with all the studied airs of a history teacher four times her age. Caroline, sides still aching from laughter, followed Georgiana to the door of her bedchamber in the hope of a goodnight kiss. She did not receive one, though Georgiana permitted an embrace which lasted for long enough to raise Caroline's hopes again.

"We should say goodnight," Miss Darcy said, though she made no move to release Caroline from her embrace.

Caroline pulled back just far enough to meet her gaze. Georgiana had once told her that she spent far too much time looking outward at everyone else and no time at all looking inward, but Caroline rather thought the same could be said of Georgiana. "I suggest we stop worrying about what we should do and pay more attention to what feels right. We are not in society now, Georgie. Did you not tell me that I may do as I wish when there are no eyes to judge?"

"One of us has to be the voice of reason here."

"And you have decided to take up that mantle, have you?" Caroline moved closer, watching Georgiana's throat bob as she swallowed. Close enough to see the pulse in her neck fluttering. "Why, if that's really the case . . ." She reached up, pressing her lips to the patch of skin directly under Georgiana's ear. "Then surely you can command yourself not to be affected by this."

A sharp intake of breath was her reward. "Who says I am?"

"The trouble with that statement, Miss Darcy," she murmured, "is that I do not believe you in the slightest."

"I don't care what you believe." The tone was brazen, the words careless, but there was something underneath that Caroline couldn't quite comprehend. She felt as if she were standing on a frozen lake and had, in the distance, heard a crack. Was it the ice or merely a distant twig snapping? Was she safe—or about to plunge to a frozen death?

Such dramatics. It was only kissing, after all.

Caroline pressed her lips to warm skin, tasting salt. "And yet, you're still allowing me to do this."

Georgiana hesitated as if torn, but acquiesced to tip her head back, allowing Caroline full access to the column of her throat. Caroline left a slow trail of kisses from left to right, then dipped down and pressed her tongue against Georgiana's pulse point, feeling the rapid beat. Her own heart rate had sped up too, though blood was thundering through other, lower parts of her with a steady, aching insistence. "Why are you so stubborn, Miss Darcy?" she murmured.

"Why are you so persistent, Miss Bingley?"

Caroline chuckled. "We are rather a well-made pair, are we not?" She pressed another kiss to Georgiana's soft cheek. "What if we did not say goodnight yet?"

Georgiana cocked her head, a look of consideration on her face, but the sound of soft voices from downstairs made them both freeze; the housemaids, probably, exchanging some vital details about the next morning's work. Caroline had expected her friend to flinch away entirely, fearing being seen or heard by the servants, but instead, Georgiana grasped Caroline's wrist and pulled her inside, shutting the door behind them and pushing Caroline against it with enough force to send a wave of desire roiling through her body. In an instant, they were kissing, and to Caroline's unfettered delight, Georgiana's hands began to roam as if Miss Darcy were mapping out her body for later study. The thought excited Caroline and she did her best to mimic the movements, squeezing and caressing until Georgiana's breath came hot and fast against her mouth.

"I was hoping you would bed me tonight, Georgie," she murmured.

Georgiana's fingers tightened hard enough to bruise on Caroline's hips, though when she next spoke, her voice was relatively calm. "You are too keen. A lady does not rush so."

A lady probably does not often feel as I feel right now, Caroline thought, biting back a growl of frustration, and cast about for a good enough reason to insist upon the matter. "Well, it is possible that I may meet a suitable gentleman any day now who will prove to be a good match for me. And I do not believe I could conduct such an affair if affianced, for that would be a discredit both to myself and my husband-to-be. Therefore it seems to me only sensible that you and I should make haste in the time that we have together."

"Ah." Georgiana was silent for long enough to make Caroline worry. "You make an excellent point." Without warning, she dipped her head and kissed Caroline soundly again, relieving her of any anxiety. "I ought not to take you, though," she added, when finally they broke apart. "For that is an act reserved for the marriage bed, as you no doubt know. But we may perform other . . . activities."

"Other activities?" she repeated, feeling dazed. She rather liked the sound of that. And was it merely coincidence that Georgiana seemed to be generally spurred on by the mention of losing Caroline to a suitor? No doubt this was simply her competitive nature emerging once more, albeit in a slightly unusual vein. "And what might those entail?"

"Have you really never—"

"No. Never. Not like this." She moved forward, walking Georgiana back to the bed, until Miss Darcy fell backwards on it with a soft thump. "Show me what to do."

"Caroline—"

"This I will not beg for, Miss Darcy," she said firmly. "I want you, and I will not apologise for it. You said you wanted me too, did you not?"

Georgiana grabbed her hand, tugging her down onto the bed. Caroline had never before been on a bed with someone whom she intended to touch or be touched by. The brief affair with the handsome neighbour in her youth had been all stolen kisses in the garden and one brief caress of her bosom, though none of it had ever made her feel breathless and desperate. At the time, she had assumed her lack of reaction to his more amorous advances was simply a product of her excellent upbringing, which had ensured that she was a modest young lady armed with every weapon of social graces and attributes needed to survive in society. However, the way she felt right now was so far from modest that it fairly took her breath away. Truly, she had no idea what to expect or what was expected of her. A lesser woman might have quailed in the face of a new venture, but dammit, she was Caroline bloody Bingley. If any old fool could make love—and certainly fools had been doing it since time immemorial—then she could surely learn how to as well.

And do it far better besides.

She pressed Georgiana back on the bed, hovering over her. "If it is your first time, then you ought to go first," Miss Darcy protested, her eyes widening in surprise.

"Never mind what ought to be done. Show me. I want to know how to do everything that you like."

"Give me your hand, then," Georgiana muttered. Her blush had brightened, making her dark eyes seem starry in the candlelight. She guided Caroline's hand down and then up, under her dress until it rested at the apex of her naked thighs. Georgiana's breath hitched as Caroline's fingers curled experimentally, the sensation of softness and dampness belonging to another person entirely new to her. "Here. Press a little and— Oh."

She stroked experimentally. "Like this?"

"Yes." Miss Darcy's gasp sent a thrill through Caroline's entire body. "Just like that."

Caroline had not Georgiana's natural grace on the pianoforte, but she could almost match her friend for technical proficiency. Her music teacher had often told her that she played very well, though she lacked heart. She had been tempted to respond that she played without thought too, since she was not much interested in the instrument, but such a retort would only have earned her a disapproving look and another half hour of dreary scales as punishment.

She had never been quite so glad about those lessons as she was right now.

"Faster," Georgiana breathed. "I mean, if you are sure. You do not have to do anything you do not feel ready—"

Her words were cut off by a moan as Caroline found what she was looking for and began to test out a few scales of her own, though these could never be called dreary. In fact, had the pianoforte made noises even half so lovely as the ones Miss Darcy was making right now, Caroline was in no doubt that she would have become a world-class musician.

"A little more pressure," Georgiana instructed, fingers tightening on Caroline's upper arms. "Oh, please, a little more." She buried her face in Caroline's shoulder, stifling another moan. Her body tensed and relaxed, flexing against the bed as need overtook her. Caroline nudged her face up for another kiss, swallowing the sound of Georgiana's pleasure. Finally, Miss Darcy stiffened underneath her, the motion followed by a muffled exclamation of pleasure and a whimper that sounded very much like Caroline's name. "Stop, stop," said she, halting the movement of Caroline's hand, which had continued stroking without any orders to cease. "I cannot bear any more pleasure."

Caroline felt half-mad with need, but she waited patiently while Georgiana blinked up at her. "My turn," Miss Darcy whispered, grinning wickedly, and for the next few minutes Caroline was lost in a blaze of passion she hadn't known herself capable of feeling. The strange dreams she'd had of Georgiana did not even remotely compare to reality; the rough drag of fingers over sensitive flesh, driving her onwards to the peak of ecstasy. When they were finished, Georgiana rolled away and lay on her back for a moment, panting. Caroline could hardly catch her own breath, so overcome was she by the waves of pleasure which rolled through her like a great, sweeping tide. It had been exuberant. It had been exciting. It had been . . .

Utterly wonderful.

Her delight was short-lived, however, as within a few moments Georgiana sat up and smoothed down her skirt, covering that which Caroline had hardly even had a chance to examine. She felt a stab of disappointment. She'd rather hoped for a few more kisses, but perhaps this was the usual way of things after one made love. Did not a man and woman usually have separate bedchambers, after all? Presumably it was the natural course of things to come together and then split apart. But if that was so, why did it make her feel so hollow? And why, despite having felt so close to Georgiana a moment before, did she still want to reach for her even now that she was satiated?

"Is it usual to feel a little strange afterwards?" she asked.

Strange was not the right word, though—*nostalgic*, perhaps? Though, how could one feel nostalgia for something one had never had in the first place?

Georgiana hesitated. "Sometimes. Do not worry, though," she added, busying herself with her dress. "I would never come between you and your goal. This changes nothing about our agreement."

Caroline, whose heart was slowing to a canter rather than a full-fledged gallop, sat up and smoothed her own dress down. "Oh. I hadn't thought it would."

In truth, she hadn't been thinking about the Great Endeavour at all. How could she, when Georgiana had been invading every inch of her body?

"Good," Miss Darcy said, her tone cool. She rose, holding out a hand to help Caroline up. "Then we are in agreement."

If that were really true, then why did it feel so much like an argument? Caroline accepted the offered hand, her legs still shaky from her earlier exertions, and made her way to the door. "Goodnight, Georgie," she said, though her companion did not turn to look at her and muttered only a quiet farewell of her own as Caroline left the room.

Caroline padded barefoot along the hallway to her own chamber, closing the door behind her with a quiet click. By the time she made it as far as the bed, the tears sliding down her cheeks were coming thick and fast enough to thoroughly wet the pillow. She wasn't even sure precisely why she was crying, though that made no difference; the hollow longing inside her ached and beckoned for a kind of satisfaction that could never come. She had given her body to Georgiana, who had taken it willingly enough, but she'd wanted to give even more than that, if such a thing were possible.

It wasn't, though.

Was it?

Chapter Twenty-Three

Dear Miss Bingley,

I realise we met only once, but Laurel and I had such a wonderful time at the party by the lake last week. We wondered if you and Miss Darcy would like to come to tea with us at Ruddock House? Perhaps Wednesday next? I have enclosed a map with our house clearly marked in case your carriage driver does not know the way, though Laurel says that all carriage drivers are born with maps of England engraved on the inside of their eyelids. I do hope not, for that sounds rather painful.

~~*Yours affectionately*~~
~~*Yours sincerely*~~
Yours, in hope,
Miss Emily Chester

The weather, which had turned grey and foreboding, succumbed to a full-fledged thunderstorm in the late morning and early afternoon. It would have been a perfect day to spend curled up together in front of a roaring fire, in Caroline's opinion, had it not been for the sting of hurt she still felt about the abrupt way in which Georgiana had sought to immediately distance herself the night before, or the way Miss Darcy had contrived to employ herself by such means that she had managed to evade Caroline for most of the day.

She finally cornered Georgiana in the drawing room. "Good grief, Georgie, will you at least do me the justice of telling me why you are avoiding me?"

"How can I possibly be avoiding you," said she, scribbling on a piece of parchment with an air of supreme industriousness, "when you follow me into every room? Avoidance suggests that I have in fact managed to shake off your pursuit, which I have yet failed to do, despite my best efforts."

Caroline stepped closer. "Forgive me for my ignorance, but I rather thought"—she lowered her voice—"what with it being my first time last night, that perhaps you might be a little kinder to me afterwards."

Georgiana looked up. For the first time, Caroline registered the red rims of Miss Darcy's eyes and the purple shadows underneath them. Evidently she hadn't been the only one who'd endured a sleepless night. Georgiana threw down the quill. "Yes, very well. You have me there. A churlish mood overcame me, but you did not deserve it directed at you." She rose, though she did not make any attempt to approach. "I had hardly thought you the sort of woman to require sweet nothings and coddling," she muttered.

"I did not say I required anything of the sort." Caroline took a step back, further stung by Georgiana's sour tone. "But I thought . . ." She hesitated. She did not know what she had thought, only that she had expected something a little softer. "Surely, Wickham did not leave so abruptly."

As soon as the words were out, she regretted them. She

really did not want to know what George Wickham had done or not done in the privacy of Georgiana's bedchamber.

A muscle jumped in Georgiana's jaw. "In fact, he did leave, after the very few times we—" She broke off, then cleared her throat. "He was afraid we would be caught by my brother, which I thought a very sensible approach. You would do well to emulate that good sense."

"I have an overabundance of good sense," Caroline retorted. "I just choose not to apply it when it comes to you, for some reason. And since your brother is about one hundred and fifty miles away at present, he can provide no excuse unless he has powers unknown to me." She straightened, pulling back her shoulders with more confidence than she felt. "I thought you enjoyed yourself last night. I know I did. In fact, I know you did, too."

"Infernal woman," Georgiana said, though her words now lacked bite and her lips twitched in unmistakable amusement. She advanced a step, then another, bringing her within kissing distance. "You give me no peace."

Relief washed over Caroline. "Had you really wished for peace, Miss Darcy, then I doubt you would have embarked on an affair with me."

"Oh, you have no idea how true that is," Georgiana breathed, her eyes brightened by passion. She leaned closer, then stopped only an inch away, waiting for a response. "Kiss me, then, and let us make up."

"No. I meant what I said," Caroline said, despite wanting nothing more than to press against Georgiana's mouth and forget the world entirely. "You hurt my feelings last night, and I cannot kiss you until we address the matter."

"Oh. I hadn't realised you—" Miss Darcy drew back, her dark eyes searching Caroline's own. "In what way? Why didn't you say so at the time?"

"You dismissed me so quickly. Was I repugnant to you after you achieved your satisfaction?"

"Heavens, no! I—" Georgiana swallowed, then raised a shaky hand to touch Caroline's cheek. "I am sorry, Caroline. Forgive me. I never meant to hurt you. I suppose I simply . . ." She shrugged, as if helplessly adrift. "Feelings which I thought I had long suppressed returned with alacrity. I suppose I felt rather exposed. You do remember that the last affair I had ended in betrayal?"

"I do." Caroline lifted her hand and placed it over Georgiana's, feeling it trembling under her touch. "I may not be the best version of myself yet, but I can promise you this—there is no version of me who would ever betray you."

"Easy to say. Far harder to do."

"I mean it." Caroline drew in a ragged breath as she tugged Georgiana closer. "I care for you."

"I care for you, too."

"Then kiss me, Georgie," she whispered.

Her heart pounded as Georgiana leaned forward. Why did this feel so different, somehow? Perhaps it was because the other times they'd been throwing themselves at each other, it had been during a fit of pique or lust or both. There was something thrilling about the idea that Georgiana was kissing her back because she wanted to, not because she was irritated or lustful or some other complicated emotion that Caroline had yet to figure out. This felt different. Intentional.

Possibly even romantic, one might say.

She gave herself a little shake. Surely, she wasn't worrying about kissing a woman with whom she'd already been acquainted in the biblical sense? Their lips met softly, sweetly, and oh, this was pleasure of a new kind entirely.

To Caroline's great surprise, when they parted, Georgiana was blushing. "Well, that was . . ."

"Lovely? Skillful? The best kiss you've ever had, I'm sure." Slipping her old arrogance on like a well-worn suit of armour gave her a modicum of protection against the strange new feelings swimming inside her chest.

"I am sure I could not possibly say it was the best I have ever had." Miss Darcy's lips twitched. "Perhaps you ought to keep trying. With practice, I am sure you will improve."

Gasping with indignation, Caroline leaned up and dragged Georgiana's mouth against her own. This was no soft, tender kiss, but a searing blaze which roared from the crown of her head all the way to her bare soles. She was quite certain she must be scorching the beautiful floor underfoot, and equally certain that the entire Pemberley estate could burn down without either of them noticing.

"Well, that was . . ." Georgiana repeated, looking as dazed as Caroline felt.

"Say 'better' at your own peril, Miss Darcy," she warned.

A slow smile crept across Georgiana's face, as inexorable as a sunrise. "I wouldn't dream of it, Miss Bingley."

"I am not Wickham, you know," Caroline said, though it hardly needed saying at all. She did not miss Georgiana's flinch. "We need not guide our affair along those lines, particularly if it did not please us to do so. I needn't have gone last night. If you'd wanted me to, I would have stayed longer."

Georgiana made no response to this but instead gestured at the letter Caroline was holding. "From Charles, I assume?"

"In fact, it is from Miss Emily Chester, inviting us both to tea with her and her sister at their home on Wednesday. Would you like to accompany me?"

Georgiana beamed down at her. "I would be delighted to."

"Excellent. I shall write back to her immediately, accepting the invitation, and then I have a suggestion for you."

"Forgive me if I am wary of your suggestions these days," Georgiana teased.

"This one you shall like very well." Caroline paused for suitable dramatic effect. "I propose we take a cake to Miss Merryhill."

Georgiana blinked several times, as if the idea required multiple mental repetitions in order to fully comprehend it. "*You* want to take a cake to Miss Merryhill," she echoed. "You want to take a *cake* to Miss Merryhill? You want to take a cake to *Miss*—"

"Miss Merryhill, yes," Caroline interrupted. "Good grief, Georgie, the sentence remains the same no matter which word you stress. It was my understanding that the lady likes cake and would appreciate such a present. Is my understanding wrong?"

"I am sure that she would." Georgiana blinked again. "But . . . why?"

"Are you not curious about what has happened since the ball?"

"I would assume very little. It has only been three days."

"But Mr Acton was so affected by the sight of his lady dancing with another man that he left the ball early. Do you think him such a coward that it has taken him a full three days to pluck up the courage to propose? Surely a confession of love, however profound, can only take a minute or so."

"A full minute, eh? How extravagant." Georgiana looked amused. "This cake . . . Do you wish to bake it also?"

"Heavens, no!" Caroline exclaimed. "I thought Miss Merryhill was your friend. One tends not to want one's friends poisoned with the creations of amateurs. Let us leave the intricacies of baking to your resident expert."

An hour later, armed with a carrot cake which Mrs Addlecombe had produced as if by magic, Caroline and Georgiana climbed into the carriage. The rain was finally beginning to taper off, and pattered against the windows with long, slanted drops which obscured the view outside. Georgiana's fingers brushed Caroline's own, making her shiver. She stole a quick kiss before they turned onto the road, knowing that it might be a while until she could safely do so again.

At Miss Merryhill's house, Georgiana was forced to knock twice before the door opened, irritating Caroline, who could never abide having rain-soaked hair. However, when Miss Merryhill finally opened the door, Caroline could not help uttering a gasp of alarm. The woman's eyes were red-rimmed, her cheeks streaked with tears, and she was clutching not one but three sodden handkerchiefs.

"Why, Miss Merryhill," Georgiana said, sounding just as alarmed, "what on earth has happened? Are you well? Is Mrs Wimple—"

"Come in," she cried, urging them into the parlour. "Come in and I shall tell you all the dreadful news." She slumped into a chair and pressed the clump of damp handkerchiefs to her face again. "Mr Acton has gone to London, and I do not know when he will be back."

"London?" Georgiana repeated. "Whatever for?"

"To make his fortune, he said."

The words landed like a punch in Caroline's gut. "Oh, Miss Merryhill," she gasped. "I am dreadfully sorry."

The lady stared at her blankly. "What have you to be sorry for, Miss Bingley?"

Even if Georgiana had not been in the room, Caroline could not—would not—have lied about her part in the mess. Kindness did not stretch so far as to cover up the truth. "I am afraid you will be angry with me," she said, bracing herself, "and you have every right to be, for I meddled in something which did not concern me. I thought if Mr Acton was jealous, he might overcome whatever was holding him back and propose to you. Mr Stan . . . er . . . the gentleman I was dancing with went along with my scheme, but the idea was mine alone."

"I thought as much," Miss Merryhill said, and blew her nose. "But I am not angry with you, Miss Bingley. Mr Acton's decisions are no fault of yours. You meant only to help him along, I am sure."

Caroline hesitated. She had meant well, but that did not excuse the consequences of her behaviour. Her stomach roiled with greasy guilt, making her feel nauseous. "That does not signify. I am sorry, in any case. And Mr Acton loves you, I am certain of it."

"If he loved me, he would have married me," Miss Merryhill said. "And since he has not, we can only reason that he does not." She blew her nose again, and Georgiana fished a dry handkerchief out of her own reticule and passed it over. "Too long have I hoped for something which shall never happen."

"Is it possible," Georgiana said slowly, "that he has gone

away to make his fortune so that he may marry? That he intends to return to—"

Miss Merryhill shook her head. "He made no promises, Miss Darcy. And I shall not hold him to words unsaid."

"But you love him, do you not?" Caroline persisted.

"Love must exist on both sides," the lady said, dabbing at a fresh stream of tears. "One cannot live in hope and anguish for so many years. My folly is my own. I did not curb my feelings when I ought to, and they bloomed too wild to garden easily." She caught Caroline's gaze and held it. "This is no fault of yours, Miss Bingley. Please, do not worry."

"Despite Miss Merryhill's protests, I maintain I have made quite a mess here, Georgie," Caroline said, as they climbed into the carriage an hour later. "Oh Lord, your poor friend. Her poor heart is quite broken."

"You couldn't have known," Georgiana protested. "Mr Acton had his choice and made it. Perhaps this is for the best."

"No," she said, determination rising. "It is not right, but I will make it so. I shall speak to Lord Ashbrook myself."

"Ashbrook?" Georgiana frowned. "What does he have to do with this?"

"Do not you recall that the viscount commissioned Mr Acton?" Caroline reminded her. "He must be persuaded to hire Mr Acton again, perhaps even to create a range of paintings here in Derbyshire, so that the man may make his fortune and marry Miss Merryhill."

"Your powers of persuasion are considerable, I admit, but do you think them up to such a task?"

"Mr Acton's talent shall do most of the work for me, and whatever gap remains, my charms must fill. I shall do whatever it takes. I simply must make the situation right." She paused, aware that Georgiana was staring at her. "What?"

"Nothing. I simply . . ." Miss Darcy swallowed. "You would go to such effort?"

"It is my duty to smooth over a situation I caused, of course," Caroline said. "Surely, you think better of me than to assume I would swan away from such a muddle with nary a glance backwards? Besides, I find that I rather like Miss Merryhill. She may not have wealth or status, but you were right: She is extremely kind, even in the face of personal calamity. She might have blamed me—and had every right to do so—yet she did not. Not everyone has such strength of character. It is to be commended."

Though they were still a minute or two from Pemberley, Georgiana leaned over and grasped Caroline's face in both hands. The kiss was briefer than Caroline would have liked, but it was more tender than any they had shared thus far. "I am not saying I did not care for you before," Miss Darcy whispered, "but I must admit, I'm rather fond of this new, kinder Miss Bingley."

Warmth bloomed in Caroline's chest. Could that possibly be pride, albeit pride of a different sort than she was used to? These new feelings were strange, and came by stranger means, but she could certainly get used to them.

"And I much prefer the new, honest Miss Darcy." She smiled back at her. "Let us both continue down our roads of betterment and improve the situations of those around us in the meantime."

Chapter Twenty-Four

Dear Self,

Despite our evening's strenuous activities—and my, they were strenuous indeed—I could not help lying awake last night thinking about poor Miss Merryhill. The lady looked so dejected, it quite touched my heart. Mr Acton did not seem the sort to drop a suit easily, so I can only assume that he is determined to return once he has made his fortune. Yet without friends from the appropriate circles in London, what success can he hope to have? That might take him years, and he promised nothing to Miss Merryhill in the meantime.

My own plan is far more direct; the product of a superior mind, wonderfully focused. Really, I ought to have been in the military.

Yours, and mine,
Caroline Bingley

On Wednesday, they travelled to Ruddock House. Though the journey took an hour and a half, weaving through small villages and towns so often that they could not reasonably indulge in the kind of embraces which had become so common to them of late, Caroline was both surprised and delighted when Georgiana took her hand, entwined the fingers with her own, and hid them artfully under the folds of their skirts. She found herself disappointed when the carriage rolled to a stop outside a large house, though she was cheered almost immediately by the bright, beaming smiles of the Miss Chesters.

After the necessary greetings and pleasantries had been exchanged, they were led into the parlour, where they had tea and cake pressed upon them in such quantities and varieties that even Caroline struggled to taste them all. Each deserved praise, though, and she extracted promises from both ladies that her effusive compliments would be passed on to their cook. The room itself was a pretty one, with blue floral wallpaper, though Caroline neither knew nor cared enough about flowers to recognise what kind they were. The furniture, though perhaps not created with particular consideration of beauty, was of a good sort, well-made and stout. These internal judgements made her realise how far she had come since her first "test" at Miss Merryhill's, and a pang of shame curled in her stomach. She had been unduly harsh on that lady and her house, neither of whom had earned nor deserved her harsh remarks.

Despite having thought of little else—Georgiana and her distracting kisses aside—Caroline was no closer to working out how she might manage a meeting with Viscount Ashbrook. Nor had she decided, in the event that she did meet him, what she might do or say to bring about the necessary outcome. It was all rather complicated. Her former self might have thrown her hands up and declared it impossible, but she had come a long way since dropping to her knees in Georgiana's bedchamber that first night and pleading for help. She blushed, thinking of the other times she'd been in that room since, although, generally, those had involved her being on her back, and once, rather memorably, on her—

"How have you fared since we saw you last?" Miss Laurel inquired, jolting Caroline from her wicked thoughts. "We had heard that Mr Radcliffe took you both for luncheon. Was it a pleasant outing?"

The nightmare inn had left a considerable imprint on Caroline, much more so than the man himself, and she took pains to detail every single horror of the place in such amusing detail that, by the end of her story, both Miss Chesters had dissolved into fits of helpless laughter.

"And what of the Mr Radcliffe?" Miss Laurel asked, wiping away tears of mirth. "Did not you desire to become his next prey?"

"I confess it has never been my wish to be hunted. I rather fancy myself more of a hunter." Caroline caught Georgiana smiling into her cup and had to bite back a grin of her own. Miss Emily Chester, who was rather sharper than her sister, looked from one to the other, a small frown creasing her forehead. "In any case," Caroline said, eager to divert attention lest her affections should become too obvious, "he is certainly not the kind of gentleman I find agreeable company. Nor do I think his sister very civil."

"We have heard as much from others," Miss Emily declared, though she hesitated when Miss Laurel shot her a reproachful glance. "I was not about to say who told us so," she muttered. "Only that we had heard similar reports."

"That is true enough," Miss Laurel conceded. "But perhaps we might talk of more cheerful subjects? Several of our horses have recently foaled. Our guests might like to visit them, for they are such sweet little creatures. One was even sired by my own Snowfall."

"You have your own horse?" Georgiana exclaimed. "What breed is he? How many hands? When and where do you ride him? May I—" She stopped, looking slightly ashamed of her excitement.

"Miss Darcy is an excellent horsewoman," Caroline supplied, sending a supportive glance to the lady in question and receiving a shy, appreciative smile in response. "I have yet to meet a horse who did not adore her on sight."

"I should be delighted to introduce you!" Miss Laurel said, rising and taking Georgiana's arm, and the two of them went off in high spirits.

Caroline followed more slowly with Miss Emily, who did not look particularly thrilled about the prospect of visiting the horses. "What about you, Miss Emily? Do you enjoy riding as your sister does?"

The girl shrugged. "I much prefer my own feet on the ground, truth be told. Even if they are forever finding something to trip over."

"Then you and I are very much in agreement."

"Of course, I can ride," the girl added. "Our parents employed a riding master to teach us at the same time, for there are only four years between Laurel and me. Though perhaps they did not fully take into consideration how frightening a horse might seem from a short seven-year-old's perspective, as opposed to a much taller eleven-year-old."

Caroline could well imagine. "What other interests have you?"

"Books, chiefly. I much prefer them to people." Miss Emily's glance flickered to her, concern evident on her face. "Present company excepted, of course. I did not invite you all the way out here merely to insult you."

"Do not worry," Caroline reassured her. "I shall not take any offense, although I cannot understand the love of books that so many seem to have these days. They rather exhaust me. And, if I may also speak plainly, I find your honesty refreshing."

The girl's face lit up with relief. "Really?"

"Oh, certainly. In my opinion, it would be a much easier world to navigate if we could all say whatever we were thinking."

"I do so struggle to know what ought to be said and what one ought to keep to one's self," Miss Emily confessed. "Laurel has tried her best to school me, but I know she fears that I might easily say the wrong thing to the wrong person. Society is so difficult to traverse, and our parents do not like to mix in company very often. They spend most of the year in seclusion at a house in the deepest part of the country and only emerge to attend such balls and events as is required for people of their rank and status. Mama and Papa do not care very much about my . . . tendencies, but it gives my sister so much anxiety that I feel compelled to curb them as much as possible."

"If you had been born a man, it would have mattered far less." Caroline sighed. "Men may say what they like most of the time, and I have heard many a fine gentleman make some silly excuse or other for his rude friend. Not that I think you rude," she added hastily, seeing Miss Chester's expression turn crestfallen.

"Do you think so? Perhaps I ought to have been born a man." She considered this. "No, I shouldn't have liked it. I like dresses too much—and cigars and whisky far too little."

Caroline laughed.

"And so . . . would it be . . ." Miss Chester bit her lip. "No, that seems like it is one of those things I ought never to question."

Curiosity flickered. "Go on. I will not tell your sister, whatever you may ask."

Miss Chester inched towards her, lowering her voice. She looked so genuinely worried that Caroline felt a twinge of sympathy. "You and Miss Darcy are very good friends, are you not?"

Apprehension spiked in Caroline's gut, but she did her best to keep her expression serene. "We are."

"Is it possible that you are more than friends?"

She swallowed, apprehension blooming into full-blown panic. What on earth was she to say to that?

"I do not judge such a thing," Miss Chester said hastily. "And I shall not tell anyone, even my sister. You have my word on that. I am excellent at keeping secrets, I assure you. It is only the niceties which I struggle with. And I have some particular inclinations of my own which . . ." She sighed. "What I mean to say is, I understand that one might occasionally find one's desires outside of the ton's expectations or approval."

Caroline forced herself to relax. She couldn't help glancing at Georgiana, who was talking animatedly with Miss Laurel, her hands waving around, a wide smile on her face. She looked relaxed, much more so than usual.

"We were friends before, and we are still friends now, but there are some . . . complications at present," Caroline finally admitted.

"Is it romantic?"

Georgiana's look of shy appreciation. Georgiana's kisses on her neck. Georgiana's hand holding hers in the carriage. Caroline's heart fluttered. *Is it romantic?* She'd been doing her best to try to avoid the question, but now that it was asked of her so boldly, the answer was impossible to ignore. She swallowed past the sudden lump in her throat. "A little, at least on my side. I know not what she feels."

"Fascinating. Now, is it possible to like men and women both, or is one required to choose at some point? I should like to know when, so that I have time enough to make the decision."

Caroline hid her smile in her teacup. Miss Emily was impossibly earnest; Caroline rather wished she'd had a younger sister just like her. "I believe that some prefer the opposite sex, some prefer the same sex, and some like both. That is the extent of my knowledge, however, and I do not pretend to know very much upon the subject."

"Hmm. That makes perfect sense." Miss Emily nodded. "I find you attractive, yet I also find Mr Dilphy attractive."

Caroline choked, spraying tea everywhere. Miss Emily stared at the herd of horses, completely unperturbed, as if she'd merely made some remark about the weather. "Who . . . who is Mr Dilphy?" Caroline managed.

"Oh, he is a cousin of a neighbour of ours. Laurel says he is not a suitable match for me, though, as he likes travel too much, and I do not. Also, he is forty." Miss Emily cocked her head. "But he does have a very pleasing nose."

"I see." She wiped her mouth. "And . . . and you find me attractive?"

"Of course. You are a very pretty woman, Miss Bingley. I am far from the only one who notices that, I assure you." Before Caroline could decide how to respond to this—how on earth did one accept such a brazen compliment from a mere girl of seven-and-ten?—Miss Emily added, "Thank you. I still have much to learn about the world, but this conversation has proved very interesting."

Relieved that it had merely been a compliment and not an overture, Caroline risked another mouthful of tea.

"Since you entrusted me with your secret," Miss Emily went on, "I ought to trust you with one of mine."

"You needn't, if you would rather not," Caroline said, patting her on the shoulder.

"I insist. It is only fair, after all." For the first time, Miss Emily blushed. "For several months, I have been corresponding with a young man. We talk of everything of importance—books, inventions, philosophy. But I shouldn't really be writing to him, nor he to me, without anyone knowing. I haven't even told my sister."

"Really?" This was far more interesting than *The Mysteries of Udolpho.* In Caroline's opinion, more books ought to be written about secret lovers exchanging passionate letters. "To whom have you been writing? Or cannot you tell me?"

"Mr Hall," Miss Emily confessed. "Teddy Hall. He is the nephew of Lord Ashbrook and was at the lake party. You may remember, for they look rather alike, although I think Teddy the fairer of the—"

"Lord Ashbrook!" Caroline exclaimed, only just remembering not to shriek the name so loud that Miss Laurel could hear. "Why, he is precisely the man I need to talk to. I have recently become acquainted with a painter, you see, and—well, it is a long story." She studied Miss Emily. "Do you think you might be able to help me? If you asked to meet Teddy, his uncle would surely attend as his chaperone. And I could chaperone you in turn."

"Oh," Miss Emily said, turning an even brighter shade of pink. "That would require me to tell my sister about what I've been doing. Writing in secret to a viscount's nephew will warrant at least a solid hour of lecturing, I am sure. Perhaps two."

Caroline followed Miss Emily's gaze. Georgiana had mounted an enormous brown horse which, to Caroline, looked far too big for her friend, but which she managed without any trouble at all, turning this way and that gracefully, with only a nudge of her knees, hands light on the reins. Miss Laurel was already astride a dappled grey stallion with a white mane and tail, looking equally as comfortable.

"I once knew a young lady," Caroline murmured, "who did not tell her brother the truth when she could have, and regretted it all her days. Secrets one may have and keep, but some are precious, and some eat away at you like rot. Be certain you know which is which, Miss Chester."

Miss Emily patted her hand kindly. "I am sure that your brother would look upon your secret well. He is known to be a gentleman of a tender nature, with great understanding of feelings."

Wait, what? Caroline gaped at her. It hadn't even occurred to her to tell Charles about her new feelings, though it made sense—of all her family, he was the most . . . the least . . . She frowned. *Well, he'll no doubt be very Charles about it. Shocked, as anyone would be, but not cruel. Never knowingly unkind.* "Would it help to know that your scolding may not be in vain? That it may in fact allow two secret lovers unknown to you, who have been unable to marry for years despite their fervent wishes, to finally be able to do so?"

"Oh," Miss Emily said, her eyes widening. "I would endure several days of scolding for such an achievement. How very romantic! I shall confess to my sister as soon as you leave, and we shall arrange the scheme as you like. I am sure that Teddy will be amenable."

"What say you to a race, Miss Darcy?" called Miss Laurel, distracting Caroline's attention.

"Oh, I do not know if that is a good idea." Georgiana, her eyes already bright with happiness, cocked her head. "I would not want to embarrass my host."

Miss Laurel scoffed, though her smile was good-natured. "You are very confident for someone on an unfamiliar horse."

"Oh, he and I understand each other quite well already, do we not?" Georgiana reached down and patted the horse's neck, receiving a soft whicker in return. "Where shall we race?"

Miss Laurel pointed east, to a field which lay like a vast, outstretched hand and only ended in a line of dark trees. Several small fences had been erected on the grass, each set apart from the others, making them look like doorways to nowhere.

"I do not think a race would be wise," Caroline called, as a slight breeze ruffled her curls. The scent of clover and fresh-cut grass which drifted over was a delightful one, but it did not alleviate any of the foreboding feeling that lay in her stomach like a stone, pressing all the previously-enjoyable cake into a tight ball of nerves. "What if one of you is hurt?"

The ladies exchanged wry looks. Miss Emily, apparently unperturbed by such wild ideas, went off inside to request more tea. Georgiana steered her horse over to Caroline and lowered her voice to a murmur. "I promise you, there is no need to worry."

"You cannot promise any such thing," Caroline protested. Up close, the horse was even more formidable—a far cry from pretty, stolid Edward, who looked more like a white barrel with legs than a real horse. Georgiana's own Swift was on the leaner, rangy side, whereas this horse was heavily-muscled and looked as if it could easily kick down a barn.

Georgiana bent down and cupped Caroline's chin, the horse's flanks blocking her action from view. "Look at me," said she, her dark eyes serious. "I promise you that I will be perfectly safe."

"Well, I . . ." Caroline began, then edged aside as the horse tried to nibble on her bonnet. "I do not trust this enormous beast."

"But you trust me, don't you?"

"With my life, certainly. I do not necessarily trust you with your own."

For a moment, a strange expression flashed across Georgiana's face, but before Caroline could decipher it, it was gone. "So?" she added, after another heartbeat had passed. "Will you let me compete?"

"Let you?" Caroline scoffed. "As if you actually would listen to me."

"I would." Georgiana's gaze turned fierce, as if trying to tell her something unspoken. "If it really frightened you, I would beg off."

"Of course it frightens me. It downright terrifies me." Caroline sighed. There was no winning here. "Yet, I would never keep you from doing something you wanted to do. A fact which you know very well."

"Thank you." Georgiana looked relieved, her fingers stroking the underside of Caroline's chin, and her smile was unexpectedly tender.

"Please be careful," Caroline murmured, though the advice was likely to go unheeded.

Georgiana clicked her tongue and the horse turned at once,

ambling back towards Laurel, who waited on Snowfall. The stallion pawed at the ground with his front hoof, evidently eager to be off. Caroline's mouth was dry, her palms clammy. She wiped them on her dress and tried to reason away her fear. It was only a short race, after all. Surely neither could come to any real harm.

"Where to?" Miss Darcy asked.

Miss Laurel pointed to the end of the field, where a large, gnarled tree stood a little separated from the rest. "What about by the old oak?"

"And what of these fences? What purpose do they serve?"

"Oh, I practice my jumps on them." Miss Laurel waved an airy hand. "But since they are only big enough for one horse at a time, they will not suit for a race."

They lined up, taking care to ensure that neither horse stood abreast of the other, and after a shout from Laurel, they were off. Georgiana's horse surged forward, his long legs giving him an initial advantage, but after only a few strides, Snowfall surpassed him. The young stallion was fleet of foot indeed, bounding over the grass as if he were descended from the swiftest of deer—the ones, presumably, who had lived long enough to outrun a wolf pack. Georgiana was not to be outdone, however, and leaned low along her horse's neck until they appeared to be one creature as she urged him onwards. The beast thundered past Snowfall in the last few moments, eking out a clear victory. Georgiana turned him in a wide circle, whooping in triumph; without stopping to congratulate Laurel on a race well run, she pushed the horse onwards at speed, back towards Caroline.

A series of gates lay in the way. Instead of swerving around them, Georgiana's horse leaped one, then another, his muscles bunching. Caroline's heart mimicked the action, choking the breath from her lungs in a strangled cry. Surely, Georgiana knew better than to attempt the final gate, which was set as high as the horse's chest. Surely, no one could make that jump without injury.

The horse's powerful haunches tensed as it gathered itself for a last great leap. As if time itself had slowed, it soared through the air and—

No, Caroline thought, instinctively reaching into the air as if she could hold Georgiana up with invisible hands as the horse—

Landed cleanly without incident, then slowed to a canter. Caroline felt a great swoop of relief, her knees weak. For a horrible moment, she had pictured the horse stumbling, Miss Darcy's joy turning to terror, a fall to the ground, a scream of pain . . .

People had died from less.

Caroline swallowed down the bitter taste of fear. Nothing had happened. Georgiana was fine. But in that moment, she had been really, truly terrified to lose her. A life without Georgiana would be no life at all, whether Caroline achieved the Great Endeavour or not.

Oh God, she thought, a terrible, helpless feeling overcoming her. *I think I might be in love for the very first time.*

Chapter Twenty-Five

In the carriage on the way home that evening, Georgiana's fingers drummed the windowsill relentlessly, her eyes bright, cheeks still flushed with excitement. "Miss Laurel has invited me back to ride with her again. Apparently, she has a friend who cannot afford to have a horse of her own, and so, stables it at Ruddock House." She caught Caroline's expression. "I shall not partake in another race, I promise you."

"Good. I fear the first one took a year or four off my life expectancy."

"I am an excellent horsewoman. You said as much."

"And you proved it today, but accidents do happen. All the skill in the world cannot overcome a moment of bad luck."

"You had better be careful." She grinned. "Or else I shall begin to think that you are worried about me, Miss Bingley."

"I simply do not look forward to being the person tasked with bringing a mangled corpse back to your brother, Miss Darcy," Caroline said. "Now, come here."

Georgiana shifted, plopping into the seat beside Caroline and laying her head on Caroline's shoulder. "You make a fair point. I would not like to face my brother's wrath." She shifted again, wriggling as if trying to find the most comfortable spot. "I rather thought you liked to watch people race," she muttered.

For a moment, Caroline couldn't think what on earth she'd meant. "Race?" she repeated. "Why, I—" Then it dawned on her. *Radcliffe, the day of the party by the lake. The rowing race.* "Do not tell me that was why you accepted the challenge?"

"No." Georgiana had gone very still. "Well, not entirely," she conceded. "I do love to ride, and I am rarely permitted to do so as freely as I did today. A young lady is especially not permitted to race other young ladies. But I suppose there might have been a tiny part of me that wanted to . . . well . . ."

"Wanted to what?" Caroline asked. "Show off? Impress me?"

Georgiana's shrug was tiny indeed, the barest motion against Caroline's own shoulder. "It's possible."

"Dear, dear." She sighed. "Well, as long as you had a good time scaring me half to death."

The chuckle against her bare skin was warm. "So, am I in danger of losing your affections to the youngest Miss Chester? She rather worships you, I think."

"You noticed that, did you?" Caroline snorted. "You may consider yourself secure enough. Though she plied me with all sorts of questions about . . . well. I blush to even repeat them."

Georgiana was silent for a moment. "She knows about you and I, then."

Dreading a fight, Caroline sought to stave it off. "I apologise. She took me by surprise and I—I ought to have denied it, I know, but she promised not to tell anyone, even her sister, and—"

"One often finds that," Georgiana interrupted, "when one

meets others who share similar natures and inclinations, that there is a tendency to keep those secrets and take them to our graves. I doubt Miss Chester will betray us."

Georgiana's hand reached for hers, found it, and squeezed it tightly. Caroline's entire body twinged with an ache, pleasant and sad all at once, which made tears prick her eyes. Holding hands didn't mean anything, really. It was merely an expression of affection and attraction, like their lovemaking. Friends often held hands, did they not?

But you feel it differently of late, the voice in her head pointed out. *And these feelings have not been friendly for quite some time now.*

She chased the thought away and reached across with her right hand to stroke Georgiana's hair. *So soft, so lovely.* Georgiana mewled, snuggling closer, and another, equally unexpected, but quite different picture came to Caroline's mind: she and Georgiana, like this, always. That was foolish, of course—they had to complete the Great Endeavour, the end result of which was to land her a worthy husband for a match of, if not love, then something close enough that it made no difference.

And if she was starting to wonder whether Georgiana was the only one who had ever—perhaps could ever—make her feel these feelings, then she had better find a way to alter that and fast. Caroline had begun this scheme with the clear intent to change, but now she was beginning to wonder whether she was changing more than she'd meant to, and worse, whether she could stop changing even if she wanted to.

She rather suspected the answer was no.

Georgiana had drifted asleep on Caroline's shoulder before they were even half the way home, for which Caroline was rather grateful. Her thoughts tumbled about her mind, leaving her restless and disquieted as she stared out at the sunset; they only slowed when Miss Darcy's fingers twitched, closing around Caroline's forearm and stroking the skin there.

"You feel cold." Georgiana yawned and sat upright. "How far away are we?"

"Perhaps fifteen minutes or so."

"Indeed?" she purred, and the tone sent a sudden jolt of desire soaring through Caroline's body. "That seems like plenty of time to get you warmed up." Her hand squeezed Caroline's thigh, sliding higher.

"I do not think I can wait until we get home," Caroline murmured.

"Oh? But what other option do we have?"

Caroline's hand slid over Georgiana's breast, cupping it, forcing her to arch her back to obtain more delicious pressure. "It is rather dark already," she pointed out, her lips pressing against Georgiana's ear. "And we are still miles from home. No one will see us."

Georgiana's head lolled back as Caroline's hand slid up and into her hair, tugging it at the roots in the way Miss Darcy particularly liked. "If discovered, our reputations—"

"It is not as if we are being followed on the road." Caroline continued to fight through the layers of fabric to reach her treasure; surely no pirate ever had so much difficulty. And ah, here was treasure indeed, driving all thoughts of brothers and husbands from her mind. Georgiana gasped as Caroline's fingers made contact, sliding up a warm thigh to find a patch of skin already slippery with excitement. "Is this infelicitous?" Caroline murmured, drawing a slow circle through soft, slick heat.

"Yes," came the strangled reply.

"Really? Ought I stop?"

"Please don't." Georgiana buried her face in Caroline's neck and tugged her closer until their bodies were flush against each other. This position made it more difficult for Caroline to move her hand. *Needs must when the devil drives*, she thought, bearing the discomfort, and stroked faster. Her reward was a delicious whimper, followed by the scrape of Georgiana's teeth against the place where her neck and shoulder joined.

"Careful," she warned. "That sort of thing will indeed be noticeable to the hordes."

"My apologies." Georgiana didn't sound sorry. She didn't look sorry either; all parted, wet lips and glittering eyes. "We shall have to be very quiet, then."

"I will be as quiet as a church mouse," she promised.

Georgiana's questing fingers squeezed Caroline's thigh again, then moved to her calf, scooping the fabric of her dress out of the way. Caroline bit her lip hard enough to hurt when Georgiana's fingers found the warm flesh of her knee and curled underneath, stroking the soft skin there. "Are church mice especially quiet? Quieter than other mice, would you say?"

"Why, certainly," Caroline managed, as Georgiana's hand skimmed over her knee and slid along her bare thigh. "One must always be quiet in a church, you see. Even a mouse must abide by the rules."

"Is that so?" Georgiana ducked her head, grasping Caroline's earlobe in her teeth. Her fingers found slick heat and dragged through it. Caroline bit back a gasp and focused on breathing rather than screaming, which was much easier said than done. "How very obedient of them."

"Indeed, the clergy are always saying so. Mice are the most tractable of all the . . . small vermin," Caroline babbled, hardly aware of what she was saying. She clutched at Georgiana's shoulders, trying to pull her closer, but before she could manage anything of note, the carriage began to rumble over familiar ground. Hurriedly she smoothed down her dress and offered her handkerchief. Instead of taking it, Georgiana cast her a coy smile and began to lick her fingers clean, one by one.

Stunned, Caroline gaped at her. *Is that a thing we can do? Why did she never mention it before?*

Cursing the proximity of Pemberley, she staggered out after Georgiana, who smoothed down her gown and sashayed into the house as if nothing untoward had ever happened to her.

The housekeeper greeted them in the great hall, but Caroline barely heard what words were exchanged. She had no idea how Georgiana could utter anything even remotely sensible right now and had to settle for smiling tightly at Mrs Reynolds before marching off in the direction of the staircase. She wasn't satiated by what had happened in the carriage. If anything, her inner fire blazed even more brightly. Georgiana followed closely behind her up the stairs, overtaking Caroline and turning left at the landing as if to make for her own room.

"And just where," Caroline murmured, "do you think you're going?"

"I was merely—"

Impish little whelp. "Don't even think about it. If you dare run, I shall pursue you to the ends of the earth."

Georgiana grinned. "Lead on, then."

Safely behind the door of Georgiana's bedchamber, where the fire crackled merrily in the grate, the first flush of lust from the carriage developed into a richer flavour, heady and wild. Caroline unbuttoned Georgiana's dress as quickly as possible, clumsy fingers shaking as she unfastened dozens of tiny catches.

She helped Georgiana out of her dress and dragged the petticoats over her head, revealing pale flesh bathed in firelight. Georgiana leaned backwards, aiming for the bed, but Caroline pulled her upright again. "In front of the fire. Your fingers are cold, and I need them warm for what I plan to do."

Georgiana obeyed, grinning wickedly. "Don't you want to take off your dress, too?" She lay down on the rug in front of the fire, hands wandering over her soft stomach and up to her considerable bosom.

"No time," Caroline said breathlessly, kneeling astride Georgiana and hiking up the hem of her dress. "Georgie, it's no good. I simply have to have you."

Georgiana's eyes widened. "What, fully? But your—" She halted, her hands stilling. Caroline knew she'd been about to say *your future husband*, and the unspoken words hung in the air between them like a bad smell.

"I need you," she growled, grabbing Georgiana's hand and pushing it under her dress until still-cool fingers brushed her entrance. "If I don't have you right this moment, I feel like I'm going to expire." It was hardly the most romantic sentiment, but she was far too afraid to voice all her new thoughts and conclusions. Half-mad with need, Caroline leaned forward and pulled Georgiana into a long kiss which she hoped spoke at least some of the feelings she did not dare to utter.

Georgiana still looked uncertain, although her body had relaxed. "You could always say it was from horse-riding," she suggested, her voice trembling slightly. "Lots of girls accidentally break that way. But, Caroline, do you understand what it means to . . . to . . ."

To give myself to you, she thought. *To give you everything you haven't even asked for.* Wordlessly, she placed her own hand over Georgiana's heart, feeling it thud rapidly against her palm. "I do."

Miss Darcy stared up at her, dark eyes wide and wanton in the firelight. Her fingers curled, uncurled, and curled again, as if Georgiana was balancing on a knife-edge and could not decide which way to fall. Then they pressed against Caroline, asking a question she was desperate to answer. Feeling relief flood her, Caroline sank down onto Georgiana's extended fingers, groaning as they slipped knuckle by knuckle into the deepest, darkest part of her body. Their gazes locked as Georgiana gasped, fully submerged inside, her eyes burning with the same desire Caroline felt.

Wincing, she rose a little as Georgiana pulled out.

"Am I hurting you?"

"No. God, no. It's just all so much." She wanted to laugh and sob and scream all at the same time. Georgiana inside her, Georgiana under her. Why did it feel like everything in the world suddenly made sense? "Please, don't stop," she begged, and bit down on her lip to keep the rest of her words from spilling out. *Oh God, don't ever stop. Use me always, just like this.*

Love me.

Georgiana set a steady rhythm, and Caroline settled into the feeling. Each thrust was an exquisite blend of pain and pleasure, building towards a different kind of finish. Georgiana's mouth was agape, her lips damp with continual licking, her own breath coming in harsh pants even though Caroline had not so much as touched her yet. The tiny part of Caroline's mind that could still formulate thoughts suggested that she ought to do something about that, and she reached down, stroking Georgiana's stomach, cupping her breasts. The thrusts became slightly more erratic as Georgiana responded to the touches, her gaze moving between Caroline's hands and her own, though the fabric of her dress covered most of what was happening.

Caroline grabbed the hem and rucked it up to give Georgiana a better view, eliciting a moan. "Shall I . . ."

"Yes," Georgiana gasped, though Caroline thought she might have agreed to anything at that moment. "Yes, please."

Caroline dragged her fingers down through soft hair, finding slippery flesh. "If . . . if you keep doing that," Georgiana said, sounding slightly strangled, "I won't be able to stop myself from finishing very quickly."

The idea excited her beyond measure. Georgiana, out of control, unable to help herself. "That's rather the point, isn't it?" she murmured, stroking Georgiana in the fashion she knew would produce the greatest pleasure, watching as her companion squirmed, revelling in the way the fingers inside her stuttered and jerked. "Wait. I'm going to—" Georgiana gasped. "Caroline, I'm going to—"

She finished with a breathy gasp, her eyes screwed shut, her fingers still thrusting into Caroline. The feeling was sublime, and Caroline's climax came moments later as she shuddered around Georgiana's fingers, grinding down onto her palm. She collapsed next to Georgiana on the rug, pulling her into a long, breathless kiss that merely stoked the blaze roaring inside her. It was immensely difficult not to whisper a confession of *amor*, though even if Caroline had felt herself free to say something of the sort, she hardly knew what that something might have been. Georgiana had made it plain from the beginning that this affair was only ever supposed to continue until Caroline had completed her Great Endeavour, and that nothing further could be offered on Miss Darcy's end, even if the scheme were not still afoot.

And you agreed to that, remember? the little voice inside her said. *You thought yourself incapable of love, did you not?*

Caroline had never been so wrong in her whole life, nor regretted any promise more. *It will all be well*, she promised herself, though she hardly knew how. *One may fall out of love as easily as one falls into it, or so I have heard.*

On that subject, the little voice was silent.

Chapter Twenty-Six

By now, they had settled into a kind of routine, though the lovemaking itself changed from night to night. Sometimes Georgiana took her time undressing Caroline, deliberating over every single button until Caroline was ready to throw all her clothes into the nearest hearth. Sometimes there seemed to be no time for any removal of clothes, only bodies propped against a nearby wall, panting and writhing in mutual ecstasy. Today had been somewhere in between, which Caroline thought she might enjoy the most—alternating between sensuous embraces and rough hands palming all the most sensitive parts of her with wild abandon.

"Closer," she gasped, wrapping her legs around Georgiana and pulling their bodies flush. "I need to feel every inch of you."

Georgiana groaned and buried her face in Caroline's shoulder, landing open-mouthed kisses on every patch of skin within reach. "You make me feel as if I am losing my mind."

You make me certain I have already lost mine, Caroline thought.

Georgiana never stayed—once they'd finished their lovemaking, they returned to one of the communal rooms downstairs or separated to their own chambers. Tonight, though,

Georgiana had looked down at her with something like longing, and the expression pierced her heart with such yearning that she could not help the words tumbling out of her mouth. "Stay," she said, when Georgiana began to slide out of bed. "Stay a little, at least."

Miss Darcy froze. "What for?"

Caroline ignored the twinge of hurt in her chest. Did she really need a reason to justify lying together once the act was over? "Could we just . . . lie together for a while? And then you may leave as you wish."

After a moment, Georgiana nodded and lay back down, though she was much stiffer than she had been only a minute before. Caroline draped an arm across her, discomfort prickling down her spine, and waited until Georgiana relaxed a little before creeping closer. Even so, Miss Darcy did not seem exactly happy about their positions. Caroline sighed. "You may leave if you hate this so much. I will not ask you to endure it again."

"I do not hate it. I simply . . . Is this not what lovers do?" Georgiana whispered. The pulse in her neck fluttered rapidly under Caroline's fingers, which was odd; surely, she could not still be out of breath from their previous endeavours.

"I thought we just did what lovers do," Caroline said, baffled.

"Never mind." Miss Darcy turned her face away.

It was clear she'd said the wrong thing—good Lord, how often that had happened of late—but she had no idea why. "You do recall, don't you," she murmured, "that I would have no way of knowing what lovers do? For you have been my only one."

Georgiana swallowed, turning back to face Caroline. The candle flame guttered behind her, casting a vivid halo around her fair hair. "I did not— I mean, sometimes I rather forget." She hesitated. "You think of me as your lover?"

Caroline blinked. *Rather a stupid question, given what we just did.* However, she'd learned by now not to say the first thing which immediately came to mind. "That depends," she said, choosing her words carefully. "What does it mean, exactly?"

"It may mean something different to every person."

That was the most evasive answer she'd ever heard. Caroline waited, studying Georgiana's face in the flickering candlelight, though Miss Darcy's expression was an unfamiliar one. Georgiana sighed. "I suppose that it might mean a person whom one takes to bed. Or perhaps a person to whom one is . . ." She trailed off, running a hand through her hair, making it look even more of a glorious mess than it already was. "Inclined?" she finished, sounding surprisingly uncertain.

"Inclined?" Caroline repeated.

"Yes. Inclined." Georgiana's lips pressed together, and she seemed unlikely to say more. In fact, she rather looked as if she were holding her breath.

"In that case, I think it fair to say that I am very inclined towards you," Caroline said, and braced for the impact her words might have. The silence stretched on and on, and just when she was beginning to think she'd made a mistake, Georgiana swooped down and caught her lips in a kiss so soft and tender that it fairly took her breath away.

Inclined, Caroline thought. *Predisposed. Perhaps even preferred.* All those words which had once seemed so silly to apply to another person were now starting to make sense.

"Will you come here, Georgie?" she asked, opening her arms. "Will you let me hold you?"

Hesitantly, Georgiana turned, sliding an arm across Caroline's stomach, bringing their bodies flush together again. They'd been skin to skin only minutes before, but this felt different. Caroline's skin tingled where Georgiana pressed against her, but the feeling left her dreamy and sleepy rather than wide awake. She wrapped her arms around the soft body, holding it to her tightly, and felt Georgiana hum with contentment. "Are you comfortable like this?"

"Very," came the quiet reply, though something in her voice suggested it wasn't a completely honest answer.

"Might we risk falling asleep together?" she murmured, aware that the edges of her consciousness had begun to blur.

"I shouldn't really, but I—" Georgiana shifted. "Are you sure you want me to stay?"

"Of course I do." The comfortable weight of sleep had already begun to descend, pulling her down into darkness. She wasn't sure why it was even a question. What could be more pleasant than holding each other after a rigorous bout of love-making? "Don't you want to?"

She was asleep before Georgiana answered.

In the morning, Caroline awoke to the shift of the mattress beneath her, the roll of it suggesting a body had recently vacated the area next to her. She blinked groggily as Georgiana gathered her clothes from the floor, evidently intending to be quiet.

"Where are you going?"

Startled, Georgiana jumped, clutching a petticoat to her naked chest. "Apologies. I was trying not to wake you."

"Must you leave?" Caroline complained. "You were so lovely and warm."

"You surely do not wish me to be bare in your bed when the maid comes in to light the fire, do you?"

It was a fair point, though when Caroline thought about it, she realised that the maid had not been coming in first thing in the morning for almost a week now. At first, she'd attributed this to the new warmth of the season, which no longer necessitated a fire to be constructed immediately, but now that she considered the idea, she wondered if there was more to it. Did Mrs Reynolds suspect the affair? And if so, had the housekeeper sought to shield their activities from the staff? Caroline frowned, thinking the matter over.

Is it possible that Mrs Reynolds disapproves so heartily that—

"Hmm?" Georgiana said, evidently expecting a response.

"Have it your way," Caroline said, spreading her limbs wide and stretching, enjoying the view as Georgiana struggled into her dress. "I shall see you at breakfast, Miss Darcy. Though I am sad to note that I shan't see quite so much of you."

"You shall be the death of me, Miss Bingley," Georgiana muttered, though she threw Caroline an amused look. With a blown kiss, Miss Darcy exited the room, leaving Caroline to drift back into the snug pink arms of sleep.

When Caroline woke that morning, she found a hastily written note pinned to her pillow, informing her that Georgiana had gone for a morning swim and might be late to breakfast.

Caroline stretched, feeling her body ache in wonderful places, then burrowed into the other side of the bed, pressing her face into the sheets which still smelled like her lover, dusky and dark as the roses Georgiana loved so much. Only a second growl of hunger from her stomach finally drove her out of bed, grumbling at the thought of having to wash and dress before she could eat. Sunshine poured through the window of the guest room when she pulled open the curtains, and she allowed herself a quiet moment of joyful reflection to bask in the warmth before turning to her ablutions. Caroline selected a rather ordinary but serviceable cream gown then dabbed a little perfume behind her ears. Her reflection in the looking glass had always shown a beautiful lady, but now she was radiant, glowing, in the full flush of gorgeous womanhood.

Unexpectedly, the sight made Caroline falter, her bright smile fading in an instant. Her affair with Miss Darcy was wonderful in so many ways, but they had agreed it was supposed to be something they did only until Caroline found a husband. Somewhere along the way, Caroline had forgotten about the purpose of the Great Endeavour. *No,* she thought, *not forgotten, for I have become a better version of myself, have I not?*

That much was demonstrably true: She had improved herself, become kinder, and shown that she was capable of love. Only . . .

It wasn't supposed to be like this.

And where did that leave her? Still unmarried, still uninterested in the suitors who had so far been presented to her, and deeply, stupidly in love with a woman whom she had promised to never ask anything more of. Even if Georgiana felt the same way—and Caroline swallowed, knowing what folly it was to hope—Miss Darcy had once been in love with a man, if one could call such a worm as George Wickham so, and therefore should be able to do so again. Georgiana could easily find a suitable match if she wished to marry and live out the rest of her life without any shadow of impropriety hanging over her.

Why, then, would she ever choose Caroline?

She would not, Caroline thought. *She made that very clear from the start.* Even if Georgiana felt something, and it was by no means certain that those feelings plumbed the same depths and dizzying heights as Caroline's own, she still had a much easier route open to her. And from what Caroline knew of Georgiana, her friend would always choose the less confrontational path in any situation. Miss Darcy was a lot of things—bold, beautiful, kind—but she would seek any escape from a situation that required honesty about her feelings; she had spent too long guarded to be comfortable opening up fully.

Caroline sighed, no longer worried about sad lung. Mrs Bingley had been strangely silent on the notion of sad heart, never alluding to it despite it being one of the most important of all organs. Yet Caroline's struggle was not merely one of adoration, but of selfishness and selflessness. Surely, it would be the ultimate selfish act to ask Georgiana to be hers and hers alone, cutting Miss Darcy off from an easy life? By even considering it, Caroline was perhaps showing how little she had actually changed.

Unfortunately, she thought, *there is only one option left to me. I must keep pretending that my Great Endeavour is still ongoing.*

No, she could not simply pretend that it was continuing; she had to actually continue it. Caroline sighed again, putting her head in her hands. The Great Endeavour had certainly changed her—far more than she had ever imagined, and in completely different ways. She had told Georgiana that she did not know what she wanted in a man, which was still true enough, but more and more, it had become clear that what she did want was Georgiana; the only person she absolutely could not have and the only person she could now ever imagine desiring. She wanted to be with Georgiana, to be the person whom Georgiana made love to each night and smiled at over the breakfast table every morning.

Selfish, selfish girl, she chided herself. *Thinking only of your own wants, as ever. Has she taught you nothing after all?*

Caroline plastered on a smile which she did not really feel, and went down to breakfast, determined to act well. She would prove that she had become a better person, that neither her efforts nor Georgiana's had been in vain.

"Good morning, Caroline," Miss Darcy said, smiling when Caroline entered the room. "A letter arrived for you."

Caroline did her best to smile back. She did not recognise the handwriting on the envelope as belonging to her family, but who else could be writing her? Opening it, she pursed her lips. *Ah.*

"Well?" said Georgiana, reaching for a plate of poached eggs and sliding two onto her plate.

"It is an invitation."

"To what?"

"The ball at Lord and Lady Percy's estate. Remember? Mr Radcliffe said he would—"

"Oh yes," Georgiana interrupted, stabbing an egg right in the yolk. "I remember very well what Mr Radcliffe said." She glared across the table. "You cannot really expect us to go."

"You know as well as I that turning down an invitation to such an illustrious ball would look odd indeed. Tongues might start wagging."

"They would wag even more if we go, for surely Mr Radcliffe will make his interest in you clear. Even clearer than he already has."

It was a fair point, but even so. Caroline set the letter aside. "Dearest, please. It's much too early in the morning for bickering."

Georgiana blinked and fell silent, blushing.

"Pass the tea," Caroline said. Georgiana made no move to do so, her blush deepening every moment. "What?" she added, baffled.

"You have never called me so before," Miss Darcy murmured.

"Oh. I suppose that is true." It had slipped out without thought, though it felt very right. She shifted in her chair, feeling rather exposed. "If you do not like it, I won't do it again."

"No, I—" The blush had spread all the way to Georgiana's collarbones. "I do like it."

"Very well, then. Dearest."

Georgiana choked back a small, undignified whimper, and swallowed hard. "Tea, you said?"

Caroline pressed her lips together and tried not to laugh. It really was impossible not to adore Georgiana. "Thank you. That would be lovely."

Unexpectedly, Georgiana rose from her chair and moved to stand next to Caroline, so close that her hip was pressed against Caroline's arm. She poured for them both, her hands trembling a little, before setting down the teapot and turning to face Caroline. Whatever Miss Darcy had been about to say died on her lips at the look on Caroline's face. For her part, Caroline could not hide her desire or her longing. Every good intention and promise she had made to herself upstairs fled her mind. The moment expanded, the air between them growing thick, as Georgiana bent down to kiss her, mouth hot and insistent against her own, and Caroline leaned up eagerly to meet her, moaning as—

The door opened.

They sprang apart hurriedly. Mrs Reynolds hesitated on the

threshold, her gaze fixed pointedly on a spot on the wall about a foot above Caroline's head. "Good morning, Miss Darcy, Miss Bingley," said she, her voice perfectly normal.

Caroline's heart, which had already been thudding rather hard, pounded until she thought it was going to erupt from her chest.

"Good morning, Mrs Reynolds," Georgiana said, her voice slightly hoarse. A long moment passed in which mistress and housekeeper stared at each other. No words were spoken, though Caroline had a feeling that an entire conversation was taking place, and she was not privy to any of its contents nor its conclusion.

"Mrs Addlecombe would like to know whether you would like her to pack another picnic today," Mrs Reynolds said. "It being such a glorious day and all."

Another silence reigned. Caroline's gaze bounced between Georgiana and Mrs Reynolds, wishing that she could comprehend whatever invisible conversation was happening in the space between them. "Mrs Addlecombe is most attentive," Georgiana said stiffly, her fingers twitching restlessly against her skirts.

"You have been taking many picnics of late," the housekeeper said. "Mrs Addlecombe merely seeks to serve the needs of yourself and Miss Bingley." The very slightest of hesitations followed before Mrs Reynolds added, "Whatever those needs might be."

"Indeed." Another silence was only broken by the sound of Georgiana's fingers drumming against her thigh. "Mrs Addlecombe is most kind to anticipate all our requirements and indulge them so."

By now, Caroline was quite sure that poor Mrs Addlecombe

was no longer actually part of the conversation. She probably ought to have left the room already, but both Georgiana and Mrs Reynolds were standing between her and the door; escape was impossible. She cast a despairing glance at her still-steaming tea, which lay untouched only tantalising inches away. No Englishwoman could be expected to broker such a delicate situation without at least one or two cups.

"Mrs Addlecombe," Mrs Reynolds said, and now her voice was softer and more hesitant, "merely worries for your health, Miss Darcy, as she has always done. Should there be anything you wish to . . . add to the menu, I am sure she would be most open to a discussion."

For the first time, Georgiana's glance flickered down to Caroline, who gave her a supportive and encouraging look, though she had no real idea what she was being supportive and encouraging about.

"Very well," Miss Darcy said. "Miss Bingley, would you give us a moment?"

Caroline grabbed her cup of tea and beat a hasty retreat to the library, where she hovered under the portrait of a bearded Darcy. "Were you all like this?" she said to the painting. "So bloody guarded?"

He did not look impressed by the question, but neither did he answer it. Caroline sipped her tea at last, though it hardly did anything to quell her panic. They had done rather well not to be discovered thus far; now that they had, she had no idea what Georgiana might do, or whether Mrs Reynolds might encourage her mistress to call the whole affair off.

She did not have long to wait. The door opened. Caroline braced herself, expecting Georgiana to burst in, to declare that everything they'd done together was merely a foolish chapter in their lives, and it was time to turn the page on it. Instead, Mrs Reynolds appeared. Trepidation rising, Caroline stared, unsure what this could possibly mean. Her surprise increased beyond measure when the housekeeper entered the room and closed the door behind her.

"Miss Bingley," she said, approaching until she stood only a foot away.

Caroline straightened. Whatever her fate, she would meet it head-on. "Mrs Reynolds."

"I have only two questions, ma'am," the housekeeper said, her mouth set in a thin line.

Oh God, what was it going to be: When had the affair started? Were they going to tell Fitzwilliam? Was Mrs Reynolds going to threaten to hunt her down with one of Mr Darcy's many guns? Were housekeepers generally well-armed and skilled with myriad weaponry?

"Yes?" she managed, clutching her teacup as if it were the world's smallest, most useless shield.

"You are aware, no doubt, that Miss Darcy's parents died some years ago, and that she was left in care of her brother. A brother who loved her very much, but who was but a young man himself, with heavy responsibilities thrust upon him."

Neither of these facts were questions, so Caroline merely nodded.

"You must also be aware, then, that Miss Darcy was alone for many months at a time. And that the servants, myself included, cared for her as if she were our own daughter." Mrs Reynolds' lips pursed into a thin line. "You should be aware, therefore, that we seek to protect her at all times, and that, having once failed to do so, it is our wish that we never fail her again."

Wickham, Caroline thought savagely, hating the man more than ever. Her hands were shaking, the teacup rattling against its saucer.

"Let me ask you now, Miss Bingley." The housekeeper's eyes were hawk-fierce, pinning Caroline with the force of a glare which rivalled Lady Catherine de Bourgh in its intensity. "If we continue to turn a blind eye to this affair, will we be failing her again?"

A complicated question, with an even more complicated answer.

"No," Caroline said, at last. "For I do not wish to fail her either. I believe our interests are aligned on that point."

She held her breath while Mrs Reynolds' eyes raked her face, the stern expression giving no clue whether Caroline had passed or failed this test.

"Very well. In that case, my second question is simply this: If you and Miss Darcy are so . . . involved"—the housekeeper nodded in the vague direction of the dining-parlour—"then why on earth cannot she win our bet about the toast? Surely she knows you better than I do."

Caroline was momentarily speechless, a thing which had happened to her only a handful of times in her entire life. She stared at Mrs Reynolds, who stared back. Before she knew what she was doing, she was clutching the housekeeper by the arm and the two of them were howling with laughter. It took long moments for Caroline to get a hold of herself, and by the time she had found a handkerchief to wipe her streaming eyes, Mrs Reynolds had lapsed back into the role of polite, inscrutable servant.

"You're good for her, ma'am, if I may say so."

Unexpectedly, Caroline's nose prickled as mirth turned to

poignancy. "Thank you. I know that she . . . that you . . ." *Good grief, why is it so hard to describe mere feelings?* "I would never knowingly hurt her. That is all."

"That is all any of us can ever ask for." Mrs Reynolds nodded. "Although, I do not think Mr Darcy will be quite as easy to convince as I."

Her words were conciliatory enough, but a lingering look in her eyes made Caroline feel like a warning shot had just been delivered across her bow. The next strike, should it come, would be grave indeed.

She had better do her best not to earn one.

Chapter Twenty-Seven

Dear Miss Bingley,

Teddy—I mean, Mr Hall—says he is very eager to help you with your scheme and asks that we visit on Tuesday around eleven on the clock, if that suits us both. It certainly suits me fine, as I have plenty to ask him about—

Never mind all that now. I shall explain on the next page. With respect to our travel arrangements, I think it best if you borrow Miss Darcy's carriage and pick me up on the way. I have studied a map closely and believe this to be the most convenient and expedient route for all parties. Do let me know whether you agree.

Yours, with great affection and admiration,
Miss Emily Chester

The rest of the letter consisted of a full three pages describing the plot of some new book Miss Emily had recently read. Hastily scribbled social niceties bookended this, as if the girl had only remembered at the end the real purpose of her letter. Caroline couldn't help but smile; she must be changing, for a few months ago, it would have seemed impossible to strike up a friendship with the Chester sisters, and now she was very much looking forward to seeing Miss Emily again. It was rather nice to have a friend with whom one could really be one's own self.

What a novel concept.

The second letter was from her mother, but she was loath to open it yet. It would surely ruin her mood, and said mood was far too good at present to be sullied. She cast an eye across the room to where Georgiana sat on the couch, her gaze sliding over the ample length of Miss Darcy's body, which was encased today in a dark blue dress, giving her the appearance of a particularly polished jewel. Caroline raised an eyebrow, her mouth already watering at the sight. "Just how long will it be before one or the other of us caves to temptation?" she mused aloud.

Georgiana raised one eyebrow in return. "Are you implying that we cannot sit in the same room together without—"

"I am not implying anything of the sort. I am stating it outright."

"Nonsense. You have your correspondence, and I have mine." Georgiana gestured to the tray beside her. "We shall be perfectly content for a while with our tea and scones, shall we not?"

For the better part of the next hour, Georgiana was right. Caroline wrote back to Miss Chester, confirming their plan, and then began a long letter to Louisa, taking care to pad it out with the kind of minutiae her sister enjoyed most, in order to make it seem like a lengthy and loving response. At least she could write honestly about how much she adored staying at Pemberley. Feeling eyes on her, Caroline looked up. "What? I can hear you thinking from over here."

Miss Darcy flinched guiltily, the tip of her quill brushing against her parted lips. "Apologies. I did not mean to stare. It was just that you looked . . . well, you were smiling rather prettily, and the sunshine was coming in through the window just so and . . ."

Caroline couldn't help smiling. "We shall make a poet of you yet, Miss Darcy."

"I doubt it. There's nothing suitably poetic about what I'm thinking. At least nothing that could be written down in a book without singeing the pages."

Caroline swallowed, holding her gaze. "I thought you had correspondence to take care of."

"I did. I mean, I do." Still, she did not move, even when Caroline rose from her seat and prowled across the room, dropping to her knees in front of the couch.

"We cannot do that here," Georgiana hissed, casting a nervous glance back over her shoulder. "What if the servants—"

"I doubt you'll last that long," Caroline said, smirking. "Not with what I have in mind to try."

Miss Darcy spluttered in outrage. "You make me sound as if I am a gun that only needs the lightest of breezes before it unloads."

"With the most wonderful trigger," Caroline murmured, hiking Georgiana's dress up past her knees.

"You are interminable, and I still have three letters to write today."

"Well, do not stop on my account," Caroline said. "Pray continue with your task, Miss Darcy."

"How can I possibly do so, when you are . . . oh, when you are doing that?"

Caroline pressed kisses along Georgiana's lower thigh, following the line of muscle just above the knee as it tensed. She really ought to insist that they spend more time in bed, so that she could devote herself to kissing Georgiana all over, every inch. And speaking of every inch, Georgiana's actions in the carriage had given her an idea.

Pressing another kiss even higher up caused Georgiana to wriggle and whimper. Fingers tightened in her hair, hard enough to hurt. Caroline bit back a groan of pleasure, humming instead as her tongue traced a line higher and higher, then began to mimic the actions her fingers normally performed. "Oh, Caroline—you can't possibly—" Georgiana writhed underneath her, tasting salty and sour and utterly delectable. "*Oh.*"

Caroline clamped onto Georgiana's thighs and clung on for dear life, determined not to stop until she'd brought her lover to the highest point of climax. The moment came sooner than she'd expected, and with a yelp only muffled by a hand hastily clapped over her mouth, Miss Darcy sagged back onto the couch.

"Perhaps we ought to have done this upstairs, for I long to hear you," Caroline murmured, licking her lips. "I confess I am quite enraptured with all those lovely little noises you make."

"Stop it," Georgiana said, though it was a half-hearted snap at best. "Good grief, you ruin me anew every day."

"I cannot possibly stop. Not when you look so enticing. So wanton." She licked her lips again. "So . . . delicious."

"You're a perfect beast, Miss Bingley."

She leaned in, intending to press a quick kiss to the side of Georgiana's mouth. "If I am a monster, Miss Darcy, it is because you made me one." She'd meant it as a jest, but Georgiana pulled back, her face strained.

"I did not make you anything." The silence lengthened. Georgiana was looking everywhere but at Caroline. "Did I?"

"Hold on a moment." She reached for Georgiana's hand, but it slipped out of her grasp. "I did not mean it like that."

"Then however did you mean it?"

"I only wanted to tease you, Georgie." She reached for the hand again, grimacing when Georgiana again pulled out of reach. "Do not take it to heart, please. I—"

Miss Darcy smoothed down her dress, taking her time. "Are you saying that you would never have done something like this, were it not for me?"

Caroline hesitated. "I do not know." She sighed, taking a seat on the couch next to Georgiana. "I think I must have come to the conclusion eventually. Certain things that I once dismissed outright as silly have become much more apparent of late."

"Such as?" Georgiana was still watching her, her expression wary.

"That I found the female form much more alluring than I ought, and not everyone felt that way about other women. That I, perhaps"—she rolled her shoulders, feeling the uncomfortable prickle of honesty making its way down her spine—"put other ladies down not simply to raise myself up or to degrade them, but to distance myself from feeling certain . . . strange feelings."

"Good heavens," Georgiana breathed. "Are you confessing you had a crush on Miss Elizabeth Bennet?"

"Well, I— No! I certainly wouldn't say anything of the sort!" Caroline spluttered. Her discomfort at the idea being voiced aloud was only partly relieved by Georgiana's giggle of genuine amusement.

"I hadn't thought her your type, Miss Bingley, but I see why she may have caught your eye. She is a very pretty woman, after all."

"I didn't know I had a type, Miss Darcy." Caroline inched closer. "Until now. Not too tall, fair hair, long eyelashes. A handsome set to the mouth. A certain wicked gleam in the eye. Those are the features I like best."

No reply came. Caroline's stomach sank with all the haste of a rock dropped into a pond. "A lady might think your silence an insult, Miss Darcy. Have you no response?"

"Well, you . . ." Georgiana swallowed, looked slightly panicked. "You already know you are beautiful."

That was worse than an insult, in a way. It stated what Caroline knew of herself, not whether Georgiana thought it or agreed with it. "I do know that," she agreed, trying to ignore the flutter of hurt in her chest. "But one likes to feel . . . desired."

"I have often told you that you looked handsome," Georgiana pointed out.

"Not often since we began . . ." Caroline waved her hand. *Whatever this is.* "Since we became intimately involved."

"It's not as if your looks have changed over the past few weeks," Miss Darcy muttered. The tips of her ears were bright pink.

"Oh, for heaven's sake, why are you refusing to compliment me? Any idiot swain knows how to flatter, and yet you—"

"What do you want me to say?"

Caroline's teeth ground against each other. "Would you like me to write out some suggestions? I am only asking for— You know what? Never mind. It was silly to suggest it. I do not even care what you think of me."

She rose, intending to storm off, but warm fingers caught her wrist and spun her back around. "I think you are beautiful," Georgiana said, struggling up from the couch, as if her knees were still weak. She looked terrified, though for the life of her, Caroline couldn't work out why.

"You needn't bother saying anything. Words under duress have no value."

"Excuse me, Miss Bingley. I am still reeling from the pleasure you just gave me, and it is difficult to think. Pray give me a moment to rephrase my words." Georgiana tugged on Caroline's wrist again, forcing the space between them to close. "Beauty is more to me than simply looks. It is how one talks, how one walks, how one acts. It is the perfume you bring with you when you enter a room. It is the way you immerse yourself in a painting or a thought, with a furrowed brow that crinkles in the most adorable way. It is . . ." She swallowed again. "The way you look when I kiss you. When you . . . lose yourself to me."

A blush burned Caroline's cheeks. Whatever she'd thought Georgiana might say, it hadn't been that.

Miss Darcy's eyes were bright and wide; the fear in them had not dissipated, but she continued regardless. "I appreciate your beauty in more than mere words, Caroline," she continued, her voice barely above a whisper. "I may not always say exactly what pleases you, but rest assured, I am more than aware of your full magnificence."

Caroline really was blushing now, the heat rising to the roots of her hair. She must look as red as a tomato, though Georgiana did not seem to notice or care. "*Magnificence* is quite an unusual word," she said, her voice sounding slightly strangled.

"I think it is accurate in this instance. There, am I forgiven?"

Caroline looked around, putting on a faux frown. "Do you think it possible that you left your drawing journal upstairs, Miss Darcy? Perhaps in your bedchamber?"

Georgiana glanced at the small table to her left, where the drawing journal lay in full sight. "Yes," she said, trying and failing to repress a smile. "I believe that I did. Will you assist me in finding it, Miss Bingley?"

"Of course I will. One can never be too careful over the placement of precious items."

Georgiana squeezed her hand, before letting it fall. "For once, I quite agree."

After dinner that evening, Georgiana poured them each a sherry in the library, but held Caroline's slightly out of reach, smiling. "Are you still afraid that you will develop sad liver?"

She considered this with all the care such a sensible question required. "I think it prudent to always be worried about what the future holds for one's internal organs."

Georgiana snorted and passed the glass over, lingering long enough to brush Caroline's fingers. Despite the fact that they'd spent almost two hours in bed that afternoon, the graze sent flames licking along Caroline's arm and into her chest. The blaze of desire was familiar by now, but the contentment which smouldered underneath was new; it made her want to curl up on Georgiana's lap like a cat and mewl for attention.

"I never asked whether it was possible to get sad womb," Miss Darcy mused.

"I used to think so." Caroline waited until Georgiana had taken a large gulp of sherry. "Though my womb feels exceedingly happy these days."

Georgiana choked on her mouthful. "You did that on purpose," she accused, when she was finally able to speak again.

"Of course I did. I live only to tease you, Miss Darcy."

"That is odd," Georgiana purred, leaning over to kiss her, "for I rather recall it being the other way around earlier."

Caroline hummed her approval of the kiss, which was short and sweet and promised more to come later. "If we only had a little music, this scene would be perfect," she said, tracing the rim of her glass. It was true—the library was as cosy as ever, the candles dotted around the room each giving off a gentle kiss of light, the scent of Georgiana's rose perfume beckoning her closer.

"You shall have music enough tomorrow at this damned Percy ball," Miss Darcy grumbled. Glancing at Caroline, her expression relented. "Though I could play something for you now, if you so desired?"

Caroline shook her head, then put her sherry down and tugged Georgiana closer, putting one hand on her waist and sliding the other up Georgiana's wrist to take her hand as she had so often seen men do when leading. "I wish we could dance together. Not even at a ball, for I know such a thing would never be possible, but simply here, at home."

Georgiana swayed into Caroline, moving to some unseen music. "My cousin Eleanor shares our proclivities and is talented enough on the pianoforte. I am sure I could persuade her to accompany our dance with a tune or two."

For a moment, Caroline let herself picture such a scene; some years from now, perhaps, she and Georgiana a little older, dancing cheek to cheek in candlelight. The image gave her a new boldness. If she could not speak her truth now, while she was so full of love and longing that she felt that she might spill over, then when could she?

"Georgie, I think I—" She took a deep breath and pulled

back just far enough to see her lover's face. "I might be developing . . . feelings."

She had braced herself for all kinds of emotions—outrage, panic, fear—but never could she have predicted Georgiana's sudden burst of laughter. "Feelings?" Miss Darcy said, grinning. "You? Surely not, Miss Bingley."

Hurt lanced across Caroline's chest, as jagged and agonising as a lightning bolt, and the thunder of anger came rumbling swiftly afterwards. Instinctively, she took a step back, her hands falling to her sides. "You have found me out." She forced a chuckle. "I know how much you like my jests."

Georgiana stared down at her. "Wait a moment. Do you really—"

She could admit that she had been serious. She could still admit all that she felt. But the words and the laughter—oh, God, the laughter—had cut her to the very bone. What the devil was wrong with her, that she should simper and swoon and fall about so, all for a woman who chuckled at the very thought that Caroline might have a single feeling? Did Georgiana still, after all this, think her so shallow that—

I thought you saw me truly, she thought desperately. *As I saw you.*

She couldn't bear it. She couldn't breathe. "I have never been able to lie very well, as you know." *To hell with it*, she thought. *It will come out sooner or later, and it might as well be now.* "The truth is that I'm in love with you."

"Caroline," Georgiana said, her expression passing through a multitude of feelings and shades, finally landing somewhere between awestruck and stricken.

"I don't expect anything from you. I want everything, of course, but I don't expect it." Now that the words had begun tumbling out, she couldn't seem to stop. The floor felt as if it were tilting underneath her, and she reached out, clamping a sweaty palm onto the arm of the couch. "I know you were hurt before, and I would never do that to you again. I know I am unsuitable as a match. I understand how unconventional this is. But I do love you, Georgie. Truly, I do. I cannot get over my feelings for you, nor do I wish to. I want to build a life together."

Georgiana stared, her face so pale that she looked on the verge of fainting. "You . . . you said you didn't think you could fall in love."

"You were the one who told me that I could, that I was surely capable of it. And you were right."

"Wait a moment. Did you not tell me once that there was . . . Let me see if I remember correctly . . . 'Not a man in the world who could elicit such feelings in me that would compel me to give up everything I have in order to love him'?"

"I don't know if you've noticed, but you aren't a man. If you were, I would have married you already." Dread and desperation prompted her to ask, "Don't you love me back, Georgie?"

Miss Darcy still hadn't moved. "We could not possibly have a life together, Caroline. We would endure immense scrutiny. Two unmarried young women, refusing all offers of marriage. Spending all their time together." She swallowed. "Even if we were exceedingly careful, there would be talk eventually. Rumours which we could never quash."

She hadn't yet answered the question; Caroline clung to that fact like a drowning man. "We'd weather them."

"Did I not tell you that we could only begin this if it went no further? And now you ask this of me!" Georgiana cried. "Don't you care what people think?"

"Of course I care. We must all care what others think of us.

We must all think of our reputations. But I"—she gestured between them, helplessly, to properly convey the depth of her feelings—"I love you. That is the simple fact of the matter. You were once prepared to give it all up for someone else, were you not? Reputation, fortune, your good name. And that relationship would have been out in the open. I am asking for far less in the shadows." It was a low blow to bring up Wickham, she knew, but desperate times called for desperate measures.

"Should anyone find out about us, society at large would give us the cut," Georgiana said, her voice trembling. "Not one person, Caroline, but everyone. Or as damn near to it as would matter."

"Even so, I do not care. I cannot care, when my feelings for you take up my entire being."

"The old you would have thought that an intolerable hell."

"I am no longer the person I was. I was selfish and unkind before, whereas now I wish to consider the feelings of other people. I was vain, but my beauty was a shallow one, not backed up by a sweet or generous soul. Once, I spoke without consequence, and now I am able to consider the weight of my words. You are responsible for that alteration, Georgie, and I thank you for it." She took a deep breath. "But you have also opened my eyes to something more. I shall ask you one last time. Don't you love me?"

"Regardless of my own . . . of anything I personally . . ." Georgiana said, unable to meet Caroline's eyes. "I will not disappoint my brother again. Forgive me. I cannot do what you ask of me. I cannot live like that."

Agony pierced Caroline's chest as cleanly and deftly as an arrow to the heart. "Very well," said she. "Then the matter is finished, is it not?"

Before Georgiana could say anything more, Caroline swept from the library, holding her battered dignity together until she could collapse in the privacy of the guest room. Each sob felt as if it were a page torn from the book of her soul, and she wept until she could weep no longer. She had once told Georgiana that she would beg, but that had been different; she'd been flirting then, driven by the desires of her body, not her heart. Caroline pressed a hand over the place in her chest which ached as if it had been scooped out. She stood up, her resolve to accept the end of their relationship ebbing away.

You cannot give in, she told herself, even while her feet took her back to the door and her fingers turned the handle. *You cannot go to her. Love cannot be begged, and doing so will only end in disaster.*

She closed her eyes, summoning strength even as she slipped into the hallway. Whispers echoed up from below, halting Caroline in her tracks.

"—heaven's sake, ma'am," Mrs Reynolds was saying, "you'll lose the lady entirely if you do not—"

"Then so be it," Georgiana hissed, her voice rougher and more pained than Caroline had ever heard it before.

"Miss Darcy!" the housekeeper exclaimed, as Caroline edged forward. She still could not see either speaker, but she dared not miss a single word. "I am all astonishment! I cannot stand idly by while you make yourself so unhappy."

"I refuse to ruin someone else's life, Mrs Reynolds!" Georgiana exclaimed. "I did that once before and I ruined my own in the process of— No, never again. Do not speak of it. Consider the subject forever closed."

The next sound Caroline heard was a slammed door. She shrank back into the shadows, though she was in no danger of being seen. The truth ought to have soothed her, but instead, the sting ached and spread until it filled her entire body. This was the worst sort of victory, hollow and meaningless; Georgiana might be in love, but she wouldn't commit herself, and the latter fact erased all the joy of the former in an instant.

Chapter Twenty-Eight

Caroline did not intend to act cool the next morning, but it was a natural consequence of her bruised heart. Georgiana gave her a wide berth at breakfast, which swiftly doused what remaining hope Caroline had of rekindling their conversation. The misunderstanding might have been a small one to begin with, but Miss Darcy did not seek to apologise or clarify the matter any further. Her lack of address spoke loud and clear, and Caroline could not bring herself to try a second time.

They spent the afternoon in miserable silence until it was time to leave for the ball. Unable to bear a silent carriage ride, Caroline allowed herself to be rocked to sleep by the motion of the vehicle—an easy task, for she had slept very little the night before. The Percy estate was vast and beautiful, and had Caroline not been in such a dreadful mood, she might have enjoyed it more. The house itself was set far back from the main road, and as the carriage passed through the large wrought-iron gates, she admired the lanterns set into each side to illuminate the entrance. They alighted from the carriage at the bottom of the steps leading up to the house, the stink of hot horseflesh mixing with scents drifting down from the open doors: the bright tang of oranges, the smooth hiss of lilies, and the rich, voluptuous smell of roasted game.

Most guests headed inside immediately, though some lingered to point and stare at half a dozen peacocks, who high-stepped haughtily around the lawn as if the entire estate belonged to them. Without a word, Georgiana began to climb the steps. Caroline followed, glad she had chosen to wear her ravishing green dress tonight, for every person she saw was dressed finer than the last. Miss Darcy was resplendent in a twilight-blue gown with a high neck, which made her dark eyes look even darker; the cream-coloured gloves she wore did not quite match, as if she'd pulled them on carelessly, her mind elsewhere. Only a keen observer would have noticed, and a lover was the keenest observer of all. Caroline couldn't help but catalogue every glance, every troubled twitch of Georgiana's brow.

One of us will have to break, sooner or later, she thought, watching Georgiana slide through the crowds with practiced ease. *Or perhaps, if one of us does not, both of us will shatter in a way which can never be repaired.* She sighed, the sound swallowed by the cheerful noise of the crowd and the lively music which preceded the beginning of the dancing, which must surely be about to start. *As long as we are on the same page,* Georgiana had once said, *then we may continue. As long as you are eager to do so, and that we shall remain friends afterwards.* Could she still be friends with Georgiana? Could she look on and smile while her heart was broken? While Georgiana moved on and found another lover, possibly even a husband?

Of course I will, Caroline told herself, tasting the bitterness of the lie even as she told it. *I will because I must.*

They had not been present even five minutes before Mr Radcliffe shouldered his way through the crowd and presented himself before Caroline. He professed how delighted he was to see her again and begged to have her first dance. Caroline bit back a grimace; she could not refuse him, as custom dictated that all ladies must accept invitations from all gentlemen or else sit out every dance for the entire evening, and Caroline had absolutely no intention of sitting still next to Georgiana for the next four or five hours. Yesterday, the notion would have sounded heavenly; today, she would rather be set upon by those hellish demons with the pitchforks and boiling cauldrons. She therefore accepted, to his obvious delight.

"I hear you are much in demand, Miss Bingley," Mr Radcliffe said, steering her through the dance.

"Am I?" She raised an eyebrow. "I know not what you mean."

"Lord Ashbrook has been asking questions about you. Many questions, in fact."

"Lord Ashbrook?" she repeated, baffled. "You must be mistaken, sir. I cannot believe that to be true, for I never met the man in my life. Either your intelligence is wrong, or he has mistaken me for someone else." She could well understand why Ashbrook might have been asking after Miss Chester, if his nephew had invited her to the house to dine, but why would Ashbrook care a whit about Caroline?

"It would be impossible to mistake you for anyone else," Mr Radcliffe corrected, smiling. "I believe he even turned up to the party at the lake to see you."

"Now I am convinced that you have the wrong woman. I am quite sure he never glanced my way more than once."

"So he is of no interest to you?" Mr Radcliffe asked.

"Well, I would not say that," she murmured, thinking of Mr Acton, and it was only Mr Radcliffe's wounded expression that made her realise that he might interpret her words in an entirely different way. "I mean, I have a question to ask him about a mutual . . ." She struggled to find the right word, since *friend* did not seem appropriate. "An acquaintance, of sorts, that I—"

"You do not need to explain to me," he said, stiffly. "I understand perfectly. Some ladies are happy with their station in life, and some desire to climb."

Stung, Caroline opened her mouth to correct him, then closed it again. Really, what would be the point in doing so? It would only encourage Mr Radcliffe to believe he had a chance to secure Caroline for himself, and would prolong, perhaps even worsen, the situation. "Indeed," she said, haughtily. "And men range in size from mountains to small hills. Is that not so?"

The rest of the dance proceeded in silence, and when it was over, Mr Radcliffe gave a short, jerky bow, hardly even half of what Caroline deserved, before taking his leave. She breathed a sigh of relief and turned to find a familiar face behind her. "Good evening, Lady Lennox," Caroline greeted the stately woman. "I wonder if you have seen Lord Ashbrook this evening? I am looking for an introduction, if it would not be too much—"

"Seek and ye shall find," said a deep voice behind her.

Turning, Caroline found the very man she had hoped to meet, yet she felt little pleasure in the moment. Up close, the viscount's eyes were hazel rather than brown, and his hair more sandy than fair, but his smile was kind. "Perhaps you would grace me with the next dance, Miss Bingley," said he, after Lady

Lennox had made the appropriate introductions. "Lady Lennox can hardly be expected to chaperone me all evening. You would be doing me a great favour indeed."

Caroline forced a smile. "I believe heartily in granting favours to the needy, my lord." She hadn't meant to say something quite so mischievous to a complete stranger and was glad that Lady Lennox's attention had already been caught by a passing knot of ladies festooned in so much shiny ornamentation they looked weighed down.

"An admirable sentiment," Ashbrook said, then followed her gaze. "My word, that is a lot of jewellery." He leaned a little closer. "They shall certainly be safe from drifting out to sea."

The comment, which was neither cruel nor superior, was so unexpectedly witty that Caroline could not help but laugh. She glanced at the viscount again, taking in his handsome features—clean-shaven, long eyelashes. He really did look exactly like the man of her dreams she had tried to picture weeks ago. *Long before I realised that there was no man of my dreams*, she thought, her amusement vanishing. *Nor woman. Only Georgiana.*

Suddenly, she could not bear to be in his company. She made her excuses and her escape, then headed to the punchbowl to slake her thirst. Georgiana was still where Caroline had left her; evidently, she had decided not to dance at all this evening, for the young gentleman standing in front of her sloped off with a most disappointed expression.

"Here," Caroline said, passing Georgiana a glass of punch, though she hadn't asked for one. "It is rather warm in here, is it not?"

Miss Darcy made no answer. They stood in silence for a few moments, watching the current set of dancers twirl and step together.

"Are you still intent on your Great Endeavour?" Georgiana blurted. "We didn't—I mean, yesterday, you did not clarify."

If she'd asked when they were alone, Caroline would have replied differently. As it was, in a bustling ballroom with three or four dozen pairs of curious eyes present, it was difficult to know precisely what to say. "As you rejected me outright, I have no reason not to continue to pursue it," she murmured. A flicker of hope wriggled in her stomach, struggling feebly to stay alive. "Do I, Georgie?"

Georgiana was pale, her knuckles white around the stem of her glass. Her eyes flickered towards Lord Ashbrook, and Caroline suspected she already knew where Miss Darcy's thoughts lay.

"'Not too tall, fair hair, long eyelashes,' you said yesterday," Georgiana muttered. "'A handsome set to the mouth. A certain wicked gleam in the eye. Those are the features I like best.' Did not you say such things?"

It was a true enough statement, but Georgiana had apparently interpreted it far too liberally, as if one person could simply be exchanged for another who possessed similar physical features. "I did. What of it?"

"I also recall that you said he was the most handsome man you ever saw in your life." Her tone was edged with a surprising amount of bitterness.

"You recall an awful lot for an uninterested party," Caroline retorted. "If you do not want me, then I am free to . . . to accept other invitations, am I not?"

Georgiana made no reply, though her knuckles whitened further.

Say something, damn you, Caroline urged silently. *Something.*

Anything. Turning back to watch the crowd, she plastered a charming smile onto her face and aimed it at the nearest knot of dancers, though her vision was too blurred to see who they were. "My offer to you still stands, if you are bold enough to accept it."

"And how do I know," Miss Darcy said quietly, "that you will not throw me over for a better option if it presents itself? When it presents itself?"

Ouch. Caroline flinched, covering it with a quick cough. The accusation was an earthquake, shattering all that she had thought steady and strong. "I am not your past lover," she muttered. "I would never do that. And you ought to know better than to accuse me of such things."

Georgiana swallowed, opened her mouth, then closed it resolutely; the move was answer enough. The music swelled to a climax around them, then ceased. Caroline nodded, blinking back tears. No one need ever know the very moment her heart had cracked beyond repair.

Seconds later, the viscount appeared at her elbow. "May I?"

She took his hand, not daring to glance backwards, and let him lead her out onto the dance floor. "I confess that I noticed you dancing with a gentleman earlier," Lord Ashbrook said, "and that neither of you looked to be having a particularly good time. I could not understand it, for if I were him, I would be delighted to be standing up with the most beautiful woman in the room."

"You flatter me too much, my lord." Caroline swallowed, waiting for their turn in the set. If she dared to glance left, she might see Georgiana through the crowd. No—she would not indulge in such a thing, no matter how desperate she was to know how Miss Darcy looked at this moment. "In turn, I shall confess that I have been looking forward to talking to you all night."

"Have you, indeed?"

Caroline took a deep breath, steadying herself. Her own complicated situation aside, she had another, more simple mess to fix, and fix it she would. "We both know Mr Acton, do we not? The painter?"

"I know him," Lord Ashbrook agreed. "I commissioned him for a painting earlier this year. Very talented fellow."

"He has gone off to London to make his fortune," Caroline said. "And, if I may be so bold, a man of fine taste such as yourself must surely be in need of more paintings. In fact, I have a proposition for you that I believe will ensure the happiness of—"

"I apologise for interrupting you, but I make a point of never talking business at a party. I hope that does not offend you." He offered a sincere smile.

Caroline bit her lip, trying to quell her frustration. She'd pursued this man for one reason, only to be blocked from her goal by the fellow himself. *Never mind*, she reassured herself. *Charm him now, press Mr Acton's suit on Tuesday.*

"Tell me, how well do you know Lady Lennox?" he asked.

"I know her only a little."

"And are you in the habit of—" He hesitated, looking at her closely. "Are you well, Miss Bingley?"

She blinked, rather surprised. Most men wouldn't have cared if she'd been on fire, as long as she'd kept smiling at them. "Thank you, my lord. I am simply . . ."

How on earth am I to convey my turbulent state of mind without bursting into tears or offending the poor man? she wondered.

"You do not need to confess anything to me, for we are but strangers," he reassured her.

Grateful for his easy manner, Caroline focused on the steps of the dance. "I am merely thinking of how complicated people are. One likes to think them simple, easily boiled down to straightforward thoughts and emotions." *And desires*, she added mentally. "Yet life so rarely proceeds in a manner which one expects. It is a puzzle, is it not?"

"Indeed. You have echoed my own thoughts exactly." Lord Ashbrook's gaze slid beyond Caroline, towards the left of the room, where one of the jewellery-laden women smiled up at a slim, red-haired man. For a single moment, yearning flashed over the viscount's features, so deep and desperate that it almost took Caroline's breath away. The next moment, his gaze was back on her, his smile tinged with apology. "And I hope you will pardon me for my assumption, but I think you understand how it feels to be denied an opportunity to work that puzzle out to completion."

"You see rather a lot for a viscount," said she, smiling, though she did not deny the statement.

"Ah." He chuckled. "It is a lifelong failing of mine to be overly observant. My mother often told me that it would lead me nowhere good, and she was correct, as mothers so often are. Will you forgive me such a transgression, Miss Bingley?"

Unexpectedly, as the dancer next to her moved out of time, stammering an apology to his partner as he did so, Caroline caught sight of Georgiana at the back of the room. Miss Darcy was staring at her with such intensity that Caroline wondered how she had not felt the force of it before. *Too bad*, she thought, a streak of her old vindictiveness raising its colubrine head. *If you will not take what has been offered, you cannot be angry when someone else does. Although . . .*

She remembered thinking, once upon a time, that a suitor who was loath to reveal his true feelings might be prompted to do so when a rival displayed an interest. The game was a dangerous one, as she'd already proven with respect to Mr Acton, but really, what did she have left to lose at this point? Caroline chattered with Lord Ashbrook for the rest of the dance, discovering that there was no need to put on any kind of performance; the viscount was witty, amiable, and charming in equal measures.

"I understand I am to see you on Tuesday?" he inquired, escorting her back to where Miss Darcy was standing. "And Miss Chester, who my nephew assures me is a lovely young lady."

"Indeed, my lord, and I am very much looking forward to the visit," she said, loudly enough for Georgiana to hear. "I am staying at Pemberley only another couple of days and shall return to my family at Hadley Hall in Lancashire soon enough."

She did not miss Georgiana's flinch at these words, nor the corresponding pang in her own chest. *Back to Hadley Hall, away from all the warmth of the only true home I have ever known.* The carriage ride back was even more miserable than the outward journey; Georgiana looked as stiff as a starched shirt the entire time, winding her handkerchief over her fingers again and again and pulling it tight, as if by doing so, she could achieve some relief from whatever storm was brewing inside her. Caroline did not offer comfort or solace; Miss Darcy might be experiencing agony, but the pain was entirely self-inflicted.

Chapter Twenty-Nine

A letter arrived the next morning in Mrs Bingley's neat handwriting, though Caroline couldn't bring herself to open it. No doubt it was another reminder that she was unwanted at Pemberley, a fact she was only too aware of now. After she returned from her outing with Miss Chester, she would have to find Georgiana and inform her that she was leaving as soon as possible. She wasn't yet sure where she would go; probably to London, to visit Louisa and see if she could distract herself with what remained of the season. It would be too difficult to stay at Pemberley any longer, knowing that Georgiana did not want her. She still held the tiniest flame of hope that Miss Darcy would confess her love, but even if that happened, it would change nothing about their situation.

I cannot do what you ask of me, Georgiana had said. *I cannot live like that.*

Caroline spent most of the day walking in the gardens, forcing herself to concentrate on the brightness of every petal and the rustle of every leaf. Several times, the hairs on the back of her neck prickled, and she turned back to gaze upon the house, sure that someone was watching her, though, from such a distance, this was impossible to ascertain. No doubt Georgiana was holed up in her precious library, her nose stuck in another book, living through characters who at least had the courage to voice their affections for one another. Caroline sank down onto a bench and closed her eyes, listening to the trill of a nearby robin, distinguishing it from the melodious call of a blackbird hidden in a hedgerow to her right. The smell of lilacs on the breeze calmed her a little, and by such means, she contrived to pass the hours until dinner, which she ate alone in her room. Georgiana did not come to her, nor did she see any trace of Miss Darcy in the house; the lady might be anywhere or nowhere at all, vanished like a ghost.

On Tuesday morning, Caroline washed and dressed with as much care as she could manage before going down to breakfast. The settings at the other end of the table were untouched. Georgiana had made no appearance by the time the clock had struck nine. Fuming, Caroline prepared to write a note, then threw down the quill in exasperation. Why should she bother with courtesy and care, when Miss Darcy was making her feelings so very plain?

Lord Ashbrook's estate was a handsome, sprawling one, stretching for—according to Miss Emily—eight thousand acres. Though the house was far grander than Pemberley, Caroline could not help comparing the two, and she found herself inexorably loyal to the latter. A manservant, dressed in a black jacket with brass buttons which had clearly been polished within an inch of their lives, showed the ladies into a large parlour decorated lavishly, though not garishly. Someone other than Ashbrook himself had chosen the furnishings, Caroline suspected, for he did not seem the type to surround himself purposefully in red velvet and brocade. Though really, she hardly knew the man; perhaps this was exactly what he liked.

Lord Ashbrook rose from his armchair next to the fire and bowed smoothly. Mr Hall rose less gracefully from the armchair on the other side of the hearth, his resemblance to his uncle clear in the fine features of his face, and bowed so low, he almost pitched forward. They exchanged greetings before the ladies settled themselves on a comfortable couch, the gentlemen taking their previous seats.

"Miss Chester tells me," Caroline began, directing her attention towards Mr Hall, "that you are interested in machinery."

"Indeed I am!" cried he. "At the moment, I am gathering all the information I can about the history of inventions, from the bow and arrow to the steam engine that has lately been built down in Pen-y-Darren. Do you know much about the steam engine, Miss Bingley?"

"I confess I do not." His enthusiasm was so genuine, she could not help smiling. "Miss Chester has graciously educated me on some matters, but I am afraid you will find me largely ignorant."

"It is a marvel indeed." He gave a darting, hopeful glance at Miss Emily. "And Miss Chester's knowledge outweighs even my own in this respect. It is my intention to write a book upon the subject, which will give a wider overview of—"

"Now, Teddy," Lord Ashbrook said, giving the boy a slightly strained smile that spoke of long days spent as the sole audience for similar impassioned monologues, "the ladies may not be interested in a long explanation before we have had tea."

His face fell. "Yes, of course. My apologies."

"Actually, my lord," Miss Emily said stoutly, "I would love to hear more."

"I shall do better than that, Miss Chester!" Teddy said. "I shall show you, for yesterday I obtained a new engine and have only taken it half apart in the workshop. That is"—and here the young man hesitated, his freckles fading as a blush spread across his cheeks—"if you would like to see it."

"Nothing would bring me greater pleasure," Miss Emily assured him. "Except hearing about the plans for your book."

"Perhaps," Mr Hall murmured, as they went off together down the corridor, "it could be our book?"

Caroline did not need to hear Miss Chester's response to know that it would be a favourable one.

Lord Ashbrook smiled, looking relieved. "As first meetings go, that was rather a remarkable one. I understand that they have been corresponding for some time, although I found it hard to believe that he had managed to locate the one young lady in all of England willing to not only tolerate his love of machinery but even encourage it."

"Miss Chester and he are well-matched, my lord," Caroline agreed. "I can vouch for her character, and though you may find her occasionally a trifle too honest, she has not a cunning bone in her body. Were he penniless with the same mind and interests, I believe she would be equally as intrigued."

"That is good to know." His gaze lingered on her face, then dropped to her collarbones.

A prickle of discomfort drove Caroline up and out of her chair. "What a wonderful home you have." She turned, admiring the room. Several paintings hung on the opposite wall, and one in particular caught her eye. Moving closer, Caroline gasped. "This must be the work of Mr Acton. I would recognise that brushwork anywhere."

"Indeed. You have a keen eye, Miss Bingley."

Caroline cast an appraising glance over the rest of the collection: several portraits bearing familial resemblance to Ashbrook, and three landscapes. Two featured the kind of bucolic beauty one might find in any country house, and which Caroline had seen repeated so often that her eyes were unable to fixate on any particular part of them, but the third was quite different; a stark forest of black and grey trees, foregrounded by something silvery that did not quite look real. It took her a moment to work out that this was supposed to be a pond of sorts, and the sudden realisation produced a jolt of horror. She had dreamed something very like this, where the trees were unreal and the land itself was a trap. Her only escape route had been through the darkness of the underwater cave, and even now, even awake, she knew that to be true beyond a shadow of a doubt.

"—a little tea outside?" Ashbrook was saying, and Caroline tore her attention away with some difficulty.

She followed him down the hallway where Mr Hall and Miss Chester had disappeared, which led to a large back door and out onto a kind of patio. Several chairs surrounded a table laden with delicious-looking treats: iced lemonade, two steaming teapots, and several platters piled high with sandwiches and fruit. The neat lawn stretched for what seemed like miles, bordered by rows of bright, if rather monotonous, flowerbeds. The day was a pleasant one, though it was rather hot without much of a breeze. *Georgiana would have called it stifling,* Caroline thought, before amusement turned into a sharp pang of grief.

"Teddy lives here, with me," Ashbrook said as they seated themselves at the table, answering a question Caroline had wanted to ask but had been wary of. "His parents died in a boating accident six years ago, and neither of us had other family, for both my parents are long dead. What about your family, Miss Bingley? And may I pour you some hot tea, or would you rather a cool drink?"

"Tea, please, my lord." He'd been close enough to lift the teapot himself, but instead, another manservant stepped forward and poured tea into two elegant cups. Caroline waited until the manservant withdrew before continuing. "I have one sister who is five years my elder, and a brother about a year younger than I."

"Are you close?"

A difficult question, she thought. "Indeed. Charles is recently married to a very sweet girl whom we met in Hertfordshire, and writes to me often. And I shall see Louisa and her husband soon, when I go to London."

Her thoughts turned again to Georgiana, who had been a large part of her life even before their affair had begun, but who now was such a huge part of her life that she could not really imagine living it without her. Would she ever be invited to stay at Pemberley again? Could their friendship ever be repaired?

Caroline shook herself. She shouldn't be thinking about Georgiana right now, not when the sun was shining and a pleasant, handsome man was asking her questions. She ought to be paying attention and trying to entice him, even if it was the last thing she currently wanted to do. If she could not have Georgiana, and that much had been made clear to her, then she must set her sights on a different target. Spinsterhood must be avoided if possible. The Great Endeavour could still be achieved. Perhaps wealth and a title would go some way towards repressing the grief and longing which threatened to drown her, though she doubted it.

"And your parents?" Ashbrook asked, offering her an iced bun.

"My father passed away several years ago. My mother . . ." *is an unfeeling shrew*, she wanted to say, but instead, bit into her bun. It was delicious, but no match for Mrs Addlecombe's baking. "Suffice it to say that she and I are not particularly close, I'm afraid."

He watched her, waiting.

"I don't think I've lived up to her expectations, despite my efforts," she finished.

"Ah. It was the same with my father. He suffered from a lamentable coldness of heart, which reduced all his relationships to mere business transactions. Hence why I preferred not to discuss Mr Acton at the ball. I hope I did not disappoint you there."

"I'm so sorry, my lord," she said, and meant it. "I understand how such a feeling can eat away at a person like rust. Yet I might also say, though I do not know you well, that you appear to have grown into a man whom any father would be proud of."

In the distance, laughter drifted on the breeze. Caroline could just make out two small figures at the bottom of the lawn, gesturing exuberantly at something large and mechanical, though she had no idea what the machine could possibly be.

Ashbrook cleared his throat. "You have a kind nature," said he, rather hoarsely. "At the Percy ball, you were always looking back to check on your friend who did not dance all night, and earlier you went out of your way to ensure that I do not suspect Miss Chester of being after Teddy for his fortune. Do not think I do not notice these things."

Surprised, Caroline blinked. *Does he see me?* she wondered, and the thought made her want to cry.

"The thing is," he continued, "and I neither wish to presume nor pry, but I have seen you in company with Miss Darcy's brother, who I lately heard married a girl in Hertfordshire." At Caroline's look of surprise, he shrugged. "Lady Lennox is a lovely woman but a terrible gossip. And your mother, though in far fewer words, intimated the same."

"My mother?" Caroline gaped at him. "You have met my mother?"

"In Lyme Regis," he said. "And I hope I do not offend when I say that I recognised some of my father's traits in her."

Caroline's pleasure in the day vanished, replaced by dawning dread. "I had heard that you were asking questions about me at the lake party." She'd assumed that Mr Radcliffe was either teasing her or completely wrong; it had never occurred to her that Ashbrook might actually have been doing so.

He bit a sugar biscuit in half and chewed thoughtfully. "I asked a few, yes. I wanted to know what sort of woman you were. The answers I received pleased me, though I wanted to get to know you a little myself."

"And what is your pronouncement, my lord?" said she, feeling worse by the second.

"Not cold, but rather distant, as if you are always thinking about something or someone else. More generous than I expected. More beautiful, too. Your character is just what a young lady ought to be: well-mannered, amiable, graceful."

Once, this list of traits would have satisfied Caroline. She could have thrown them in Mr Darcy's face—from a viscount, no less!—as proof that she was not the inferior creature he claimed. Now, she could find nothing in it to please her. There was only one person in the world whose good opinion meant anything.

"Your mother led me to believe that you were a practical woman," Lord Ashbrook went on. "So I hope that you receive these compliments in the spirit they are intended."

"They sound like a thorough assessment," Caroline managed.

"The thing is," he said again, "that I wish to propose an arrangement which I believe would be beneficial for us both. I believe you also understand what it is like to be in love with someone now married and out of reach."

She flinched, dread spiking to panicked levels. What on earth did that mean? *She was correct*, he'd said at the Percy ball about his own parent, *as mothers often are.* Had he been thinking then of Mrs Bingley's advice? Had he been calculating when and how best to propose? Had it all been arranged to everyone's satisfaction long before he had ever set eyes on Caroline?

He gave her a soft, comforting smile. "I do not fault you for your feelings. Mr Darcy is a fine, upstanding gentleman."

"Excuse me?" She stared at him, not able to believe what she'd just heard. *He thinks I am in love with Fitzwilliam?* The idea made her want to throw her cup at the wall and then the contents of her stomach all over the viscount's fine lawn.

"I myself have some experience with loving a person who did not love me back. Not in the way I had hoped, in any case." He ran a hand through his hair, his voice suddenly bitter. "The heart is an errant horse, Miss Bingley. It can rarely be steered the way one wishes."

"May I ask the lady's name?" she said, not really knowing what else to say.

"Josephine," Ashbrook said, after a pause.

"And why didn't—"

"I never told her how I felt. Not in so many words, anyway."

He picked up his cup of tea but didn't seem inclined to drink it. "So she married my best friend instead. He at least was able to put voice to . . . Well. No matter." He forced a smile. "Which brings me to my point. I wondered if perhaps you would consider marrying me."

Wordlessly, Caroline stared at him, then around at the estate. *He cannot possibly be serious.* "I . . . You could marry anyone, my lord. I am sure that hordes of women—"

"I do not wish for hordes, Miss Bingley. I do not even wish for one woman who could love me, for I could never love her back. No, my list of requirements is more specific than usual, and requires a very particular kind of woman to fulfill them. I am looking for someone who I am certain is in love with someone else she cannot have. The two of us may form a lasting friendship, which is more than many can hope for. And then there's all this." He gestured at the admittedly beautiful grounds. "You would have my fortune and my name. If you find my character at all deficient, I am sure that those will more than make up the spare."

I would be Lady Ashbrook, she thought. *Wife of a viscount. Oh, Mother, you have played the game too well this time.* "Why marry at all, then?"

"An heir or two to secure the inheritance, with as little fuss about that side of things as possible. It is, as you know, the done thing. And I desire lifelong companionship with a woman I can trust and respect."

Caroline could not deny how flattering Ashbrook's attentions were, especially in the wake of her repeated rejections from Georgiana. His interest was not romantic, nor did it cure her of any of her pains, but it was pleasant enough to be reminded that someone might want her—not simply for an affair, but for a marriage. A life; the exact offer that Georgiana had rejected. Ashbrook's was a pragmatic one. They might never be happy together, but they could be content. Caroline would have married up in the world, so her family would be delighted. There really was no downside, apart from the fact that the idea made her want to throw herself into the nearest body of water. "May I have some time to consider your offer?" she choked out, hardly knowing what to say.

"Of course, Miss Bingley. You do not know me at all, and I would be more than happy to meet with you as often as you like, so that you can ascertain the details of my character."

Get a hold of yourself, woman, Caroline thought, biting back tears. "Your character is not in question, my lord," she said. "Only my own heart."

"Ah, Miss Bingley." His smile was regretful. "How our hearts do pain us. I wonder sometimes whether, if I had the option, I would choose not to have one at all."

"Really?"

He gave the matter some thought. "No," said he, staring down at the small figures of his nephew and Miss Emily, who were pacing about the large machine as if working out all the secrets of the universe. "I think I would rather have the pain of knowing I had loved once, than the emptiness of never having loved at all."

Caroline hated that she knew exactly what he meant. "Speaking of the heart, may we now circle back to Mr Acton? For he loves a lady but cannot afford to marry. Money is all that keeps them apart, which seems a far easier gap to bridge than the ones you and I face."

"Indeed? I had no idea he harboured such passion." The viscount studied her. "You know, some people might not wish anyone to have love if they cannot have it themselves. Envy is a tempting vice."

"Some may," she agreed. "But I am not so churlish. And I do not think you are, either. Will you help him, my lord? Commission another few paintings so that at least someone of our acquaintance might know what it is to be happy?"

He chuckled, and the sound was no longer bitter. "That I can do, Miss Bingley. That I can do."

"I have a question," Miss Emily said in the carriage, when Caroline relayed the details of the proposal. "Actually, I have several. Beginning with, why on earth did not you turn Lord Ashbrook down immediately if you are in love with Miss Darcy?"

In love with Georgiana. Saying it herself had been one thing; hearing it said aloud by another person was something else entirely. Caroline closed her eyes and counted to five, then ten, then fifteen.

"I do not understand it," Miss Emily pressed, sounding as distressed as if someone had informed her that all grass was in fact purple, not green. "When last we spoke, I was under the impression that you and Miss Darcy—"

"Miss Darcy has made it plain that our relationship will never be—" Caroline snapped, and Miss Emily's eyes widened. "I apologise," she added, more calmly. "It is a rather sensitive subject at the moment. Suffice it to say that I appear to be in one place, and she another."

"Have you asked her how she feels? Laurel is forever saying one should ask people how they feel rather than assume."

"Unfortunately, Georgiana refused to confirm or deny whether she loved me."

"How odd." Emily gave this some thought, staring out of the carriage window as they rolled down the road at a comfortable pace. "How does she expect you to know what she is feeling if she refuses to tell you?"

Caroline sighed. "Miss Chester, if the world thought and spoke as we do, it would be a far less complicated place indeed."

"Indeed." Miss Emily nodded. "What a comfort it is to have your friendship, Miss Bingley. I hope that mine can be a comfort to you, too."

"It already is," she said, surprised to find that this was true.

Chapter Thirty

Miss Emily chattered about Teddy's book all the way home, and by the time Caroline returned to Pemberley, her own mind was still so full of inventions and names from history that it took her a moment to register who had opened the front door. Not Mrs Reynolds, but Georgiana, who stared down at her with a scowl more stormy than Caroline had ever seen before.

"How was your outing?" Georgiana asked. Her voice was steady, though the hand which held her cup of tea quivered slightly.

"Excellent." Caroline swept past her, taking off her gloves and hat with over-exaggerated care. "We had a delicious spread, and I think Miss Chester may soon be married to Lord Ashbrook's nephew. They are very like-minded young people." The silence lengthened. "The viscount was a very attentive host," she added, when it became clear that Miss Darcy did not intend to ask any follow-up questions.

"I am glad that he amused you," Georgiana said stiffly.

"Indeed, he did. I was most . . . entertained, all afternoon." It was a sly comment, to be sure, but it gave her a feeling of satisfaction to see a look of consternation cross Georgiana's face. *Why should I be the only one to suffer here?*

Down went the cup, clattering onto the side table in a manner guaranteed to spill, and here Georgiana came across the room, striding as if going into battle. "You," she breathed, pinning Caroline to the wall, eyes seething with desire. "You were entertained by him, were you?"

Caroline was playing with fire, and she knew it, but Lord, how she needed to feel something burn. "Not nearly as entertained as I could be right now," she ventured.

This was no longer the heady passion that had once scalded Caroline so blissfully, nor was it the torrent of tenderness from only a few days before. Now, Georgiana looked savage, as if she'd wrapped up whatever weakness she possessed in enough layers to hide it fully from view.

"Upstairs," Miss Darcy ordered. "Or I shall take you right here on the floor regardless of who sees."

Caroline couldn't help a whimper bubbling up. She had just enough sense to consider disobeying, and just enough hope left to give in to the demand without argument. They didn't even make it as far as the guest room before Georgiana pounced, pushing Caroline hard against the wall, her hands and mouth desperate, drinking every kiss down as if she'd never get another.

Caroline fumbled for the door handle, missed it, and found it on the second try at the exact moment Georgiana's teeth sank into the flesh of her neck. Gasping, she flung open the door, and they stumbled into the room, still kissing, unable to take their hands off each other for even a moment. She tore at Georgiana's dress, not caring a whit if it required mending, and Georgiana pushed her backwards onto the bed. Caroline landed with a thump, Miss Darcy on top of her an instant later, hips already rolling in a familiar motion.

"I need—" Caroline choked, everything inside her boiling up into a tangled mess of emotions and desire, "Georgie, I need—"

"Tell me," Georgiana said, her breath coming in hot pants against Caroline's neck. She pressed her face into the pillow, sounding half-choked. A woman stretched as taut as a violin string, ready to snap at the slightest provocation. "Whatever you want."

You, Caroline thought helplessly. *Only give me yourself and I should be forever happy.*

"Inside," she panted, and before she could plead, Georgiana was there, exactly where Caroline needed her, sliding in with delicious friction, filling her up with a sensation she could never get enough of, not if she lived a thousand years. When she finished, shuddering, they stayed motionless for long seconds, and just when Caroline opened her mouth to utter a final plea, Georgiana pushed her to the side and slid out of bed, grabbing her petticoat and wriggling into it.

Aghast, Caroline turned to stare at her. "You're leaving? After we just—" All at once, the floodgates were open, the stream of Caroline's words building in her throat until she could no longer hold them back. She swung her legs out of bed and stood up, completely naked and blazing with fury. "Absolutely not. I have held my tongue far too long, Georgiana Darcy. You must let me speak before you dare leave me again."

"I cannot believe you are shouting at me when you have not a stitch of clothing on. Only you would dare do something so utterly ridiculous." Georgiana paused in the act of picking up her dress from the floor. "And I have never known you to ask permission to speak before."

"I am not asking it now. I am ordering you to listen to me."

"Then it seems I have no choice." Miss Darcy straightened,

glaring at Caroline. "Out with it, then. Make your declaration. When are you to marry Lord Ashbrook?"

"What?" Caroline stared, entirely thrown. "How did you—"

"Do not tell me that he did not propose to you today," Georgiana snarled. "I heard rumours enough at the Percys' ball that the viscount came looking for a wife and had found himself a suitable bride indeed. Go on, then. Tell me." Her hands were trembling worse than ever. "Tell me what I already know."

A Bingley does not run from battle like a coward, Caroline's father had always said. *A Bingley stands their ground and fights.* True, this was an unusual sort of battle, but a battle it was, nonetheless.

"You once told me that some people put themselves in discomfort for the sake of others whom they love," she retorted. Miss Darcy was wearing only her petticoat, just like she had done in Caroline's dreams about the lake. It was odd, when Caroline thought about it, that she had never felt so much like she was drowning as she did at this very moment, awake and on dry land. "I did not understand what you meant at the time. I mean, I heard the words, but I did not truly comprehend their meaning. I . . ." She hesitated. "I have lived a very selfish life, Georgie. In fact, I rather revelled in the idea. I thought it something to be proud of, when I know now that nothing could be further from the truth. If you truly do not love me, then say so, and I shall never speak of my feelings again. I shall not pursue you, nor harangue you, nor flirt with you in any way. We shall be friends, though never as we once were. Merely friends. Will that satisfy you?"

Miss Darcy's jaw worked as if she were grinding her teeth together. "And if I say nothing, will you marry Ashbrook?"

"If you say nothing, whatever I do or do not will be no business of yours."

Georgiana turned and strode away a few paces, then came hurtling back as if she could not bear to be more than three feet from Caroline. "You delight in cornering me, Miss Bingley!" she cried. "You give me no quarter. Very well, then, I confess it: You have cut through all my defenses with your persistence and your charm and your incessant bloody candour. I have watched you learn and fail and improve and—" Tears spilled down her cheeks as she wrung her hands, the very picture of anguish. "I cherished the acquaintance that I had, but I am utterly besotted with the woman you have become. And I cannot give you up, though I know what that means for us both." She grabbed Caroline's hands, pressing them tightly between her own. "I love you, Caroline. I have loved you longer than I knew and in ways I still scarcely understand. Please don't marry someone else, for I could never bear it. You are mine and I am yours."

Caroline stared at her. Georgiana stared back, tears dripping onto her bare collarbones.

"Say it again," Caroline whispered, tugging Georgiana closer. Perhaps she was dreaming now. Perhaps she had simply fantasised the words which she had wanted to hear most in the world.

"I'm sorry for what I said at the Percy ball," Georgiana said instead, swaying on her feet. "It was awful. You didn't deserve that. I've been so caught up in the past, and I'm—I'm so afraid, Caroline. I feel as if I am walking in darkness, like Orfeo. How can I ever be sure that you're beside me? How can a person ever truly trust another?"

"Say it again," Caroline repeated. "Say it again and you have me."

"I love you." In a moment, she was smothering Caroline's face in quick kisses, each too fast for Caroline to respond to. "By God, how I adore you. I tried not to, for I knew you wanted your Great Endeavour to—"

"To hell with the Great Endeavour!" she cried. "If you love me, nothing matters but that."

"Oh, darling, my darling," Georgiana said again, half-sobbing, and the next moment, her arms were around Caroline's neck, and they were clinging to each other as if adrift, though it was the most tethered Caroline had ever felt in her entire life. "You are an impossible, infernal woman, and there is no one in the world with whom I would rather be."

"That may be," Caroline choked out, through sobs of her own, "the nicest thing anyone has ever said to me."

They fell backwards onto the bed, kissing frantically. By the time the passion had slowed, though not cooled, Georgiana caught Caroline's hand and guided it under her petticoat, aiming her fingers lower than usual.

Realising what was meant, Caroline hesitated. "Are you sure?"

"I took your maidenhead, did I not?" Georgiana rested her forehead against Caroline's, looking as terrified and as hopeful as Caroline had ever seen her. "Would you not take mine in return?"

Caroline urged Georgiana to sit up, peeling her petticoat off and laying her back down. If she was going to do this, it could not be a hurried, panicked affair. She needed to feel everything, skin against hot skin, the memory branded forever into her own flesh. She wanted this so badly, she could barely breathe, and yet, she held back. "Do you know what it means,

Georgie?" she asked, mirroring what Miss Darcy had asked her right before the first time she'd been inside Caroline. "What it would mean to me?"

"I know what it means," she whispered. "And I give myself to you, as you have given yourself to me countless times."

Caroline eased forward, relishing the way Georgiana felt under her, against her, around her. The heat of her, the slick joy of taking what Georgiana gave so willingly, was enough to drive Caroline almost to the edge herself. Miss Darcy's eyes were screwed shut, her lips parting as she drew in a ragged breath, as if coming up for air after a long dive.

"Look at me," Caroline panted.

"I am half-afraid to." Georgiana blindly pressed a clumsy kiss to the curve of Caroline's shoulder. "Seeing you is one thing. Seeing me is quite another."

"Be brave for me, Georgie," she breathed. "Remember Euridice? I will always walk behind you, and I will never let you go."

Georgiana's eyes were a fury of wild emotion, savage and tender all at once. Caroline rocked forward slowly, refusing to speed up even when her lover whimpered and begged underneath her, nails scoring down Caroline's back hard enough to make her gasp. Georgiana breathed her name, the word a kind of prayer she repeated again and again until her final, ecstatic shudder.

"I love you, sweetness," Caroline said again, dropping kisses into fair curls as they snuggled impossibly closer. "I swear to you that I will be constant and true, and all the other things which a marriage entails."

"Let us run away together," Georgiana suggested, grabbing Caroline's hands and holding them tightly, her dark eyes imploring. "Perhaps to Scotland? I know we cannot be wed in the traditional sense, but we could rent a small place and—"

"Dearest, no." Caroline shook her head. "I won't be another George Wickham to you. You have faced yourself and accepted yourself for all that you are and are not. Do not you think it time you faced your brother in the same way? It is long past time you stopped being kind and started being honest with him."

"Are you serious?" Georgiana squinted up at her. "I suspect you've gone quite mad, Miss Bingley."

"I'm saner than ever, Miss Darcy." Caroline smiled down. "You know perfectly well that he would never reveal your secret to anyone, not even his wife, if you asked him to keep it to himself. He may be many things, but your brother is a man loyal to a fault."

"Lord, how I hate it when you are right. Which, incidentally, is not nearly as often as you think." Miss Darcy buried her face in the crook of Caroline's neck. "Very well. I shall write to him and ask when he is coming home."

Caroline stroked Georgiana's hair, marvelling that she was allowed to touch, to caress. To love and adore, fully and completely, without pretense. "We will face him together if you so desire. Or if you prefer to tell him alone, then I shall be there waiting for you afterwards."

"What if he does not approve? What will we do?" Miss Darcy shifted uneasily in Caroline's grasp. "Where shall we live?"

"I do not know," Caroline admitted. If Mr Darcy did not want them at Pemberley, then Charles and Jane would surely take them in for a while, although their sudden appearance at Netherfield would require some explaining. The idea of Georgiana being banished unceremoniously from her childhood home simply for loving Caroline was almost enough to make her want to give the relationship up entirely. No, she would never let Darcy do such a thing to his sister; Caroline would get on her knees and beg first. "Let us cross one bridge before we worry about the next, hmm?"

They exchanged final kisses, and within minutes, Georgiana's breathing had evened out. Caroline held her long into the night, fearing that her lover might turn to mist if she loosened her grip even slightly. *Down into the underworld we go*, she thought ruefully. *Too bad the descent was the easy part.*

Chapter Thirty-One

Dear daughter,

I am returning early to Hadley Hall, where I await your happy news. I assume the gentleman was not so coy as to keep my involvement to himself, and I trust you are suitably grateful for my intervention. A viscount, Caroline! If only your father were alive to receive such glad tidings. You shall be the envy of all my friends. Come at once, for we shall have much to arrange.

Yours,
Arianna Bingley

Caroline stared down at the letter. If she'd only opened it before she'd accompanied Miss Chester to Lord Ashbrook's, she would have gone forearmed against the scheme. Though, really, what difference had her ignorance made? It had all been arranged without her, as if she were simply a prize cow handed from one hand to another. At least Ashbrook had not hid Mrs Bingley's involvement, and he had given her time to consider the offer. He was a decent man, all told, but even Caroline's old self would have baulked at the reasoning behind the offer. It would have taken a certain combination of fortitude and ambition to ignore her husband's obvious love for another woman; surely all the wealth and fortune in the world could not have made up for a lack of preference. Had Ashbrook really thought her that kind of woman?

And was I? she wondered, the question turning her stomach.

"What's wrong?" Georgiana murmured, slipping both arms around Caroline's waist and resting her chin on Caroline's shoulder.

Caroline leaned back, taking comfort from the heat of Georgiana's body. "I must leave for Hadley Hall tomorrow, dearest," she said, and turned when Georgiana stiffened against her. "Please don't be mistaken—I do not want to go, but Mother has called me home in no uncertain terms."

She showed the letter to Georgiana, who skimmed it, her eyes widening. "She knew? Your mother orchestrated this?"

"Ashbrook already confessed this news when he proposed. He may not be much of a lover, but at least he is not a liar."

"I would rather hear nothing at all about what kind of a lover he is." Miss Darcy's smile was tinged with jealousy. Her hands slid down to Caroline's waist, tugging her closer, eliciting a sharp intake of breath. "Or need I remind you what kind of a lover I am?"

"Did not you show me twice already this morning?" Caroline grinned. "And you have no reason whatsoever to worry. You know that you are all I think of. I am not so easily swayed as all that."

"My stubborn darling." Georgiana's hands slid down to Caroline's waist, fingers tapping an anxious rhythm. "What are you going to do about your mother?"

"What I ought to have done before now. I'm going to stand

up to her." Caroline straightened her shoulders. "I shall tell her that her scheme has failed and that I shall not marry."

"As easy as that?" Georgiana asked, pressing a kiss to Caroline's cheek, then another against her jaw, and a third just under her earlobe.

Caroline shivered. One did not simply say no to Mrs Bingley, though she did not wish to make her love more anxious by saying so. "Whether easy or not, it must be done." She pulled Miss Darcy close, savouring the feel of the embrace, the sharp scent of newly-cut roses. "I will return. Please do not doubt me."

Georgiana relaxed a little. "You told me last night that you would always walk behind me. Ought I call you Euridice?"

"I think I'd rather be Orfeo, and show him how the thing is properly done. Trust in love and never look back." Caroline tilted Georgiana's chin down. "What say you to that?"

"Absolutely," Miss Darcy breathed, and the next few minutes were lost to the sweetest kiss Caroline had ever known.

The Bingley family home in Lancashire was at least three long days away by coach, and there didn't appear to be a single rut in the road or loose stone which the coachman did not discover and drive over on the way. By the time Caroline had reached the inn, which marked the halfway point on her journey, she felt as bruised as a schoolboy's apple. She could have taken an overnight coach to continue her journey, arriving in Hadley Hall by dawn, but the dread of the forthcoming confrontation tempted her to prolong it as much as possible.

After a disappointing dinner of flavourless beef stew, which could only be described as an excellent exercise for one's jaw muscles, Caroline retired to her room and wrote a letter to Ashbrook. The draft took several attempts, but eventually, she had a version she was happy with; kind and appreciative of his proposal, but a clear rejection nonetheless. She slept fitfully, dreaming of dark caves and watery things again, before waking in a cold sweat. Still, turning down Ashbrook's proposal had made her feel slightly better. Whatever Mrs Bingley had schemed, the offer had now been declined and the matter closed. They would all simply have to move past it.

The next morning, she watched the coach come and go outside the inn, unable to coax herself onto it. The second morning found her courage likewise depleted, and it was only the knowledge that Georgiana was waiting for her back at Pemberley that eventually forced Caroline to board on the third day for the final stretch of her journey.

Hadley Hall had been the Bingley family home since Caroline was three. They'd rented the estate from a local lord, which was not unusual. *Land-wealthy and coin-poor*, her father had often said, though never in the man's presence. This was of no real significance to Caroline, for gentry who had fallen on hard times, for one reason or another, often rented their estates out to wealthy families, but Mrs Bingley was sensitive around the matter of not having their own inheritance.

By the time Caroline arrived outside the gates of Hadley Hall, her bruises had grown bruises of their own, and her nerves blazed as if someone had set her alight. *Remain calm*, she told herself. *Do not lose your head now. Remember all that you have been through, and why you are doing this.*

She took a few deep breaths, though the unhelpful air did nothing to assuage her anxiety, and pushed open the front door just as the housekeeper pulled it open from the inside. A moment of stumbling confusion followed, and by the time both had righted themselves, the lady of the house had appeared in the hall.

"You took your time, Caroline," Mrs Bingley said, eyeing her daughter with ill-disguised impatience. Her hair was as dark and as neatly-curled as Caroline's own, her eyes a pale, searching blue which matched her dress. In such an outfit, she looked very like a doll Caroline had adored and which had been given away without her consent when she was eight. "And let the servants work for their keep, for heaven's sake. I did not raise you to go about opening doors for yourself."

"Good afternoon to you, too, Mother." Caroline shot an apologetic look at Mrs Wendel, who kept her own gaze firmly on the floor.

"Come in, come in," Mrs Bingley urged. "Wendel, do not stand there gaping, for heaven's sake. Bring in Caroline's bags."

Without another word, Mrs Bingley turned on her heel and flounced down the right-hand passage, evidently expecting her daughter to follow.

"I have only the one bag and there's no need to have it taken upstairs yet," Caroline whispered. "I fear I bring a hurricane to your shores today, Mrs Wendel, and I likely won't be staying to weather it."

The housekeeper looked surprised at being addressed so, and Caroline realised with a jolt that she'd never actually had a conversation with Mrs Wendel before. She had no idea if the woman's husband was still alive, whether she had any children, nor what her opinions were on how brown toast ought to be. Regret unfurled in her stomach, but she pushed it down; at present, there was no time to consider the myriad mistakes she'd made in this house.

"That's . . . that's alright, ma'am," Mrs Wendel said, eyeing Caroline with curiosity. "Forewarned is forearmed, or so they say."

Caroline deposited her sole bag next to the stairs, intending to take it up to her chamber later if things went well—although of the foolish hopes she'd harboured in the last few weeks, this was surely the most foolish one of all—before following her mother towards the dining room.

Hadley House was a beautiful home, though it glittered without warmth. The walls were painted an angelic, shimmering cream, and every surface was adorned with expensive, gilded trinkets. Long gone were the pretty green vases Caroline had so admired as a child, replaced with more fashionable blue plates and bowls. Everything sparkled, polished to a high degree, but that was likely the only human touch those objects ever enjoyed. There was not one spot in the entire house that could reasonably be thought of as *cosy* without stretching the meaning of the word beyond all recognition. Georgiana's favourite well-worn couch would never have survived a single hour in this place.

Caroline trudged through the corridor which linked the dining room to the great hall, which was lined with paintings of the highest quality and the lowest interest. These included a portrait of her parents dressed in their best, her mother pouting, her father smiling blandly. If Mr Bingley were here, perhaps her mother might have had a rider to rein in the worst of her ambitions. As it was, she had been allowed to roam unchecked, pleasing no one but herself and the highest of society. Caroline had once thought that attitude rather marvellous, but now she saw it for what it was; a hollow outlook based solely on ambition, stripped of any genuine feeling. She had been well on the way to becoming a younger version of her mother, before the Great Endeavour had thrown her off course.

She shivered. *This could have been my life.*

When Caroline entered the dining-parlour, Mrs Bingley was already sitting ramrod straight at the other end of the lengthy table. She took a seat appropriately far from her mother and cast a surreptitious glance around the room. Gone was the familiar bustle and warmth of the Pemberley staff—here, the servants glided in and out as silent as shadows, depositing plates and filling glasses. They were so quiet that Caroline found herself straining to see if they were even breathing. Possibly Mother had forbidden breathing in her presence; it wouldn't have surprised Caroline, though it was possible that holding one's breath caused sad lung. Then again, she couldn't imagine her mother caring if a servant got sad lung, other than to complain about the brief distress replacing them would cost her.

Caroline stared down at the plate of braised greens, topped by an unseasoned and overcooked lamb shank which had been delivered to her by a pale boy with dark circles under his eyes, and felt a deep longing rise inside her for Mrs Addlecombe's cooking.

"I beg your pardon?" she said, realising she'd missed her mother's last comment.

A short, icy silence warned her not to make the same mistake again. "I said, and how are the Darcys?"

"They are well. Mr Darcy is lately married, as you know." Once, that statement had stung her, but she had long ceased to care. Now, she could only think of Georgiana, of her sweet kisses and the kindness she had shown when Caroline had felt at her most lonely. The pale footman poured her wine, then melted back into the shadows. Caroline took a sip, then a much larger gulp; a little liquid courage must surely help here.

"Hmm. Does his new wife have any brothers?" her mother inquired.

She nearly choked. "No, only sisters. Four of them. The eldest is married to Charles, Mother."

"Ah." Mrs Bingley's expression did not change, but the atmosphere thickened noticeably. "Another Bennet. They do spread themselves around, do they not? Marrying all the gentlemen they can find."

Caroline stared down at her plate again, then picked up her fork simply to have something to do. Once, she would have laughed heartily at that remark and contributed something unkind—albeit correct—of her own. Now, she felt sorry she'd ever done so. The Bennets were not the perfect family by any means, but they seemed to genuinely love each other. That was more than she could claim had ever happened under this roof.

"If you are too overcome by joy to engage in polite conversation, then let us get to the heart of the matter," her mother said, sounding more indulgent than Caroline had ever heard her. "I was thinking an August wedding. July would be better, but there is so much to do. September would be too late, for the leaves will have begun to fall and will insist on creating that dreadful mulch you know I cannot stand."

Caroline's fork slipped through her fingers, clattering against her plate. Despite the considerable distance, she heard her mother tut.

"You needn't worry about my blessing. I approve the match most heartily," Mrs Bingley added. "It is about as well as you could possibly do, given the circumstances."

"The . . . the circumstances?" Caroline echoed, baffled.

"Caroline, do not play coy. Everyone knows you were chasing after another man for some time and failed to catch him. That sort of thing reflects badly, you know. A hunter ought to always catch her quarry."

"I wasn't— I didn't—"

"It is no matter," Mrs Bingley said, waving a gracious hand. "Now you have a viscount. My, my, what a fine man he is."

Caroline closed her eyes for a moment, seeking inner strength. This was not going to go down well at all but too bad. She had made her choice, and she would stand by it. "Mother, I came here to tell you that I cannot marry Lord Ashbrook," she said, and hated the quaver in her voice.

"Nonsense. He is a perfect match for you."

"I am in love with someone else, Mother."

"Love?" Mrs Bingley repeated. "I thought we were talking of marriage."

"They are not mutually exclusive ideas these days," she muttered.

"Love is a silly, newfangled notion. Upon my word, it'll never catch on." Mrs Bingley eyed her. "I'm surprised to hear you talk such rubbish, Caroline. Of all my children, you are the most like me."

Caroline gaped at her mother, unable to summon a coherent response.

"Your hunger to climb ought to take you far in life," Mrs Bingley went on. "At least, you were hungry when you first debuted. I had expected better of you by three-and-twenty, truth be told. Consider that Charles fell to the foolish affliction you call love, while Louisa made a more sensible, if rather mediocre, match. One despairs to see one's children making poor choices. But you have a fabulous opportunity in your grasp now. A titled gentleman, no less. You may be many things, Caroline, but you are not impractical."

"The viscount seems to be a good man, but he . . . I could never be happy, Mother."

"Happiness is fleeting. Security lasts. Besides, I have heard rumours," Mrs Bingley said, her voice dropping several degrees, "of untoward behaviour on your part."

The hairs on the back of Caroline's neck prickled. "Untoward?" she repeated, dread pinning her to the chair. Had someone seen her and Georgiana together? No, it wasn't possible. They'd been careful. Even the occasional kisses stolen inside the carriage had been performed with secrecy.

"The best way to eliminate such rumours is to marry at once and marry well. Ashbrook is the solution to your problems."

"I do not have problems," Caroline said, forcing herself to stay calm. "To whom do you attribute these rumours?"

"Oh, but you do, daughter mine. Without me, what fortune do you have? What dowry? Without Hadley Hall to return to, where will you live? Do you imagine that people won't talk, if you plan to be a spinster all your life? Or do you intend to live upon the charity of your precious Darcys?" Mrs Bingley's expression was glacial. "He doesn't love you, Caroline. It is frankly embarrassing to have you lingering around Pemberley, waiting for him to return with another woman in tow. I raised you to have dignity, not to act like some simpering mistress who—"

"Oh bloody hellfire!" she swore. "I am not in love with Mr Darcy. Why does everyone think that?"

"Do not curse in this house." Disbelief lined every haughty wrinkle of Mrs Bingley's beautiful face. "And do not lie to your mother, child. It is unbecoming. I taught you better than that."

"What you taught me," Caroline said, rising to her feet and wishing she could upend the entire table, "was how to be a hunter. A wolf, always looking for her next meal, always keeping abreast of the pack."

For the first time, her mother looked pleased. "I'm glad

you hold my lessons in such high esteem. Finally, we make a little headway in our conversation."

"You misunderstand me, Mother. I would rather be a sheep." In her mind's eye, she saw Mr Acton's painting again—the lamb, wandering from the safety of the flock. Why had she known that there ought to have been danger in the skies overhead? Was it because she had lived that way? She'd never known a moment's peace from her mother's eyes, nor from her unceasing, oppressive judgement. It had pressed her like coal, turning her into a diamond; beautiful, certainly, but hard and cold and unfeeling. No wonder Georgiana had thought her—

"A sheep? I cannot believe it," her mother snarled. "What a silly thing to say."

Caroline's fury faded, leaving her exhausted. She hated this place, with its beauty and grandeur and lack of any real emotion. Where was the fondness, the intimacy, the compassion that she saw in other families? "I cannot marry Lord Ashbrook," she repeated, gathering her courage. *Do it now*, she told herself. *You are many things, but you are not a coward, Caroline. You never have been.* "I love another. And she . . . She is waiting for me."

The words tumbled into the silence like stones down a well, and Caroline waited, heart hammering, for them to land.

"She?" Mrs Bingley stared at her. "Whatever do you mean?"

"I love another woman. I might have been able to love a man one day, had I not fallen in love with her. I really do not know. Nor shall I ever know now, for I am in love with her and her alone, and she with me. We intend to be together." She held her head high. "That is it. That is all."

The silence might have been five seconds or five years, Caroline could not tell. She'd expected wrath, but when

Mrs Bingley spoke again, her voice was as calm as if Caroline had merely asked her to pass the salt. “You shall marry Lord Ashbrook, and that shall be the end of it.”

“I cannot,” she gasped. “Mother, did you not hear me? I have already written to him to turn him down. And I love—”

“Then you shall write to him now to beg him back. If you do not, then you are no longer part of this family, and will never darken our doorstep again.” Mrs Bingley picked up her wine, looked at it appreciatively, and took a sip. If Caroline didn’t know better, she would have thought her mother entirely composed. Instead, she noticed the tightness of the jaw, the corded muscles in the neck, the slight twitch under one eye, all tiny indicators of extreme displeasure from which there could be no return.

“Mother, please. I beg of you to simply hear me out. I know this is not what you want, but I—”

“You heard me perfectly well the first time, Caroline Bingley. Do not make me repeat myself.”

The silence stretched on and on. “And if I do not acquiesce?”

“Then I expect you to leave this instant and never return.” Mrs Bingley’s gaze met hers, and it was colder than ice. “Choose now. Never speak of your disgusting, sordid affair again, or never speak to me again.”

Caroline picked up her fallen fork and arranged it neatly by the side of her plate. *The point of no return*, she thought. In her dreams of Georgiana and the lake, the only way out had been through the darkness of the underwater cave. Perhaps something inside her had known all along how this would turn out. She rose to her feet, smoothed down her dress, then took a deep breath. “Gladly. Farewell, Mother.”

Before Mrs Bingley could say another word, Caroline swept out of the room.

Chapter Thirty-Two

Caroline dashed down the corridor and up two flights of stairs, skidding on the corner and almost crashing into an elegant bust of Vespasian, before flinging herself through the door of her old bedchamber. It looked no different from the last time she had been here, but even in her haste, she marvelled at how little it showed of its occupant's personality. It contained no trace of her childhood, not even a single doll or blanket to mark that she had once been small and in need of comfort. *Entirely unlike Georgiana's bedchamber*, she thought, opening the door of the dresser and grabbing several necklaces which her father had given to her. These were not the most expensive of her jewellery, but they were the most precious to her.

"What are you doing?" Mrs Bingley snapped from the doorway. "Theft, Caroline? Have you stooped so low?"

"These are mine, Mother," she said, holding up the necklaces in question. "I can hardly steal that which already belongs to me."

Mrs Bingley studied the handful for a moment, her lip curling. "You do not even have the sense to take the best in your collection."

Only her vast self-restraint stopped her from flinging the

necklaces directly at her mother's face. "Which is it? Am I a thief or am I too stupid to be one? Are these items dear to you, or worthless? It cannot be both."

"Are you quite finished?"

"Quite." Caroline pushed past her mother, unsurprised when cold fingers wrapped around her wrist.

"You will regret this, Caroline," Mrs Bingley warned. "I shall never speak to you again."

"Oh, Mother," Caroline sighed, tears already brimming. "Is that a promise?"

Mrs Bingley's grasp loosened in surprise and Caroline wrenched free. Not daring to look back, she hurried down the stairs, hot tears already trickling down her cheeks. In the great hall, she picked up her bag, stuffed the necklaces inside it, and dashed outside, straight into something tall and surprisingly firm.

"Ouch," she said, reeling backwards. "What the devil—Charles!"

Frowning, her brother held her at arm's length. "Caroline? Where on earth are you going in such a hurry? Good heavens, are you weeping? My God, has someone died?"

"What are you doing here?" she cried, embracing him.

"I might ask you the same thing."

"Then perhaps you might ask me in the carriage," Caroline said, jerking her chin at his waiting driver. "I fear that my presence is no longer welcome here."

His eyebrows rose, but he complied, ushering her forward and taking her bag to pass up to the waiting footman.

"I apologise," Caroline continued, once they were settled inside and the carriage had begun to move. "You only just got here, and now you are leaving again. Wait—are not you supposed to be in Bath with Jane?"

"I was, but . . ." He hesitated, scratching at his stubbled cheek. Clearly he'd ridden hard for at least a couple of days. "I think it best that you tell me your tale first. Why on earth is Mother so angry with you?"

"Someone proposed to me. She arranged it all behind my back." She dabbed at her eyes with her sleeve. "And I turned him down."

"Ah." Charles sat back in his seat, grimacing. "Yes, I can see why that might upset her. Was there nothing about him which pleased you?"

Caroline shrugged. "He is a handsome and wealthy viscount. Everything a young lady ought to want."

Charles studied her. People often thought him less shrewd than Mr Darcy, perhaps because of his more openly cheerful manner, but her brother was far from a fool. "But not what you want?"

"Oh, Charles," Caroline choked out, dropping her head into her hands. "I must throw myself on your mercy, at least for a while."

"My mercy is yours to use as long as you like," said he, looking more confused by the second. "Caroline, forgive me for saying this, but I would have thought a handsome and wealthy viscount would suit all your desires."

"I am in love," she confessed. "With someone else."

"I knew it!" he cried. "That letter you wrote me, asking what love felt like. I knew it could not be simply idle speculation. With whom are you in love, dear sister? Is it anyone I know?"

Whatever he said, it couldn't possibly be worse than Mrs Bingley's response. Caroline swallowed. "I am in love with Georgiana Darcy."

She braced herself for more shouting, but Charles merely studied her for long moments, head tilted to one side. "And is that why you're crying?"

"No. I mean, yes, but not exactly." She stared at him. "You don't seem upset. Or shocked. You do understand what I'm saying, don't you? I am in love with another woman."

"Come, Caroline," he said, with a consoling smile. "Do you think that none of my fellow students at Cambridge ever tussled with one another under the sheets? I didn't personally indulge, of course, but I certainly had offers enough. Why, Jane has even told me in confidence that one of her sisters—" He broke off, then cleared his throat. "I mean, sometimes these things happen between men and men or women and women. Though I confess I am surprised to hear you say it, since you always seemed so—"

"Concerned with men?" Caroline suggested.

"Detached," he finished, looking apologetic.

"Good heavens, did everyone think me made of ice? I do have feelings, you know."

"I can see that," he said gently, pulling out a handkerchief and passing it over. "Some of them are leaking out of your eyes at this very moment. And you love her?"

"Completely and utterly."

"And she loves you?"

Caroline couldn't help smiling, though the question brought on a fresh flood of tears. "She does."

"There!" Charles exclaimed. "What more can you want?"

"Spoken like a man," she chided him. "Have you forgotten

that without Mother's approval, I have no wealth to speak of? No dowry, either. I cannot give Georgiana what she deserves."

"I do not think any Darcy needs our money," he said, smiling at her fondly. "She will not want your dowry. And if she does, I shall provide it myself."

Her sobs took a while to subside, but he bore it patiently, patting her on the knee until she was able to speak again. "I do not deserve you. You are the very best of brothers."

"I'm sure I don't deserve such praise." All at once, he looked uncomfortable. "Speaking of brothers, I now understand why Fitzwilliam bade me ride like blazes to find you."

Caroline's relief turned to dread in an instant. "Georgiana said she would write to him, but she did not say she would reveal our affair. I had thought she'd wait until he was present, and I had returned, so that we could do so together."

"I do not know what she wrote," Charles admitted. "All I can tell you is that he came down to breakfast holding a letter and told me to ride to Hadley Hall at once."

"He did not say why?"

Her brother shook his head. "I dared not ask any more. Not when he looked like that."

"Like what?" Caroline asked, though she had never wanted an answer less.

"By Jove, like absolute thunder." Charles swallowed. "Take heart, dear sister, for I fear whatever conversation you just had with Mother is about to look like child's play in comparison."

Caroline had imagined that her return to Pemberley would be triumphant, if tinged with grief. She'd imagined running into Georgiana's arms, holding her close, and having time to discuss how they might best present their case to Mr Darcy in order to gain his—well, if not his blessing, then at least his agreement to leave them be. She hadn't expected three days of panic and dread, only to be greeted on the steps of Pemberley by the man himself, his expression a perfect storm of rage and betrayal.

"I must speak with you immediately, Miss Bingley," he snarled, then whirled on Charles. "And I must do so alone."

Charles backed away at once, looking alarmed. "Er, well, I'm not sure that seems entirely—"

"It's fine," Caroline muttered. "Go forth. I shall see you shortly."

"My study," Mr Darcy said. "Now."

Ordinarily, Caroline would have met his temper with her own but now did not seem to be the best moment to begin the fight. "Lead on," she said, watching as he turned and marched away without a backwards glance.

Chapter Thirty-Three

Caroline approached Fitzwilliam's study with the same amount of trepidation she would feel regarding the doorway to hell itself. As if sensing her presence, Mr Darcy appeared just beyond the entrance; his glower had not faded any but seemed to have concentrated in the very little time it had taken her to gather her wits and pat her hair down.

"Remind me," said Caroline, turning sideways to present as small a target as possible as she inched closer, "just how many guns do you keep in that room?"

"Four," he said, with no hesitation.

"And how many are within arm's reach?" she asked, stepping over the threshold.

"All of them," Darcy snapped. "And do not think I shall stop there. I can obtain more guns if need be. Close the damned door."

"You shall not require any," Caroline retorted, as the door clicked shut behind her.

"Shan't I?" He regarded her coolly. "I will be the judge of that."

She waited while his eyes raked her face, the clock in the corner ticking an endless beat without a melody. "You do not need to put on such a performance, sir," said she. "I am no common country swain, come to whisk your sister away to a life of poverty and ruin."

"Poverty, no. Ruin? That is yet to be seen." His fingers tapped the arm of his chair while Caroline seated herself opposite, even though he had not invited her to do so. "The last time I saw you, I told you that if you did not mend the error of your ways, then you would never find love as I have done."

"Indeed, you did."

"And now . . ." His fingers ceased drumming, then started again. "You think you have found love with my sister?"

Ah. So he already knows. "As difficult as that may be to believe, yes."

"It is not difficult at all," he said immediately, a loyal hound to his last breath. "My sister is an absolute delight."

The implication hung in the air: *and you are not.* Caroline refused to rise to the bait. Instead, she crossed her legs at the ankle and folded her hands in her lap.

"I have no desire to prolong this pain on either side. So let me ask you plainly." Darcy's fingers tightened on the arms of his chair. "You may already know that I once offered George Wickham a great deal of money to leave her alone and he took it. I shall offer you the same now. As many thousand pounds as you require to leave and never look upon my sister again."

She could not possibly have heard him correctly. "Excuse me?"

"Name a number, and it shall be yours."

She wondered whether she could refrain from slapping him. The urge had been building for some minutes and was now almost impossible to repress. It was bad enough that he had once thought Caroline shallow enough not to be capable of falling in love, but to also have him ask how much money it would take to buy her off, as if it was a foregone conclusion and all that was required to agree on was the precise amount, was too much for her to bear.

"Do not dare insult me so, sir." She very nearly spat her next words. "I do not want your money. I do not need your money."

"Perhaps not," he said, stroking his chin. The motion producing a slight rasping noise. Evidently he had not yet been shaved that day. "Everyone wants something different, do they not? For Wickham, it was money and freedom. For you—"

"Only your sister." Caroline's tone was ice. Slapping was too good for such a man. Stabbing might do.

A long, slow stabbing.

He studied her, those familiar dark eyes roving over her face, searching for any weakness. This was not the Fitzwilliam Darcy she knew—neither the haughty, self-contained version, nor the softened husband. "Not status? Not a marriage match worthy of royalty? For I could manage such a thing easily, you know. I could charm my aunt into taking you on one of her tours. Lady Catherine de Bourgh's reach is . . . extensive."

She said nothing. The clock ticked on. Darcy got up from his chair and began to pace the room. "You would have status," he continued. "You would have power. Are those not the things you once prized more highly than anything else?"

"I did, once." Caroline swallowed. He knew her well enough to probe her weakness, and to exploit her new vulnerability to his advantage. The dreams she'd once held of her own importance, sparkling on the arm of someone wealthy and handsome, the envy of every ballroom, faded when she thought of worn couches, tender kisses, dark eyes fierce with unspoken longing. "That was before I knew anything else existed."

"And where will you go, if my sister decides she no longer wants you?" His dark eyes watched her every move. "For I know that you have no desire to return to Hadley Hall to live with that cold-hearted wretch you call a mother. The only option you have left is to accept this viscount who has made you an offer of what must surely be a loveless marriage. And trust me, when Georgiana comes to her senses, she won't want you, nor whatever domestic felicity you claim two ladies can have together. It would be but a half-life, Caroline. You must see that."

Liar, she thought, and hadn't realised she'd said it out loud until she saw Darcy's eyebrows rise. Despite her rebuttal, she swallowed down a wave of panic. She was certain of Georgiana's feelings, but she could not quite shake how it had felt when her lover had refused to commit. Suppose Miss Darcy renounced her promise, if only to placate her brother, whose happiness and peace she had so often prized above her own?

I must be Orfeo, she reminded herself. Walking away into the darkness, not looking back to see whether love followed. Devotion was a test of faith indeed, but not a test for the object of one's affections.

A test of myself.

"I am here whether she wants me or not," Caroline declared. "I couldn't stop loving her if I tried, and whether she decides to be with me or not"—she broke off, gulping down a swell of panic—"is both of no consequence and the greatest consequence of all. I love your sister, and I will never stop loving her. You cannot induce me to do otherwise with money or status or power or anything else you can think to bribe me with." She rose, drawing herself to her full height. "I am no George Wickham, sir. I cannot be bought. I will not flee. And I will never be hunted."

His voice dropped; softer, more cunning. "Would you acquiesce to be helped, then?"

Tick. Tick. Caroline's heartbeat pounded rabbit-fast, but she refused to look away from him. She would meet her fate head-on, whatever it was, and he could not trick her when she had nothing to hide. "Not by you. I have already turned the viscount's offer down. I have already been disowned by my mother. If those facts do not convince you of my undying love for your sister, nothing will."

He sat back in his chair, brow knitted. Something had changed in his expression, though she knew not what it was or what it heralded. "There are two doors in this room." Fitzwilliam gestured behind him. "This one leads to my sister and certain ruin." He pointed over Caroline's shoulder, at the door she'd entered. "This one leads to stability and security, though you will never see Georgiana again. Choose now. Which will it be?"

"Without Georgiana, I am already ruined." She stared him down unblinking. "No amount of money or power could ever make up for her absence in my life, and you cannot take anything from me which I wouldn't gladly give for her. I had already chosen my fate before I ever entered this room."

"Really, Miss Bingley?" he said, the hint of a sneer curling his upper lip. "You, who once cared so much about fortune and rank? To say nothing of your precious reputation? Now you say you do not care at all? You understand how that is an exceedingly difficult thing for me to believe."

"I . . ." She hesitated, biting her lip. It was a fair point, she had to admit. He had been there when she had presented her argument to Charles against his pursuing Jane Bennet, when she had talked of status, of wanting only the best for him and their family. "I understand how that might look to you," said she. "And perhaps I shall never be able to convince you. But let me put the same question to you. For you joined me in advising Charles to drop his pursuit of Miss Jane Bennet, and I believe, given what he said to me later that week, that you and he had also had some private conversation away from us ladies, where you argued even more strenuously for his giving up the match entirely. You were not an innocent party in that matter."

An angry flush painted Darcy's cheeks. "I did so. I do not deny it."

"So then," she challenged. "What say you to that?"

"I say nothing. I was in the wrong."

"And so was I," she cried. "How can you hold us to different standards when you yourself made the same decision I did, based upon what you thought was right for my brother? And when you realised your mistake later, when once you fell in love yourself and understood all the happiness which you had kept from him, how did you feel?"

"I know very well how it made me feel," said he, his eyes glittering. "How did it make you feel?"

"Nothing at first," she admitted. "It was only once I developed feelings for your sister and understood the great happiness and joy that love can bring, that I truly realised the depth of my betrayal of Charles. I chose my own status and comfort over his happiness."

"As did I."

"So we understand each other," she said, watching him carefully. "As we did then, so do we now, though for very different reasons."

"Then to keep you apart from her would be to simply commit the same error of judgement again as I did with Charles, would it not? By doing so, should I not prove that I had learned nothing? Is that your argument?"

"I would not hold it against you, if you did," said she, despite feeling as if her stomach had fallen into her shoes and was even now seeping between the floorboards. "The situation is . . . rather different."

"Indeed." He leaned forward. The chair creaked under his weight, and the sound reminded Caroline of a tree being felled. "Then let me alter my question, since you will not agree to my terms. I am asking, as a brother and as a friend, for you to let Georgiana go. This affair can only lead to her ruin, as well as yours. If news of such a relationship should ever get out, neither of you would be allowed back in society again. Surely you would never put the woman you purport to love at risk?"

"I would let Georgiana go if I thought that it was the best thing for her."

"Do not you want her to be happy? Secure? Safe?"

"Of course I do," Caroline snapped. "But I believe myself best placed to provide that happiness." She closed her eyes for a moment. "No one could ever love her as much as I do. I can assure you of that."

"And if that should ever not be the case?" he pressed, looking at her keenly. "Would you let her go then? Would you free her if she wished to marry someone else?"

It was a question she had asked herself many times over the last few weeks. "That is an impossible question. I know that the answer—the right answer, the one you want to hear—would be yes, that I would let her go. That I would rather she be happy with someone else than with me." Caroline took a deep breath. She couldn't believe she was about to admit the one thing that would give him grounds to forbid the union entirely, but she simply couldn't lie about a subject this grave. "I have changed over the last few weeks, and I believe I have become a much better person, but a leopard cannot change his spots, sir. At heart, I am still that stubborn, selfish woman who demanded the truth from you when she was not ready to hear it. I give you honesty, as I have always done, even if it secures my doom. The truth is that while I love her so much that I would do anything for her, the one thing I could never do willingly is give her up. Therefore, no, I cannot imagine myself without her, and I cannot do what you ask."

Darcy's glower was so extreme, and his fingers twitched towards her and for a moment Caroline really did think he was about to reach for the nearest gun, but a split second later, he'd grabbed her by the hand, pulled her in close, and was—

Shaking it.

What?

Chapter Thirty-Four

Caroline stared up at him, completely baffled by what had just happened, and by the sudden change that had taken place, transforming Fitzwilliam's face from the sternest judge to the most exasperated of countenances.

"I had to test you," said he. "I had to know that you wanted her beyond all else, that you would give up everything for her. Love is a selfish act, Caroline. It drives us mad with desire. It can be selfless too, in that we would do anything for the one we love." His eyes grew distant for a moment, and she knew without a doubt that he was picturing Lizzy in some private moment. "It is my familial duty and the honour of my life to protect my sister by any means necessary."

Caroline's knees were weak. She held on to the back of the chair, steadying herself. "Was it also necessary to frighten me half to death in the process?"

"Both necessary and amusing," he said, unable to repress a brief smirk. "You must have known that whatever my feelings on the matter, I would never have let your name be ruined, Caroline. I have saved lesser men from far worse."

"I knew no such thing. You absolute devil," she breathed. "I thought you were really furious with me."

"Oh, I was. Until I understood what you truly meant to my sister. She has told me everything, which makes you entirely unlike her first match. Georgiana has always been . . . different, and though I did not foresee her happiness linked to a woman, I have suspected that she would never be satisfied with the kind of life and love that the ton considers appropriate. Her feelings cannot be confined to a neat box." He sighed. "And had I been sought after to provide a female suitor for her amongst all the ladies of our acquaintance, trust me when I say you would have been the absolute last on that list."

Ouch. She hoped that was his last barb, else she would have to revisit the idea of a stabby demise.

"But to quash the flame in her that you have lit would be both barbaric and brutish," he went on. "I am her brother, not her jailer. If she cannot help loving, then she cannot help loving. All I have ever wanted was to see her happy. I doubted she would ever . . ."

He trailed off, then shrugged helplessly. *He doubted it would ever happen*, Caroline thought, her heart aching for Georgiana. "Where is she?"

"Waiting for you out there." He pointed behind him, to the doorway leading to the private room. "Had you failed the test, I would have had Mrs Reynolds, who is waiting there"—he pointed at the hallway—"escort you to your room to pack forthwith. You would have been on a carriage within a quarter hour, and you would never have been permitted to set foot on my estate again."

"You thought of everything, I see."

"Not everything." He cleared his throat, looking slightly ashamed. "I confess I was . . . Well, suffice it to say that I doubted your character and your constancy both. You are, in fact, a much better woman than I once thought. Forgive me for that, Caroline. I shall never underestimate you again."

"When last we saw each other, you listed my flaws," she said, her voice shaky. "You were right about them, of course, but you mistakenly included stubbornness, when in fact it may be one of my few virtues. I am determined, sir." She swallowed. "When I set my mind on something, I will pursue it to the ends of the earth."

"Hmm. You know, I think you and my wife will get along rather well. You have a lot in common."

Caroline couldn't help the laugh that bubbled out of her throat. Darcy watched in bafflement as she clung to the chair, half-hysterical and completely unable to explain why it was so funny.

"Long story," she gasped eventually, in response to his raised eyebrow. "Yes, I believe that Miss Eliz—I mean, Mrs Darcy and I shall henceforth get along very well indeed."

He nodded, striding to the door which led to the hallway. "I shall leave you be for now and shall expect you both later for dinner."

Caroline waited until the sound of his footsteps had died away before she turned the handle of the adjoining door, took a deep breath, and entered the private room. She had never been inside this one, for it was Fitzwilliam's own domain. Georgiana, who had evidently been pacing the room in some agitation, froze upon seeing Caroline. The moment stretched on, neither willing to speak. The air was ripe with cedar and woodsmoke, but Caroline found herself searching for the dark scent of roses in every breath.

"Did you know I'd come for you?" she asked.

"Yes. No. I don't know." Georgiana's throat bobbed. "Love is a leap of faith, is it not?"

Caroline crossed the room in two steps, pulling Georgiana to her in a tug so violent the impact almost knocked the breath from her lungs. "I told you once that I would never look back, were it my own heart on the line," she breathed. "At the time, I thought it simply a sensible course of action. Now, I believe it the only course." She pressed a tender kiss to Georgiana's temple. "Dearest, I have but one question to ask you. Will you promise to always follow where I lead?"

"Always, darling," Georgiana sobbed, a warm trickle of tears on Caroline's shoulder. "As long as you will do the same."

"I promise," Caroline murmured, her own eyes stinging. "Let us only ever look forward."

Dear Self,

It is not always easy to improve, is it? In fact, it may be the hardest thing we have ever done, made harder by the knowledge that the journey is an endless one. There is no point at which we will achieve the most perfect version of our self, no point at which we might rest our tired feet and say, aha, the thing is done!

That lack of true destination should not discourage us, though. Far from it. We should not try to better our self to prove someone else wrong, nor should we advance only to impress another. We ought to improve only in order to become the person we wish to be: kind, generous, unselfish, but with the strength to hold on to our convictions and values despite external pressures, and with the courage to follow love wherever it leads us. I think we finally understand that, do we not?

And, of course, one may do all that and still maintain one's excellent tastes and opinions, even if one has learned to share them a little more . . . sparingly. Did not someone important say that "enough is as good as a feast"? If not, then consider the phrase coined by my own hand.

Hmm. Perhaps I shall write a book after all.

Yours, and mine,
Caroline Bingley

Epilogue

My dear Miss Darcy,

I can hardly write, my hands are shaking so. Mr Acton returned from London last night and proposed to me! We are to be married tomorrow. I owe Miss Bingley a debt which can never be repaid, though I shall certainly try. My new husband and I—Lord, how odd it feels to write such a thing—cordially request the pleasure of your company the day after. Please bring Miss Bingley, too!

Yours affectionally,
Miss Merryhill

On their first visit to see the Actons, Georgiana and Caroline brought with them a large basket of fresh fruit and cheese, as well as one of Mrs Addlecombe's pear cakes, all of which were joyfully received by the happy couple. Caroline could not help comparing this lunch with the first she had attended at Miss Merryhill's, and although the attendees were the same, she found herself enjoying this encounter far more. The Grimleys had improved markedly, being now several months into their marriage and rather less inclined to be ridiculous in company. Privately, Caroline admitted that perhaps she was now more disposed to see them in a favourable light, having experienced love for herself. Mr Grimley was courteous and attentive, while Mrs Grimley's kindness and eagerness to please did not stop at her husband, but extended to everyone in the entire party.

The Actons were also in the full flush of love, though theirs was a quieter, gentler sort. When Caroline caught them looking at each other from across the room, there was nothing untoward in the glance, but the adoration emanating from each was enough to avert her eyes.

When the Grimleys finally left, Mr Acton brought out a large cloth-wrapped package. "This is for you, Miss Bingley," he said, presenting it with a smile.

"For me?" Caroline blinked. "I deserve no present, sir."

"I disagree. Were it not for you, I never would have taken the necessary steps to secure my future. And were it not for you, I would not have been commissioned again by Lord Ashbrook."

"Ah, but I have heard," Caroline said, wagging a finger at him, "that some Northern painter is all the rage in London now. Even my sister, who cares nothing for art, has heard the gossip. I may have given you a push, Mr Acton, but you flew the nest yourself and soared higher than I could ever have imagined."

He pushed the package towards her again, his grin broadening. Caroline unknotted the string and pulled the cloth aside to reveal the painting she'd given her opinion on weeks before. The same sloping hills remained, the same shepherd with a broad-brimmed hat shading his eyes, the same lamb who had wandered away from its flock. Only now—as if it had always been there—high on the far left of the painting hung a large tawny bird with wings outstretched as if soaring. A pale shadow on the grass underneath matched the bird, and Caroline held her breath, feeling as if, at any moment, the shadow would move, those curved talons would descend, and the lamb would be carried away forever. *Nature may be cruel*, she thought, *but it is also kind. The buzzard seeks to feed her young by any means.*

"I see you took Miss Bingley's excellent advice," Georgiana said.

"Indeed I did," he agreed.

"And what a marvellous job you did," Caroline exclaimed. "The addition of brutality elevates it from the commonplace pastoral pictures that one may see in any home. It is an honest representation of the world."

"I am glad you think so. I also took it upon myself to make another small addition."

Puzzled, Caroline scanned the painting, her gaze finally alighting on two tiny figures in the bottom right corner. Leaning closer and squinting, she made out two ladies, seated on a picnic blanket, who were—

Kissing.

Oh no, she thought. *We are discovered.* Horrified, she glanced at Georgiana, who had frozen in place.

"I meant no harm by including you both," Mr Acton said hastily. "I was on the hill one day, and saw you both from a distance, but it was clear that, er—" His cheeks pinked.

"What my husband means to say," Mrs Acton cut in, "is that we are aware of the true nature of your relationship, and you need not hide when you are with us, if you do not wish to."

Georgiana let out a long, slow breath. "That is exceedingly

kind of you to say." She glanced at Caroline, anxiety written across her face in a large, scrawling script.

Caroline could very well understand why—they were not amongst family, but friends. Society, of a sort. Not the ton, of course, but respectable, good company—and really, was there any other sort that mattered? She reached out, her fingers trembling, and grasped Miss Darcy's hand. "I think I speak for both of us when I say that we appreciate your friendship most heartily."

Georgiana turned Caroline's hand over, entwining their fingers, and let out an equally shaky laugh. "Indeed. And if there is a place where we may safely show affection in the way other couples do . . ." Miss Darcy swallowed, her eyes filling with tears. "Please excuse me. I find myself quite overcome."

Caroline moved closer, one arm wrapping around Georgiana's waist. "Don't cry, dearest. Remember, you'll get sad eyes."

This produced a laugh, and soon enough, the tears were dried and replaced with smiles.

Back at Pemberley, Georgiana stopped Caroline the moment Mrs Reynolds closed the door behind them. "Fitz suggested to me this morning that he could buy us a place of our own, in lieu of a wedding gift."

"Let me guess," Caroline said, taking off her gloves. "You accepted."

"Well, I—" Miss Darcy looked surprised. "I didn't suppose you would want to live alongside Lizzy."

"I lived with my mother for twenty-three years, sweetness. I think I can tolerate Miss Eliz—I mean, Mrs Darcy, for a while." Caroline did not miss the way Mrs Reynolds' lips twitched. "I do not want you to have to leave Pemberley. It is your home."

"You are my home," Georgiana said, with unexpected

fierceness. "You gave up everything for me. Besides, it is not just a house. It is a life, Caroline." Miss Darcy turned to her, and Caroline was surprised to see nervousness in her expression. "Would you like to build a life with me?"

Caroline pressed her lips against Georgiana's knuckles, too overcome for a moment to speak. "Dearest, I can think of nothing sweeter."

"I believe," Georgiana said, turning to the housekeeper, "that you would be amenable to accompanying us to our new abode, Mrs Reynolds?"

"That I am, ma'am."

"Not that I do not appreciate your considerable talents, Mrs Reynolds, for I do," Caroline said, unable to help her wheedling tone, "but do you think there is any way that we might also poach Mrs Addlecombe?"

To Caroline's utter astonishment, the housekeeper blushed. "Where I go, Mrs Addlecombe might . . . might also like to go. Though you should ask her directly, for I do not claim to speak on her behalf."

"What?" Georgiana gasped. "Well, I never! I had no idea that—you never said anything!"

"It—it is . . . quite a new thing, ma'am," Mrs Reynolds stammered, ramrod straight, her face now dangerously close to the colour of a beetroot. "And that is all I may say upon the matter."

"My, my," Caroline said, as the housekeeper all but ran from the room. "I did not see that coming. Do you think we shall ever hear the tale in full?"

"Give them time to find themselves first. Then I shall press Mrs Addlecombe for every morsel."

"Speaking of pressing Mrs Addlecombe for morsels . . ." Caroline said hopefully.

Georgiana gaped at her. "You cannot possibly have more room for cake! You had three slices at the Actons'."

"One must keep one's strength up, Georgie," she purred, advancing until a grinning Miss Darcy was backed against the wall. Only the sound of footsteps on the stairs drove them apart, though Georgiana still held on to Caroline's hand.

Mrs Darcy, clad in a light blue gown, descended into the great hall and headed for the front door. "Ah, Miss Bingley. I wondered if you would like to accompany me for a turn around the garden. I have been told that you enjoy long walks as much as I." Her eyes flickered to their entwined hands, her expression surprisingly fond. "Unless I am disturbing you?"

"Indeed, Mrs Darcy," said Caroline. "I heard that we have a lot in common. Perhaps it is time we got to know each other a little better."

"Remember, be nice," Georgiana murmured, as Caroline put her bonnet back on.

"Dearest, I'm always nice." Caroline considered this. "Well, no, I'm not, but I am always myself, and that should be enough for anybody."

She swept out of the door without waiting for a response, and joined Mrs Darcy, who was waiting at the bottom of the steps. Turning her face to the sky, Caroline sighed with pleasure. The day was warm and fine, the sunshine brilliant, and the air was tinted with the dark, sultry smell of freshly-cut roses.

★ ★ ★ ★ ★

Acknowledgements

Thanks to my darling wife, Z, who kept me fed and watered and on a reasonable sleep schedule (despite my protests) while I wrote this book. It's not often that the love of your life turns out to also be the best first reader, and I feel so blessed. Truly, you're the gentle, romantic Charlotte Lucas to my unhinged, chaotic Caroline Bingley, and I appreciate you more than mere words could ever convey. Thank you for letting me subject you to excited monologues on operas including *Dido and Aeneas*, various mythologies, and gothic literature, although I note that you still haven't allowed me to read you any fascinating passages from the real book of *A Dissertation on the Chief Obstacles to the Improvement of Land, and Introducing Better Methods of Agriculture Throughout Scotland*.

Tsk. You're really missing out, babe.

To my friends, especially the "library day" folk—Alex, Annie, Charlotte, Claudia, and Elizabeth—thank you for supporting my descent into ferality, bringing baked goods, and generally being awesome people.

Heartfelt thanks go to my brilliant editor at Harlequin, Stephanie Doig, whose giggling in the edit margins kept me going, and to my agent, Laura Zats, without whom I might never have dipped even a single toe in the deliciously warm waters of romance; I admit, I do love swimming here. Thanks to the art team at Harlequin, who have created yet another banger of a cover, as well as to nineteenth-century scholar and extremely cool Austen nerd Emma Butler-Marr, who suggested naming the white horse after her grandfather. I hope your Edward would have been proud of this inclusion.

I must thank Jane Austen, for creating the wonderful character of Caroline Bingley in the first place, but thanks must also go to Anna Chancellor, who played Miss Bingley so haughtily in the 1995 BBC version of *Pride and Prejudice*—you will always be my one and only Caroline.

To Caroline Bingley herself: thank you. I stan you so deeply, my haughty, obnoxious, confidently-incorrect queen; may we all experience even a quarter of your unshakeable self-esteem.